The Mystic Diaries:

The Whispered Secret

Lexi unearths secrets never meant to be shared.

By: Lilibeth Muscato

Edited by: Wendy Mardas
Cover Photo by: S. Sagmiller

Book 1 of The Mystic Diaries Series

First Edition

DEDICATION

After many obstacles, dead ends and turn arounds, there was a very dim light at the end of the tunnel. I want to say a huge thank you to my publishers, Freedom of Speech Publishing.

To those who said I can't, I'm showing them that I can.

To those who said I won't, I'm showing them that I will.

I love my friends who have pushed me, when I've felt that it was too dark. I can say, with best friends by your side, they'll push you until you fall. Because they know that you'll get back up (once they're done laughing at you). When you cry, they'll cry right along with you. I've also learned that a true friendship is your guide in your darkest hour. When you want to give up, they're right there, not allowing it. You find faith that you didn't think you had. Whether you succeed or don't…true friends will be there every step of the way.

Some words I will leave you with. It doesn't matter if you succeed or not. You have gotten further than if you didn't try at all. Don't be one of the one's that sit back and 'wish' they could do something, without even seeing if you can.

A journey may begin with the first step...
The adventure starts with the second.

The Mystic Diaries

The Whispered Secret

By Lilibeth Muscato

For more books like this one, visit the Mystic Diaries page on my website
at:

http://lilibethmuscato.com/

or visit the series pages at:

http://themysticdiaries.com/

2012 copyright by Freedom of Speech Publishing, Inc.

Printed in the United States of America
The publisher offers discounts on this book when ordered in bulk
quantities. For more information, contact Sales Department, Phone 815-
290-9605, Email:
sales@FreedomOfSpeechPublishing.com

Freedom of Speech Publishing, Leawood KS, 66224
www.FreedomOfSpeechPublishing.com
ISBN-13: 978-1470046163
ISBN-10: 1470046164

A SPECIAL THANK YOU TO YOU!

On behalf of everyone at Freedom Of Speech Publishing, thank you for choosing The Mystic Diaries: The Whispered Secret for your reading enjoyment.

As an added bonus and special thank you, for purchasing The Mystic Diaries: The Whispered Secret, you can enjoy discounts and special promotions on other Freedom of Speech Publishing products. Visit www.freedomeofspeech.com/vip to learn more.

We are committed to providing you with the highest level of customer satisfaction possible. If for any reason you have questions or comments, we are delighted to hear from you. Email us at cs@freedomofspeechpublishing.com or visit our website at http://freedomofspeechpublishing.com/contact-us-2/.
If you enjoyed The Mystic Diaries: The Whispered Secret, visit www.freedomofspeechpublishing.com for a list of similar books or upcoming books.

Again, thank you for your patronage. We look forward to providing you more entertainment in the future.

Contents

The Beginning 1

Chapter 1 – Strange Occurrences 3

Chapter 2 – The Beginning 20

Chapter 3 – The Dreams Reality 34

Chapter 4 – State of Confusion 47

Chapter 5 – Too Much, Too Fast 61

Chapter 6 – Back to Reality 75

Chapter 7 – Part of the truth is better than none... Right? 88

Chapter 8 – The Truth about the Witches 100

Chapter 9 – The Kiss 116

Chapter 10 – The Spoken Truth 129

Chapter 11 – Curse, or Coincidence? 147

Chapter 12 – The Dance 165

Chapter 13 – The Interference 180

Chapter 14 – Irony 192

Chapter 15 – Off to College 206

Chapter 16 – The Picture 223

Chapter 17 – Jealousy Comes a-Knocking 239

Chapter 18 – The Break-Up   254

Chapter 19 – It was just an accident...or was it?   270

Chapter 20 – Acceptance   284

Chapter 21 – The Story   297

Chapter 22 – One Dream Comes True   308

Book 2 Preamble   320

ABOUT THE AUTHOR   321

Warning!

This book is not like any other you will ever read. The main character – who is based on a real person – shows us that sometimes we cannot keep up with the workings of the human mind…that not everything is clear until the dust settles, and even then, it is never really clear.

Can you imagine a place where all the myths, legends and stories we have heard were more than just stories?

Do you have to believe to see?

Do you believe what you see with your eyes?

Or do you believe what you see with your heart?

(Is it better to be kept in the dark or to face the unknown head on?)

The Beginning

I grew up in a small town - not too far from the major city. But far enough away that, as far as the rest of the world was concerned, it was nonexistent. My town was so small that you couldn't even find us on a map. If you happened to blink while driving through, you would miss us altogether. Everyone who lived there knew everyone. There was nothing you did or said that wouldn't make it back to your parents by the time you got home from school. As annoying as that could be at times, I somehow enjoyed it.

I wasn't known for my looks, my wits or even my brain, for that matter. I was the "easy" one - the one that bullies turned against because they knew I would not fight back. To ward off my despair, my fear of having my dreams come to nothing, I looked for reassurance outside myself. I tried sports, hoping that I could overcome my reputation for having two left feet and being totally accident prone. I was complimented on the agility of my hands, but just about anything I touched seemed to fall apart or die. I tried everything I could think of to find my talent in life, but I just couldn't seem to come up with one. Everyone kept telling me that I would find my place, but how could I believe them when in the back of my mind I knew it wasn't true?

I remember when I was growing up, I dreamt of wanting to love – and to be loved in returned. I am not saying that I had a troubled home life. In a way, I was very sheltered – but not sheltered from my own thoughts. I could blame all those stories that portrayed happily-ever-afters for the dissatisfaction I often felt, but what was the point? This was something that I truly longed for.

I remember pretending with my friends that we were being chased after blood-sucking vampires who would steal our souls if they caught us. We would run through the meadows, looking back and giggling every time our feet touched the earth. When the hills were covered with snow, we would pretend we were riding the waves on our sleds along a warm, sandy beach.

With endless imaginations, we came up with new things to do as the years went by.

Growing older, we knew we could not escape what was coming for us: reality. Although I never really lost focus of what I truly wanted, each passing year pushed the dream further away, until it was hidden in the back of my brain as if sealed behind a steel door. Eventually, the dream became nothing more than a childhood memory, one that retreated into a world of fantasy as other things came into play. The dream would have to wait.

So our imaginations seemed to fade further and further away with each passing year, until they seemed to be nothing but a laugh. We had always thought about how cool our fantasies would have been if they were real. But we knew that they could never exist; after all, if they were real, you would think that everyone would know. If they were true, it would have defied all of the laws which our parents had taught us. There are myths, rumors and legends, but that's all they really are. If any of them were true, the stories we were told would not have started out with "A long, long time ago;" Instead, they would say, "And this is how it goes…"

This is the story of my life and this is how it goes…

Chapter 1 – Strange Occurrences

This past summer went by way too fast. I picked up as many hours as I could doing odd jobs at the farm. Not my favorite thing, but it helped put some money in the account I kept for special trips during the school year. It was like no other summer I could remember. I had two left feet and two right hands, and as clumsy as I was, I would fall down trying to do the simplest of chores; but then I could take on the most complex tasks without a hitch.

This year on the farm was worse than all the others. Strange events had gone on that I couldn't explain; nor could anyone else who had been there to witness them. The first happened one time when I was lifting hay over a fence. I lost my grip on the bale, and by all accounts, the hay should have landed on me. Keywords "should have." But it just rolled over in the air and flopped to the ground next to me.

The next one was when a horse got out of the paddock and headed straight for where I was standing. Being the natural idiot I am, everyone was screaming at me to run; but I just stood there, staring, as it came charging at me. That horse was within inches of me when all of a sudden, it just changed course for no apparent reason. It looked as though someone had yanked its head away and kept it from running me down. But even though a bunch of witnesses were there, not one could say for certain what had really happened.

Another event was luckily no one was there to see. It was raining on and off, and I wiped out on a mud patch on the way to the barn. On the way down, I put my hands out to absorb the shock of my fall, like any natural person would do. But my hands never hit the mud. It felt as if someone had caught me and pulled me back up, all in a single, swift motion.

The scariest event of that summer happened on the same day as the almost-fall. I was walking home in the rain, since I was already wet and the farm wasn't that far from where I lived. The rain had started to come down pretty hard by this time. I had to take a different road than usual, because the regular way had puddles no matter which way I stepped. I was minding my own while I walked, when suddenly, the horn of a car made me jump. The driver had lost control, and the car was headed right for me! Again, like an idiot, I stood there in shock.

Just seconds before what would have been girl meets bumper, I felt a violent shove. I landed on the side of the road as the car flew past and then came to a stop further on. The driver came running back to see if I was OK. He was totally freaked out and kept apologizing over and over, but I wasn't physically hurt, not as I would have been if I'd been hit. I told him to take it a little easier and kept on walking.

But he felt so bad that he followed me home and explained to my parents what had happened. My parents wanted me to file a police report, but I said no. I wasn't hurt, at least not by the driver and his car, so I felt that there was no need to punish someone for what hadn't happened. Dad reluctantly sided with me and thanked the driver for doing the right thing. After all, how could I explain to the officer who came out to file the report that I was pushed out of the way by something I didn't see?

That was my exciting summer.

It was time for reality as I got ready for another day. Homework, tests, being on a set schedule, and the dreaded chore of choosing a college. This time I couldn't say, "I have a couple more years to decide," or "I'll do it next year." Next year was now *this* year, and all of the choices that were now in front of me made everything I had gone through before seem like nothing.

Junior year started off to be just like the last two. Now the only difference is I would have to start applying to colleges. Did I even want to go to college? My grades were just above passing, and I still didn't even know what I wanted to do with my life, let alone start making the choices to prepare for it. I had thought some about becoming a lawyer, but then again... After the events of that summer, I knew I had to start preparing for something.

The school year started off with the normal overload of homework, pop quizzes and tests. With our friend Mike Harts off to college, it made reality seem even more real. He wasn't there anymore to offer his support to the rest of us. Mike, who was tall, light hair with a surfer built had been accepted with a full ride because of his test scores. It felt like a link that was missing – and next year, two more of our friends would be headed off to college, as well.

The one thing I do enjoy is photography, but only as a hobby. My first camera had been an old 110 mm that just snapped pictures when you clicked the button. Then my dad gave me the 35mm camera that he had bought back when he fought overseas during Vietnam. With this camera, you could changes lenses, manually focus, and all that good stuff. I absolutely loved it. There was a clearing in the middle of some trees that I euphemistically called a forest. I would spend hours there, just relaxing in the summer's warmth on days when I wasn't working, taking my camera with me on many occasions to test out all of the different functions.

I am an only child, which was great in some ways, but also sucked in many others. I had no one to understand where I was coming from, no one to talk to, to share my secrets. Sometimes, a best friend is not the same as a sibling. Like, if you had an issue at two o'clock in the morning, you would know you could sneak into your sister's room and talk to her about it. There was a plus side to not having siblings. If you wanted to be left alone, no one was there trying to pry anything out of you.

I checked my watch as I walked down the stairs. I had set it by the clock at school. Luckily, I only had to walk right out the door to catch the bus. Something glittering on the kitchen table caught my attention just as I was heading out the door. *Happy 17th Birthday,* the card read.

I mumbled to myself as I held the box in my hand. "I can't believe that I'm 17 years old already..."

I opened the card, already knowing who it was from. *Love, Mom and Dad. August 28, 1998.* The box felt heavy and light at the same time. I carefully removed the birthday paper, and to my delight, there was a portable CD player. It was awesome! Now I could concentrate on my own thoughts instead of the mindless chatter on the bus. I ran upstairs to grab my favorite CD and locked the door behind me as I fumbled with my new gift.

My mom and dad – Andrew and Christina – were usually gone before I got up for school. I rarely saw them in the mornings. My parents trusted me to get up and get to school without supervision. They had instilled the fear of God in me. I knew if I ever crossed the line, I would feel their wrath. They trusted me to do the right thing. I had never really received much praise from them, but I didn't want to seek attention by doing something wrong. I value my freedom and privacy.

Mom works as a receptionist for a dentist, while Dad works as an electrician. They were pretty laid back until you crossed the line. Mom is one of those who wait for something to go on sale. Dad is one who has to do all the research on a product before he buys it. So I guessed the CD player had been a great buy for the price.

I had to take the bus to school, because we lived outside the city limits. The bus ride dragged most days. Especially listening to what others had done the night before or what they had planned for the upcoming days. I usually blocked out the mind-numbing chatter by getting lost in a book I had borrowed from the library. Now I had the CD player to keep my mind occupied, as well.

When I walked into the school building, most of my friends were already there.

"Hey! Alexandra!" A sweet, over-hyper voice called from behind the people standing nearby, yakking away. I strained my neck trying to see where it was coming from.

"Hey, Val!" I called back, after seeing her wave above the clusters of heads.

"How are you doing today?" She asked, hugging me. Valliria Befuss was a girl who danced to her own tune. She was shorter than the rest of us, and her black hair was naturally spiky. Her style was completely different from anyone else's, because she liked to come up with her own outfits.

"It's a new day!" I laughed back. I looked around to see who else was here. My class consisted of pretty much all the usual cliques that you would find in any given high school. Geeks, athletes, brainiacs, freaks, etc. All the regulars were there.

Terry Huder was wearing his football jersey, and his blonde hair was a mess. Lately, his eyes always seemed tired. You could tell that he would rather be anywhere else than on the football team. It didn't used to be like that. He used to love playing football, but he had one of those fathers who lived vicariously through his son. So instead of playing for fun and the love of the game, Terry had begun to see it as an obligation or a chore.

Aaron, who was getting extra help in one of his classes, was the only kid who wasn't there. Aaron was Val's boyfriend. He was a senior and had been accepted to a prestigious college on a baseball scholarship. He was cute, if you like those muscle-bound dorks. He always kept his hair super short. Unless he got lazy, the only way you could tell what color hair he had was by his eyebrows. He was shorter than the average player, but his size allowed him to maneuver easily and gave him the upper hand. He was the typical high school jock.

I wasn't jealous of their relationship, but I just couldn't see the two of them together past high school. I was happy for Val, and I never said anything to her about my fears for her. They had, after all, made it past my first prediction of six months – they had been together since the middle of her freshman year.

"Have you decided on which colleges to apply to yet?" she asked.

"No. Not sure. Heck, I don't even know what I want to do yet!" I smiled back.

She already had a handful of college material. "Well, you better hurry," she smirked.

7

"So, what are you going to college for?" I asked, as she flipped through the different brochures.

She answered with a huge grin. "Fashion designer."

Yeah, I could see her doing that.

"I would really love to go to law school, but…" I said, with a sigh.

"You don't think you'll be able to get in," she said, finishing my sentence.

"That, too. The cost, mostly."

"Apply for a scholarship. You're really smart - and a lot braver than me," she said.

First bell rang, letting us know that we were back to the real world. Everyone took off in a hurry, heading down the halls to their homerooms. I was relieved, but disappointed at the same time, that no one had remembered my birthday. I walked to my locker to put away the books I didn't need. Although I was in a building with almost three thousand other students, I felt somehow alone.

"HAPPY BIRTHDAY!!!" I heard, as I opened my locker door. The inside was filled with crepe paper, streamers and balloons! My mouth dropped open when I saw how great it looked.

"You didn't think we forgot, did you?!" Val shrieked, as she bounced up and down.

"No, but there was always a chance." I smiled and hugged her back. "Thank you!"

"We all knew you would like it!" She gleamed back, happy with how my locker had turned out. There were about fifteen people there waiting to hug me and wish me a happy birthday. Everyone scattered off to class after their hugs.

"Happy birthday!" Dave said, the last one to give me a hug. Dave was my best guy friend and the only one that I could confide in. He lived in the subdivision kitty-corner from mine, but because of the way the school districts were made up, we had gone to different elementary schools. Dave

Kravic was tall and athletic-looking. More so a geeky athletic type. He didn't play any sports, although with his height you would think that he could be great at basketball.

He was a senior and about a foot taller than me, with black hair that just seemed to stand in place no matter what. If we weren't best friends who shared everything together, I might have seen him as something more than a friend, but there wasn't that type of chemistry between us. Well, for me, anyways.

"Thank you," I said, returning the hug.

"Any plans for tonight?"

"Just the usual," I said, holding up the book I was reading from earlier.

"Sounds exciting," he said, as he glanced at the book.

"Very."

"How about I'll give you a call or stop by after school?"

"Sure." We exchanged another hug, and I headed off for homeroom.

"I'm happy for you." I turned around looking to see where the voice had come from. It had seemed like it was in surround-sound. I looked around to see who had spoken, but no one was there.

I thought out loud to myself, "*That was weird.*"

"Happy Birthday, my Angel." Same voice. I looked around, but again, there was no one there.

OK. I'm losing it. I thought to myself, as I hurried to class.

The classes seemed to drag by, yet the day passed quickly.

Finally, I got to my last class of the day: photography. I loved photography, the idea of capturing something that you see and hoping that others get why you had taken the picture in the first place. That was my vision, anyway.

"What are you two rambling on about now?" I asked, as I sat down at my assigned table.

Russ Breck had real bad acne that broke out about a year ago. We used to tease him by saying that puberty finally caught up with him. He was a lot taller than me, but was a very slender, bleach blonde-haired surfer type of guy. I've had a crush on Russ ever since we were in elementary school. Back then, we had been the best of friends, but ever since we started high school, we don't talk or hang out any more.

Will was kinda the oddball. He and Russ were about the same height. He could never decide on how to wear his afro from day to day. He was as sweet as they came, but you would never have known it by the way he acted. He would act all big and tough, which was funny if you really knew him. Put these two together, and they were very outspoken.

"Oh, that's easy! We're gonna win the game tonight," Russ replied to Will.

It almost looked like the two of them were staring each other down, and who ever lost, it would mean that their team was gonna lose. I'm not into sports, so I just sighed and got my homework out. Besides, I couldn't understand what I was watching when any team played. I stared at the roll of film that I had brought in. We would be developing it ourselves today. I had completely forgotten about the voice I had heard earlier. I didn't want to start thinking that *I* was going crazy.

"Good afternoon, class," Ms. Kohel beamed, as she walked into the room.

"Ms. Kohel? I have a question?" I heard one of the students ask, from an adjacent table.

She loved it when students asked questions. "Go ahead." She always said that it showed that students were taking an interest in her class. It was the days they didn't ask questions that worried her.

"What is going to be the point of developing film once we are able to view a picture as soon as we snap it?"

"Ah. Good question. Well, one, that technology hasn't been invented yet, and I honestly don't think it will for a couple more decades. If and when it does come out, there will still be things you will only be able to capture with regular film." She seemed confident in her future prediction.

The student was now challenging the teacher. "Like what?"

"The color and vibrancy of the images."

"Ummm. OK," the student replied, still not really understanding. And, in all honesty, neither did I.

"Did everyone bring their film?" She asked. No one spoke, just held up their film. "Good." She then proceeded into the darkroom, motioning for everyone to follow.

"Will we be working with color or black and white?" I heard one of the other students ask.

"I'm leaving that up to your imaginations," she beamed.

You could hear chattering as everyone went to their stations. I got to work right away. I loved taking nature shots. The peace, the serenity, the tranquility frozen in time, all seemed in harmony when you just sat back and enjoyed the view. I wasn't confident with the color yet.

As I unrolled the negatives, I looked for my favorite five to use. Once I decided, I placed the negative on the machine and started with a simple 4x6. Then I played with the colors. Getting it to where I wanted it, I finished the process and hung the paper up to dry. I repeated the process with the other four. I went through all five and picked my favorite one to put on an 8x10. Paying little attention to the other students, I was always off in my own little world when I was back here.

"Wrap it up, class," Ms. Kohel called, from the doorway.

Already? I thought to myself.

I gathered my film and photos and walked out of the darkroom. I was curious to see my pictures, even though they were just of everything and nothing. I sat at my table and noticed that we still had ten minutes left. Enough time for me to admire my work.

I went through the smaller photographs first. I admired them silently – they had turned out great. I put the smaller ones down and began to study the larger one. I was making mental notes of what to improve analyzing the photo like I was reading a book line by line. I had never made a picture that large before and with color.

"Who's that?" I heard Ms. Kohel ask, from behind. I didn't know what she was talking about, since I had taken all nature shots, and I knew no one had been there at the time. As if reading my mind, she pointed to a spot on the film.

"I don't know," I answered, as she indicated a part of the photo I had not yet reached with my eyes. "No one was around that I know of when I took these."

"Sometimes you get that when you shoot nature. You concentrate on the scenery and forget that there is anyone around you."

She patted me on the back saying good job, as she went to another student. I pondered who the person could have been. I was in my favorite remote location, and I had *never* seen or heard another soul there before. Something was odd about the person in the picture though. It had been a windless day, and everything stood still in the picture but this figure. The thing was although you could see him clearly, he was still a distorted blur. The way he was positioned, it looked like he was further away than where he was actually standing.

RIIIIIIIIIIIIIIINNNNNNNNNNNNNGGGGGGGGG...

There was nothing like the annoying sound of the school bell to snap you back to reality. I gave no more thought to the pictures as I threw them into my portfolio. I headed off to my locker to throw what books I didn't need before catching the bus.

The ride was boring but at least short.

"Finally home," I mumbled, under my breath, as I walked through the door.

I stared around my room, trying to decide whether I liked this arrangement better than the old way. I was constantly rearranging my room. Unless I was wrapped up in a book, I never sat still. I grabbed my CD player from my bag, a new CD, and the book I had started the night before and threw them onto the bed. I looked out my bedroom window and started to daydream.

Our house – the kind that builders call a quad - backed up to a luscious pond and park. To get to the front door, you had to walk up the steps; the formal living room and a large eat-in kitchen sat on that level. From there, three bedrooms and one bath were up a flight of stairs. If you walked down the stairs, you were in the dining room/family room combo. In the back sat a fourth bedroom, another bathroom, and the door to the two-car garage. If you continued down another flight of stairs, you were in the basement.

My daydream took over as I wondered what it would be like to be loved in *that* way. I'm not talking family love; I'm talking about someone you can't live without and they can't live without you. A love that makes the world so complete everything else just falls into place.

"What the…?" I asked, out loud in disbelief.

A silhouette of a tall, handsome dark-haired boy stood next to the old oak I used to climb when I was younger. He was waving. I blinked… hard. When I opened my eyes, I saw… nothing. I knew I was tired from staying up late reading the night before, but I didn't think I was *that* tired. I staggered to the bed, threw on my headphones, and started where I had left off in my novel.

"Alexandra?" I heard my name being called over the sound of music.

I took my headphones off and listened again to make sure I wasn't hearing things. Silence. I put my headphones back on and started reading again.

"ALEXANDRA!" I jumped up, because I *knew* that I wasn't hearing things this time.

"Yes?" I called back, turning the CD player off and headed downstairs.

"Just making sure you're home," Mom said, as she laid her keys on the kitchen table. "So…?"

"Thank you for the present, Mom! I love it!" I replied, giving her a quick hug and starting towards my room again.

"You're welcome!" I heard her laugh from downstairs. I placed my headphones back on.

Before I knew, it was time to eat.

After dinner, I put on my running shoes to take my nightly jog around the neighborhood. My little town may not be on the map, but the neighborhoods were so spread out that you could take a different path every day if you traveled through the various subdivisions. I quickly switched to a new CD and headed out the door.

I loved my neighborhood. If I actually ran the whole diameter, it would take me a full thirty minutes. My parents didn't care if I was out after dark. After all, the town being so small, if anything happened, someone in the neighborhood would know someone in another neighborhood who knew someone that knew my parents, and it would get back to them by the time I got home. Confusing, huh? And it would take them a whole five minutes in their car to come and get me.

Stories and myths filled this little town, so that people always had something to talk about. I believed in ghosts, even though I had never seen one. I believe in the sixth sense. But if I couldn't get all five of mine to run on all cylinders, how could I operate a sixth?

There is one house that I always make a point of running past. I will even go out of my way and run an extra mile or more just so I can see it. It's an old Victorian style with a covered front porch. The house is dark blue, with medium gray trim. Although that may sound pretty normal, it was out of place sitting in this part of the neighborhood. This part was mostly built up in the past year with contemporary homes painted in lighter colors. The builders that had developed the area never strayed from the five basic models that they offered.

The Victorian house intrigued me. It was beautiful. It was a house that you might see in a book about witches, vampires and werewolves. I

14

always laughed to myself when I make that comparison. I never stopped to gawk, just jogged past it like it was any other ordinary house in my neighborhood. I would though, secretly peeked at it every time I ran by. The house certainly didn't fit in with the motif of the others. It looked as if the builder had had to build around it. The other strange thing was that the house was always dark. Like as if though no one had lived there for years.

There was an old saying about my little town of Greneville. That if you dated someone in high school and it went well, you found the person you were going to marry. A lot of kids in school were paired up already. Granted, most of them broke up within those four years, because they had started so young. Those who made it past high school usually ended up getting married. I knew I was too young to actually settle down, but I still yearned for that feeling of being loved and having something to fill the emptiness. Dang fairytales.

"Phew!" I stopped to catch my breath. I lit the light on my watch to see what time it was. "Crap!"

I had been running for almost ninety minutes. My normal runs last only an hour. They can take up to two if I am really steamed about something. I wasn't mad about anything tonight - not that I knew of, anyways. I decided to finish my course and head home. I took a deep breath in and smelled the freshly-cut grass. Fall was right around the corner, and everyone was trying to get their yard work done before the first frost.

"Hello, beautiful." There was that voice again.

I could hear it over the music, so loud and so clear. It felt like someone was standing right next to me and talking through the music. I stopped and looked around. By this time, it was already dark. Even though the street lights cast some light, I still couldn't see anyone. Instead of sounding stupid and answering the voice back, I just continued on my way. I really don't remember how much time had passed; I was just concentrating on my run and the music floating in my head when I heard it again.

"I do apologize," the voice said, with a sweet tone.

OK, that was it! I'd had it! I stopped and looked around. I saw a shadow move on the street that I had just passed. I took off after it at full speed. Whoever was playing with my head was going to pay for it! It probably took me less than a few seconds to reach the street.

The road was long and straight, so it wasn't like anyone could avoid me by turning a corner. I saw no one. I heard nothing. There were no other kids, no cars, no birds, not even a dog barking. Not even the wind was blowing. Everything was perfectly calm.

I'm not a confrontational person. But I don't run away from things, either. But I decided to head home so my parents wouldn't send a search party after me. When I looked around again, the old Victorian house caught my eye. For a moment, I thought I saw a movement inside. I just ignored it... for now... and started off back home. I'd had enough for one day. The rest of the run was quiet, as though nothing unusual had happened.

When I reached my street, I saw Dad's truck parked in the driveway. I had always wondered why my parents had chosen the house we live in now, but I'd never thought to ask them. It was just the way life was, why would I question that?

"Something wrong, Lex?"

I shuddered, as I walked in the door. I hated that name. "Nothing, Dad, why?"

He sat at the kitchen table, looking up from the newspaper. "You were gone longer than usual."

Dad didn't look like a dad. He was forty-seven, but he could easily pass for someone in his late twenties-early thirties. Mom was the same. I guess it was a good thing when you got older, but at my age everyone mistook me for being a lot younger that I actually was.

I held up the CD player they had bought me for my birthday. "Lost track of time."

"Ah! Glad you're using it," he grumbled. Not much ever made him smile.

"I'm headed off to bed," I stated as I started up the stairs.

My *off to bed* meant getting ready for bed and then snuggling with a good book. I had done all my homework during study hall, and even though I'm barely passing, I really didn't care.

"LEX!" I heard my dad call from downstairs. "Dave's on the phone!"

"Thanks," I called back. I hurried down the stairs, grabbed the cordless and headed back to my room. "Hey, what's up?"

"Not much. I wanted to apologize for not calling or stopping by sooner."

"Eh, it's cool," I shrugged. I had actually forgotten that he'd said he would.

"You shouldn't be alone on your birthday," he said with sympathy.

"It's the middle of the week. I don't expect that much to happen."

"I'm glad Renee isn't bothering us anymore," he breathed, with gratitude.

Renee tried *way* too hard to fit in, always going from group to group to add her two cents where it didn't belong. She was a pretty heavy-set girl and knew it. It wasn't her weight that was keeping people away. It was her personality. Eh, it's hard to explain.

"She wasn't all *that* bad," I mocked.

"Yeah, she didn't look at you like you were something to eat," he groaned.

I couldn't help but laugh. "Oh, stop that."

"Really, she would just stare at me. It made me uncomfortable."

"Maybe she has a crush on you?"

"Ew. I hope not! Don't even joke about that!" He demanded, with all seriousness.

I couldn't help but laugh out loud. "Out of how many times you all tease me! I have to get one in there somehow!"

"Fine. It's over, can we *please* move on?" he begged.

17

"Fine," I said, with playful sarcasm. "So what else is going on?"

His tone sensed he was dying to tell someone. "Oh, a lot."

"Spill," I demanded, in anticipation.

"Mike likes Lynn, and…"

Lynn was about my height, with light brown hair and blue eyes. She wasn't as thin as the rest of us, but that never stopped her from having fun. We never paid attention to her weight. She didn't make an issue out of it like Renee did.

"Whoa, wait a minute, Mike likes Lynn?" I asked, astounded. "When did this happen?"

He sounded as incredulous as I was. "I guess sometime over the summer, but neither one of them would admit it."

"Then how do you know for sure?"

"Mike told me last night," he beamed.

"I wish them luck," I said. I'd always had a hunch that they would get together.

"Luck? What luck, they ain't together yet," he protested.

I sighed deeply. "No, but if they like each other as much as you say, they will be. I just hope it doesn't end badly *if* it does."

"I think that's why they ain't saying anything about it yet."

"How's Terry been? Haven't really seen him lately," I asked, speaking the truth.

"He's been slammed with practices. Honestly though, I think he would rather hang out with the jocks than with us." How Dave spoke surprised me but didn't at the same time.

"That doesn't surprise me. He always seemed distant when he hung out with us."

"Yeah, he does miss us, but since none of us are really jocks or really care about sports," he continued. "He sort of feels alone. Not to mention the fact that he can't stand Aaron."

"He's always welcome to come chill with us whenever he likes," I said, offering support.

"Yeah, I told him. It seems like there's something else bothering him, but he won't say."

Terry used to be inseparable from the group. I paused for a moment. "I take it he's not coming with us this weekend."

"Nope," he said.

"Oh, well. It won't be the same. It's not like he's been around lately either."

You could tell he was trying to shrug it off. "No it won't. But life goes on, right?"

I agreed. "Right." And that was the sad part. Life goes on whether you want it to or not.

"Well I gotta head off. I'll see you tomorrow?"

"Of course. Where else would I go?" I kidded with him.

"Just making sure," he chuckled. "Later."

"Later," I said clicking the 'off' button.

Dad hated it when the phone wasn't plugged in when no one was using it. I ran downstairs to put the cordless back on the charger, went back to my room, set my alarm and curled into bed with another book from the library.

Chapter 2 – The Beginning

"Alexandra!" Val hollered, across the room. Nothing could keep her free spirit down.

"Hey, Val," I said, putting a happy expression on my face. I had been putting one on for almost 17 years. So it had gotten real easy to fool people. I made sure the power button was off before I put the player away in my bag. I didn't want the batteries dying.

"Awesome CD player!" Again, everything was an exciting high for her, no matter how small.

"Yeah. I got it yesterday. You know, parents had to get me something so they couldn't hear my music," I teased. Not that they hate my music, but Mom liked oldies, and Dad liked AM talk.

She laughed, as she jumped up and down in anticipation. "You still coming this weekend?"

"Yeah. Don't have that much saved up, but window shopping should be fun," I said, faking a smile. "Who all are coming?"

"The usual," she replied, motioning with her eyes toward the table. "*Hopefully Renee doesn't find out*," she mouthed.

Probably not – Renee had ventured off to torture a new group of kids. We were going to the mall to shop for the upcoming Homecoming dance. It was coming up in just a couple of weeks, giving us girls a reason to shop for clothes and our guy friends an excuse to check out the sports and electronics stores. Most couples were already paired off. I was the least likely to appear at any of our school dances. I would usually go just to hang out with my friends when the dance was over. Afterward was always more fun than the dance itself. It would have been funny to watch us from an outsider's point of view - a bunch of giggling teenagers crammed into a booth in a corner of our favorite restaurant. Living in a small town, there weren't many places that were open late, but we always had a blast.

I could see David coming through the doors. "I'll talk to you later?"

She nodded and returned to the debate that was going on about last night's game.

I felt myself wanting to run over and ask him a question that was burning in my mind. "Dave!"

"What's up, sexy?" He gave me his normal big grin.

I shuddered. I always hate it when he tries to pay me a compliment like that. I didn't see him the same way he saw me. And I was just not used to that kind of attention.

"What can you tell me about the history of our town?"

Dave's family had been one of the first to live in the town, and he loved history. This was a subject I cared nothing about. Right now, I had questions that needed answering. He knew everything about the town. If there were any stories, his parents would have heard them, and they would have passed them on to him.

He smiled like a lion, realizing that he could stop time to catch his prey. "You know you are setting yourself up for real punishment."

"Yeah, I know," I smiled, throwing him off guard. I love it when I do that to him. "Have time during study hall or after school?"

He loved any excuse for spending time with me. But this time, I didn't mind. "How about after school?"

"Sure. What time and where?"

I could tell I was going to be in for a long night by the cheesy smile and the tone of his voice. "I'll call you when I get home and we can meet somewhere."

"Sounds good. I'll catch you later," I agreed.

We hugged like we always did, and I headed for my locker. My mind was racing, thinking about the early history of the town. I really hated history as a subject. The stuff they teach you in school is mainly about the major wars and other earth-shattering events – nothing I was interested in. But Dave *loved* to talk about history. Especially about our town, every minute that he could. I heard the chitchat of the other kids around me as I finished at my locker and headed towards homeroom.

"Hey! Slow down!" I heard Lynn behind me, running to catch up. "Where's the fire?"

"Huh?" I didn't realize I was walking that fast. I was almost at homeroom already.

"Have you see him?" She asked, with her eyes full of wonder.

"Huh? See who?" Surprisingly, I had no clue about what or whom she was referring to.

"The new kid, duh!"

I replied, as uninterested as I could be. "Oh. He's starting this week?"

"Yeah, and everyone is curious about him," she said, out of breath.

I really didn't know why. And I couldn't have cared less. Parents were probably moving here to escape the violence of the big city or something.

I just rolled my eyes. "You would think with a school this large that no one would notice another body."

"I hear he's cute. More than cute! Drop-dead gorgeous!" I rolled my eyes again. This time she saw me do it. "What? You aren't at least *half* way interested?"

I laughed. "Why? I don't know or care to know every member of the four-thousand-student body that's already here. Why would I want to know about a newcomer?"

Her anticipation was killing her. "True. But maybe something interesting will actually happen, instead of just the normal gossip. I hope he attends here and he's not a freshman."

I nodded in agreement. Nothing exciting ever happens in our part of the state. Three thousand students crammed in one school while the freshman class crammed in the older school.

"You know he'll be the talk of the town for the first couple of weeks, maybe a month, and then everything will die down and become boring again."

"Agreed. But at least it's something!" She waved, as she walked into her homeroom.

Part of me truly regretted that I had never listened when Dave talked about our town's past. And he talked about it a *lot*! Like I said, I find history extremely boring and I tune it out as much as I can. Would Dave think I'm nuts for wanting to know about it now? Probably not. Most of what I do or say he takes as the most thrilling news he's ever heard.

Well at *least* my mind is quiet today. No voices. That's always a good sign. Right?

I took my seat and started writing a note to Val. We figured that keeping a notebook of our notes to pass back and forth was safer than actually writing on a single piece of paper and risking it getting lost. How do I explain this to her? She is one of my good friends. Not best. I had about five notebooks from friends that I had to write back to, Dave being one of them.

Dave

Is it possible that our town is... has ghosts? How far does our town actually date back? Who was here before us? Yeah, I know, you most likely think that I'm nuts. But I couldn't help but wonder...

OK, now he'll know I've gone off the deep end. I finished writing to the others just as the bell rang for the next class. Since we don't have time to stop and talk, we just grab the notebooks as we pass each other in the halls. Dave was always eager to read his right away. I could hear him laughing from down the hall. *Oh great!* I thought, as I started to feel myself blushing. By grace I was naturally tan, so no one really noticed.

School had ended, and the bus rides home were becoming a lot easier with my CD player. I had it continuously playing and never paid much attention to where we were along the route. My mind always came back to reality when it turned onto my street.

I hopped off the bus and went inside, and straight up to my room. Ding... Dong...

23

I raced down the stairs to get the door. "Dave! I thought you were going to call?"

"Why waste electricity?" He asked, as he turned away from the door towards the sidewalk. I grabbed my purse, made sure I had my keys, and followed out behind him. "Where to?" he asked.

"I just thought of something, be right back," I said, holding my finger up and racing back into the house.

I grabbed my portfolio and left a note for my parents so they would know that I had come home from school. They loved Dave. They never questioned when, where or how long I stayed out with him.

"What's that for?" he asked, as he noticed the camera in my hands.

I had a sly smile on my face as I looked up at him. "You'll see."

"Uh-oh. Now I'm scared," he grinned. "Where to?"

"Follow me..." I instructed, as we started down the street.

We headed in the direction of my favorite out-of-the-way clearing in the forest. It was right across the street from our neighborhood, but it was secluded enough. One of the local myths was that wild animals like to roam in there – just one of the many rumors made up by people who lived here. There was a nice, cool, crisp breeze flowing through the trees.

"Are you trying to get us eaten?" He teased, with amusement.

I just grinned back. "Yeah. I brought you as bait so I could escape."

We both laughed. I felt so much more at ease with him than I did with my other friends. Not that our friends judged me or anything. Nothing like that. It was just that he and I were best friends. We knew we could count on each other for anything. But the problem I was facing, how could I make it not sound strange, even to my strange group of friends?

"Now I see why you always come here..." His astonishment did not bewilder me. After all, that's why I come here in the first place. "This close to our houses and I've never been here before."

"So... tell me about our land..."

"In answer to your question from earlier... yes," he said, sitting on a stump that looked like it had been strategically placed there just for that purpose. I went to sit next to him, carefully setting down my portfolio and camera. "Before the houses you see now were built, there were crops and empty land."

I interrupted him. "Woooo, crop circles!?"

The corners of his mouth started upward. "No." He was always serious when he talked about history. I looked at him apologetically and motioned for him to continue. He continued. "There is nothing in the history but some old tales that were passed on from traveler to traveler. Even back in the early 1800's, before the first settlers came and planted roots. Before that, many different Indian tribes lived here."

I knew this was going to be a long story, so I settled in, trying to get comfortable.

"No one knows for sure which tribes lived in the area – only that they were here because the soil was so rich. You know where the old, old, old part of town is located?"

I nodded. It was somewhere in his neighborhood. Over the years, each new resident had changed a part of the land, no matter how small, to make it his or her own.

"Well, it's been said that it was the site of the original village built by the new settlers after the Indians had left. Legend has it that it wasn't a completely peaceful transition. But once the village was established, everything calmed down. At least until two unwed women – sisters – showed up from no one really knew where. Then the trouble started, and the rumors began to fly."

Nothing's changed there, I thought. Dave smirked as though he could read my mind.

"Not long after the sisters arrived, the villagers began losing crops and livestock; even some of the people died mysteriously. Although this time period was much later than the original witch hunts of the 1600s. The people who lived here were highly superstitious, and misfortunes and tragedies like this were often blamed on "witchcraft." The villagers were convinced that the sisters were behind these tragedies. They accused the newcomers of practicing black magic. An ultimatum was given: leave the village and never return, or be burned alive.

"The sisters were as different as night and day. Each was beautiful in her own way; one sister had hair as pale as corn silk, and the other had rich, dark tresses. But they had one trait in common - their green eyes. The legend says that the dark-haired sister was a good witch who tried to protect the village from her sister's wrath. She is said to have been weary of moving constantly from one settlement to another and wanted a place to call home.

"Some said that she had fallen in love with an Indian named Lakota. Their love was forbidden by the laws of his people. When the tribe learned of the illicit love, they commanded their brother to return to them and never to see her again. But he knew that she was carrying his child, and he could not bear to be separated from her. He told his tribe that he was truly sorry and ran to her side as she fought to save the village from being destroyed by her sister's rage.

"Lakota would never believe that his love was evil. Even with the tales of how the witches controlled people with their eyes and forced them to do their bidding. Because the villagers had dared to cast the sisters out, the evil witch had sworn her vengeance. As he watched the resulting inferno, Lakota knew that all hope of saving his love was gone. The villagers either fled or died trying to save their land. In the midst of his despair, Lakota heard a cackle; whirling around, he caught sight of the flaxen-haired witch, who was staring right at him. He was so consumed with hatred for her that her powers were useless against him. In all of the settlements that she and her sister had encountered, they had never crossed another person who was able to withstand their powers. Yet Lakota, seeing red in his fury, went charging after her and killed her before as she stood in shock. His anger abated, he watched helplessly as the town burned; when nothing was left, he turned away and returned to his tribe.

"Although the tribe was remorseful for failing to offer their assistance, they knew that they could have done nothing to aid the settlers against the witch; but the land itself was another story. The chief, knowing that he could not heal the earth on his own, called two forth two spirit animals – a dog and a cat – to carry a message back to their fellow creatures. The spirit animals placed a spell on the land. That if the settlers should return, the witch would no longer be able to wreak her havoc. But although they came back to salvage what they could, they left as quickly as they came, fearing the promised return of the evil witch. It was rumored that the dark-haired sister escaped unharmed, but since she didn't know how to find her love, she went after the fleeing villagers in order to protect them. Sometime in the 1830s, a new wave of settlers arrived. Although they had heard the rumors of the disaster that took place only decades before, they did not take the legend of the witches to heart. All that remained of the original village were a few homes that had survived the holocaust.

"Lakota was heartbroken and never recovered his spirits – he would never see his love again as long as he lived. He vowed that after his human life was over, he would remain to protect the land. Moved by his sorrow, the other members of the tribe added their vows to his. So it's been said that if you are quiet enough, you can hear the tongues from the past – not only at night, but during the day as well. But because none of his people remain, no one knows how to interpret what the voices are saying. It has also been told that the evil witch lived on after everyone else was long gone. There are those who still say that they can hear the evil sister call out to her coven. No one knows for sure the exact location where all of these events took place. Since new homes are being built here, the older residents have kept the rumors of "seeing" and "hearing" things on the down-low. Everyone who has lived here for any amount of time knows that this town is haunted to some degree, but no one really likes to talk about it.

My eyes grew wide. "Why is it kept on the down-low?" I was thinking that I had always known something else was here besides us, I had just never known what.

"Well, this is the wealthy part of town, as you know," he reminded me. "Since no one else mentions unusual activity in the rest of the town, the people who live here don't want to be thought of as crazy."

"Isn't it possible that bizarre things of this nature happen in the other towns, and they are all thinking the same thing we are?" I asked.

"Possible," he shrugged.

"Have you ever heard or seen anything bizarre?" I asked, wanting desperately to show him my pictures.

"The only thing bizarre in this town is you," he teased, with a big grin.

I rolled my eyes. "Ha. Ha. Seriously, though. Do you believe in all this hoop-la?"

"Yes, I do, and no, I haven't encountered any flying ghosts." He started to put his arm around me. "Whatever is scaring you, I'm here now and I'll protect you."

"I am *not* scared!" *Am I though?* "Just frustrated with something." He glanced at me, not like I'd lost it, but with a what-in-the-world-is-she-talking-about look in his eyes. "Promise not to laugh?"

I rolled my eyes again and smiled as he signaled an X on his chest with his finger and grinned. "Scout's honor."

I grabbed my portfolio and handed the photos to him. I didn't say anything about what he was to look for. I wanted to know if he could see the same thing I had seen. I sat back to enjoy the lively scents that surrounded us and watched as Dave tried to picture which spot they had been taken in.

"These are really good, Lex. No wonder why you love coming here so much." For some reason, I never cringed when he used my name like that. Even though I hated it, I knew my name could be a mouthful at times. He finished going through the smaller photos and handed them back to me as he studied the larger one. I placed the ones he returned back in my folder so they wouldn't get damaged. "What the...?" I heard him start to say.

"So it's just not me?" I sighed, with relief.

"There is another rumor about our town," he started to say. We both stopped short when we heard a faint growl.

"What the...!"

We looked at each other and pretty much thought the same thing – it can't be possible! I could tell something was wrong with Dave. He's the bravest person I know. Nothing ever scares him that I've seen. So it frightened me that much more when I heard the tone of his voice.

"See, that is what I don't know," my voice was about to crack, but we still didn't move. "What other rumor were you going to tell me about?"

He tried to appear brave. "I better get you home."

Maybe it was just me, but I could tell that something was wrong. He completely ignored my last question. So I just nodded and didn't press the issue. I took him back out by a different path. Thinking I might want to return to figure this one my own without him knowing where I was. I still wanted this place to remain a mystery to others.

I think Dave was like me. He *believed,* but he didn't at the same time.

"I'll see you in school tomorrow," he said, as he gave me a quick hug goodbye and started off home with wonder in his eyes. Since he didn't give me time to respond, I waved behind him as he took off down the street. I couldn't get over what Dave had said, or actually didn't say. He hadn't finished telling me about the last rumor he had mentioned.

I knew that my parents were home, because both of their cars were in the driveway. I could smell that dinner was almost done as I walked into the house. There weren't many meals that Mom made that I didn't like. Mom and Dad used to be all lovey-dovey. I can't exactly tell you when that all stopped. I just like to think that they got into the routine of married life. Then again, I knew other couples who never stopped being affectionate with one another, no matter how long they had been married. Routines were great when it came to certain things. Other times not so much.

"Hey, Dad?" I asked.

He replied without looking up from what he was doing. "What's up?"

"May I go online for a little bit?"

"Sure. Not too long, though."

"Thanks."

He started up the computer and walked away. I just sat there, waiting for it to boot up. Technology was great, but not so much. Especially when it took you longer to log in; than to just write something down with a pen and paper. Once the computer was booted up, Dad came back and logged me onto the server. Mom didn't even know how to turn on a computer, and I wasn't allowed to touch it unless he was there to supervise.

I browsed the Internet for a little bit. Since it was still so new to the public sector, there wasn't really that much out there. The chat rooms were for the most part boring, depending on who else was on. There were many chat rooms to choose from. I decided to try a generic one for now.

Please wait while connecting to General Chat Room 15

I finally got in and started reading what everyone was typing. Every few lines you would see a/s/l, meaning that age/sex/location was the current pick-up line for the chat room, which varied in ages and locations of its users. I replied the normal 17/f/Greneville, and then got up to get a drink. When I came back, I had an IM waiting.

There was a box to click yes or no.

Accept IM from Lynn2155?

I clicked yes, and a box opened up in front of the chat room.

Lynn2155: Hey Lexi! It's me!

FCG95: Hey Lynn!

Lynn2155: My parents finally broke down and bought a computer!

FCG95: Awesome!

I really wanted to tell her I knew about Mike, but I decided not to. I had picked my screen name by the fires we had whenever we always got together, country because I loved country music. The girl part was a no brainer.

Lynn2155: Yeah I know! So what do you normally do on here?

FCG95: Not much, LOL

Lynn2155: Yeah, the chat rooms seem boring. Which one are you in?

FCG95: General 15. Nothing exciting happening in here. Gonna check out another one.

Lynn2155: K. Let me know which one and I'll be there.

FCG95: K.

I clicked the *leave chat room* button and clicked on another chat room.

FCG95: I'm in General 439

Lynn2155: Be right there

Soon, Lynn was in the chat room with me. Same old a/s/l was popping up. I answered as usual, and then started laughing when I saw what Lynn had typed in: 21/f/Greneville

FCG95: Why did you put that?

I typed in our private IM box.

"What's so funny?" Mom asked.

Lynn2155: Just to mess with people.

"Lynn is messing with people in the chat rooms," I explained.

FCG95: IC

"How so?" mom asked.

Lynn2155: Oh crap, now some 35 yo is asking if he's too old for me.

I laughed out loud at what Lynn had typed.

"She's telling everyone she's four years older than she really is," I explained.

FCG95: Well, duh, since you are only 17 LMAO

"You guys can't wait to grow up," Mom mumbled.

Lynn2155: Mom says I have to get off. See you tomorrow.

FCG95: Laters.

Hope her mom didn't catch her doing what she did. She would never be allowed back on.

"So what's going on in the chat rooms?" Mom asked looking up from her book.

"Oh, nothing. The usual. People seeing if there is anyone the same age who lives near them."

Since there was nothing else going on, I clicked *leave chat room* and closed all the windows.

"I'm done, Dad!" I shouted, downstairs.

"OK, did you sign off?" He called, from the downstairs bedroom.

"Doing it right now!" I answered back.

"I'll turn off the computer later!" He hollered back.

"OK!" I stood up from the table and decided to go for a run. "Can I go for a quick run, Mom?"

She glanced at the time. "A little late, don't you think?"

"I won't be gone long, promise."

Her hesitation was making me nervous. "Well, OK. Have fun."

"Thanks."

I threw on my shoes and headed out the door. The air was getting cooler by the day, and the leaves were starting to change and fall off their branches. It was very peaceful here in autumn. I also couldn't wait for Christmas. I love it when everyone has their decorations up, and as you run past, you just can feel the spirit of Christmas in the air. Now, though, people were just starting to prepare for Halloween; some took that just as seriously as Christmas, if not more.

I took the fast way, since I had promised Mom that it would be a quick run. I ran by the old Victorian house, which was just as dark and lifeless as the day before. Nothing ever changed much in this town. With the exception of the seasons, but even so, everyone still did the same thing they had in the years before. This town was so predictable - way too routine.

I started past the park behind my house. Nothing seemed out of the ordinary at first, but as I got about halfway through, I thought I saw something moving. I slowed down to look, but didn't see anything. I played it up to just my eyes playing tricks on me in the dark and continued towards home.

When I got there, Mom and Dad were getting ready for bed. I did the usual and headed off to bed myself. I made sure my alarm was set and started in where I had left off in my book.

Chapter 3 – The Dreams Reality

The week had flown by – I couldn't believe that it was Friday already! I hadn't heard any more unusual voices, and I hadn't been back to my private spot since that afternoon with Dave. So I think I'm doing pretty good.

Today had begun as any usual day.

"Hey, guys!" Terry smiled, as he approached our table. "Sorry I haven't been around much lately."

"It's cool," Aaron replied.

Terry shot him a look when Aaron looked away.

"Yeah, we know when we're not wanted," Lynn winked at him.

"It's not like that at all," he said, feeling bad about not hanging out with us more.

"We know," I said, trying to smooth things over. "You've been busy, we know that."

"Yeah. I just don't see how *you* have so much time," he said, glowering at Aaron.

"I play baseball, not football. They don't run us ragged," Aaron gloated.

"Do you mind if I sit with you guys today?"

Why would he ask permission? He knew he didn't need to ask.

"Don't see why not," Lynn said.

"Thank you. Again, I'm really sorry."

"OK, what's going on?" Dave asked, sensing that something was up.

"Nothing," He insisted, and then hesitated. "It's just that the new captain is being a pain. He's letting the *power* make him think that he's king."

"Knew there was a reason," Val commented.

"Again, I'm sorry…"

"Oh, stop that," I blurted. "You're always welcome here."

"Thank you guys. Have I missed anything much?" We all looked at one another and shrugged. "Ah. The same old same old. I miss that."

"Yup, we're just another boring group," I said, taking a sip of my soda.

"Hey, nothing wrong with that." We all glared at him. "That's not what I meant, and you know it."

"What are you doing tomorrow?" Dave asked.

Terry shuddered. "I have an away game."

"Ah. So you wouldn't be interested in joining us for some *boring* homecoming shopping."

"That sounds like fun!" His excitement vanished as quickly as it came. "What time?"

Aaron answered as he took a bite of his pizza. "Late morning."

"Crap. My game is early afternoon."

"It's OK, really," I said, putting my hand on his arm to comfort him.

"I wish I could quit football," Terry dejected.

"Your dad won't let you do that," Aaron said, shoving another bite of the pizza in his mouth.

You could tell the tension was growing.

"Yeah, this I know," he deeply exhaled.

"Just think though, once you are off to college, you can do whatever you want," Val encouraged.

"If it was that easy," Dave answered, for him.

"All this talk makes me want to go to college sooo bad," Lynn joked.

"At least you don't have such a strict dad," Terry mumbled, under his breath.

"Yeah, but at least you're going to college for free," Lynn retorted.

"OK, enough arguing," I groaned. I grabbed some food off Dave's plate. We do that quiet often when one of us orders something different.

"OK, ummm," Val said, tapping her finger against her chin. "HOMECOMING?"

Terry just groaned. Homecoming was the worst, because it's like an unwritten rule that the homecoming games were the most important of the season.

"Oh, get over it," Lynn cracked. "We'll be there to support you."

"I know. But Dad heard there are going to be scouts there. That's the only reason I moaned."

"Wait, weren't you already accepted into a college?" I asked.

"Yeah. But Dad wants to see whether any other schools want me."

"That sucks. We're really sorry, Terry." Dave spoke, on behalf of all of us.

We sat and talked about other things for a while, trying to get his mind off the seriousness of football. It was a real shame that his father had killed his love for the game. It wasn't as if their family *needed* the scholarship. Everyone called his dad El Cheapo. By the end of the lunch hour, we had Terry smiling. It looked like he was even enjoying himself a bit.

The rest of the day went by without me hearing voices, and I went about my normal routine. The bus ride home sucked. My batteries died halfway home. I had to listen to the mindless chatter again. Since I almost always got home before my parents, I had complete peace once I was there. Not much to do besides enjoy the silence or blast my favorite music.

For the most part, it was an uneventful evening. Mom came home and started dinner. Dad worked on one of his projects. We ate and cleaned up, and I played on the computer for a little bit.

"Mom?" I asked.

"Yes?" She answered, without looking up from her book.

"Do you mind if I go prom dress shopping with everyone tomorrow?"

Now she set her book down. "Yeah, no problem. Do you have a date?"

"Yeah, right," I snorted.

She looked surprised. "Dave didn't ask you?"

I felt like I was being left out of some big secret. "No. Why, was he supposed to?"

She went back to her book as I made a face and groaned. "No. I don't know," she said, shrugging. "You're with him all the time, so I just figured that you two were going together."

"Ew. Mom! I don't see him like that. He's only a friend."

She pretended to be taken back at my comment. "Oh, OK. Sorry I mentioned it."

"Do you mind if I go out for a run?"

"That's fine," she said, already absorbed in her novel again. "What time are you going shopping tomorrow?"

"Probably late morning," I answered.

"OK. I work the afternoon shift tomorrow, so most likely I won't be here when you get home."

"That's fine. I'll be back in a few."

I got ready for my nightly run. I made sure to replace the batteries in my CD player before taking off. Tonight's run was no different than any other. I had the strangest sensation that I was being watched. But every time I looked around, no one was there. I only ran for about thirty minutes or so. I knew I had a lot to do at home, since I would be gone for most of the day tomorrow.

Back in my room, I picked out clothes for our shopping trip. We would be trying on dresses for the upcoming homecoming dance. I wanted to pick an outfit that would be easy to put on and take off. After I found one that worked, I sat down at my desk to straighten out my portfolio.

Ms. Kohel had offered to submit my work to a college to have it critiqued, but I had refused. I knew her intention was to have a college offer me a scholarship. As much as my parents would love that, photography was not something I wanted to do for a living. I had almost finished rearranging my portfolio when I came across that odd picture again. I couldn't help but think about how this guy had ruined my frame. I would have to take another picture to replace it. I tossed the photo aside and put away my portfolio. I got comfortable in bed and picked up the book that I had been reading.

Dreaming is the best way to occupy your nights. Often, my dreams were full of odd details; they just didn't make any sense. The dreams would continue on like that until I woke up. In one recurring dream, I am inside a house with stairs leading to all different doors. A fun house, one might consider it. I never opened any of the doors, just tried to find my way out by taking the stairs. If I did manage to open a door, it would lead to another room with more doors, and so on.

I love dreaming so vividly, just as if I were really there. The only part that sucked was trying to remember all of the details when I woke up. One dream wasn't so much a nightmare but confused the living day lights out of me. Was when, one of my favorite teachers was there. He said, "You are who you are. Only you can change who you are." Out of all of my dreams of dinosaurs, weird houses, and jumping from location to location in a blink of an eye, that dream was definitely the strangest.

The sun shone bright and inviting on my secluded forest clearing. I had my camera with me so I could take some more photographs. I really wish I had one of those nice cameras with a zoom lens, where you don't need to be an inch away from your subject to take a picture. But I manage with what I have. I was lying there, perfectly still, waiting for any "wildlife" to come by and sit still for a minute so I could capture it against the green of the foliage. When I say "wildlife," I am referring even to insects. I was stretched out motionless in the grass when it happened.

"Hello, my sweet Alexandra."

I jumped to my feet and looked around. I saw no one. There was no wind, no breeze, so I knew I hadn't just imagined the voice. It had sounded sweet, inviting and welcoming.

"What do you want?" I asked, making a complete circle as I tried to see to the owner of the voice.

"I do not mean to frighten you."

"You're not!" That was a lie. I could feel a scream starting up in my chest. "Who are you? What do you want? *Where* are you?"

"I will show myself to you if you promise not to run." The voice sounded almost as if it were begging me to stay.

"Umm, OK," I nodded, still trying to figure out which direction this voice was coming from. "GASP!" I clapped my hand over my mouth. I didn't know what to say, what to do, or even what to think! The boy standing in front of me was, without a doubt, the one in the picture I had developed at school.

"I am so sorry to have frightened you," he said, as he slowly approached me. "I was trying to send you signs so you would not be afraid."

"W…h…y?" I felt like I was whispering, if you can call forming syllables with your mouth whispering. "What signs?"

"Please, oh please, my dear Alexandra," he stopped where he stood and just gazed at me. Not like a deer-in-the-headlights gaze, but with such compassion, such benevolence. Part of me wanted to run, but a bigger part of me was filled with curiosity. He began moving across the open space between us.

"Please do not be afraid. I simply had to speak with you." His speech sounded oddly formal, confusing me.

I could not take my eyes away from his. They were the most beautiful brown. His composure was something that you would see in an old black and white film. His dark, sandy brown hair was neatly combed to one side. I would guess he was at least nineteen, by the way he carried himself, but his vocabulary was not of this time. Even the college students I knew never spoke in this manner.

"Who are you?"

"My name is Jay." His eyes gazed back at me with such intensity - I don't even know the word that would be used to describe it.

"Hello," I replied, dumbstruck.

Stupid stupid stupid!

"No, you are not stupid," he replied, as if reading my mind. His smile was like no other. It was absolutely perfect. "I know our two worlds can never be one, but you are so beautiful, I just had to speak to you." I looked around in complete confusion. He laughed the most beautiful laugh I have ever heard. "Even though we are not of the same world, I would still like to converse with you." By now, he was only a few feet away. There was something so strange and outlandish about him. "It would be such a pleasure to converse with you for a little while."

He bowed, lowering his head with his arm in front of him.

"Why me?" I asked, finally able to speak. "You keep mentioning worlds. What worlds are you talking about?"

I was thinking that either I'm losing it, or this guy, this incredibly gorgeous, melting brown-eyed guy who I had never met was playing a very bad trick on me.

"I am afraid that you will just have to trust me. I cannot explain more at this moment." He looked at me with such intensity that I was compelled to know more. "I am what mortals refer to as a spirit guide."

"OK," I gulped, trying not to sound like an idiot. What was a spirit guide? "What would you like to know?"

"My sweet Alexandra, you act as though this were an interrogation." The smile slowly vanished as he seemed to wonder whether he had made a mistake in addressing me. "Please, accept my apologies for disturbing you."

I tried to sound like *I* knew how to speak properly. "May I ask you a question?"

My parents mostly ignored me when I used the word "can" instead of "may."

"Within reason, I shall respond to whatever you wish to ask."

He had moved to a sitting position in the middle of the clearing. I edged closer to this creature about which I knew nothing, trying to think of questions that did not involve the "other world" issue.

"Why me?" That was really the only question that came to mind.

"Because, my love…"

That snapped me back to reality. Did he just say what I think he said? "Whoa! Hold up! Don't call me your *love!*" His sweet, angelic look turned instantly to hurt. "I'm sorry. But how can you call me your "love" when we've technically never even met?"

His sweet voice was an octave lower. "You are right. I am sorry." He bowed his head.

I knew I had sounded more sarcastic than I really meant to. "OK, *Jay*, so why did you seek me?"

His eyes looked deep into mine. "I could not find the strength to speak to you again."

I was so taken aback by his sincerity. Whatever thoughts I had before about this guy standing in front of me, were gone. I wanted to know why he had picked me. Why was he here, and what did he mean about having the strength to speak to me?

As terrified as I was, I no longer had the urge to run. I was compelled to know more about him. "So why now?"

"I prayed that in this way…" pausing… "You would not be frightened. Yet I can see that you are very much so."

I lied. "No, I am not." Actually, I wasn't exactly frightened, but I just couldn't put my finger on the word for what I was feeling. Then the curiosity that had killed the cat came to mind, and I shuddered inwardly.

"You are not a very good liar," he said, flashing me a smile that I could have sworn made my heart miss a beat.

No one but Dave had ever been able to read me like that; so how could he?

"OK, answer this for me." Somehow, this felt like a dream but didn't at the same time. "Who are you? Where do you live? Why do you want to talk to *me,* and who are your parents?"

That should do for a start. Everyone knows everyone here. I figured if any parents didn't know them directly, a friend of a friend would. He looked at the air like someone out there was telling him what to say. After what seemed to be forever, he started:

"I live here. You are so beautiful - I just had to talk to you. I do not know what happened to my parents." The last sentence was barely audible. I lowered my face, unsure of how to respond.

"Okay," I was the next to speak up after a short silence. "What is your last name? What part of town do you live in? And who are you staying with? I've never seen you at school."

He seemed rather affected by my tone. "From the sound of your voice, you are no longer afraid of me."

"I am, a little," I admitted. "Should I be?"

"No, you should not," he said, smiling that beautiful smile and making my heart skip another beat. "I have never done th..." He started to say.

Curious as to what he had been about to say, I asked, "Done what?"

Was I dreaming? Through all the thoughts and questions I had racing and barreling into each other in my head, I knew one thing for sure - no man of this magnitude had ever approached me like this. Not that I was ugly, but I was hardly beautiful. I considered myself average. Not fat, not skinny. Athletic. Not too short, but not tall, either.

"Yes and no, about whether you are dreaming." His faced relaxed into that smile that never seemed to end. *How could he read my thoughts?* "I see you still have a lot of questions."

Well duh! But I don't think you need to be a mind reader to know that! Somehow I was afraid to even think, in fear that he would hear or read my thoughts.

"I want more than anything in our worlds to be able to speak the truth." I felt a chill in the air as he let out a sigh. *Worlds? What in the world does he mean by* worlds? *Okay, so now I* know, *I'm dreaming.*

"You keep referring to *worlds*," I said, staggering. "What do you mean by worlds?" When he turned to me, his face was filled with agony, as though I had hurt him somehow. What was I supposed to think? Let a mind-boggling question go unanswered? "How can you *love* someone if you don't trust them enough to tell them the truth?" I asked somewhat sarcastically.

HA! Threw it right back at him. I still think that this was nothing but a mean joke. As fast as the anger came across his face, it disappeared again. He knew I was right.

"I can see that you are wise beyond your years," he said, with that sweet smile. I felt like I was going to have a heart attack in my sleep. "The time will come when all the answers that you seek will become clear."

I don't know what made me say it, but I did. "I know I'm dreaming, that I cannot deny, so how can I say what is real, when it's only in my head?"

"If you have the insight to ask such a question, you already know the truth," he said, and then turned toward the naked trees behind him.

I suddenly felt another sharp chill. *Great!* Not only did I sound like I was trying to insult him, but my questions must have sounded like they were being asked by a petulant five year-old. He was not dressed like a normal teenager. He was dressed so much more formally, in a strange outfit that was brown and looked like a step down from a tuxedo. For some reason, I did not want this time to end, even if I was only dreaming.

"You speak as though you are not from this time period," I remarked, wondering if I was saying too much. The change of expression on his face told me that I was getting close to the truth.

"You are most correct," he said, looking intently at me. His brown eyes had me memorized. "I know you could never love someone such as me. Not in this lifetime."

"Love is such a strong word," I replied.

Looking into those eyes, I lost track of whether it was day or night. Love *was* such a strong word when it came to another person. I loved pizza. But if I fell out of love with pizza and fell in love with pasta that wouldn't hurt anyone.

"Again, you are correct. It is. It is the most powerful emotion there is." By this time, we were only several inches away from one another, and the air seemed to chill my bones; yet I was not shaking.

"I'm…" I was just able to say.

"Your heart is pure, that I see. You are wise to perceive the things you do. I wish that I could explain the things you cannot yet see, but at this present time, I am bound and cannot say more." His face fell, again in despair.

"I am sure I will figure it out." In fact, I was determined to figure it out. "Will I see you again? If so, when?" I knew I was pressing my luck after acting, as it seemed to me, like a five year-old.

"Whenever you wish my dear." He was clearly delighted at the idea that I wanted to see him again. "But I must warn you before we part," now looking down, "Seeing and conversing with you the way we are now, is the easiest way for me."

I had no idea what he meant by that.

"Will you be here tomorrow afternoon?" I asked, knowing that he would say no. I couldn't really blame him. "I don't know what you mean by "in this manner"."

But his eyes lit up. "Yes. But you should know that, even if you do not see me with your eyes, I will be here. I will let you know of my presence. I must also warn you – there is another entity that is seeking your attention, as I am. But this one is in a form that you will not recognize."

Still not sure whether I was dreaming or awake, I wanted to at least appear like I knew proper grammar. "As it seems that you must leave, may I know when we can talk again in this manner?" He bowed his head. *Hopefully* I would get at least one straight answer from this mystery man.

"We may converse in the present way at any time you wish," that sweet smile appeared on his face once more, and then started to fade away. "In the other state, you may not always see me with your eyes. I will try to summon the strength to appear clearly to you at least once each week." His eyes wandered, seeming as though they were about to fill with tears. "I cannot explain outright, as others may hear me who will not tolerate this. You will need to learn to understand on your own."

I wanted to throw my arms around this gorgeous creature as we stood together in the clearing. I didn't want to stop looking in his eyes - deep brown eyes that twinkled and glowed in the light and shadow. They seemed to see only me, as though there were not another soul among us.

We stood not more than two inches apart, but it felt like a mile. I took a step forward and lifted my hand. I needed to touch him to make sure that he was real. His hand, with the utmost hesitation, slowly reached for mine, and I began to feel a chill. But it did not chill me as the fall winds have. It was sensation I could not explain -a warming chill as our hands grew closer together, our eyes never leaving each other's.

I heard a shallow beeping in the background. I knew that sound, but I could not pinpoint what it belonged to. He froze, and the connection between our eyes was broken; and he looked around as if a semi was headed straight for him.

"What's wrong?" I asked, still keeping my hand where it was.

"Not a thing, my dear. Time flies faster than the wind when I am with you," he started to smile again.

Will someone shut that stupid noise off! I thought. I did not want this day or night to end. I could not tell what time it was, nor did I care.

"I will always be by your side, no matter where you go. You will not know I am there, but I will be there unless you tell me to go." He spoke with such sincerity that I felt my heart skip a beat.

The beeping sound became an octave higher.

My hand rose towards his, so I could at least touch him before whatever was coming could find us. Our hands were just about to touch, I could feel the cool air against my tongue, an air I have never tasted, and the chill that was around me seemed to turn even colder. Yet it wasn't the cold of the fall air that was rolling in. It was a cold I have never felt before.

That beeping sound seemed to be getting closer, no matter how hard I tried to block it out.

"This is not goodbye," he said, with a smile that started to arch into a frown. "Until we meet again."

"NOOOO!" I couldn't believe that he was gone.

Chapter 4 – State of Confusion

"ALEXANDRA!"

Beep…beep…beep… I bolted upright, trying to figure out at what had just happened.

I was no longer in my clearing – I was in my *bedroom*. As my eyes adjusted to the daylight, I spotted my alarm clock.

Crap, I'm late!

"I'LL BE RIGHT THERE!" I screamed.

I turned off my alarm clock and raced to get ready. I threw on my clothes, brushed my teeth, ran a brush through my hair and raced down the stairs.

"Have fun!" Mom said, laughing as she pressed something into my hand.

"Mom!" I groaned. She knew that I was well aware of the financial situation. Even though we lived in the upscale side of town, ever since my Dad had lost his full-time job a while back, money had been an issue. "It's fine. Really," she smiled. "Now, go have fun with your friends." I sighed and ran out the door.

Half of our group lived on the other side of the city where our school was, which was closer to the mall. The rest of us had made arrangements to carpool over. Lynn, Mike, Dave and I were all riding together. Val and her boyfriend Aaron were meeting us at the mall. Even with Mike off at college, he never acted like he was better than anyone else. We didn't see him as often as we had when he was still in high school, but that didn't change anything.

On the ride over, I droned out the endless babble of what colors and accessories they would be sporting at the dance. I stared off in the distance, still thinking about last night. Had it been real? Normally, I have a hard time remembering all the details of a dream after I wake up. But this was different. I remembered everything so vividly – like it had just taken place.

47

"So, what do you think?"

"Huh?" I stared at Dave with a dumbfound look.

"Do you think I should go as vampire and scare everyone?"

"You don't need to dress up to scare anyone, Dave," I joked.

Dave was sweet, and we could all rag on each other without anyone feeling hurt.

"Yeah, you're right," he grinned as hard as he could, squeezing his eyes closed.

He was cute, no doubt about that. No one could understand how I wasn't attracted to him. But I just didn't see him that way. To me, he was like an older brother. "*There are lines that can't be crossed once you reach a certain stage,*" I had explained one time to everyone. "*You have the infatuation line. That crosses into relationship, and if that ends, there's no going back. Or the friendship stage, where if you end up getting into a relationship, things never seem the same. And then you lose a friend.*" Dave had always promised we would still be friends, no matter what. But I had never wanted to take that chance.

"So what type of dress are you hunting for?" Lynn asked.

"You make this sound like a battle," I groaned.

"In some ways it is," she giggled. At this point, Mike and Dave were wrapped up in their own conversation. "So I know for one, not to be looking for the same thing, so we don't end up looking like twins." The guys stopped talking, and we all burst in laughter. We knew what the guys were thinking when Lynn said the word twins. *Teenage boys,* I thought to myself. Lynn and Mike were in a debate over the radio, and Dave looked at me as I stared out the window. That shouldn't really bother him. I had never been much of a talker in large groups.

"What's on your mind?" Dave asked.

"Just a dream I had." I wasn't lying. But *was* it a dream?

He sounded overly curious. "What was it about?"

I really didn't want to get into it, not with the other two in the car. I know they would mean well, but I would be the running joke up until school restarted next year. So I just glanced towards Mike and Lynn, hoping they didn't see me looking.

"Oh. Okay. Later," he quietly finished.

I was always glad that I didn't have to say much for Dave to understand me. We pulled up into a parking spot and started towards the entrance. Val and Aaron were already waiting for us.

"Geez," Aaron impatiently coughed. His finger was tapping his watch. "Did you guys lose a horse on the way here?" Now he smiled and laughed.

"Never mind him, guys," Val said, elbowing him in the side. "He's thrilled to be here!"

"Yeah, I just *love* dress shopping," he said, rolling his eyes.

"Remember," Mike reminded him. "*They* are dress shopping. We men are *tool* shopping."

"Even better!" Aaron agreed.

Val, Lynn and I headed off to start in the discount stores. After all, why pay retail for something that you are only going to wear once? We were giggling as we strode into the first store. The guys hung back and waited for us right outside.

Everyone was so pale compared to me. It was harder for me to find a dress that wouldn't make me look like a freak. A lot of colors just didn't look right with my skin tone. It made me feel really uncomfortable, as though I were a huge fashion mistake or something.

"How does this look?" I asked Lynn.

I am not very creative when it comes to dressing up. In fact, my idea of dressing up is wearing a flannel shirt over a white t-shirt with jeans. Purple is my favorite color and I found a purple dress that glittered and had accent rhinestones. I thought the dress was beautiful. I put it on and stood in front of the mirror. Even though I loved the dress, it just somehow seemed to clash with my dark thick hair, deep brown eyes and tan skin. I sighed. It didn't help that I didn't have a figure either. I had large hips. It made it impossible to look right in anything. And made it impossible for anything to look like it actually fit.

"It's...ummm..." You could tell she was looking for the words. "The dress is beautiful, but the color..." She was right.

I looked at the price tag. More than double what I wanted to spend. We changed into our regular clothes and headed off to the next store. This time, we hit a major retailer. We knew we would spend more money there. If we picked something that we could get away with wearing twice, it might be worth it.

"Why didn't you model for me, hunny?" Aaron asked, playfully, pouting at Val.

"'Cuz nothing I saw in there I liked," she shrugged, ignoring his immature behavior.

He wrapped his arms around her, and she rolled her eyes as he whined, "It's not about what you like, it's what *I* like."

We rolled our eyes in sympathy as we went into the next store. The boys went to oogle over the electronics, while the girls headed off to the clearance racks.

Val picked up probably the most hideous dress in the store. "Ooooh, isn't this pretty!"

"Oh, that's so you!" Lynn agreed. "Why don't you try it on?"

We all giggled. We knew that even though it was hideous she would end up buying it and making it into one of her own creations.

"I might just have to do that," Val said, swinging the dress over her arm.

This should be interesting. She hadn't even checked the size. From between some other dresses that just seemed to be thrown together on one rack, a glitter caught my eye. Something about the dress looked familiar. I couldn't believe it.

"LOOK AT THIS!" I cried, holding up the dress.

The girls looked my way. I never really get excited about much, and I *was* excited!

"That's the same dress, but in royal blue!" Lynn was holding the dress up to examine it. "And your size!" I flipped over to check the price." And half the price!" She was just as excited as I was.

"Well let's make sure it fits. And doesn't make me look like an overgrown blueberry."

We all giggled again. I held the dress up in front of me in front of the mirror. *Not bad.* I thought. *But I wonder what it's going to look like when it's actually on.*

We were all giggling, talking about who was going to be there, what type of music they were going to play, whether they would enforce the six-inch rule and if there would be anything new on the menu. We always went to the same place after all of our dances – the *only* place that was open 24/7 in our town.

I slowly crept towards the mirror. Lynn was already there, with some pink dress that I could only dream of wearing. Val had on the gaudy dress she had picked up, and I had on the blueberry one.

Those two were playing with their hair to see what would look good with the dresses they had on. Val really seemed to be enjoying her find, which, surprisingly, looked good on her. You could just see what she was planning on changing.

"Well… what do you guys think?" I asked, standing as stiff as a statue.

"Now, that looks awesome!" Lynn said, with a big smile on her face. "Yeah. That color is much better!"

"If you wanted to be a blueberry…" Val teased. "You would put all the other blueberries to shame."

I looked in the mirror. Even though my skin tone was natural, it was still hard for me to see the beauty in whatever I wore.

"I would kill to have your skin tone," remarked Lynn.

"And I would kill to have yours," I whimpered, smiling back at her. "You know how hard it is to find something that doesn't make me look like a freak or a *blueberry*?"

"Oh, please," she said, rolling her eyes. "You spend the afternoon with me, and I could make you look like a model."

"She's right," Val agreed. "You don't give yourself enough credit."

"You know I'm not the one to go to school all dolled up." In fact, I hated the idea. I loved being natural and not have to worry about whether my makeup was on right.

"That's right, you're not. That's why the guys like you," Lynn commented, with a hint of envy.

"Yeah. Whatever," I could feel the warmth in my cheeks.

"It's true. I could name five guys right now who want to ask you out, but they don't think that they are good enough for you," Val stated, still looking in the mirror and imagining what hairdo would look the best.

Lynn chimed in. "You have this mysterious thing going for you. But at the same time, you aren't afraid to speak the truth."

"I hate to say it," I wanted to change the subject as fast as I could. I hated being the center of attention. "But, Val, that awful dress looks great on you."

Lynn turned to Val to see what I was talking about. "It really does," she agreed, looking over the dress.

"Once I do some fine-tuning, it will work," she agreed, nodding her head as if she had just won a major award.

Even though Val bought off the rack, she always made adjustments to her wardrobe. She could be standing next to someone wearing the same outfit, and you would never know it. Her creativity and imagination was a never-ending sea of wonder. I envied her for that. My imagination is not what it used to be.

We found the dresses we wanted and accessories to match. After we paid for our stuff, we went looking for the guys. Wondering where we should start, we all looked at each other and blurted out, "ELECTRONICS!"

We were right. The guys were drooling over a new big screen that had just come out.

"You guys done already?" Mike asked, looking at his watch. "I can't wait for when the TV's are thin and don't take up so much room. I would love to have this one in my dorm."

We just held up our shopping bags, looked at each, and started giggling like the school girls we are.

"I was wondering why I was hungry. I didn't realize it was that late already," Dave said, glancing at his watch.

"I'm so hungry I could eat a cow," Aaron agreed, feeling up his stomach. "I need to keep up this beautiful figure somehow."

"That's my man!" Val declared, kissing him.

"Eeeeewww, gross!" the rest of us pretended to gag.

"What are you all in the mood for?" David asked as we headed towards the food court.

"Chinese," Val stated.

"Something grilled," Lynn said.

"Pizza," I voted.

"I want," Aaron started.

"We know you want an uncooked cow," Mike teased.

"Just a little cooked. Eating raw meat is bad for you," Aaron teased back.

"The redder the better," Dave threw in.

The good thing about the mall was that everyone could get what they wanted. It was a little more expensive, but it saved on having to drive anywhere. We ordered what we wanted and found a table to accommodate all of us.

"Poor Terry," Dave flinched.

We all could see it now, his dad screaming at him to do better. Ridiculing him for not scoring a point or whatever. His dad was overly harsh on him. I personally think that it had to do with his dad living his own dream through his son.

"Yeah I know. Poor guy, I bet he would do better if his dad wasn't living vicariously through him," Lynn said, echoing my own thoughts.

"I just hope he does well when he goes off to college," Dave said, taking a drink of his soda. "I heard you mess up once and you're out."

"That's not true," Mike disagreed. "But yes, if you do mess up a lot and don't play to their expectations, they will kick you off the team."

"How is college life, man?" Aaron said, swallowing.

"Eh. It's OK. A lot more homework, tests and lectures. As long as you pay attention, you should be fine."

"I haven't picked a college out yet," Val declared. "I'm still undecided."

"So am I," I agreed. "I really want to become a lawyer, though."

"You would do great at that," Dave encouraged.

"Yes, you would," Lynn also agreed. "You don't buckle under pressure. That's always a plus."

"There's pressure?" I teased. "What pressure?"

"See!" Lynn pointed out. "You don't even know when there is pressure!"

We finished eating while making small talk back and forth. After we were done, we cleaned up our spot and headed out, new purchases in hand. We said goodbye to Val and Aaron and headed towards the car. The car ride home was the same as it had been on the way to the mall. This time, the guys rode in front and we girls sat together in the back.

Mom will be so proud of me and how much money I saved! I could tell by the look on Lynn's face that something was bothering her.

I softly whispered. "What's wrong?"

"Oh, nothing," she whispered back. "I'll tell you about it later, OK?"

"OK," I nodded, as we pulled into the driveway.

"See you guys later!" Dave and I called, as we exited the car.

"Laters," Mike and Lynn said, in unison.

She had gotten out of the back seat and was now sitting in front with Mike. She looked nervous.

"Be right back," I told Dave, as I ran to the house to drop off my purchases.

Ever since Dad got laid off from his job, Mom had been working full time, and Dad took whatever jobs he could. I threw the bags onto my bed and left my parents a note. They didn't care what I was doing, as long I left them a note saying where I would be.

"So...?" He asked, as we walked down the street.

"So... what?" I asked, completely forgetting about earlier.

He wasted no time getting straight to the point. "So what was your dream about?"

"Oh." Duh. "I completely forgot." Then it hit me.

"I'm not buying that. I see the expression on your face."

"Honestly, I just remembered," which was the truth. Dave knew just about everyone, not only in our town but the surrounding towns as well. "Does the name Jay ring a bell?"

"Jay? What's his last name?"

"I don't know. Ummmm," I said, biting my lower lip. "He's about your height. I think. Has these gorgeous brown eyes and dark brown hair."

"You know how many students have those same features?" He laughed, knowing I had just described about half of the student population at our school.

"Yeah. I know," I said, with a heavy heart, not knowing if I would ever see him again.

"What's with this guy? You like him?" He was becoming defensive now. Not just because he liked me, but he saw the wreck I had become after the last crush.

"I can't say that I do. I don't even know if he's real."

OMG I just sounded like an idiot!

You could tell he was trying not to laugh. "What do you mean, you don't know if he's real?"

"In my dream," I was beginning to wonder whether I should tell him the truth or not. But I had already started, so I might as well finish. "I don't know how to explain it."

"Do your best," he encouraged.

I knew the *dream* part was hard to get past. "Remember where I took you the beginning of the week?" He nodded. "Well, in my dream, I was there, only not alone. There was someone there. He said his name was Jay. I really don't know how to explain it, Dave, I really don't."

He smirked, trying to hold back his laughter. "You are probably just fantasizing about the new kid that is moving to town."

"I really don't think that's it. You know me all too well, Dave. When has a new kid ever done this to me?"

He just smiled and shrugged. "True. You normally don't care."

"Just another body to add to the overpopulated school district."

"Yup," he agreed, as we walked in silence for about two streets. "It was just a dream. Could mean one of two things..."

"Like?" I was dying to know his reasoning.

"Well, you are either worried about finding Mr. Right," winking at me. "And you don't think you ever will," winking at me again. "Or you are going to meet him very soon," another wink.

I ignored his winks. "Either way, the dream freaked me out."

He started laughing so hard we had to stop walking. "Why on earth would that freak you out?"

"I don't know, really. I just... I just don't know." I put my hands in my pockets, taking a breath of the fresh air. "I've never had a dream that felt so real before."

"It's a dream, Lexi. It's just your subconscious trying to tell you something."

On any other day, I do believe what he says. It's weird, in a way. He acts older and wiser in some ways than he really is. Today was different. As much as I wanted to believe him, part of me just couldn't deal with an answer that maybe fit. We walked to the street where our sub divisions met.

"If you need me, just call."

He gave me a hug and headed home. I stood there in a daze, not sure what to think. I felt something hit me on my shoulder, but when I turned around, I saw nothing. Then I started to feel it – the storm we were supposed to get was getting close. I started walking home, thinking about whether I should go to my spot tonight or not. By the time I got inside, Mom and Dad were already there.

"So? Did you find a dress?" Mom asked, as soon as I entered.

"Yup. And it was on sale!" I was excited!

She was as excited as I was. "Let's see it!"

"Alright. Hold on," I said, as I ran upstairs to fetch the bags. When I came down, I gently took the dress out and held it up for her to see.

"That's pretty," she said, admiring it.

Dad had come walking up the stairs. "Nice," he said, without taking much notice.

Now if I were a new electronic gadget that had just come out, I knew he would have been interested. Well, at least he would have cracked a smile, anyways.

"Any ideas for college, yet?" He asked, as I put the dress back in the bag.

"I sent off for a few brochures," I affirmed. He grunted as he headed back downstairs.

Dinner was ready a short time later. We sat there as a family while Dad went on about his new project. After dinner was over, I decided to call Lynn to see what was wrong.

Ring...ring...ring...

Normally, she picked up on the first ring. I started to hang up the phone.

"Hello?" The voice on the other end asked.

"Lynn?" I wasn't sure if it was her or her mom. They both sounded the same on the phone.

"Hey, Lexi! What's up?" She seemed in a better mood than from earlier.

"Just seeing what was bothering you."

"This stays between us, OK?" She became all spy-like, lowering her voice.

"OK," I agreed.

"Promise?" She begged.

I had to giggle. Spy was an understatement. "I promise," I reaffirmed.

She whispered even lower. "I sort of like Mike."

"Really?" I tried to play it off as if I didn't already know.

"Really, I just don't know what to do," her tone raised a bit, as if coming out of spy mode.

"Well, does he like you?" I asked.

"I think so," she paused. "I think it's our age difference that scares him"

"Well, just keep things the way they are and let him make the first move," I suggested.

"I want to invite him to the homecoming dance," she nervously admitted.

"As friends yes, anything more I would personally hold off."

"I'll ask him next time I talk to him," she said, with confidence. "Just as friends."

"That sounds like a plan," I laughed. The reason I didn't tell her what I knew was because if for whatever reason he changed his mind. It would break her heart.

"Mom's calling, gotta run."

"Laters," I said, as I hung up the phone.

Even before I had a chance to put the phone back on the charger, I heard the doorbell ring. *What now!* I thought to myself.

"Dave? What are you doing here?" I asked, shocked, since we had already seen each other not too long ago.

"You have a minute?" He sounded like he had forgotten to tell me something.

"Sure, I'll be right out." I went to hang up the cordless and threw my coat on. "What's up?" I asked, when I was finally outside.

"I know you said you didn't want a birthday present this year, but…" I had told him not to get me anything. He usually outdid himself when it came to trying to make me happy. I was just glad that he was in my life. "I didn't get a chance to give you your birthday present before, because I didn't have it yet," he shyly added.

"I told you not to get me anything," I said, reassuring him.

"I know," he said, with an evil grin. "When has that ever stopped me?"

"Never," I said, as I rolled my eyes.

"That's my point. So here," he said, handing me a large, wrapped-up square.

"You promised!"

"I promised that I wouldn't spend a lot," he looked down with his sinister grin.

"Ugh," I groaned.

You could tell he wanted to see my expression. "Just open it already, will you?"

The package felt like a book. But it seemed too light-weight to actually be a book. As I opened the gift, I could see the reflection of the night sky - the same way diamonds flicker in the light. I finished unwrapping it and held a photo album. It was so beautiful! Different blue crystal accents, with a plain white row on the cover. Inside, the pages were blank.

"It's awesome!" I hugged him as tight as I could.

"See, knew you would love it!" he said, returning the hug.

I gasped in admiration. "Where on earth did you find one this nice?"

I had been searching forever to find an album like this. The only ones I could ever find were already arranged with pockets in them.

"I stumbled across it at a store, saw it, and thought of you."

"You know, if I found out you spent too much, I'm going to hunt you down and hurt you!" I was still sifting through the pages. There were a lot of pages that I could start out with.

"I know. I know. You know where I live. So what?!" We cracked up laughing. "I gotta go. I'll see you in school tomorrow?"

"Yeah, where else would I be?" He gave me a peck on the cheek, wished me a happy birthday again, and headed home.

I was thrilled that he had been able to find an album like this. I liked everything to match, but as pretty as the cover was on this one, I knew it would be impossible to find another one like it when this one was full. I ran inside and showed Mom what he had got me, and then proceeded to my room. I sat at my desk to decide how I wanted to set up the pages. I was becoming lost in my photographs when a cold breeze glided past me followed by…

"Hello Alexandra…"

Chapter 5 – Too Much, Too Fast

The next week went by in a blur. Everything was back to normal. No more voices. Mike was busy with college and Terry with football. There was a new rumor floating around the school that the new student's parents had decided to wait until the end of the school year before transferring in.

The weather was getting colder, and the frost had hit. Time does fly, whether you want it to or not. You better get on with it, or you will miss whatever is thrown your way. More often than not, you don't get a second chance.

What was the point of going to college? What was the point of learning half the stuff we were learning? Just because someone said we had to? College wasn't cheap. It didn't guarantee a future in life. But nothing that took place now guaranteed a good future.

Once, we almost lost a student to a drug overdose. But I didn't feel bad for him – no one forced him to take the drugs. He did that on his own. He has to live with what he did. He almost lost his life to something stupid. Why? To feel good for a few minutes? Not me, no thank you.

I had so much other things on my mind. I had to decipher an act from *Romeo and Juliet*, by William Shakespeare, lots of other homework, colleges to pick, and now this dream. I didn't care if it was raining or not, I had to take my run before my head exploded. The only thing that sucked was that I couldn't bring my music. But with the way my brain was racing, I don't think I would have heard it anyway.

I changed into my running gear and headed outdoors. Mom and Dad didn't say anything as I headed out the door. *Odd.* That wasn't like them at all. But they are used to me running no matter what the weather is like. At least the rain was nothing more than a light drizzle. Felt good.

OK, I thought to myself. *What to work out first.*

I tried to let my mind relax before thinking about the first thing. Well, *Romeo and Juliet* was out, since I had yet to actually read the play. Homework was out, since it was raining, and it would get wet. Next topic, colleges.

I couldn't stand that what I did with the rest of my life rested on a decision I had to make now. I had always loved ghosts and ghost stories, but it's not like there's a ghost-hunting college out there, or anything. Also, proving that they existed was another thing. How could you prove something that no one can see? I also loved knowing the behind-the-scenes details about why things happened. But there were no colleges for that. The one thing I loved that made sense was Law. *Matlock,* in all honesty, was and is my role model. Just something intrigues me about the law. I'm always fascinated to know more.

The only thing was that my grades were too poor to get me into any decent law school. The bad part about it was that if I actually just paid attention, I would do well. If I focused and did my homework right, I would do great. Everyone says to go to a community college to get your general education courses out of the way. Cheaper and easier. I hate change. I lived in the same house I was born in. All the kids had gone to the same school as the years went by. I couldn't even imagine what it would be like to move on. On my own, I can't wait for that! Be on my own, on my own. But yet I was terrified just thinking about it.

Luckily, my watch was waterproof. I thought I had been running longer than I actually had. It had taken me the same time to do the whole neighborhood that it usually did for my normal run around just the perimeter. I had run down every street. I had figured that thinking about college would kill time and distract me from the last item on my mind. I had never gone to my spot when it was raining, let alone when there was no light. Never needed to before.

"Might as well get this over with," I said, heading towards the opening into the clearing.

I hope it's where I think it is. Stupid me, forgot to take a flashlight. All I had was the light from my watch, which wasn't very helpful.

Curiosity killed the cat. I was probably the most curious kid out there. If there was a logical explanation, I was always determined to find out the cause. I never took no for an answer.

Glush…glush…glush…as I walked through a few puddles.

Oh, great! Not only am I soaked, I have not a clue if I am even going the right way! Slopping through puddles that I couldn't see in the dim light.

A voice called from the dark. "This way."

I know that voice!

Why is my heart skipping beats? I kept following the voice through the dark until it landed me right at the edge of my private clearing. I could just hear Dave now, *'You're such an idiot'.*

"Hello? Jay?" I called.

I couldn't even describe the words I felt as I called out. The words were beyond *stupid.* I was calling out some guy's name that I didn't even know whether he really existed.

"Hello my Angel."

My heart skipped a beat. "Where are you?" I called out. The trees did a good job of keeping the rain out, but not great. Plus they blocked the light from the street lights. "I can't see you."

He was trying not to chuckle. "I'm over here. Open your eyes my dear."

Were my eyes closed? I didn't think so. I wiped my rain-soaked hair away from my face and everything came into focus. The rain was coming to a stop, but it was still too dark to really see anything.

"Better?" He asked.

"Yes. A lot." Well, not really, but it was better than before. I still can't believe I had my hair in my face and didn't even know it.

His eyes lit up with delight. "I have missed you so terribly. But now here you are, standing in front of me."

Why was he interested in me?

Again, I probably sounded harsher than I intended. "I still have a lot of questions to ask, and they need answers."

"I know you do. Let me start by saying that I care for you so that words cannot express how much." The glow started to fade from his voice. "I know that everyone has their own road. They make their own paths to follow, making their choices along the way."

"You've lost me again."

"I saw you today," he remarked.

I was completely confused. "Saw me where? Running?"

"At the mall with your friends," he vouched.

"Why didn't you come up to say hi?" Growing even more annoyed now.

"I wish I could. I would have tried, but just like you, they would have been too afraid to see me."

"Well, it's not like I can tell them about you," I started to chuckle. "They would have me committed. Why am only I allowed to see you?"

"I know," he frowned. "I am truly sorry. I have meant you no harm. But I have been watching the life you live, and you don't seem happy in the least. You are the only one I trust because you see with your heart, not your eyes."

"Isn't that my problem and not yours?"

He looked like I just had just run over his beloved pet. "You speak the truth. But you neither hear nor see the truth."

My patience was growing thin, and not being able to understand what he was saying, was getting on my nerves. "OK, well, speak the truth, so I can hear the truth. You said you have been watching the life I live."

"That is correct," he answered, without hesitation.

"How long have you been watching me?"

"Not as long as you must think," he said, looking away.

I placed a hand on my hip. "Well, humor me."

"I will speak the truth when the time is right. For now, it is still early, and I am afraid."

"Afraid of what?" I questioned.

"Of your not understanding. Because I cannot speak to make you understand."

"Will you tell me soon?" I was dying to know right then and there.

He walked out further towards me, and I was compelled by some force to walk towards him. As I saw him clearly, I wanted to be even closer.

"The truth is that you will have doors open for you in the future. I cannot tell you which doors you will open and which ones you will close," he said, as though he were looking straight into my soul.

We were now about five feet from each other, and I felt that chill again.

"Well if you would tell me which doors I should open, wouldn't it make it easier on both of us?"

"That I cannot do. You hold your own fate. You hold your own destiny in your hands," he said, leaning against the air. "For you own the board, and I am merely a pawn in your life. The part you play is your own. But I could no longer hold back from speaking to you."

"OK," I actually had to laugh at his analogy. "I'm horrible at chess. I couldn't play it if my life depended on it."

He chuckled, and then looked out at what appeared to be the light growing even dimmer."

"Please forgive me when I say," he took a deep breath and exhaled. "That part of me does not want you to choose me when the time comes for you to make the choice. Yet the other part of me cannot stand to not know what would happen if I did not approach you."

"Then why do you come here to confuse me even more?"

"I do not mean to confuse you at all. I just…" He stopped.

"Just what?" I needed to know more. I wanted to know more.

"Just that this is one of those doors of which I was speaking."

"How about this," really not knowing what I was thinking. "We start off getting to know one another. Then maybe you can see that I may not be your Angel."

As soon as I said the word *Angel,* my heart sank to the bottom of my stomach. I really didn't know why.

"Fair enough," he agreed, with a glitter of hope in his eyes.

"So," I started.

I wanted to ask him something, because it seemed like he would know the answer, but I didn't want him thinking I was just using him, either.

"Yes?" His anticipation was growing, since I had not yet run off and even said I wanted to get to know him. Whoever *him* was.

"I can tell by the way you speak, you might know something about *Romeo and Juliet*," I hesitated, biting my lower lip.

"I know very little. Why do you ask?"

"Well..." hesitating again.

"Just speak, my dear."

"Well...I have a paper due on it, and I have to decipher it."

"I shall help you if you wish."

"Awesome!" Any help I could get would be great; I was barely passing, and I needed to pass this class in order to graduate.

"Have you picked out a verse which you would like to translate?"

"Not yet. It was raining when I left the house, and I didn't think that I would see you tonight," I chirped. The air still felt heavy, as if it was going to rain again.

"When would you like to get together?" he asked, delighted that he would be able to see me again.

"If it is not raining, how about tomorrow? It's Sunday, and I don't have school."

"The rain bothers you?" He was completely dry, as if not one drop of rain affected him.

"No," I giggled. "The rain does not bother me. It's just that my books do not like the rain."

He looked up, as if remembering some long-forgotten bit of information. "You are right. Please forgive me."

"You are forgiven," I said, smiling back.

I was horrible at flirting. It was like a cat that had a piece of tape stuck to its paw. Hilarious watching it walk, but you feel bad for it at the same time.

"You looked very beautiful in the dress you chose," he said, looking at me lovingly.

"Thank you. The dance is right around the corner. The girls wanted to go and get the shopping out of the way."

"You will be the most beautiful one at the dance," he said, moving closer to me.

I looked at him, wondering why he was watching me with such intensity. I decided to ask him. "Why are you staring at me like that?"

Not that I was freaked out, but at the same time, I wanted to know what was going through his mind.

"I am mesmerized by your beauty inside and out."

"You never told me how old you are," I said, smiling at him hoping to catch him off guard.

His face turned an odd color of pink. It worked! "You would not believe me, even if I told you the truth."

"Try me," I smirked, as I was trying to guess.

"My age at present is 21."

"You do know that I am only 17?"

My heart dropped, knowing the age difference and the law.

"I do. But age is nothing more than a number. You speak with more wisdom than your years."

I felt at ease. He was so easy to talk to. Easy to look at, OK drop dead gorgeous. *Is he for real?* I thought. Does he even know about the law?

"Yeah, OK. Whatever you say," I said, busting out with laughter.

"You are more modest than you need be, my dear."

"No one has ever told me that before," I conceded.

"This is where you speak untrue." He took another step forward. I realized that I couldn't hear him splash through the puddles, as I had.

I was dying to know, since no one had said a word to me in school. "OK, then, who has informed me of such?"

He grinned as if he knew the answer to the million dollar question. "The boy you call Dave who adores you so."

"Oh, him," I frowned. "We are just great friends. Sometimes I don't know whether what he says is the truth or if he's just saying it to make me feel good."

"He does speak the truth," he said, unsure of how I would take the news.

"Dave's just a friend and nothing more. I don't see him the same way as he sees me." I had to make sure he knew that.

"His heart is pure, just as yours is," he sincerely stated.

"I have a question for you," I said, feeling rather stupid about asking.

"I will speak the rightful answer if I can," he had a worried expression.

"One of these doors you speak of, does it refer to Dave?"

"That question I cannot answer. For I do not know which path you will walk."

He had to give me some type of clue. Being lost and confused in his presence seemed to be the normal state affairs.

"Yes, I'm completely lost in life. Is there any hint you can give me to know which way my life is supposed to go?"

"I am truly sorry again. For I cannot answer that. You are the only one who can decide which way you feel is right for you."

"A little hint?" I begged. He smiled. "Please?"

"My hands are tied. I am sorry," the sadness darkened his face as he looked away.

I needed know whether I was dreaming. "May I see something? I promise it won't hurt."

"What would you like to see?" He asked, with burning curiosity.

I lowered my eyes. "I would just like to see something and I'm afraid you'll say no. But I promise I won't hurt you."

I hope I wasn't breaking a promise or that what I wanted to do was going to hurt him.

"I know for certain that you will not hurt me. But if I do agree, I must ask one thing."

"That depends," I smirked, trying to do the same thing to him as he has done to me.

"Please, if you do become frightened, please let me know at once," he spoke, with such hesitation that I wondered what I was agreeing to.

"Yes, I will," I promised, smiling so hard that my cheeks were starting to hurt.

"Alright. Then I agree," he said, smiling back.

"Close your eyes."

"What for?" He asked, jerking back by a step.

"I promised you I would not hurt you. I promised you that I would stay and talk if I was frightened afterwards. You said you believed that I will not hurt you. So please have trust?" He nodded his head, somewhat nervous as he didn't know what he had gotten himself into. He slowly closed his eyes. "Stay still," I said.

I moved closer and slowly raised my hand towards his face. There was a glow I had not noticed before. Not a bright one, but one enough to make me take notice. Time seemed to move in slow motion. No matter how hard I tried, I couldn't seem to move any faster. When my hand was just inches from his face, he began to open his eyes.

"I told you, you had to keep your eyes closed," I said, somewhat frustrated, yet amused.

"I am sorry," he closed his eyes and held them shut.

I knew he saw what I was doing. He started to become a little uneasy, which made me start to be uneasy. I needed to know if he was real or not. My face was only inches away from his, and my hand was just a breath away from his cheek. The chill ran colder than before. I hadn't realized that I had goose bumps. I slowly placed my hand against the side of his face. His face was cooler to the touch than the air around us. He relaxed, and his anxiety seemed to fade away.

Woooosh! A cold wind blew through the clearing, whipping through my wet hair. As soon as the breeze began, it stopped.

"You can open your eyes on one condition," I couldn't help but smile.

"Agreed," he seemed pleased with my promise of trust.

"If you are frightened, you tell me." I found it amusing to use that same line on him.

"Agreed. For I know that will not be the case," he agreed, with a warm smile.

When he spoke the coolness became more pronounced. He slowly opened his eyes, meeting mine, which were just inches from his. Time seemed to stand still. We both sat there just looking at each other, with smiles on our faces. My hand was still touching his face. I wanted to kiss him, but I have never kissed anyone besides family in my life.

"See, I did not hurt you," I whispered.

"I did trust you when you said you would not. But this I did not expect," he spoke so softly, I could barely hear him.

"I'm sorry," I said, removing my hand from his face and leaning away.

"No. You have no reason to apologize."

The look on his face told me that he was sorry I was not as close as before. "I didn't mean to make you feel uncomfortable," I fluttered.

"You did not. In fact it did just the opposite," he said, with those eyes that you could get lost in. "May I ask you a question, if it is not too rude?"

"Uh, sure," I said, not quite sure how to take that.

"Why did you want to touch me?" He daunted me, but at the same time, I was happy.

"I wanted to see if you were real," I answered.

"What did you see?" He remarked, curious about what my answer would be.

"It's not what I saw, it's what I felt," I admitted.

"What did you feel?" He asked with hopefulness.

"I felt you," I smiled.

"Now, if you would do me the honor of closing your eyes. You have my word that I will not hurt you."

"I know you won't hurt me. Or should I say you can't. I know karate!" I laughed, as he looked at me awkwardly. I stopped laughing when I realized he didn't know what I meant.

"I am a man of my word. Now, please close your eyes." I did as he asked. "No peeking!"

I could hear him trying not to laugh.

"Oh, you mean like you did with me?" I said, laughing back at him.

Once again, time seemed to freeze. I felt a large flash of coolness, and then warmth against one side of my face; then a smaller coolness then warmth on the other.

"Wow!" I gasped. I opened my eyes to see the cool air that I breathed out.

"I'm sorry. I did not mean to hurt you."

"What makes you think you hurt me?"

"When you said *wow*," he hesitated. "I merely assumed."

"Trust me. Number one, it was a good *wow*," I said. I felt like I was floating on air. "And two, the second emotion I can't even begin to describe. For three, don't ever assume."

"So you did like the kiss that I have offered?" He looked like I had said no. So I played with it.

"No, I do not like what you have done." He started to move away. "I *LOVED* it." I could not help giggling. His expression turned from remorse to curiosity, and then to complete bliss. "Can I be honest with you?" I asked.

"Please," he pleaded, as if there were no other way he would have it.

I blushed, looking away. "That was the first time I have ever been kissed."

I didn't consider Dave kissing me on the cheek anything more than I would a family member.

"Now you must surely be lying," he said, looking at me in disbelief.

I'm not," I said feeling my cheeks get even redder. "How long have you been watching me?"

"The night is full while the time is empty," he looked up at the trees with sadness.

"I don't want this night to end," I said, following his gaze.

I wished we could see the stars, but the clouds were blocking them.

When he breathed those words, a sweet chill swept over my face. "I do not want this night to end, either."

We sat next to each other, just looking ahead of us. I wanted to hold his hand so bad, but I was afraid that was going too fast. I was in complete bliss. I sat next to this guy who I had only just met, but already felt so comfortable with.

I felt another cool breeze, then warmth on my hand, and I looked down. He was holding my hand, still looking forward but with a smile on his face. I looked up at him as he moved his body to the side, still keeping my hand in his. As I moved closer, I didn't notice he had held his breath. I began to contour my body to his. Again, the warmth encompassed the coolness.

We just sat there in silence, listening to the beating of our hearts. His heartbeat – now I know that was a sign to let me know he was real.

"I could stay here all night," I whispered, breaking the silence.

"I know," he sweetly breathed again.

"You know there are a lot more questions that I have."

"I know." My heart skipped another beat as he smiled. "We are running low on time to have all your questions answered tonight."

My heart sank as I looked him in distress. "What do you mean, 'low on time'?"

"When in this state, time passes twice as quickly. There is no explanation as to why. It's just the way it is."

"ALEXANDRA!...LEXI!"

I jumped, as I heard a muffled voice in the background. "What was that?" I jumped up, looking around. I whispered softly, as my eyes cringed closed, "*Who could possibly know where I am?*"

"It is now time for us to part," he said taking my hands in his.

"Just a few more minutes?" I begged.

"It is not that easy. You must go now, or you will be late."

"Late? Late for what?" I demanded, confused.

"This is farewell until we meet again," he said, as he brushed his hand across my face.

The cool air was no longer cool. It was now warm. Then I felt a cold breeze.

Then, I started to hear a loud banging. He vanished quickly than he had appeared.

"WHAT?" I cried out loud. "Just leave me alone!"

The banging was growing louder and louder.

I stood there in the clearing, waiting for the banging to disappear and for Jay to return. There were so many questions that still had not been answered. I know he said I had to wait, but part of me couldn't and needed to know now.

The banging seemed to cease. I ran through to the edge of the clearing to see if he had returned.

"JAY?!"

Silence was all I heard.

Chapter 6 Back to Reality

I don't know why, but I started to cry. My hair was still damp from the light rain before. I took the hair tie that I always kept on my wrist and tied my hair back into a ponytail. The light started to come through the trees. I could see more clearly than I had before.

BANG... BANG...

"LEXI!"

I cried even harder. I wanted the banging to stop. I curled up into a ball, throwing my hands over my ears.

"ALEXANDRA! IT'S ME, DAVE!"

I slowly opened my eyes, realizing that I was back in my own bedroom. I jumped out of bed when I saw what time it was.

"I'M LATE!" I screamed, racing down stairs.

"LEXI! I KNOW YOU'RE IN THERE!"

Why was Dave here? How did he know I would be home? *How did I get home,* was probably the most important question. I didn't remember coming home last night. The last thing I remember was being in Jay's arms. I felt the same way as I had after the first dream. Only this time it felt so much more real than before.

I know I'm not losing it. I know I'm not. I know I'm not having conversations with myself or with someone who's not really there.

I flew down the stairs and opened the door.

"Are you OK?" He sounded as if I was in danger. "I called you yesterday and your mom said that you were asleep," Dave explained. "You never go to bed early unless you're sick, and your mom said that you weren't. So I knew there had to be something wrong."

"I fell asleep?" I said, just below a whisper.

"Yes! She said you were sleeping. Come on, let's go so we're not late for school, and you can tell me what happened along the way," he said

75

motioning with his hands. Stunned, I grabbed my bag, threw on my shoes and locked the door behind me. Dave was already waiting in the car with the engine running. "OK, now tell me what happened," he demanded.

I just remembered! "Wait! Today is Sunday! We don't have school on Sundays."

He had this really worried expression on his face. "Lexi, today *is* Monday."

"Are you sure?" I was still trying to make sense of what happened Saturday night, but where the heck did Sunday go? "Are you telling me that I slept all through Sunday?"

"Yes!" He screamed back. "What's wrong?"

"Nothing," I wasn't lying, except for the part where I was missing an entire day.

"Stop lying to me," he accused.

"Seriously, I'm not. I'm just worried because I slept through Sunday and didn't even know!"

That part was the truth.

His tone was coming down to earth. "Why did you sleep all day?"

We were now passing into the city where our school was.

"Dave, if I had known that I was asleep, I would have…" my voice started to trail off.

"Would have what?" He asked, in a demanding tone. I've never seen him like this before.

"I didn't know I was asleep. You want me to apologize for sleeping?"

It was the truth. Even *I* didn't know I was sleeping. So how could I let others know not to bother me?

He took in a deep breath. "I guess not. I just didn't know you were that tired."

"*I* didn't know I was that tired," I mumbled.

I smiled at him to let him know that I was fine.

"Don't ever do that to me again!" He demanded, with genuine concern.

"Do what? Not tell you that I'm sleeping?" I had to laugh at that comment.

"True. I guess you couldn't tell me that you were sleeping when you *were* asleep."

There was no way around keeping what happened from Dave. He would eventually put two and two together. "I saw Jay Saturday night," I blurted, without even trying to sound dignified.

"Jay who?"

"OK, now don't freak out." I sucked in air to get the story in as fast as I could. I couldn't help but smile. "That guy I asked you about before?"

"I'm trying not to freak. But first you tell me there is nothing wrong, and then you tell me that you saw Jay Saturday night."

"Well after you went home, I went home to change and go for a run..."

"In the rain?" he asked, cutting me off.

"Do you want to hear this, or not?" I demanded.

He angrily breathed, "Go on."

"After I ran my usual course, I still had a lot of on my mind, so I decided to go to my spot," I knew I was talking a mile a minute. "And I heard the voice again and this guy appeared. His name is Jay, and we just talked all night."

"So let me get this straight. You hear a voice, some strange guy appears and you stay to *talk* to him?"

"Yeah, I know it sounds weird," I still couldn't wipe the smile off my face.

"So I'm guessing that this *Jay* guy made sure you got home OK." I could tell by his voice that he was not happy. I wanted so much to tell him *everything,* but he was already being paranoid.

"See, I'm fine," I said, holding my hands out at arm's length. "I'm all here, alive and talking to you. Right?"

"Yes. I see that you are," he sighed. "So when do I get to meet him?"

"Meet?" My heart was now in my throat, and the smile that wouldn't go away vanished.

"Yes. Meet him. Jay. You know, face-to-face?" Pointing his fingers to his eyes, then to mine, and then back again.

"Soon," OK, I lied now.

"Will he be at school today?"

I bit my lip, fearing what he would say. "He doesn't exactly like go to school."

"What do you mean he doesn't go to school? Does he go to private school?"

"Yes. He's away at college," I lied again. College won't be so farfetched, considering the area we live in.

"When will he be b...." he started, but I cut him off.

"How about this? I will let you know when he's back in town so you can meet him. OK?" Dang, I lied again. I hope he couldn't see the cringe on my face.

You could tell he was mad. "OK."

"What's wrong?" I asked, since he still hadn't calmed down.

"Well, I have never seen you smile over a guy. Not even when you dated what's-his-name last year. And now here you are, smiling and happy," he must have seen the look I flashed him, "but...you are acting...well...not like you. And that is what's bothering me about him."

I couldn't disagree with his reasoning. It did make sense. I know I wasn't being me either. But how could I explain it to my best friend who knew me inside and out? When I didn't even know how to explain what was going on to myself.

We sat in silence for the rest of the way to school. Luckily, it wasn't too long, since we were almost there.

I was happy. I was truly happy, and for the first time in my life, I felt complete. There was one little problem. Was this guy even real? Should I be hoping for something that was just part of my imagination? Was this guy actually real?

We barely made it to school before the final bell.

"Alexandra!" Val ran up and hugged me.

"Val!" I said, repeating her excitement.

"Are you OK?"

"Yes, I'm fine," wondering how she knew.

I turned to look at Dave. She must have seen the look I gave him. "Now don't be mad at him. He was worried. Truly worried," she said, feeling relieved at actually seeing me. "Did your mom tell you about anyone calling?"

"Ummm..." How do I put it that I was sleeping but didn't know that I was sleeping? "I actually slept all day Sunday."

"Are you sick? Are you feeling OK?" She seemed just as worried as Dave was.

"Yeah. Yeah. I'm fine. I don't know. Must have been all the hours I put in over the summer finally catching up with me," I lied again. Dave shot me a *you actually lied* look. I gave him the shut up look.

"My dad was saying that with work picking up, he might need more people. I can tell him about you if you like?"

I really didn't know what to say. "Thank you for the offer." With the look on her face, I couldn't say no. "Yes. Thank you."

"We still have time, so I'll let you know as soon as I know," she assured me.

"Sounds great." I hope she didn't catch the lack of enthusiasm in my tone.

The rest of the day continued on as usual.

We sat around our usual table at lunch, chatting about Saturday. Val was telling us how Aaron was hungry again when he got home and ate the cow in the backyard.

I could hear all the voices as distant blurs as I started to daydream. It felt so real. It was more than I could have guessed that someone actually wanted me. I was still unsure of the actual events that took place. I physically remember going to my place in the forest, I remember seeing him and talking to him. I remember sitting by his side with me in his arms. His scent that, I couldn't describe. It was sweet. Like right after it rains mixed with fresh linens that just came in from fresh cut grass. A mixture of all three scents, but yet none of the three. So surreal.

"So, Alexandra," I heard Lynn's voice breaking in on my daydream.

"What's up?" I asked, looking at her.

She knew she had caught me off guard, and there was no use in hiding it. "What do you think?"

"Think about what?"

"I told you she wasn't paying attention," Dave said, half annoyed, and half pleased that he was right.

"Oh. Sorry," I could feel my cheeks get hot. "What's going on?"

"Oh, cut the girl some slack," Lynn grinned. "She's in love!"

"What? No, I'm not," I denied. I couldn't believe she was saying that!

"Oh please," she said, rolling her eyes. "You're a bad liar!"

"What?" I said, shrugging my shoulders.

"No one is going to take our little Lex away until I've had a chance to meet him," declared Dave.

I hated that name. I flashed him a look, and he knew what he had done wrong and just smiled.

"What, are you her father?" Aaron asked.

"No. Better. Bestest friend," he flashed his toothy grin.

"Dave has a point," Lynn chimed. "If anyone is going to declare Lexi...I mean *Alexandra* as their own, we *ALL* have a right to meet and interview this guy."

I crossed my arms over my chest and pretended to be offended. "Don't I get a say?"

"NO!" They all answered back.

"*Great,*" I said sarcastically.

All my friends were in an uproar.

I couldn't say he was part of my dreams. Nor could I say that he was real. Because I didn't know which one. I also knew if I held onto the fact that he was real, it would end up being all in my dreams. If I said that he was in my dreams, well, yeah, then I'm the fruit loop. The teasing would never end.

"So when do we get to interrogate... I mean *meet* lover boy?" Val asked, laughing.

"When he comes back from college," I answered. I knew I had to keep up the lie, or Dave would really start questioning. Lynn was right, I am a bad liar. I didn't know how long I could keep this up without some more difficult questions being thrown my way.

"OK then. It's settled," Aaron announced. "You let us know when he comes into town, and we'll all be there. Deal?"

I couldn't object. Then they would really know something was going on. So I had no choice but to agree. "Deal."

Lunch was over, and we headed to our classes.

I sat in study hall, trying to concentrate on *Romeo and Juliet.* The teacher had each of us pick out of a hat for an act to decipher. I picked Act 2 Scene 2. Lovely.

ROMEO

He jests at scars that never felt a wound.

JULIET appears above at a window

But, soft! what light through yonder window breaks?

It is the east, and Juliet is the sun.

Arise, fair sun, and kill the envious moon,

Who is already sick and pale with grief,

That thou her maid art far more fair than she:

Be not her maid, since she is envious;

Her vestal livery is but sick and green

And none but fools do wear it; cast it off.

It is my lady, O, it is my love!

O, that she knew she were!

She speaks yet she says nothing: what of that?

Her eye discourses; I will answer it.

I am too bold, 'tis not to me she speaks:

Two of the fairest stars in all the heaven,

Having some business, do entreat her eyes

To twinkle in their spheres till they return.

What if her eyes were there, they in her head?

The brightness of her cheek would shame those stars,

As daylight doth a lamp; her eyes in heaven

Would through the airy region stream so bright

That birds would sing and think it were not night.

See, how she leans her cheek upon her hand!

O, that I were a glove upon that hand,

That I might touch that cheek!

'He jests at scars that never felt a wound' *ummm, I had no clue.*

'But, soft! what light through yonder window breaks?'

Something about the light that breaks the window? Oh, wait, no! The sun is soft so it must be early dawn or dusk. The sun rays coming through the glass of the window. That's it! I hope. The sun from dawn/dusk rays are coming through her window.

'It is the east, and Juliet is the sun' A*gain, I had no clue.*

I was hoping to get some lines done before my brain shut down.

Why did we have to do *Romeo and Juliet*? Some kids who have talked to kids from other schools said they had to do the same thing. Maybe I was trying too hard? Maybe I just didn't care? Maybe I am that dense I can't figure out what they are saying in plain English? I don't know.

All I know is I have been looking at the same sentence for fifteen minutes and still can't decipher what it's saying.

I closed my eyes for a brief moment to try to relax my thoughts.

The voice broke through my thoughts, and I opened my eyes. He was kneeling beside me, with his hand on my shoulder. "My Angel, please do not fret."

"I don't..." He held his finger to his lips to silence the rest of what I was going to say.

"I can see you are quite distressed. Please, you need not be."

I pointed at my homework. His smiled told me that I was making a mountain out of tiny speck of dirt. He must have read the first line where I had written *no clue,* because he put his hand to his mouth to hide his laughter. *See,* I said with my eyes.

"Let us proceed line by line. He stands by everyone. Jest means to joke," he looked at me like he just given the one word that would cause everything else to make sense. When my bewildered expression still did not change, he continued. "Scars that never felt a wound… meaning the wounds that you may conceal, others just simply would not understand for they have not the same type of scars."

I picked up my pen and crossed out the *'ummmm, don't know'* and wrote: Not everyone feels the hurt we have because they have not gone through it.

"Most excellent!" He whispered. "I must go. I shall return."

"Tonight?" I mouthed.

"Of course," he graciously said.

"Alexandra."

"Yes?" I answered, to the sound of my name.

I was sad that he was already gone. And I was confused about who was calling my name.

"Wake up! You'll be late to your next class."

"Huh?" I asked, opening my eyes to the brightly lit classroom.

"You fell asleep," I recognized the voice clearly now. It was my study hall teacher. "Is everything okay?"

"Uh. Yes. Everything is fine," I said, a little disoriented.

"Well, you better run before you're late," she said, walking back to her desk.

"I will. Sorry, I didn't mean to," I said, starting to throw my things into my bag.

"If you need anyone to talk to," she interrupted me. "Come see me any time. Okay?"

"OK. Thank you," I said, avoiding her line of sight. I threw my books into my locker and hurried to class before the bell rang.

The rest of the day flew by.

I started walking to the bus when I heard my name being called.

"Lex!"

"What? You know I hate that name," I groaned.

"You want a ride home?" I just looked at Dave with confusion. "Remember? I drove you to school today."

Oh, that's right!

"Sure. That would be great. Thanks," I said, following him to his car.

I was dreaming again. That so sucks. If anything good came out of my day dreaming, though, it was that I figured out at least one line from this stupid play.

"Where you going?" Dave asked.

I looked around. I had totally walked by his car. "Uh. Sorry, just out of it," I said back tracking.

"What's wrong?" He asked, as he started the car. "I heard you fell asleep in study hall."

"Who told you that?" I demanded.

"Lex," the expression 'if looks could kill' was an understatement for the look I shot him.

"No, I mean how did you know that I fell asleep?"

He just laughed. "Remember news travels fast here?" He was right – you could do something as soon as you walked into school, and the whole school would know about it at the end of homeroom.

I was getting irritated that he wouldn't say who told him.

"My parents personally know your study hall teacher, and she told me what happened."

"Oh," was all I could say.

His tone was soft and concerned as he spoke, "I'm really starting to worry about you."

"Don't," I snapped. His eyes got wide. "I'm sorry. I don't know. I just have a lot going on. School with this *Romeo and Juliet* thing and college."

"I wish I could help you with *Romeo and Juliet*. But I never understood it myself. So I don't think that I would be much help."

"It's OK," I sighed, looking out the window. Would I be lucky enough to see Jay again?

His tone came back to that of a caring friend, "For the college thing, just take a week off thinking about it. Take one thing at a time."

"Yeah. I know. Easier said than done."

"Well try. For me?" He said.

His expression told me that he was really worried.

"I'll try. No promises."

"That's all I ever ask," he grinned, his cheesy grin at me.

He dropped me off and headed back to his house. I couldn't remember much about study hall, just the fact that I was pissed that the teacher told Dave. Now he's never going to leave me alone. The phone was in the middle of a ring when I walked through the door.

"Hello?" I asked, as I picked it up.

"Hey Lexi! It's me, Lynn!"

"Hey, hold on real fast. I gotta grab the cordless."

"OK," she said, as I quickly hurried downstairs, grabbed the cordless and switched phones.

"OK, better," I said, clicking the cordless on and hanging up the cord phone at the same time.

"OK, good. Now tell me what is going on with you," she giggled.

"What do you mean?"

"I mean you have been acting odd. Who is this Jay guy?" She was dying to know.

I couldn't tell her the truth, when I couldn't tell Dave all of the truth. "He's this guy I met..."

"Met? Where?" She started throwing questions at me even before I could finish her first one.

"On one of my runs," I just have to remember that next time someone asks me that question.

"How old is he?"

I cringed, thinking about what she was going to say. "He's 21."

She screamed so loud I had to hold the phone away from my ear. "He's 21!?"

"Yeah, it's not like what you think, though," I tried to reassure her.

"Mike's only 19 and he's having an issue with the age, and you find a 21 year-old who doesn't? Where do I find me one of those?"

I couldn't help but giggle when she said it like that. "Again, it's not like that. Right now he's just a friend."

"A friend. I don't believe that for one moment," she said.

"Why not?"

"Because, I know you oh too well. A guy is just not *friends* with you. He either dates you or wishes he could date you."

"Yeah, OK, like who?"

She hinted with a *duh* in her voice, "Ummm, Dave, for a prime example,"

"Dave is a different story," I said, annoyed.

"He's still a story, nonetheless."

"But I don't see him like that and you *know* that," I pointed out.

"Yes *I* know that and so does everyone else. *But* that doesn't close the door that he likes you more than just a friend," she playfully stated.

Why did she have to say that about closing doors?

"Can I call you back later? Or see you tomorrow in school? I got some things I have to take care of here. I just walked in the door."

"Sure, if you need anything, call. This conversation about *Jay* is not over," she teased.

"Will do, thanks."

I hung up and tried to decide what I wanted to do.

I enjoyed the peace and quiet while I gathered my thoughts.

Chapter 7 – Part of the truth is better than none... Right?

The week seemed to whiz by. The homecoming dance was in just a couple of days, and the students were getting impatient. I didn't have a date – nor did I really care. A lot of kids wouldn't go without a date, but I had my friends.

Things were back to normal again. I didn't even look at the *Romeo and Juliet* piece I had to decipher. I was actually taking Dave's advice and concentrating only on the homework that was due in the next few days. For the time being, I had managed to put everything else aside in my mind. My runs weren't lasting as long as usual, because I was actually doing my homework in the evenings.

The idea was to pick up my GPA just a bit before I started applying to colleges. I knew my parents wanted me to continue my education, but they never forced the issue. As much as I loved them and was grateful that they didn't hover like most other parents, I rarely got any type of encouragement.

I picked up the brochures I had sent for and flipped through them. I had only received four so far, but that was enough to give me an idea of what was out there. I wondered what they would say when I actually told them about the colleges I had picked out. Guess we'll find out soon enough.

I gathered my courage and walked downstairs, brochures in hand.

"Mom, Dad?"

"Yes, Lex?" Mom answered, over her book she was reading.

I groaned. "I hate when you call me that."

"Why?" She asked, looking up.

"I don't know, I just do."

She repeated sarcastically, "Okay, yes, *Alexandra*?"

"Can I talk to you about... ummm... colleges?" I asked.

Dad beamed over the computer he was working on. "Sure!"

"Well, I don't know which one to apply to," I said, giving two of the brochures to Mom and the other two to Dad. I took a seat on the stairs to await any questions they might have.

"Law school?" They said, both in unison.

"Do you think that you'll be able to get in with your grades?" Mom asked.

"I know my grades aren't the best. I'm working on bringing them up."

"You know we want you to go to college," Dad said, carefully studying each page. "We know you can do well. You are very smart."

Dad giving me a compliment? Now that doesn't happen all the time. There was an uneasy silence.

"We're just afraid that, well, we see how you handle high school homework," Mom started to say.

"Hon," Dad interrupted her. "College is not like high school."

"Is it the money?" I asked. I knew it would be about that.

"We'll manage, *if* this is something you really want to do," he said.

They had exchanged the brochures between them. "Would you plan on staying on campus or commuting?" She asked.

"Well, probably stay in the dorms. You know how I hate driving in the city," I answered.

It was the truth. I really didn't do well on the expressways. Plus the population was a hundred times worse than the small town we lived in.

"It wouldn't hurt if you applied to them all – it would give you a better chance of being accepted at one of them," Dad suggested.

"Well," I started to say. "There's a little issue if I apply to them all."

"Oh. I see," he said. "Application fees."

I breathed with disappointment. "Yeah."

I knew this was a bad idea. I had some money saved up, but applying to all four schools on my own would leave me completely broke. I could tell what Mom and Dad were thinking. I hadn't even applied to college yet, and it was already starting to cost money.

"Tell you what," Mom started to say. "You do everything you need to do to apply to each one, and we'll help you with the application fees."

I wasn't expecting that!

"Mom, you don't need to do that. If I can just narrow it down to one, or maybe two…"

"Don't worry about the money," Dad reassured me. "We'll find a way."

"We're just excited that you will be going to college," Mom said, seeming to forget that I hadn't been accepted yet.

Mom and Dad had never gone to college, although they were always telling me how important it was. Sadly, I have never been close with my parents, except when I was very young – back before Dad lost his job. I realized that I had never known much about them. How had they met? What had their lives been like as children? What were their hopes, their dreams? They never seemed to look at the past – they were always focused on the present and how to work it into the future.

They never put out family photographs like you see in most homes. There was a large painting of a ship that looked like it was in the middle of the storm above the fireplace. My favorite, though, was a painting a country lane; trees surrounded the path, and an old farm house sat far back in the picture. The colors had always intrigued me.

I tried painting once. Yeah, it looked like a mess of colors that threw up.

"Are you going for your run?" Dad asked.

"Most likely."

Dad hinted answering my silent question, "Okay. We will be going to bed soon - early work day tomorrow."

He handed me back the college brochures.

"See you later," Mom said, going back to her book.

I ran upstairs to put the brochures away and changed into my running clothes, heading out the door to begin my run. I decided to take my route backwards this time.

Oh crap. I said to myself. I had forgotten to take my CD player. *Oh well.*

"Hey!" I turned to see Dave running up to me.

"Hey!" I waved back.

"I called your house, but your mom said that you'd already left," he said, out of breath.

"You're fast."

"It's only a block away!"

"True." I said. "So what's up?"

"Just wanted to see if you wanted some company?" He asked, keeping in step with me.

"Sure," I said, half-lying.

"So this week flew by, didn't it?"

"Yes, it has," I said, nodding in agreement.

"Alexandra?" Dave stuttered.

Oh great, what does he want now?

"Yes?"

"I know the *guy*," his voice was sour when he said the word guy. "But I was wondering if you would be my date for the homecoming dance?"

"Dave..." I said, slowing my pace a bit.

"I know. I know," he broke in. "Just as friends."

"Why don't you ask Lynn?" I asked.

"I don't want her getting the wrong idea." He looked away, scratching his head. "Plus, she already asked Mike," he admitted.

Even though there was no rule about dating each other, no one in our group had ever done it until now.

"Oh," I swallowed.

"What?"

"Ummm, nothing…" I gulped.

"No, not nothing. You know something. Now spill!"

"Hey, that's my line!" I cracked.

"Yeah, well I'm stealing it. What do you know?"

Dave was obviously thinking the same thing I was, but just wasn't about to be the first to spit it out. "The same as you," I smirked.

"And that would be?" He asked, raising an eyebrow.

"What you told me before," I said, slowing down.

"I wasn't even supposed to say anything," he fussed.

"And you didn't," I reassured him.

"What do you mean?" He was confused. It was nice to have someone else confused for a change.

"Lynn told me," I confessed.

He didn't seem to believe me. "What did she exactly tell you?"

"She told me that she likes Mike, but she doesn't think Mike likes her, and blah blah blah," I said, mimicking with my hands.

"Phew," he answered, pleased.

"What do you think Mike's going to do?"

"I don't know. It is sort of his fault for not acting sooner," he said, placing the blame on Mike for not speaking up.

"Well, if they're at the dance together, maybe they'll see it for themselves," I joked.

"Yeah, maybe. Who knows? So what do you say?"

"Just as friends?" I reconfirmed.

"Just as friends," he reassured.

"OK, just as friends," I agreed, to his offer.

I could tell by his tone that he was relieved the worst was over. "Have you talked to your parents about colleges yet?" He asked, changing the subject.

I sighed, "Yes."

"Didn't take it well?"

I spoke the truth. "Just the opposite. They took it too well."

"So which ones are you applying to?"

I answered, my voice rising a bit, "They want me to apply to them all!"

He was just as shocked as I was. "All? Do they know about the..."

"Yes, they know," I said, cutting him off.

"They must really be excited, then. Where are you going to apply?"

"I don't know. Two of the schools I've been looking at are the major city, and two are out of state."

"You know if you go out of state, I'll miss you."

"I'll miss you, too," I said, with a heavy heart. I knew that our friendship would change if I went away to college. Dave was planning to stay local and attend the community college in the next town.

"Why don't you come with me to the same college, that way you'll know someone? And since I'm a year ahead, I can help you with your classes."

"What if we don't have the same classes?" I objected.

"For your first year, you'll most likely just take general education classes. That way, your parents can save money, and when you transition to a traditional college, things won't be as over whelming."

He was right. "I'll think about it," I said. "I would still like to check out the law schools to see which one I would need to do after the community college. *If* I take your suggestion..."

"I have no issues with that," his tone was a bit more uplifting than before. "I can go with you to check out campuses if you want me to."

"We'll see," I said. "My parents may want to take me."

"True," he sighed, feeling left out.

"But you would be welcome to come," I quickly added.

"Yeah, your parents adore me!" He slyly added.

"Yes, I know they do," I couldn't disagree.

"Now only if you could adore me, as well," he winked.

"I adore you," I looked away, smiling. "I just don't adore you in the way you want me to."

"You will one day!" He said, pointing his finger at me.

"You're mighty confident about that," I bantered.

"Yes, I am. You know how I feel, and that's never going to change."

"You say that now."

"I mean that, now and forever."

"Dave," I cautioned him, "We're still young."

"It's this *Jay* guy, ain't it?"

"I like him, yes. But I don't know if he likes me the same way."

"Oh, whatever," he rolled his eyes.

"Seriously, it's hard to explain."

"Well, explain," he pursued.

"I don't know *how* to explain." And that was the truth.

"Well, try. For me," he said, batting his eyes. I had to laugh. He looked like a toddler who wanted something from his mother. "See, I make you laugh," he said, trying to put his arm around me.

"Yes, you do. And as much as I hate it at times, I do secretly enjoy it," I teased.

He motioned with his hand, "So, spill."

"Have you ever been so sure, but not been sure about any of it at the same time?"

"Now I'm going to play a Lexi. I am confused," he said seriously.

That's what they say when someone is confused. *They play a Lexi.*

"Well, it's just that, with him in college and where I am in life, I am not looking for anything permanent right now."

"No one said things had to be. You act like whoever you date right now is going to be the one you are stuck with."

"*You* would like to be stuck to me," I joked.

"Now what would give you that idea?" He smiled brightly. "You know I would wish for nothing more than to be stuck with you."

"Yeah, you say that now," I said, giving him a *get over it* look.

"We've known each other for how many years?"

"A lot. You know all my secrets, and you know everything about me," I sighed.

"And I'm still here. Ain't I?"

"Yeah," I answered.

We walked in silence for a couple blocks. I couldn't have asked for a better friend than Dave. I loved that we didn't need to talk all the time to be at ease together. We made a loop around my subdivision and came back to the spot where he had caught up with me.

"I should get going. Don't want my parents to worry," he said.

"Yeah. I should get some work done on my *Romeo and Juliet* paper."

"I'll see you later." He gave me a quick hug and started walking back in the direction of his house.

"Later," I replied.

I watched him round the corner before I started heading back to my own house. *Romeo and Juliet.* Yuck. The week had gone by so fast that I had completely forgotten about what had happened during study hall. I wanted this paper to be done already so I wouldn't have to think about it anymore. I walked into the house, took off my shoes and headed upstairs to shower and change.

Afterward, I took out the play and my binder from my book bag and laid them on the desk. I wasn't really tired, but I knew if I listened to my music, it would put me to sleep. The house was silent, as both of my parents had already gone to bed before I got home.

I opened the play to the section that I had been assigned and then began to open my binder.

GASP!

I couldn't believe it. Was I dreaming?! I could have sworn I had only deciphered one line, but here I was, looking at the second line already deciphered on the page. *How was that possible?* I had fallen asleep during study hall. Could I sleep and write at the same time? *Wouldn't that be lovely?* If only things were that simple.

"Good day, my sweet Angel."

I froze – I had not dreamed the whole thing in study hall; he had really been there. But no one else had mentioned seeing him. I was starting to wonder whether the only time that I could see him was when I was sleeping. It seemed like just when things were starting to make sense, they went back to making no sense at all!

I loudly whispered, "Where are you?"

It was bad enough to have Dave thinking I was off-balance. I didn't want my parents thinking the same thing.

"I'm sorry, my dear. Truly I am. But remember I explained that you may not always be able to see me with your eyes, and you would have to be patient with me."

I did remember him saying something like that, but I had always been able to see him before, so I really hadn't paid much attention. *And I wanted to be an attorney?*

"Yes, I remember," I said, still whispering.

Lucky for me, my parents are sound sleepers.

"Would you like more help with your paper?"

I nodded. The faster I finished my paper, the sooner I would be able to actually talk more with him.

He went through each line, explaining Shakespeare's English in a way that I could understand. As dense as I seemed as we went through the text, he never once lost his temper. I am a hard person to get along with – even *I* knew that. My patience was thinner than tissue paper. I loved hearing his sweet voice. We had just deciphered the last line when I let out a long yawn. I hadn't even paid attention to the time.

"Sleep, my beautiful, for you must be weary," he said. "It's early in the morning – I should not have kept you for so long."

I looked at the clock. It was already 2:30. But I didn't care. "I don't care. I want to talk to you."

He gave a light chuckle. "Ah, more questions?"

"Lots," I smiled back.

I turned off the light, crawled into bed, but kept the radio on low. I could feel that he was happy to be near me.

"Come and sit, if you can," I softly whispered. "You told me that another familiar would be seeking my attention."

"That is correct," he said. I felt a weight press down the corner of my bed. The air was chillier than I had remembered.

"When? I haven't seen anything out of the ordinary."

"Hmmm. That is strange," he replied thoughtfully.

"Maybe he saw that it was hopeless," I said, trying to be upbeat.

"Maybe," he half-heartedly said. "Yet this other soul is not one to give up easily."

"Well, his loss," I teased.

"What do you mean?" He asked, confused.

"Now it's my turn to have a secret that you will find out in time," I beamed. I heard him sigh. "What? You think you are the only one that is allowed to have secrets?" I challenged.

"No, it is not that, my dear," he sorrowfully said.

"Well, what is it, then?"

His voiced lowered with genuine concern, "I am afraid."

"Afraid of what?"

"Afraid that this familiar will succeed in gaining your attention over mine."

He was saddened by the idea that I would choose this someone over him. But whoever this person or whatever was, I couldn't care less about him. I was happy where I was.

"Stop talking like that. Stop being insecure," I said. "Either we have trust, or we don't. It's that simple."

"You never have any doubts of your own?"

"That's different. My doubts pertain to myself, not to others."

"I see."

"No, you don't," I softly giggled.

I hated it when people said *I see*.

He sighed again, "You are correct."

"Where are you?"

"At the foot of your bed," he responded.

I quietly crept towards where I felt the pressure on the mattress. I could feel a sharp cold sensation as I set my hand down for support.

"Is that you?"

He sounded as if he were about to cry, "Yes."

"I just wanted to make sure," I said, reassuring him.

"My presence does not bother you?"

"No. Should it?"

"Most normal mortals, yes."

I smiled. "Remember, I'm not normal."

"That could be a reason I am drawn to you so."

"That's the only reason?" I asked, teasing.

"No, I did not say that was the only reason. I merely meant that it was *one* of the reasons."

My bad. "Oh."

"Now, if I may ask you a question?"

"Yes, you may," I said, with a smile. I was glad he was finally the one asking questions.

"What draws you to know more about me?"

I yawned again, "Where to start."

"I am sorry to keep you up at such a late hour."

"It's OK. Really. Well, for one thing, you don't speak like other guy your age. You are different. You are sincere. You're like no one I have ever met before."

"And that draws you to me?"

"What draws you to me is your beauty within. You see things as they are and not how they are perceived by the naked eye."

"Now you have me confused," he snickered.

"How can I explain it? I am at ease when I am with you. I don't have to pretend that I'm someone I'm not. I know I can tell you my fears, my hopes, my dreams, and you will be there to listen. Does any of that make any sense?"

His voice was more upbeat. "Makes perfect sense."

"Will I see you tomorrow?" I asked, barely able to keep my eyes open. I wanted him to stay. But if I wasn't really dreaming all of this, explaining to my parents about a strange guy in my room wouldn't go over too well.

"If you wish. I will wait for you in the clearing," he responded.

I couldn't believe how tired I was, because what he said just didn't make sense. I began to feel a cool sensation. I lay back down, pulling the covers over me. I then felt a pressure on the bed next to me. I started to feel a cooler sensation, followed by warmth on my forehead.

"I do wish," I said, fighting sleep.

"Sweet dreams, my sweet Alexandra." His voice was becoming more distant. "For tonight, I will try to show you what you want to know."

Chapter 8 – The Truth about the Witches

The land went on as far as my eyes could see. There was nothing around except for some old-fashioned looking buildings. The buildings were made of some type of stone, almost brick-like. Smoke was wafting from the rooftops. The trees were in full bloom, and a rich, earthy scent filled my nose. Nothing looked familiar to me! I needed to find out where I was and how to get back home.

There were no roads, so no street signs. I walked towards the group of buildings, hoping maybe I would find someone who could tell me which way to go. As I got closer, some of the buildings began to look somewhat familiar – but I couldn't quiet put my finger on where I had seen them before. I had a feeling I had a long walk ahead of me.

But it didn't take as long as I had thought. In fact, although I knew I was walking, it didn't really feel like I was – it was more like I was drifting closer. The town that had seemed so peaceful from a distance was in fact in an uproar. I could hear people screaming. Babies were crying, and a male voice was shouting, "Get the women and children out of here!"

The clothing that people wore was not like anything I had seen. Although some of the men were dressed in the same type of clothing as Jay wore. I looked around to see if I recognized anything at all, but no luck – I was the only thing that was out of place. No one seemed to pay any attention to me. They acted as though I wasn't even there.

The women and children were running away from the town toward horse-drawn wagons. Some of the men were gathering as many weapons as their hands could hold. Off in the distance, I could see a darker-skinned guy talking with a light-skinned girl. It looked as though they were arguing. I crept closer to see if maybe the girl needed help.

"GO!" The darker skinned guy demanded.

He was wearing a light tan garment that only fell below his waist. He stood quite tall and composed. His long straight black hair was pulled in a single pony tail that lay flat against his back.

The girl was crying. "NO! I SHALL NOT LEAVE YOU!"

She looked to be about my age. She was glowing and very beautiful, and her long brown hair seemed to be perfectly in place in spite of all the confusion going on around us.

"YOU MUST, FOR I CANNOT LOSE BOTH OF YOU!"

Both of you? I only see her. Then I noticed her belly. She had to be ready to give birth at any moment – how could I have missed that! Again, from someone who wanted to be a lawyer?

"PLEASE, LAKOTA!" Begged the woman. "I CAN HELP! I CAN HELP STOP MY SISTER!"

"NO! Teresa, you must not put yourself in harm's way," he scowled. "You must protect our unborn child."

She was sobbing through her hands. "I love you, and I am so sorry! I've destroyed your world."

"Never say that!" He demanded. "I love you. You have opened my eyes to more than I had thought was possible."

She embraced him tightly. "I love you!"

"I love you, too. I shall return with my tribe to help the village." He wrapped her in his arms. "I must go," he told her, as he climbed on his horse and rode off.

She wept as an older man came whispered something in her ear, and she slowly rose to her feet.

"We shall return once it is safe," the older man said, taking his coat off and putting it around her shoulders. "And you shall be reunited."

He swiftly but carefully lifted her into one of the wagons. His face held anger, but also regret. It almost seemed as though he knew the end was coming and he was not ready for it.

CRASH!

"Where are you taking her?" Another woman demanded furiously, coming into view from behind one of the houses. Her corn silk hair flowed in the breeze. Remembering the story that Dave had told me, I realized she must be Teresa's sister. She had the same beautiful features, but her face was transformed by the pure evil in her expression.

"Sarah! Your battle is with us! Not her!" A younger looking boy scowled back at her. "We're ready to fight you!"

"Oh, you are, are you?" She cackled and pointed her finger.

The boy screamed in agony as his body flew backward and struck the closest building, where he lay motionless in an unnatural position.

"Leave the boy alone!" Another man shouted.

He was pointing a long rifle at her; he fired and missed. Ten or so other men were racing towards this beautiful woman, various weapons in their hands. Some stayed close to the houses to take shelter with their weapons; some went to check on the boy who had been thrown.

I squeezed my eyes shut for no more than a second, trying to think of what I could do to help. When I opened them, I was no longer in the village. Instead, I found myself on the outskirts of an Indian camp; the village was no longer in sight. This was too strange! Was I dreaming? It didn't seem like a dream. It felt more like watching a movie.

"My brothers!" The same man I had seen with Teresa, whose name was apparently Lakota, was frantically talking to the others around him. "Please, I beg you, we must help the white man!"

"We cannot," said an older Indian. Some of his black hair was tied behind his head, while the rest lay across his broad shoulders, a handful of colorful feathers twisted into his topknot.

"This is not our battle," agreed an even older Indian, who seemed to be the chief. His straight black hair was twined with beautiful feathers that nearly trailed on the ground. He sat in the middle of four other men, who seemed to defer to him. "Her magic is more powerful than ours."

"I love this woman," Lakota declared. "I cannot stay back and watch her be destroyed. If I cannot stop this war, then I will die trying."

An older woman came up and stood beside the first man who had spoken. Her hair was tied back behind her head in segments running down her back. She was older, but the words she spoke were so sincere that her beauty surpassed her age. "We know that you will go." She lowered her eyes to the ground. "We are deeply regretful, but you know we cannot help you."

Lakota bowed his head before the council, then ran to his horse and took off.

"He must understand that, only he can fix what he has broken," the chief stated, to the older woman.

"What if the roles had been reversed?" The older woman asked. "And the white man came to help us?"

"I must look out for my own people," he said, not meeting her eyes.

"I know," whispered the woman. "But this war *is* about our people. And the unborn child of ours will never know the truth."

There was silence, and then black. I struggled to see anything as I stood motionless, not wanting to disturb anything.

I don't know how much time had passed, but finally, I began to hear screaming and mumbling, and then saw a soft glow of a candle's light under an old wooden door.

"Breathe! Come, Teresa, breathe!" I heard what appeared to be an older woman.

"ARGHHHHHH."

I guessed that the screaming was coming from Teresa. I slowly walked towards the light. My feet did not make any sound as I walked forward. I stood right outside, holding my breath, as I slowly opened the door.

The woman lay on a bed, her legs arched up in a way that made me think of an OB-GYN exam – something that makes all teenagers cringe. I knew this was no exam. There was the beautiful brunette, lying on her back with her legs open to her chest. Her hair was in disarray, and you could see the movement from her enlarged abdomen. Her face held such agony that I began to feel for her.

"Teresa, I need you to push," came the same voice as before. An older woman with grey in her hair was kneeling in front of Teresa" I can see the head. I need you to give a push, as hard as you can!"

I hadn't gone through the Miracle of Life yet in school. In fact, I hadn't taken any health classes yet. My eyes burned – I realized I hadn't blinked in some time. As horrified as I was about what was happening before me, I could not turn away.

"THE PAIN!" She screamed. "SHE CURSED ME!"

"No," the midwife reassured a calm voice. "You are not cursed. Everywoman experiencing the miracle of life suffers what you do now."

I tuned out all the voices that were yelling back and forth. There were other people in the room. A couple of the women were trying to help her by holding her hands; a girl scrambled to get what the midwife needed. Everything seemed to be happening in slow motion, although in truth only a few moments had passed.

My eyes were bouncing from one person to another. *Did they even know I was there? If I said something, would they hear me?* I decided not to take the risk. I just sat in the shadows, watching the events unfold before me. My eyes leered towards some women huddled in a corner, crosses clutched in their hands. They looked like they were terrified of Teresa.

The sound of a baby crying brought my attention back to the bed.

"Teresa, welcome your baby boy to the world," the midwife said, holding the baby up to lay him in her arms.

The infant had his mother's eyes and nose. But although his skin was darker than his mothers, it was fairer than Lakota's, who I assumed was the boy's father.

"My breath is taken away by such beauty." Her eyes were a softer brown now. She stared at the baby lovingly, all of her pain replaced with tenderness. "I will call him… Justin."

"*GASP!*" I cried.

All noise stopped the instant I cried out. The room grew quiet, and everyone looked around. I wondered if they heard me. Could they even see me? The atmosphere in the room grew tense. I started to feel sick to my stomach. Had they heard me? All the people looked around at one another anxiously for a few moments. Finally, the conversation picked up once again.

The midwife went back to her patient. The new mother said a few things in a language I had never heard. The older woman looked puzzled at her.

"I placed a spell on him to keep him safe always." She smiled lovingly at the child in her arms. "Please, you must put a stop to my sister's evil."

Then, all at once, her body went limp. The midwife scooped up the baby and had swaddled him in blankets with one fluid motion. She passed the tiny boy to one of the women that sat by Teresa's side.

"What do we do?" The woman holding the baby finally asked.

"Surely, by the color of his skin, his father is not one of us," called one of the women from the corner, still clutching something to her chest.

The midwife whispered sadly, "We'll take him to the orphanage at day break." .

She pulled a sheet up over Teresa's body, covering her face.

One of the women cried an outburst, "You can't take him away!"

"What other choice do we have?" The old midwife replied.

"I will take him," a woman sitting on the other side of the bed replied calmly. "My beloved husband and I have wished for children of our own for many years, but we have never been blessed. We will take the infant and raise him as though he were our own."

I saw a slender man sitting in a room just outside the door, nodding his head as he listened. The woman, who had spoken, rose to take the child. She then joined her husband as he stepped into the room from where he had been sitting with the others.

"As you wish," the midwife said.

An older man, evidently a judge or magistrate of some sort, joined the group. "I will draw up the necessary papers. That way, there will be no question if the father ever comes looking for his son." The magistrate sat at the desk at one end of the room, taking out a quill and an inkwell. He wrote away, dipping the feather in the ink every now and then.

"What if the father does come looking?" The husband asked.

"Then we will do what is right," said the wife, with a sorrowful look in her eyes. "If he chooses to claim his son, then we will surrender the baby to him."

"Are you sure you can do this?" Her husband asked, concerned.

"I'm sure," she said tearfully. "Although I would be heartbroken to see him leave, I would ask for the same consideration if our roles were reversed. I would not have it any other way."

The scene went black again. It felt like riding a roller coaster with a full stomach. Bouncing back and forth, not knowing which direction you were going in – the only difference was that I wasn't actually moving at all.

Was this Justin the Jay that I knew? I couldn't help but wonder. My Jay did not have dark skin from my memory. Yet I had never paid that much attention. His voice always claimed all of my emotion when we were together.

The light came back as fast as it had disappeared.

Now, I could see dead bodies twisted in unnatural positions around me. The dead ranged from young children to adults, and they were scattered everywhere. I could hear a horse galloping in the distance, and fires had engulfed nearly all of the buildings in the village. Then I saw the blond witch throwing her hands up in the air as if in celebration of victory.

"YOU! WITCH! STOP!" Called Lakota – it was the same man I had seen before – throwing himself off his horse.

"Why should I stop?" Sarah cackled. "You see, I have already won!"

"You have won nothing, yet!" He glared at her.

Her voice was as high and shrill as a school girl's. "There is no one left to fight me."

"That is where you are wrong!" With that, he shot an arrow from his bow in such a quick motion that she was taken completely off-guard.

Her eyes went wide – she had not expected that an Indian would defend the white man. And if he had not been in love with a white woman – one who had just given birth to his child – she would have been correct.

"My sister will avenge my death!" She declared as she pulled the arrow from her heart.

She slid to the ground, clutching her heart as her blood flowed out onto the ground. The Indian looked around to see if there were any survivors. Not seeing any, Lakota set fire to the dying woman before he climbed back onto his horse and rode off in the direction he had come.

"I CURSE THIS LAND!" the witch vowed, with her last breath. "I shall curse the children of all who settle here, so their parents may feel the pain I have, of the loss of my sister whom you have selfishly stolen away!"

"We shall see about that!" The Indian called back over his shoulder.

It was black again.

I didn't know where I would end up. Was it over? Was there still more to see? Could someone really curse a land? Was there such a thing as a curse? I remembered Dave telling me the legends about our town, but aside from the present situation with Jay, I had never seen or heard anything out of the ordinary. Not that I was skeptical or anything, I had just personally never experienced what others had reported.

The picture was slowly coming into focus again. I was back at the Indian encampment; it seemed that no one had moved since I had seen them shortly before.

"The white village has been lost," declared Lakota, as he leaped from his horse.

The chief bowed his head, "We have seen the end of the battle."

"I have killed the witch," Lakota told them defiantly.

The members of the council seated before him raised their heads in amazement. "How is that possible?" One of the members demanded.

"I put an arrow through her heart." He beamed with pride, but his heart was heavy with fear for his love. He did not yet know that she had died giving birth to his son.

"Just an arrow..." one started to say.

"And I lit her on fire before I left."

"We admire your bravery," the woman standing next to the chief solemnly stated. "We regret that we could not help. As you know, it was not our battle to fight."

Lakota's eyes welled with tears, "I do understand."

"There is more?" Another council member inquired.

"Before I rode away, she vowed that she would curse the land."

The council rose to their feet as one and began to walk past the tearful Indian.

"You stay here," the chief ordered him.

The rest of the council followed behind him as he entered a nearby dwelling. As soon as the last council member entered the hut, the door swayed shut. You could hear a lot of "no's" and "that is forbidden," amid a lot of other mumbling.

Lakota could no longer contain his tears. They were now flowing down his cheeks. The rest of the tribe gathered behind him to see and hear what was going on in the hut.

After what seemed like forever, the council emerged and resumed their former positions. There was silence as everyone waited to hear what the council had decided.

"We will ask the members of our tribe individually," the chief announced, "for it would not be right to decide their fate for them."

Lakota nodded once in agreement.

"My people," the chief rose and began to address them. The other council members remained seated. "Our brother has killed the witch who would not leave our land in peace. The white man has fought a heavy battle to defend the land."

You could see the Indian warriors had stern expressions, as if they were ready to fight. The chief gestured with his hands that they should remain quiet.

"It was not our battle," he continued, answering the questions on their faces. "But one brave soul, who cared more for his love than for his life, went by alone and took the life of the one who would rob us of ours. But not before she cursed all those who would walk the land in the future."

Another pause. He closed his eyes as to think about what he would say next. A brief moment later, he reopened them.

"Now as you all stand before us, we," he motioned to himself and to the council, "have decided to come to the defense of the white men who were brave enough to risk their lives to save their land. To defend them, we will continue to protect the land long after we have passed out of this life. We now ask you if you will do the same."

There was silence and eyes looking back and forth at one another. Some nodded in agreement, while others just shook their heads as though they couldn't believe what they had been asked to do.

"The choice is yours to make," he continued. "We will not cast you away if you decline. Our young one will understand the path you choose for yourselves. For he has chosen his fate, as we have chosen ours."

"What I have done was wrong," Lakota declared, before his peers. "I will take full and sole responsibility for my actions. I have fallen in love with a white woman, and she carries my child. I do not know if she survives, or whether she disobeyed me and stayed to fight against her sister. I have lost the one I truly loved regardless of our differences. I will never again be complete. There is a part of me that I may never find. I will stay with my people and fight with all I have, and more, to protect our people and our way of life."

"I will give my soul to protect those whom you have tried to save," a younger member of the tribe spoke up. Turning to the others, "I have spoken to his love and know she meant no harm. In truth, she held more hatred toward her sister than anyone. Love is more powerful than any magic that any one of us possesses."

The rest of the tribe considered what their brother had said. The majority cheered and raised their weapons as if in agreement. One young man looked at a girl who appeared to be his partner and lowered his eyes. He proceeded towards the two men that stood before the tribe.

"I regret that I cannot pledge myself." He bowed his head before Lakota and then looked at the council. "I have made a promise to protect the one I love, just as you have done. I hope that you will understand."

The council and the two that stood alone bowed their heads as if to show that they understood. The one who had spoken slowly walked back to the girl who was waiting for him.

"Then it is final. For those who have pledged to protect this land, we will hold a ceremony to ask the spirits to help us." The chief raised his hands, and everyone departed.

Lakota slowly walked away to a hut that sat apart from the rest.

It became pitch black again. If I was dreaming, it was like no dream I had ever had before. The evil witch, Sarah was dead. The good witch, Teresa was dead. Lakota's soul was lost. This seemed more like a nightmare than a dream. The light started coming into focus again. I was once again back at the village where this had all begun. I could hear a commotion as a group of villagers appeared to be assessing the damage.

"The witch is dead!"

"Good riddance!"

"But look at all the lives that were lost!"

"Let us take care of this before any more are lost."

I wasn't sure what they meant by that. If the battle was over, why would any more lives be lost? Some men started to dig holes away from the village. Others began moving the bodies to the graves, setting them with space between each body.

"Where is the evil witch?"

"I don't know, and I don't care just as long as she's far away from here."

"What if she comes back?"

"I don't think she will," someone said, just loud enough for the rest to hear.

"Why do you say such?"

He breathed pointing to the ground, "Look here."

The fire was still consuming her body. Through the flames, you could still see the Indian's arrow.

"Go back and retrieve the others," ordered the man who had discovered her to one of the younger men. "It is now safe for their return."

The youth nodded and took off. The rest of the men got back to work. I was amazed by how they lived. I was spoiled by all the technology I was used to seeing. I couldn't imagine living as they did, with the lack of modern-age equipment. I watched with wonder and awe as they worked.

Once again, it felt like some had hit the fast-forward button. A horse-drawn buggy came to a standstill just a few feet from where I stood. The man who had agreed to adopt the baby emerged, leaned back inside, and then stepped back with something carefully held to his chest. His wife followed him out of the buggy, reaching to take the baby from him.

"Is the fight over?" The husband asked. "Is the Indian still here?"

"Yes, it is over," answered a bystander. "But the Indian is nowhere to be found."

"Welcome, newcomers," a younger man appeared.

"Thank you," answered the husband. "We bring Teresa's son. She has died giving birth to the child."

"It is safe to return, for the evil witch Sarah has been destroyed." If you choose to stay, you are welcome. And if Lakota does return, he will not have far to seek for his son."

"That is kind of you, sir," the wife responded. "We have claimed the child as our own if the Indian does not return to take him."

The young man nodded.

"EVERYONE! PLEASE!" The man bellowed. "Please welcome Mr. and Mrs. Noynur. They have offered to raise Teresa's son. Lakota does not return, they will care for him as their own. I expect that you will honor their wishes."

"Hear! Hear!" The villagers cried out.

Another man approached the husband to shake his hand. The husband asked what he could do to help, and he led him away. Time seemed to whirl by, and suddenly the village was restored. The women and children had returned. It was as though the battle had never taken place.

Then everything went pitch black and silent again.

The light started coming into focus as before.

Was I home? The place now looked familiar to me, but it appeared to be the middle of summer. The trees in were in full blossom. I noticed a familiar face. I moved closer to see if this was the place I thought it was.

Yes!

I was on the farm where I had worked last summer. I saw everyone else who had worked there, as well. I walked around, not knowing whether they could see me. I purposely walked in front of them to see if they would react. Nothing. They had always been friendly towards me, so I knew I still had to be dreaming. I *think,* anyway. Why had I been brought back to this point in time? Whatever time it was... Walking around the barn, I saw something completely unexpected.

ME!

I was hurling a bale of hay over a fence. *Why had I been brought back here? Why am I watching* myself *throw hay over the fence?* I saw myself struggling with the bale. It looked like there was someone standing on the other side of the fence. *That's strange. I know there was no one around me then.* As soon as I threw the hay, I noticed that the someone wasn't just an ordinary someone. It was Jay! I bent down and picked up another bale and started to toss it over the rails. Somehow I lost my grip.

I remember that!

The hay started to fall on me. I was putting my hands up to avoid being hit in the head with the bale, and I saw Jay put out both hands. It looked like he was pushing it away from me! *No wonder it hadn't hit me! He was the one!*

All was slowly going black as I watched the other workers racing up to make sure that I was OK.

The light brightened again, and I saw everyone in a panic. I looked around to see what the commotion was about, and then I noticed the ropes in their hands. This must be when the horse had gotten loose. I ran to where I knew I would be standing.

When I finally found myself, I saw that Jay was standing in front of me, perfectly calm and without a trace of fear or any other emotion. When the horse came closer, he put out his hands to stop the charging animal, but it kept coming. When it was just inches from us, he leaped forward and pushed its head, redirecting the horse away from me.

Once again, the scene darkened, and then brightened on another incident. Everything seemed fine at first – nothing out of the ordinary. Since it had been raining on and off for pretty much the entire day, I had given up trying to avoid the mud puddles. My foot slipped in one of them, and I held my hands out to catch my fall – and there was Jay again. Even though I was now watching him as he helped me back to my feet, I still couldn't get over what I was witnessing.

Just as before, the light grew dim, until it was pitch black. This time, it stayed dark longer than before. I looked around, wondering whether I had woken up. I couldn't see or hear anything.

Then the light started coming in slowly once again. As the light grew brighter I was standing in front of some trees. It was raining, but I wasn't getting wet. Nothing was happening. I stood there, listening to cars kicking up water as they passed over the wet pavement. I still didn't see anything unusual, so I waited a little longer before trying to decide where to venture off to.

Then I heard the sound of feet sloshing through water. I waited a little longer as the sounds drew near. A few moments later, I saw myself walking along the street. I looked in the other direction and saw the car that had almost hit me that day. I looked back at me and noticed that Jay was walking beside me.

Why hadn't I seen him before?

I looked back at the approaching car. Still, nothing was happening. The driver seemed to be in perfect control. Then, suddenly, it spun out and headed straight for me. This time, Jay held terror and fear in his face. I saw the same fear on my own face as I stood there like an idiot.

Why wasn't Jay pushing me out of the way?

When I looked back at the car, I realized why. He couldn't tell where the car was going to end up. With the same terrified expression, he stood right next to me, never taking his eyes off the careening vehicle. When the car was just inches away, he threw his arms out, pushing me out of the way as the car went right through him.

Then it went completely pitch black and silent. I waited, completely still, to see what would happen next.

Nothing.

"Hello?" I called out.

Silence and complete dark surrounded me. *Was this what it was like to be dead?* I sat there a little longer, trying to figure out how to wake myself out of this state of sleep.

"Now you know the truth," I heard a very faint voice – so faint that although the words were clear as day, I had to struggle to hear.

"Hello? Who's there?" I asked just a bit louder.

Silence and peace surrounded me. "Jay? Is that you?" I asked again. No answer.

"Thank you. Why didn't you tell me before?"

Again, there was no answer. I felt a sweet, cool breeze and I started to see…

Chapter 9 – The Kiss

I lay in bed, trying to make some kind of sense out of what had just taken place. The sun was blazing through the window, lighting up every corner of the room. I wanted to get up, but for a while, I just kept lying there. It *had* to have been a dream. Or had my wild imagination finally gone off the deep end?

I had to find answers to all of this. There was no more waiting. I had to find the answers, not just about the stuff I'd just seen, but about everything. I had to find out what was going on before someone decided to have me committed.

I jumped out of bed, changed my clothes, and scribbled a note, then threw it on the table as I flew out the house. I climbed on my bike and rode as fast as I could to the library. Luckily, it wasn't that far from our house.

In a stroke of luck, the library was actually open – I had completely forgotten to check the time before I left.

I looked for anything that had to do with the history of the surrounding area. There really wasn't much to go on. I was getting frustrated at not being able to find what I wanted, so for giggles I catalogued 'ghosts'. There was quite a bit of information on the topic. Ghost stories, ghost Hauntings, the Girl Who Cried Ghost and so on.

One of the books was titled *Ghosts A-Z*. Luckily, it hadn't been checked out. I searched for a quiet area and started thumbing through the pages.

One of the questions was, 'What are ghosts also called?' Spirits.

Another question was, 'How to know if you are in the presence of a ghost'. The answer was simple. You would feel extreme cold or have a strange sensation. You might feel what the ghosts are feeling now, what they were like when they were alive, or what they were doing the day they died.

Another question was, 'Are ghosts hostile towards the living? The answer was not as simple. Depends.

Well, that's helpful.

The book went on to talk about residual hauntings – ghosts that still "live" in the time they had passed away, doing the same thing over and over again as if they were still alive. They are not even aware that you are there. Then there were the intelligent hauntings, ghosts who try to communicate with you. Among these, the bad ghosts are called demonic. Demons want to hurt the living.

Another section was about how to go about capturing ghosts. One technique is to use a recorder. Since ghosts speak on different wavelengths than we do, they are sometimes hard to hear with the human ear, but it may be possible to catch them on audio tape. A camera might also be used to capture a ghost. Most of the time, you can't get a clear picture, but if you do, it referred to as an apparition. A camcorder is really only good for recording objects that a ghost is moving.

Another question in the book was, "Why do ghosts haunt the living?" The answer was that ghosts mainly do not haunt the living; it is thought that they have unfinished business that they need to take care of before they can cross over.

I went back to trying to research the land in our area. All I could find out was about the time period after the first settlers came; not much about anything before that time.

Finally, I checked out a few of the ghost books, dropped them in my bag and headed back home. When I got there, I could hear the phone from inside. I threw down my bike and got to the phone on the last ring.

"Hello?" I answered, out of breath.

"Hey, Alexandra! Everything OK?"

"Oh. Hey, Dave. Yeah, everything is fine. Just got home from the library. What's up?"

"Not much. Was seeing what you were up to today."

I lied. "Have homework to finish."

I wanted to get to my secret spot as fast as I could.

"You really want to get into college, don't you?"

"Uh. Yeah. But I'll probably take your idea up," I was trying to get him off the phone as soon as I could.

"Really?" he asked. "Why the sudden…"

I sharply cut him off, "Hey, I really gotta go, can I call you back later?"

"Sure. If you need any help besides on the *Romeo and Juliet* thing, I'm here."

"I'll let you know, thanks." I hung up the phone before he could say anything else.

I unloaded the books I had checked out onto my bed and covered them over with my sheets. I then grabbed my recorder and camera. Dad would kill me if I took his camcorder, but anyway, I didn't know how to operate it.

On the note I left earlier, I scribbled out the part about the library and said that I would be at the east park, studying. It's not like I was actually lying – I *was* studying, trying to figure out this mystery. I headed back out of the house, stopping to put my bike away, since I knew it would not make it through the trees. I hurried to the clearing as fast as I could.

When I finally reached my spot, I swung the bag off my shoulder and lightly placed it on the ground.

"Jay?" I asked, in the air.

Nothing.

"Jay? Are you there?"

Again, nothing.

"Come on now," I demanded. "I'm not scared. I'm here, aren't I?"

Crack.

What was that? I straightened up, startled. When I realized that I had nothing to be afraid, of I relaxed a bit. I stood still, listening to the sounds around me, then took a long breath in through my nose. Nothing.

"Fine. Do me a favor and leave me alone!" I picked up my bag and started walking out of the clearing.

His voice traveled low and soft, "Wait."

My heart skipped a beat. I stopped. Turned around and headed back. His voice was so soft it could have been mistaken for the wind.

"What?" I asked.

"Please don't go," still low and soft as before.

"Why are you playing around with my emotions?"

He answered in a low whisper, "I am sorry."

"Show yourself," I demanded.

"On one condition."

"What's that?"

"That you will not be mad at me and remember what I have told you – I can't always appear the way you want me to."

"That's two conditions. But fine," I agreed.

I don't know why I was losing my patience with him. The sun was trying to make its way through by the branches as he slowly emerged from the other end of the clearing. He was even more beautiful than I had remembered. He smiled slightly, and I completely forgot about being mad at him.

"Better?" He smiled.

"Better," I returned. "Now tell me," suddenly remembering why I had come. "Was the baby you?" He looked at me with such intensity. I realized that all the questions I had when I got here weren't important any more.

"The answers you seek with your eyes may not be the answers you hear with your ears."

"Why do you play with my emotions?"

"I am truly sorry if you believe that I am merely toying with you," he said sadly. "You must believe me when I tell you this."

"I wanted to say thank you."

He tilted his head to the side. "Thank me for?"

"Thank you for helping me with my *Romeo and Juliet* play."

He smirked, as though he had forgotten and only remembered now that I mentioned it. "You are most welcome."

I lovingly expressed my gratitude, "And I also wanted to say thank you for pushing the hay off of me and saving my life."

"You are welcome again," he said, lowering his head with a smile that melted my heart.

"You stand before me, in the state you are in," I really had no idea where I was going with this. "Can you answer me a question?"

"I will. For you now know the truth. I have no secrets from you."

I sat down against my usual wooden log and waited for him to join next to me before I asked my question. He slowly walked across the clearing and sat down next to me – we never took our eyes off one another.

"My question now," I took a deep breath in. His sweet aroma filled my nose. "You told me that you loved me…"

He chuckled. "On the contrary, I called you my love. But you are not far off."

I was embarrassed. "So I had it wrong?"

"Yes and no. I have loved you since I first laid eyes on you. But I have never told you straight that I loved you," he cheerily replied.

"You got me on that one," I could start to feel myself starting to blush. "OK, so how did you know that you loved me when you first saw me?"

"I just knew," he said, shifting his body towards mine. "Did you not feel the same?"

"That is hard to answer," I spoke the truth.

His smile started to fade. "How so?"

"Love at first sight is hard to go on," I began to explain. "You can't know if you love someone just by seeing them for the first time."

"Explain something to me, if you will," his eyes had me completely turned around.

I nodded.

"If you do not feel the same, why continue conversing with me?"

"Well," how to explain without sounding like an idiot. "If you heard voices, wouldn't you want to know where they came from? If a person appeared out of thin air, wouldn't you want to know where they came from? Who they were?"

"I will give you that," he smiled. "But tell me, if you do not mind, what do you think now?"

"Truthfully, I cannot yet call it love. Maybe infatuation." His smiled was slowly disappearing. "Don't get me wrong, I do *like* you. But…"

Our eyes met. When I didn't continue, he prompted me to go on. "But what?"

"But, how can I fall in love with someone who can't be where I am?"

"I am here now," he protested.

"Yes, now. But you said before that you cannot always be this way."

"True," he frowned. "But there is always hope."

"Jay," I started to say.

"Yes, my dear?"

"I really do like you. I will admit, more than I probably should."

"If it makes you uncomfortable when I tell you that I love you, I will stop." He put his hand on my arm. The cool sensation was replaced by warmth. "But how I feel inside will never change."

"I would like to take things slowly," I said, placing my hand on his.

"I would ask for no less." He pressed his lips together and pulled away his hand.

"Why did you save me?" I asked.

He gracefully gestured, "It was not your time."

Now I was confused more than ever. How could he know whether it was my time or not? "If it was not my time, then why did those things happen?"

He was silent.

"I'm just wondering."

He looked at me, trying to make me understand. "It is hard to explain. I thought that by showing you and letting you see, you would understand."

"I understand and I don't at the same time. If that makes any sense to you?"

"I am sorry, I do not follow."

"I saw what you showed me. I just don't know why it happened."

"No one ever knows exactly why things happen," he said calmly.

"I guess that will always be a mystery to me then."

"A mystery to myself, as well," he smiled.

"What's wrong?" I asked.

"I know you said you want to take things slow, but," he hesitated. "But there has been something that I have wanted to do since I first laid eyes on you."

I was scared. "What is that?"

I was more than scared, actually, but I wasn't going to let him know that.

"I would rather show you than tell you," he smiled, making my heart skip a beat.

"Will it hurt?" After I asked, I shut my eyes, knowing that he wouldn't do anything to hurt me.

"I cannot promise that it will not. I have never done this before," he said nervously.

When I opened my eyes, I saw the look on his face and knew that whatever he wanted to do with me would not hurt.

"I will let you, on one condition," I smirked.

"Agreed."

I grinned from ear to ear. "You take a picture with me."

"I will. But you must not be disturbed when the pictures come out. For the pictures may show my true form."

"Agreed."

OK, now I was scared. *True form* – what does he mean by that?

"Please close your eyes," he said, in his sweetest voice. "And no peeking! It will take me a moment or two."

I closed my eyes tight and waited for him to show me what he was talking about. I was afraid, but not afraid at the same time. I knew he would not hurt me. But that didn't make me any less afraid of what he had in store. My mind was racing and trying to figure out what he was talking about. All of a sudden I felt that cool sensation on my lips, followed by warmth.

He was kissing me! I pulled away.

"I'm sorry. I should not have… I was hoping that it would not hurt."

"Please, don't be sorry," I blushed. What could I say but the truth? "I've never kissed anyone before. And no, it did not hurt."

"You have not? And you do not lie when you say that it does not hurt?"

"No I have not. And I promise you it did not hurt," I wasn't fibbing – it hadn't hurt a bit. At the same time, I knew somehow I had to be dreaming all of this.

"I did not hurt you?"

"No," I said laughing. "You only startled me."

"I did not mean to startle you," he said, looking away.

I put my hand on his face to make him look at me. "It's not a bad thing. I promise."

We stared into each other's eyes for what seemed to be hours. I was trying to find a way to remember every detail.

"Now it's your turn to keep up your end of the bargain," I said, as I jumped up to grab my bag. I worked the controls on the camera so that all I had to do was click the shutter button. I slid in beside him, contouring my body to his. "Smile," I said.

I snapped the button.

"Did you smile?" I teased.

He held me tight with one arm. "I am always smiling when you are near."

"Since I know what I am to expect, do you mind if we try one more time?" I knew I was pressing my luck.

"Whatever do you mean?" He seemed confused about what I was referring to.

Yup, I was dreaming.

"The… ummmm…" I wasn't normally shy. But I had never been in this position before. "Kiss."

His eyes grew wider, and a smile even bigger than the last one came across his face. He held me in both his arms, our noses touching each other as he looked deeply into my eyes. It seemed completely natural. As our mouths grew closer, my eyes slid closed. His lips were so soft. His breath was so sweet. Moments passed before we slowly pulled away from what I could only describe as a piece of heaven, his kiss.

"That was," I said trying to catch my breath. I could see my breath condense in the air. "That was awesome."

"Your sweet lips are like forbidden fruit."

"I wish you could come to my dance with me."

I was devastated that this gorgeous boy wanted to be with me, and I couldn't introduce him to my friends.

"I wish I could, as well. When the time is right."

"What do you mean, when the time is right?"

"We shall see," he said pulling me in closer. "I will not make a promise that I may not be able to keep."

"Life is so boring without you in it," I said, not sure where those words came from.

"Always remember, life is what you make of it," he said.

I had pushed my face against his chest, and I could feel his heart beating. That's why I knew this had to be a dream.

"Remember, I don't have much of a life," I laughed.

"Yes, you do," he said, laughing back.

"My friends want to meet you," I declared, changing the subject.

He looked shocked. "You told your friends about me?"

"Well, not exactly." I wasn't lying. "They sort of figured it out."

He pulled away a bit, and I knew he was wondering just how much they had guessed. "Figured what out?"

"They saw my change in personality." That was the best way I could describe it. "They saw how happy I am all the time."

"You deserve to be happy."

"Let's say you are right," I said. "That I deserve to be happy. But what if I am *not* happy with my life?" He pulled away with from me with a sorrowful look on his face.

"I was hoping that I would have made you happy," he said.

"Besides you," I exhaled. "I'm happy that *you* are in my life now."

He held me in, closer than before. "Please, my dear, take it one day at a time."

It felt so nice to be in the arms of someone who cared for me deeply. Even if this was just a dream, I'll take it. It was different than with Dave. I knew he cared for me deeply, but I just couldn't bring myself to hurt our friendship. Sure, there were kids in school that had dated, and then they were still friends afterward. But they had started dating before they became friends, not the other way around. Even though Dave always promised that if things did not work out, we would still be great friends, I just couldn't see it that way.

"I am a little worried," I admitted.

"Worried? About what?"

"You say that you knew I was the one when you first laid eyes on me," I began. "What if you lay eyes on someone else and have the same feeling?"

He laughed. "To put your worries to bed, I know for a fact that shall never happen."

"How do you know?" I quizzed.

"You see, I have waited a very long time for you."

"There are more beautiful girls out there. They would love to be able to call you theirs."

"I know," he sighed with disgust. "But those girls are not the ones I want."

"May I ask why?"

"It's rather hard to explain. They look for the beauty on the outside, rather than the beauty within," he frowned. "I want to be more than someone's trophy on their arm."

"I just wish…" my voice traveled off.

"I know," he exhaled. "The time is not right. You will know when the time comes."

"My best friend Dave asked me to the school dance," I said, biting my lower lip.

"I know," he chuckled.

"I said yes," lowering my eyes and adding quickly. "But only as friends."

He chuckled again. "I know."

"You are not mad?"

He acted like it wasn't a big deal. "Why would I be upset?"

I felt like an idiot. "Oh."

"I trust you," he kissed me on the forehead. "You have reconfirmed my fears by your friends' words. I am the one who is afraid."

"Fearful of what?"

"Of you wanting more than I can ever offer you."

"Then you don't know me too well, now, do you?" I chuckled.

"You say that now, but at a later time you shall see that what I speak is the truth."

"If that is how you feel, then why bother?"

"Bother?"

"Yeah, why do try if you feel that way?" I challenged.

"I live on hope, my dear."

"I believe we all do," I said, looking into those eyes that took my breath away. "Sometimes, hope is what gives us strength."

"I hope you are right about that."

"Oh, shut up already and kiss me," I said, pulling his face towards mine.

His lips turned upward into a warm smile that made my heart skip another beat and another. I turned my body towards him and held on tight. I never wanted this moment to end. I ran my fingers through his dark, sandy soft hair, messing it up. He held one hand on the side of my neck, with the other hand softly pressed against my back.

When he pulled away, I exhaled and I could see my breath again.

"I'm so, sorry my dear," he said. It seemed like he was out of breath.

"Sorry about what?" I asked, out of breath as well.

His warm smile turned to a cold frown. "It is time that you must be on your way."

"Why do I have to go?"

He looked over the treetops at the edge of the clearing. "It is getting late." He was right. The sun was starting to lower on the horizon.

"When will I see you again?" I asked.

"Soon. I am a man of my word," he smiled again. "There are things I must take care of before we meet again."

"I will miss you," I said, holding onto him.

"I will miss you, as well." I could feel his heartbeat growing stronger. "Please don't fret if you do not hear or see me for a while."

My voiced cracked, "Are you seeing someone else?"

"No," he said quickly. "Of course I am not. You are my one and only. Please believe that I shall always be near, though you may not be able to see or hear."

I looked at him intently. "If I find out that you are playing games…"

He wrapped me in a large bear hug. "I promise I am not. I am the one that will be anxious about you."

I returned his hug. "Do you mind if I get a few more pictures of you?"

"Yes, you may. But I warn you, they will not come out the way you think."

"That's OK," I smiled. "I have a few more pictures left before I can develop this roll." He let me go and stood poised against the log. I snapped the remaining pictures on the film. "That wasn't so bad, was it?" I asked with a giggle.

"No, it was not bad at all," he laughed. "Until we meet again?"

"Until we meet again," I agreed.

He kissed me on the cheek and walked back to the place where he had entered the clearing. I stood there, just rolling the camera over in my hands. His words danced around in my head. I couldn't wait to develop the photos – that way, I could show Dave and the others that it wasn't just in my head.

I put the camera gently into my bag, swung it over my shoulder, and headed home.

Chapter 10 – The Spoken Truth

Homecoming week was finally here. Each day had its own theme: for instance, Monday was pajama day. Some kids didn't go along, because they thought it was too immature. Whatever. You only get to dress like an idiot once a year – although in our school's case, some dressed like an idiot every day for a week. Some kids took it to the extreme, with extra messed-up hair and toddler-looking pajamas; some of them even carried blankets with them.

Thursday was class color day. Each class had its own color, and all the students were supposed to dress in it. The freshman groaned; they were afraid being hazed by the juniors and seniors. But that was only a myth – the worst thing a freshman really had to worry about was a junior with a yellow marker in hand; they would use it to mark their year somewhere on a lower classman's body. You would know if a senior had gotten to anyone, too – that person would have a red mark on them. It was pretty funny. The freshmen would react as though they'd been branded with a hot iron, while the upper classmen would laugh as they walked away.

I couldn't wait until photography class. I was both excited and nervous about how the pictures would turn out. What if Jay didn't show up in them? What if I looked horrible? I must have been showing my anticipation more than usual – I heard giggles in every class. I even heard one student whisper, 'She's been like that all day'. The time seemed to drag on longer than usual. I did my homework during class so I wouldn't have any later on and could concentrate on more important issues when I got home.

"*Finally!*" I said, as the bell rang for last period. I jumped out of my seat and ran out the door before anyone else had time to react. I threw my books into my locker and grabbed my camera and portfolio.

"You're here early," Ms. Kohel stated.

I held up my camera. "Just excited!" I exclaimed. "I have a new roll of film waiting to be developed."

She smiled and started going through the papers on her desk. "I wish I had more students like you. Go ahead in and get started."

"THANKS!"

I ran off to the dark room with my camera in my hand. I slowly wound the film into the container, popped the latch open, and slid the film out onto my palm. I stood there for a few moments, wondering what the film had captured. I slowly undid the canister lid and gently unrolled it, holding it up to the black light to see which negative had both of us in it.

I started with the larger 8x10 first. I carefully laid the film down on the machine and started to enhance the picture. It came out perfectly; there was no blurriness, the trees were in range, I was in range. I started playing with the colors to enhance the picture. There was one thing missing – Jay. As I started playing with the colors, I could see a blur where Jay had been sitting next to me. You could make out the shape of where he sat. While everything else was in clear focus, where he sat the branches and colors were distorted where he had been.

When I got the image as good as I could, I looked for the frames on the end that had just him. There had been five shots left when I took them. They were all the same as the first: every branch, every leaf, every stump was in clear focus except for where he had been standing.

The teacher came in after she had handed out the assignments to the rest of the class. "What's wrong?"

"Oh. Nothing. I thought the pictures would have come out better."

I had known they might not show anything, but I was hopeful.

"Let me take a look," she said, carefully taking the first one I had developed. She analyzed it for a few moments before speaking again. "These turned out great. Except…"

I knew what she was referring to. "I don't know what happened," I lied.

"These are quite interesting. Where were they taken again?"

"At... ummmm," I really didn't want to tell her the truth. But she wouldn't know where it was, anyway "A forest preserve." I told her.

"You have quite a gift, Miss Smith." She set the first photo aside and looked through the rest. She flipped through them as though she were analyzing a diamond. "What do you think the blurry spots are?"

"I don't know," I lied. "Maybe the wind moving the trees? Remember, I have my dad's old war camera. It could be malfunctioning."

"Yes. Possibly," I could tell she wasn't buying my sad excuse. "I can't wait to see your portfolio," she beamed.

What could I say or do? I was stuck. I hadn't thought that the pictures would draw so much attention from her, but my grade was on the line, so I couldn't make up a stupid excuse; nor could I afford to tell the truth. I was really disappointed the photos had not come out, though.

The bell had already rung to dismiss school for the day. I gathered my photographs, stuck them in my portfolio, and headed off to my locker.

I had forgotten to bring my CD player that day, but I was too lost in the thoughts in my own head to even pay attention to the mindless babble of the other kids.

As soon as the bus came to a stop in front of my house, I stood up and hopped off. Mom and Dad weren't home yet. I unlocked the door and went inside. Taking the stairs two at a time, I threw my book bag on the floor of my room. I took out the portfolio and grabbed the book that talked about capturing ghosts on film. I slowly flipped through each page to see if I could find a picture that resembled the ones I had taken.

There were stories with each picture about where and why they were taken, but I wasn't interested in any of that. I was almost done flipping through the book when the words "How to catch a ghost" caught my attention. The instructions were simple:

1.   Buy a camera and film
2.   Visit a cemetery

3. Visit a haunted location

4. Start taking pictures

5. Get them developed

6. See if anything appears abnormally

OK, that was stupid. The book went into more detail about how to capture a ghost's voice. Again, stupid. It talked about how tricks of the light can make you think that you've caught a ghost. It talked about dust being mistaken for orbs, and how people like to pretend that they had captured a ghost just to gain media attention. The book never mentioned why a ghost could not really appear on film; it mainly says that if you can see a 'ghost' clearly, it is probably a hoax.

I opened another book that offered a description of how to lure ghosts. But in my case, they came looking for me! I didn't need to lure them. Apparently, ghosts need energy – and they prefer electrical devices to charge up. Supposedly, when a ghost draws energy from an electronic device, it drains the battery, so this is one sign that lets you know that a ghost is in your presence. Ghosts sometimes take the energy from people, as well, in order to be able to communicate. This makes people feel weak, sick or even angry for no apparent reason.

It talks about how the human senses know when there is a ghost present. A cold breeze was the number one sign; or it might just be a cold spot in a room. You might smell an aroma that had no apparent source – a scent left from whatever the ghost had been doing when it passed. Goosebumps might appear on your body for no apparent reason, or you might have the sensation of being watched. The presence of a ghost might have a negative effect on the body or no effect at all. Each person is different. OK, that scenario fit my case. Sort of.

The next chapter mentioned listening to ghosts. It says that you could only hear words, not complete sentences, because ghosts have to scream in order to be heard by human ears, and doing so takes a lot of energy. It also said that young children's minds are more open, allowing them to see and hear to what adults can't.

The last chapter talks about what ghosts were capable of doing. The number one thing they could apparently do move objects around, making people think that they were losing it. I tried to relate the information to my own case, but nothing seemed to fit the normal ghost profile.

Part of me believed that I was really communicating with a ghost, while the other part was denying the fact: I could hear Jay without any type of electronic device, and I could feel his skin as if he were really standing right next to me. One thing he had mentioned which made me question his existence was that he had said that he could not always show himself in the form that I wanted. What didn't make sense was that during the times that he had shown himself; I hadn't had any electronic devices on me. Nothing really seemed to fit, from what I could tell.

Finally, I slammed the book closed and got ready for my run. My parents would be home by the time I got back, so I grabbed my CD player and a new CD before heading downstairs to leave them a note. I threw a note on the table and headed out the door.

I started off at a full stride, not even paying attention to where I was going.

I must have been running for at least twenty minutes when I finally slowed down to catch my breath. I looked up and noticed that I was passing by that house that stood out from the rest – the old Victorian. With everything else going on, I hadn't even thought about it, but now I could see that there was something different about it. I was upset at myself for not noticing before, but I could not for the life of me put my finger on exactly what was out of place.

I continued at slower jog so that no one would notice me looking.

When I reached the older section of the neighborhood, I slowed down to a walk and removed my headphones. I don't know what I was trying to hear. *Was I listening for Jay? What was I trying to listen for?* I really didn't know. All I could hear was the usual hustle and bustle: dogs barking, kids playing, cars driving by. I left my headphones off and started into a jog once again.

I was about two blocks away from my house when I noticed a light flickering across the way. It appeared to be coming from my clearing. I looked at the time and saw that I still had some time to kill before my parents would be home, so I headed off in the direction of the light.

I stood right outside the clearing to see if I could hear or see anyone else around, but there was nothing. It was eerily quiet. The sun had just started going down, so I figured I would be safe, and I could always run if anything was wrong in there. I started into the forest. It was darker than I thought it would be. Even with no leaves on the trees, the thick branches blocked out a good portion of the setting sun's rays. I sucked up my courage and called out.

"Hello?"

No answer. I tried again.

"Hello?"

I could hear something. People talking? I couldn't be sure; I was still a good distance from the clearing.

"Hello?" I repeated, louder this time.

The response came in such a soft whisper, "Hello?" I wasn't sure if it was him.

"Who's there?" I asked.

"It's me," was all the voice said.

"Me who?" Sounded like I was playing a game of marco polo.

"Lexi?" The voice asked.

OK, now this was getting creepy. Jay never calls me by my knick name.

"Who wants to know?" I demanded.

"Where are you? I can hear you, but I can't see you." The voice sounded more familiar as it got closer.

It wasn't Jay. Maybe Dave? The voice was too muffled to hear it distinctly through the trees. I slowly crept closer to the clearing. The voice repeated my name again. By this time, I was right on the edge of the clearing, hunched down so as not to be seen. I looked around in the dim light to see who was calling my name. I didn't see anyone.

"OK!" I said, leaping out into the clearing to catch the person off guard.

"LEXI!"

I turned around and screamed. Dave screamed right along with me.

"DAVE!" I managed to say through gasping breaths. "What in the world are you doing here?"

"I tried calling your house, and you didn't answer." He was also gasping for breath and leaning against a tree. "So I stopped over and no one answered, so I figured you had to be here. "Where ever here is. This place is hard to find."

"I went for my run," I explained. "I saw the light and had to see what was going on."

"Do you mind if we get out of here?" He asked, looking as though expecting a magical door to appear. "This place is creeping me out."

"This way," I said, pointing. "Why does this place give you the creeps?"

"I have no idea. Maybe because it's dark and my flashlight is about to die."

"The only thing that creeps me out is the bugs," I said laughing.

"I can deal with the bugs," Dave said brushing one away from his arm.

"So, why did you come here?"

"You bolted from school pretty fast, and I wondered what was up."

"Oh. Nothing, I just needed some time to think. About the college thing," I said, lying to him again.

"So what have you decided?" He asked, holding a branch out of the way.

"I'll cram in as much community college as I can in a year or two and then apply to a real college."

"So you aren't going to apply to law school?"

"I can't. Not yet. I need a bachelor's degree, first. I'll only have my associates if I do community."

He sounded amazed that I would need all that extra schooling. "Really?"

"Yup. But I'm still going to check out the law schools, so I know which one I want to apply to when I'm ready."

"I'm happy for you," he said, grinning.

"Huh? Why are you happy?"

"Because you aren't going to leave me just yet!" We both laughed as we entered my subdivision.

"Well, I should get going, the 'rents should have dinner ready," he said.

"Yeah, so should mine," I agreed.

We gave each other a quick hug and began walking toward our separate homes. As I approached the house, I saw that both cars were in the driveway. I knew my parents were home and starting dinner, so the door would be unlocked.

"I'm home," I called, as I walked inside.

"Hey, Lexi," Mom greeted me from the kitchen. "How was your run?"

"Same old, same old," I answered. "I saw Dave along the way."

"Really? How's he doing?"

I shrugged like it wasn't a big deal. "He's doing fine."

"That's good."

"Where's Dad?"

"He's downstairs, working on another project."

I called down the stairs. "Hey Dad?"

"WHAT?" He screamed back.

Uh-oh, something must be broken that he can't fix. That's the only time that he becomes eccentric.

"You got a minute?" I screamed back.

"Yeah, in a second!"

"What's wrong?" Mom asked.

"Oh, nothing is wrong." It really wasn't. I was thinking it would be great news to them. "It's about college."

"You still plan on going, right?" Mom asked, sounding concerned that I might have reconsidered.

"What about college?" Dad was standing at the top of the stairs.

"Well, I was thinking, and I also did some research," I started to say. "I need a bachelor's degree to enter law school. So I was thinking of taking my gen eds at community college and then doing my last two years at a real college."

"That would be perfect!" Mom exclaimed.

"Yeah, it would," Dad said. "Is that it?"

"Uh, yeah."

"Let me know when dinner is ready," he said, as he turned around and headed back down the stairs.

"Never mind your father," Mom said, stirring something in a pot. "He's just been under a lot of stress lately."

"Why?"

"His company is making cutbacks."

I gasped softly. "Oh no!"

"Yeah, he's up against the boss's son, the boss's nephew, and two guys who have been there for a long time."

"How long have the son and nephew been working there?"

"They just started," she said, without much tone. She already knew the answer to the silent question.

"Ouch." I said.

"Yeah. So say a prayer that he doesn't get laid off."

"I will."

"Tell your father dinner is ready, please," she said, setting the table.

"OK." I ran down the stairs to let him know.

After dinner was done and cleaned up, Mom went back to her book, and Dad went back to his computer. I headed off to my room to pretend do to homework. I had done everything already, hours before I was ready for bed. I wasn't used to having so much free time. I lay on my bed and just stared off into space.

"Lexi!" I heard my mom call me.

"Yes?" I answered back, running down the stairs.

"Phone," she said, passing me the handset.

"Hello?" I asked.

"Lexi?" It was Lynn.

"Yes. What's up?"

"Hey, it's me, Lynn," she giggled, like I didn't recognize her voice.

"Hey! What's going on?"

"Not much. Just called to chat."

Something in her voice told me otherwise.

"I heard that Tim asked you to the homecoming dance."

I didn't know much about Tim, except that Lynn had mentioned he was in one of her classes and she thought that he was stealing glances at her.

"Yeah, he did," she said.

Her tone sounded less than thrilled. So I had to ask her. "What's wrong?"

"Oh, nothing. It's just that I'm regretting saying yes, and I don't know how to back out of it."

"Why would you want to back out?"

"I think he's kind of cute..." She started to say.

"So...what's the problem?"

"I've just been thinking about what if things don't work out," she admitted.

"Well, you could always tell him afterwards if he says anything that you just want to be friends."

Lynn deeply sighed. "Yeah, I just wish I knew what his intentions were."

"Hey! Don't look at me!"

"I'm not," she giggled. "I'm talking to you."

I rolled my eyes. "Ha ha. You know what I mean."

"Yeah, I know," she said, with a heavy sigh.

I knew there had to be more. "What else is going on?"

"Can I ask you a question?" she asked.

"Sure, what's up?"

"Dave told me," you could tell in her voice that she didn't know whether she should know or not. "Hope you're not mad that I talked to Dave about it."

I was lost. "About what?"

"Well," she paused. "About ghosts."

"Oh, that!" *Thanks, Dave.* "I'm not an expert or anything. So I don't know what I can help you with."

"Do you believe in them?" She hesitantly questioned.

"Yes and no," I truthfully answered.

"Can you define for me please?"

"Well, I believe there are ghosts, and no, I have never seen one." I wasn't really lying. "Why do you ask?"

She sounded hesitant to say anything more. "Well, I have been hearing creepy stuff lately. I don't know what to think."

Nothing could be as creepy as what I have been going through. "What type of creepy stuff? And how long has this been going on?"

"Just recently, I have been hearing knocking, whispering, just weird stuff that I never heard before," she admitted.

139

Could it be that she's experiencing the same thing as me? "It's probably your imagination playing tricks on you."

"How can you be so certain?" She asked.

"Well, why would they all of a sudden start now?"

"Ummmmm, good point," she said, really thinking about it.

"Plus, didn't you have neighbors that moved in not too long ago with those younger pre-teens?" I asked.

"True. You know what? I hadn't even thought about that."

"You want to get them back?"

"Hell, yes I do!" She sounded relieved to know that she wasn't losing it.

"Get some flour and spread it around under your window," I started.

"Flour? Why flour?" She sounded as confused as I am half the time.

"Because when they come by at night… I'm presuming that is when this is taking place?"

"Yes," she said, as if a light bulb had gone on.

"Well, they won't see the flour at night, and they'll step into it and tracking it back to where they came from. And you can follow it in the morning."

"Awesome!" She cried. "I can't wait to try that!"

"And if that doesn't work, we'll work on something else to catch them. Sound good?"

"Sounds great! Thanks for listening. I didn't want you think I was going nuts."

I couldn't help but laugh. "Nah, I never would think that."

"Or if *I* was thinking that *I* was going nuts myself," she laughed. "I'll see you in school tomorrow."

"See you then," I said, hanging up the phone. Well, I'm up and wired with no place to go. "Hey Mom?"

"Yes?"

"I'm gonna go out for a walk, if that's OK."

"Sure. You know the rules."

"Yup," I said, as I got my shoes on, grabbed my coat and headed out the door.

I couldn't stop thinking about what, exactly, Dave might have told Lynn. Had he just played it off? By her tone, it didn't seem like he had told her everything that was going on. I don't even think he knew everything that was going on. I hadn't brought my CD player this time, because I wanted to take in the scenery.

During each season, I have a favorite moment. In the fall, it is when the leaves start to change colors. Winter is for the first snow fall. Spring is for everything starting to come to life. Summer is where there is no school and you don't have to be stuck indoors unless it rains.

I made my way into the newer section of the neighborhood, where the old Victorian house stood. I started up the street towards the house and saw something there that I never noticed before. Two cars were sitting in the driveway.

As I got closer, the creepiest sensation overtook me. I felt as though I was being watched. I was just on the boundary line of the property when a couple emerged from alongside of their car and just watched me. It was the creepiest thing. They had to be about my parents' age. They didn't smile. They didn't wave. They just glared at me as I walked by.

Creepy.

I headed home right after that. I was talking to a person that I couldn't see. Creepy people were moving into the neighborhood. I really didn't want to know what was next. But I was hoping that I would at least be able to speak to him tonight.

When I got inside, I showered and changed for bed, then turned my radio on low to hide my whispering. I believed him when he said that no one would be able to hear him, but that didn't mean when I spoke to him that no one else could hear me. My anticipation was growing as I wondered whether I would be able to hear him tonight. I still couldn't believe that I had received my first actual kiss. I couldn't help but smile; I could feel myself glowing and wondering when was the next time we would be able to kiss again.

"Hello, my dear." I looked around, but couldn't see him.

I softly whispered, "Hello." I didn't want to wake my parents.

"It is OK," he chuckled. "You may speak normally."

"I don't want to wake my parents," I spoke, still whispering.

"They cannot hear you," he reminded me.

I looked around my room just, to make sure. The music was still on low. I shrugged – if they did hear me, they would probably think that I was talking in my sleep or something. *Not* being a normal teenager, I did that quite often.

"I've been thinking a lot about you," I said, looking around the room.

"What are your thoughts?" He asked, as I felt an impression on the mattress next to me.

"About," I hesitated, wondering if I should tell him the truth. "Our kiss…"

"Was it not good?" He asked, slowly materializing in front of me.

I nodded, "It was."

I was amazed by the different states that he assumed before taking on human form.

"I have been thinking a lot about it too," he looked deep into my eyes.

"OK, now I know you're lying," I half teased.

"I speak the absolute truth," he insisted. He spoke with such sincerity, and from the look he gave me, I knew he was telling the truth. I wanted to move closer to him, but I was afraid to. I could smell his sweetness, and part of me wanted to be in his arms. The other part was still cautious about what was going on. "What is it that you wonder about?"

"Nothing," I smiled at him as if I knew something was going to happen. Something good.

"Can I ask you a question?" He inquired. I nodded. "What is your perception of love?"

"Love?" I was taken aback by the question. "Love is a feeling that depending on how you use it, it can either make or break you."

"That is a strange analogy, I must say." He was surprised by my response. "Please explain?"

"I have seen *love* make people do stupid things," I admitted. "I really don't know how to explain it. You could be so far in love that you lose all sense of reality. It would make you lose sense of who you are." I wasn't sure exactly how to explain it.

"I must say I have never heard it described like that before," he admitted, leaning back. "Real love should not be like that all. Would you say that you describe might be infatuation?"

I thought about it for a moment. "Yeah, I guess it would, to some degree."

He looked at me curiously. "To some degree?"

"If you are listening to your heart and your heart is saying love…"

He seemed bemused by the line of discussion. "Your mind, body, heart and soul must all be in agreement over that feeling. Then and only then will you know it is right."

"Besides it being just a feeling, how do you know if all four are in unison? Is it possible for all four not to be in synch right away?"

"It is," he collaborated. "All four must be in agreement from the very beginning, if only for a brief moment. It's a sense, a feeling that comes from within. The reason they may fall out of unison is due to the obstacles you have faced on your journey."

He seemed pretty familiar with all this for someone who just had their first kiss. "How do you know so much about this?"

"Well," he chuckled. "You hear with your eyes and see with your heart for your mind to hear your soul. You hear with your ears and see with your eyes for what your mind wants to apprehend. It is learning when to use them all when needed that is the most difficult."

He was still leaning against the wall as I was sitting against my headboard; we were just looking at one another. It was like we didn't have to say anything to be heard. I couldn't stop staring into his brown eyes as they glistened in the light. The light? I looked behind me and through the blinds I could see that it was sunny.

"Do not fret, my dear," he grinned, when he noticed my expression of shock. "You still have plenty of time."

"How?" I looked at him, confused about what he meant.

"In this world," his face drew down. "Things at times are reversed. It is when the sun descends here that your world will wake as normal."

"So I'm in your world?" I was nervous, but excited at the same time.

"No," he laughed. "It is easiest for me to appear to you in this world so you may view me as you wish."

"Oh," I said, lowering my eyes.

I felt a cool breeze, followed by his sweet scent, and I closed my eyes to embrace the aroma that flooded my nostrils.

"Alexandra?" He asked, worried.

I slowly opened my eyes. "Yes?"

His eyes, just inches away, stared deep into mine. "Are you alright?"

"Why wouldn't I be?" I whispered. It was like we couldn't stop looking at one another. We both wanted to know. I wanted to know more about him and these worlds he kept speaking of. "Will I ever be able to see your world?"

His eyes grew wide as he leaned back. "No."

"Why?" I leaned into him, drawn to him by some type of chemistry that I couldn't explain.

"When it is your time, you will but, that is not for a very long time," his look inquired why I had asked such a question.

"You come into my world; why can't I come to yours?" I thought it was a fair question.

"It is not as easy as that," he leaned away again. "Once in this world, you are bound to stay until…"

"What do you mean 'you are bound to stay'?" I couldn't imagine a world where they 'make' you stay. "Even you have said that we all have choices."

"Yes. Choices about whom you choose to be with and the path you will take. You do not choose who you are or where you live."

He looked away as if I had just hurt him. I leaned in again, touching his face with my hand. There was no cool sensation this time, just warmth. He gave me a look, as if to ask me why I hadn't run off yet.

I smiled, answering his silent question. "Because that's my choice."

He slowly smiled back as I placed my hand on the back of his neck, bringing his face towards mine. I could hear his heart race as mine skipped. I set my forehead against his. He seemed to welcome my advances, and I tilted my head just a bit to kiss him. His lips were so sweet that my taste buds were going into overtime. I kept my eyes closed, listening to him breathe through his mouth. His shoulders moved up and down as he wondered what to do. I kissed him again. I could tell he was enjoying every kiss.

"I…" he started to say as he pulled his lips away.

"My choice," I breathed.

He leaned in to kiss me this time. A sensation went through my body like I had never experienced before. I ran my fingers through his hair. It was soft and silky to the touch. I was so lost in his sweet scent and his taste. He pulled back, looking away as though something had caught his eye.

"I must be on my way, my dear."

"Why?" I turned to see what he was looking at; the sun was starting to descend in the horizon.

"Until we meet again?"

"Until we meet again," I hopefully repeated.

I threw my arms around his neck. The warmth of his skin slowly turned cool. I didn't want to open my eyes, for fear that he would be gone, but the sun grew brighter and brighter, leaving me no choice.

I slowly opened my eyes.

Chapter 11 – Curse, or Coincidence?

We used to laugh whenever adults told us that these four years would fly by – we never believed them. But out of all three years of high school so far, only freshman year had really seemed to drag. This weekend was already homecoming. Fortunately, most of our teachers were cool and hadn't given us any homework, since the dance was tomorrow.

I couldn't help but wonder if someone was playing a joke on me. I didn't hear from Jay at all for that whole week. As hard as I listened, trying to hear his voice, there was nothing. I had even gone to the clearing to read after school, just in case, but he never appeared.

The temperature had been dropping, and winter was definitely in the air. Not that this winter would be any different from any of the others – it just seemed like it was coming earlier than I ever remembered. Things had changed so much since I was a kid. I missed how we used to play, full of imagination - piling into our snowsuits, barely able to walk, and staggering out into the snow.

Everything was changing. The times had changed. We were growing up. Our crayons and markers and blank paper had been replaced by pens and paper and lined paper. Instead of drawing what we wanted liked, we were told what to write. Watching cartoons without a care in the world had been overshadowed with homework and wondering whether anyone would ask us to the school dance – wondering whether any of your friends from this small town would be in any of your classes, so you would at least know someone. Now, the changes were coming even faster, going one step further. Friends were moving away or going to college out of state, parents were getting divorced = your whole life could change in less than a year.

When we were younger, if we didn't like how something turned out, we could simply erase it or crumple the paper up and start over. But now, there was no more redo. Every path we chose made our future more concrete.

Even my best friend would not be in school with me next year. Although he was going off to community college and staying close to home, things would not be the same. And everyone seemed to have it all figured out – to know exactly what they wanted to do with their lives.

Everyone except me.

Friday was like any other school day. The cliques were all in their normal spots, talking about the dance in addition to all of their normal crap. My friends collected at our usual table, also talking about the dance. Time moved relentlessly forward, never pausing to let us catch our breath. Yup, it was just another ordinary day in this thing we call life.

"Hey, Lex!" Dave called, as he pulled out a chair for me to sit.

"What's up with this?" I asked.

"Can a gentleman be nice?"

I giggled. "Yes, a gentleman can be. But you're not a gentleman."

His look showed that I had hurt his feelings. "You're Dave," I simply stated.

"I'm gentleman Dave," he proclaimed, holding his elbows out with his hands on his waist.

"Yes, you are a gentleman," Lynn giggled. "But you ain't no superman."

We all burst out laughing.

"Everyone ready for the dance tomorrow?" Val gloated.

Everyone cried in unison, "NO!" Her smile faded.

"Just kidding," Aaron said, giving her a hug.

"It's just another dance," I said, calmly.

Dave high fived Aaron. "It's the last homecoming dance for us."

"No, it's not," I rolled my eyes and shook my head. "You know you'll be back here next year for our dances."

"No…" Aaron started, to say. Val gave him the look. "Uh, yeah, I mean. This isn't my last year."

"In that case," Dave said, putting his arm around me. "This isn't my last year, either."

"Oh, please," I groaned. "Like you guys would want to party with us high schoolers."

"That's not true!" Aaron playfully looked upset.

"Yeah! You're our high schoolers!" Dave finished.

"I belong to no one," Lynn declared, smiling.

"You belong to me," I said elbowing her.

"That's right! I belong to Lexi!" We burst out laughing.

The bell rang, and we all headed off to class. I wanted this day to be over with so I could see Jay. If he was there.

I heard his voice in the crowded hallway, "You're mine." I smiled to myself, because I knew no one else had heard him. The emptiness that had filled my body all week long was no longer there. I was starting to feel complete; I had never believed until now that the emptiness I had felt for so long would ever be filled.

The first half of the day went by so fast that it was already lunchtime before I knew it.

"So I take it things are great between you and Jay?" Val asked, at lunch.

"Huh?" What made her bring up Jay? "Yes, why?"

She laughed and pointed to my notebook. "You're scribbling his name all over your stuff."

"Don't get too attached to him," Lynn said.

My face began to grow hot with anger. "Why?"

"Because we haven't met him yet," Dave answered.

"Oh, yeah." I felt stupid. "You will soon."

Val piped up, breaking off her conversation with Aaron. "When?"

"Uh, I'm not really sure," I couldn't believe I was lying again. "It depends when he comes home next."

"He'll probably be home for Christmas," Lynn said, as she took a bite of her pizza.

"Christmas?" I hoped that no one noticed the anxiety in my voice.

"College students always have a break at Christmas time," Lynn said. "I think it's a law, or something."

Dave rolled his eyes. "A law?"

"OK, OK, not a law, but you know what I mean," she snapped back.

"Do you mind if I sit with you guys?" A voice asked, behind Lynn.

It was Tim. Why was Tim asking to sit with us? I couldn't understand this one. It's not like we had anything against him, but he wasn't exactly part of our clique, either. I didn't know much about Tim, except what Lynn had mentioned about him being in one of her classes and thinking he was stealing looks at her. Then it dawned on me.

"Yeah, that's fine," answered Lynn, as she scooted aside to make room.

"Everyone looking forward to the dance?" Tim asked.

Everyone just looked at one another. We had already cleared that topic. But if it would get people off my back about Jay, I'll be happy revive it.

I pretended to be thrilled. "Yes! I'm really excited!"

"No, you're not," Val joked. "You hate dances."

"I don't hate them hate them," I smiled. "I just tolerate them for what comes afterwards."

"That's the best!" Aaron said, taking a drink of his soda.

"Yeah, because you get to eat another cow," Val groaned.

"A cow?" Tim asked, horrified.

"How is Terry doing?" I asked, trying to change the subject.

A familiar voice answered. "I'm doing just great!"

"Oh, hey, you!" I said, looking over my shoulder.

"Come join us," Dave said, pulling another chair up to the table.

"Sorry, I can't, guys," he said, apologetic. "Mind if I sit with you on Monday?"

"Yeah," Val piped up.

"Thanks. I gotta go."

We waved as we said our goodbyes, and he went to sit with the rest of the football team. We all felt bad for Terry. What was should have been an exciting time for him felt more like confinement. It was pretty funny, actually. You actually had to be in our clique to understand our strange sense of humor. Val explained the cow joke to Tim, as the others went back to talking about other things. I piped in here and there, just so they wouldn't catch me day dreaming.

School had ended, and the bus ride was over sooner than usual. Not many kids were on the bus today – probably walked home with a friend, or their parents had picked them up for a sleepover.

I hopped off the bus as fast as I could. Since it was Friday, I was hoping that I would be able to see him. Then I noticed Mom's car in the driveway, although I hadn't remembered it being her short day.

Fortunately, she was always reading a book or into one of her hobbies – knitting, sewing, junk like that – to take too much notice of what I was up to. I unlocked the door and went in.

"Hello? Mom?" I asked, as I stepped into the house.

No answer.

I ran upstairs to my room to throw my bag down. As I was halfway back down the stairs, I heard the door open. Mom looked sickly white.

"What's wrong, Mom?"

"You remember Kim?" She managed to say. "The girl living down the street on the north side?"

"Yeah," I knew her a little. We weren't best friends, or anything. "What happened?"

"She committed suicide today."

I gasped. "She what?"

I hadn't noticed any commotion on that end of our street. Then again, the bus had gone another way to drop us off.

She hobbled to her usual spot at the table and sat down. "She couldn't cope with the death of her sister."

"I just saw her last week!" I did. "She looked fine to me."

"Her parents said they should have seen the signs." Mom's eyes were red from crying.

"What signs?"

"Kim put up a front. She was doing things a lot of suicidal people do," she paused. "To make people think that everything was fine."

Kim's sister Carol had died in a horrible car accident the year before last. It was tragic. From my understanding, she had been driving in horrible weather when she shouldn't have been out. Lost control and flipped her car. She was wearing her seat belt, but that had only prevented her from being killed upon impact. Carol was in a coma for several months, until the family had to make a decision. Their insurance had run out, and they couldn't afford the care any longer. Kim had taken it really hard, to begin with; she had been really close to her sister.

Mom and I both looked up when we heard a knock on the door.

"I'll get it."

Might as well. Mom didn't look like she was in any condition to walk, and I was closer to the door.

"Hey."

"Hey, Dave," I said. "Do you mind, Mom?"

"No. Go ahead," she said, waving me out.

"Are you sure? I can stay."

"No, I mean it. Go." She looked like she was ready to break down, but her tone was serious enough that I knew she would yell at me if I didn't go.

"I'll be home later."

"Take your time."

"Later, Mom," I said, still hesitant, about leaving.

"Later honey."

Honey? She rarely calls me anything like that. I gently pulled the door closed and started walking with Dave.

"So you heard," he said softly.

"Yeah. I just found out."

"Let's get out of here," he replied, steering me in a different direction from what we normally took.

"Where?" I asked.

"Let's take a walk in my neighborhood."

"OK," I said, putting my hands in my pockets.

In his neighborhood, the houses were spread further apart. It was also quieter there. Dave's face wasn't pleasant. Not surprising, considering what had just happened. Everyone knows that people die, but usually it just happens to the elderly. That I knew of, anyways. We were a few blocks into his neighborhood and just strolling side by side.

"I didn't tell you the full story," he started to say. "The part I had started to mention the other day, but we got sidetracked."

"The full story?" I asked, startled.

"Remember when you asked about the history of this land?"

"Yes, I remember it well." Of course I did. "But you never got around to the other part you had started to mention."

"You remember the witch part of the story?"

"Yes, the one who put a curse on the kids?" I asked.

He looked at me, puzzled, silently asking me how I knew. "I never told you about that."

Oops.

"I, umm, did some research," I lied.

What was I supposed to say, that I had a dream that showed me everything?

"Where did you find that information?" He demanded. "No one has ever been able to locate any information from back then."

Busted.

153

"I don't remember." I had to think of something fast. "I forgot where I read it. Next time I come across it again, I'll let you know."

"I would really like to know!" He was upset. "I want copies of whatever you read, as well." His ancestors had been among the early settlers, and he was really into history. So for me to know something about the town that he didn't was aggravating to him. "I was told that there was nothing in writing. Just word of mouth."

"I promise you I'll get you copies. OK?"

"OK," he reluctantly agreed. I had to change the subject fast.

"Now, what did you not tell me about the history of the witch?" I asked. His eyes softened, and he looked away. My strategy had worked.

"Well, I guess you already know the main part," he said, with his voice slightly lower than usual.

"Main part? I'm not following."

"The part about how she cursed all of the children who would live on this land."

"What about it? You don't believe in all that witchcraft crap, do you?" I asked, trying to throw him off.

"Yes and no," he admitted.

"Same here."

After all, I had to believe. To some degree, anyways.

"A lot of the people here know that Carol's death was no accident."

"How could they think that?" I asked.

"Yes, the roads were bad, but they were not as bad as people say they were," Dave mused, trying to remember back to that day.

"What about Kim?" I asked.

I got it about the curse, but the choice to commit suicide had been hers, not anyone else's.

"Kim," he sighed. "That was an ugly aftermath."

"Aftermath?"

"People here don't like to talk about it. They will always make up something believable so that no one starts talking."

"Talking about the curse?" I asked.

"OK, now I really want to know where you found this information," he demanded.

"You just mentioned it earlier."

"I know, but I would like to know how you found out before I even mentioned it," he quizzed sternly.

"The information was pretty vague." To a degree, it had been. "I promise, as soon as I relocate the information, I will show you."

"Fine," he said, in a low tone. "Deaths on your street have been occurring since they first started building homes there."

"Really?" I tried to remember the last death that had taken place.

"Really. No one has ever mentioned anything before or raised a stink about it, because they didn't want to say that the street was haunted."

"Haunted?"

"More so cursed," he continued. "But things started happening, and people had no choice but to pay attention. It started with a man who was mowing his grass on his riding lawn mower. People said that he was being stupid – he had his toddler on his lap while he was mowing. Everything was fine until the last patch; then the mower flipped over and the baby was thrown underneath."

"Gasp!" I cried.

"Yeah. That was way before our time. Everyone just blamed it on the stupidity of the father."

"I would never!"

"That's what everyone else said, too" We walked in silence for a few moments. "But there have been lot more 'freak accidents' since then. They come in spurts, and then everything is quiet for a year or two. You know Aiden, on the south end of your street?"

"Yes." Aiden was a sweet boy who walked with a limp and could barely talk. I had always thought he was just born like that. "Something happened to him?"

"He was once what you would call an 'Aaron.' He was great at sports, and he had his whole future ahead of him. Colleges were throwing scholarships and money his way. They say that he was out partying, had a lot to drink, and on his way home, he lost control and rolled his SUV into an embankment. He wasn't wearing his seat belt, so he went straight through the windshield."

Aiden had been that way as far back as I could remember. "I always wondered what had happened, but no one ever said anything."

"Do you remember the family that moved in, and then moved out within the same year?" He asked.

"Vaguely," I admitted.

Our street seemed like it constantly had people moving in and out.

"Well, their little girl, Ariel, drowned in the swimming pool. They don't know how, because when they found her body floating in the water, the ladder was still against the side of the house. One of the older residents actually told them about the curse. They eventually moved out, probably thinking about the safety of their other two children. But most of the adults around here won't talk about there being a curse. Every time there's been an unexplained death, they come up with some kind of rational explanation.

"OK. Let's say that there really is a curse." Even I found myself trying to find an explanation. "If all the adults know about it, how come they are still living here with their kids on the street instead of moving away?"

"Various reasons, I guess," he said shrugging. "Can't afford to sell, don't want to believe the rumors, or they think that it won't happen to them."

I whispered, "I guess the same could be said about my parents."

"The 'killings' only happen every so many years. But I can guarantee you that there will be at least three homes that go on the market by the end of next week. What I haven't mentioned is that there is another myth – but it's just a myth – that if you are the first family to own the house you live in, then you will be safe." He didn't sound too sure that it was only a rumor...

"Phew," I let out a breath. "My parents are the original owners of our house, so I should be good."

"You should be," he grinned.

"So after this accident, there shouldn't be any more deaths taking place for now?"

"There shouldn't." His confirmation wasn't all that convincing. "Not for a while, anyways."

"Is there any way to know? I mean to know about if and when the next..."

"Sadly, no." He answered before I could finish. "No one knows when or where or even who the curse will strike next."

We walked on in silence. I knew what he was thinking, and he knew what I was thinking – the adults had kept us kids in the dark, or so they thought. The witch, Sarah, had been pretty clever if you really thought about it. The ways that the children had died seemed like freak accidents or just plain stupidity on the part of their parents, like the guy with the lawnmower. As long as there was some other explanation, no one had to believe in the curse, and kids would keep dying.

We turned the corner, entering the part of his subdivision that had a lot of older houses. We had been walking for a few minutes when I realized something. I knew that I couldn't let Dave know about my dream, not yet anyways, but I couldn't believe what I was seeing.

"When were these homes built?" I asked casually.

I hadn't thought about it until now, when they were right in front of me, but some of the houses here looked a little too familiar – they were the same ones I had seen in my dream! I tried my best not to freak out – then Dave would really start to question my sanity.

"Oh, those?" he said nonchalantly. He looked around at the older brick homes like he was just now seeing them.

"These were the very first homes that were built here."

"They look like they are brand new," I countered.

"Yeah, but they are built out of blocks and clay," he explained. "They are some of the best-built homes here, and the owners do a lot to maintain them."

"Wow, they do look old, but they seem modern at the same time," I gawked.

"Well, a lot of the owners have added their own touch," he said with disgust. "It takes away from the originality of the construction."

"Times are changing," I commented.

"Yes, they are," he agreed. "Lexi, there is something else I was going to tell you about our land."

"What's that?"

"The Indians that used to roam here before the first settlers." He paused, uncertain if he should continue, and then pointed at an empty plot. "That was supposed to have been an old Indian burial site."

I breathed, "So the story was true." I cringed hoping that he didn't hear me. "So that's not a myth or a rumor?" I asked.

"Nope. That part of the story is true," he said, looking straight ahead. "A lot of people nearby hear things that they can't explain."

"So I take it that whatever is making the noise isn't harmful?"

"No one could really say that they are harmful. Playful, maybe, but not dangerous in any way," he agreed.

"What do you mean by playful?" I questioned.

"You know how most people have a table by the door and they put their keys there?" I nodded. "Well, when they go for their keys, knowing that they had very well set them down there, they are missing."

"Maybe their kids took them to play with them?"

"That would be a logical thought," he said, smiling. "Except that it has happened to people who don't even have kids. And with those who do, the kids deny it up and down, saying that they didn't touch them."

"That's strange. Do they ever find the keys?"

"Yeah, usually in a place they would never have put them."

"Like," I asked, raising an eyebrow.

"In the bathroom, on top of a bookcase, stuff like that." He shuddered. I wasn't sure if it was because of the cold air or the fact that the subject was making him uneasy.

"Maybe they just forgot," I figured. "You know, subconsciously forgetting that they put them down somewhere else, since they were so used to putting the keys in the same spot every day."

"Who knows," he shrugged. "Anyway, we should start heading back."

I looked up at the sky to see the sun sinking behind the horizon. Dangit. I thought angrily to myself. I hadn't realized that we had been out for so long. There was no way that I would be able to make it to the clearing tonight.

We were nearing the entrance to my subdivision; cars I had never seen before were lined up along my street.

"They must be here for Alan and Marge," Dave said answering my silent question – Carol and Kim's parents.

"I'll see you tomorrow?" I asked, hoping that he wouldn't be offended that I was ending my time with him so abruptly.

"Of course. Remember, tomorrow is the dance," he smiled.

"Of course. I knew you wouldn't let me forget," I chuckled.

He gave me a hug and headed off toward home. I hoped my parents wouldn't be upset at me for being out so late, but they probably wouldn't mind. They adored Dave. A while back, they had tried to push me into a relationship with him. But they've backed off some, since it's been so long and they finally realized that I only like him as a friend. Not that that stopped them from asking about us every so often.

When I walked in the door, dinner was already on the table.

"How was your walk?" Mom seemed to be doing a little better.

"It was fine." I didn't want her knowing what I just found out. "Just the usual."

"So we hear that you are going to the dance with him tomorrow," Dad said.

"Yeah. Just as friends."

"Just as friends," Mom said sarcastically.

"Yeah, just as friends," I reiterated.

"Uh-huh," Dad said, grinning.

We sat in silence while we ate. After the strange events that had taken place over the last couple of months, I had grown more curious. After dinner was done and everything was cleaned up, I sat back down at the kitchen table.

"Mom? Dad?" They both looked at me. "I have a question."

"What's that?" Dad asked.

"What made you decide to move into this house?"

"Well," he started. "We originally looked into store fronts."

"See, your dad has a certificate for a VA loan, and the realtor didn't want to touch it," Mom added.

"So we went to a different realtor inquiring about a store front we had driven by that was up for sale," he continued. "He asked us why we were looking at store fronts instead of single family homes."

"We really thought it was hopeless," Mom said, taking a sip of her coffee.

"So we explained the situation about the VA loan. He said that he would show us store fronts if we wanted, but he could work with the certificate and get us into a single-family instead. So we humored him."

"What made you decide on this area?" I asked. I knew they had moved from a good distance away.

"The realtor had friend who lived out this way, and he knew the contractor who was building some homes in the area," Mom said, setting down her cup.

"So we decided to give it a shot and came out to look at the models. The realtor said that if we didn't like the models, to drive around the area where your friend Dave lives and take a look. We looked at the models, but we had a certain requirement that had to be met."

"Our old house was pending sale, so we had to find something we could move into right away," she added.

"We viewed a house similar to this one, but we didn't like the lot that it sat on," continued dad. "It sat up right behind another house that was being built."

"Why didn't you buy in Dave's area?"

"We should have," Mom said.

"Your mother wanted a two story."

She replied smugly, "Yes, I did."

"If we knew then what we know now, I would have listened to your mother. But the houses out that way were more expensive," Dad finished. "A few days after we had checked out the models, we received a phone call. The contractor explained that the original buyers had some problems; their financing fell through, and the house was up for sale with an immediate closing and move-in date."

"So we're not the original owners of the home?" My heart stopped for a second.

"We are and we're not," explained Dad. "We are the first ones to live here, but the house was not built for us. We did have some things changed, though, since it was not yet completely finished."

"Like what?" I asked.

"The fourth bedroom in the original plans that was all open space was connected to the family room. Plus, with the price they wanted for central air and some other little extras, we decided to pay separately and hire out the work for them. Everything was already roughed in, so we had it finished after we moved in."

"Why did you want to know?" Mom asked.

"Just curious, that's all," I answered.

"You know we're not going to kick you out after your senior year," Dad chuckled.

A lot of kids had been complaining that they needed to live on campus or find somewhere else live after they graduated, because their parents were going to kick them out or start charging them rent.

"I know," I said, smiling. "You guys are the best! Anyways, I gotta get some sleep for tomorrow."

"Night, little one," Dad said. I hated that almost as much as I hated them calling me Lexi. "Night," mom chimed.

"Night, guys." And I headed off to my room.

I was a little worried about the fact that we weren't the original owners of the house, after all. I looked at the time. It wasn't too late to give Dave a quick call.

Ring…ring….ring…

Please pick up. Please pick up, I thought over and over as the phone continued to ring.

"Hello?" A woman's voice answered.

"Hello, Mrs. Kravic. May I please speak to Dave?" I asked.

"May I ask who's calling?"

"Alexandra," I answered.

"Oh! Hey, Alexandra! Didn't recognize your voice. Sure, hold on, I'll get him for you," she said. "DAVID!" I heard her yell away from the mouth piece.

"Yeah, Mom!"

I heard some crackling as she handed the phone over. "It's Alexandra, on the phone."

"Hey, Lexi! What's up?"

"Remember earlier, when you told me about the original home owners should be safe?"

"Yeah, I remember," he laughed. "I told you that just earlier today."

"Yeah, yeah. Well I found out we are not the original owners of the house," I explained.

He sounded concerned. "What do you mean?"

"Well my parents informed me tonight that the house was actually built for someone else, but their financing fell through."

"Well in theory," he paused. "You technically are the original owners of the house. Since the first people never technically lived there."

"Ummmm," I said.

"The rumors," he started. "Well, the kids who have died were all under the age of sixteen."

"Kim was my age though. Seventeen," I said quickly, correcting him.

"Lex, like I said, she was an aftermath. She wasn't killed in some freak accident," he said, trying to reassure me.

He was right but wrong at the same time. Kim wouldn't have committed suicide if her sister hadn't died.

"Well, anyway, I'm going to bed. I'll see you tomorrow?"

"Yes, ma'am. What time should I pick you up?"

"Dance starts at 6, right?"

"Yeah," he confirmed. "Do you want to go out to dinner beforehand?"

"We're eating afterwards, remember?"

"Yeah, I know," he said, as if that had nothing to do with it.

"Guys. You can eat whatever you like and not gain a pound," I mumbled.

"Just in our nature," he laughed. "Pick you up at 5?"

"I'll be ready."

He replied enthusiastically, "See you then."

"See you," I said, hanging up the phone.

I put the phone back on the charger and crawled into bed, hoping that I would see Jay.

Even if he was only in my dreams and my imagination, at least I wouldn't have any more nightmares. At least, that's what I was hoping.

We'll see, right?

Chapter 12 – The Dance

I woke up to the sun shining through the blinds into my bedroom. *That's odd.* I hadn't dreamed at all. I was somewhat disappointed. It was still early, and I had a lot of time to kill before getting ready for the dance. I decided to do my nightly run during the day instead, since I wouldn't get home until late. I started getting washed up, and then I changed my mind. I was going to go to the clearing to see if Jay would be waiting there. After all, it was usually on a Saturday or Sunday that I would normally see him.

I don't know why, but I was happy… almost giddy. Was this what it felt like? To be in love with someone who loved you back? I had no frame of reference, since I had never been in love before.

My parents were already gone for the day. Mom was working, and Dad was running errands. So I left my usual note and proceeded out, started off at a jog. The neighborhood parents were extremely nosey; I acted like I did on any other day.

After making my way into the forest, where I knew I couldn't be seen, I kicked it up to a sprint. I must have been running full steam, because I made it to the clearing in no time.

"Hello?" I called out.

No answer. My heart sank.

"Hello? Jay? Are you there?" I called again.

Again there was no answer.

Then something occurred to me. I took off out of the woods again and ran back to the house. In one swift motion, I unlocked the door, ran up to my room and grabbed my recorder, heading back in the same way. I didn't care who was watching me now; I took off like a rocket and was back in the clearing in no time.

I made sure the tape was rewound to the beginning. I really didn't care what had been recorded on it. I remembered reading in the book that ghosts like to drain batteries; I had forgotten to bring an extra set, but I figured I would press my luck.

I pressed record.

"Hello?" I asked again, holding the recorder away from me.

I waited a few moments.

"Jay? Are you here?" I asked again.

I waited a few more moments.

"I've missed you. I miss you right now."

I waited a few more moments, not knowing what else to say. If anyone could hear me, they must have thought that I was some kind of nut job. I hit the stop button, rewound the tape and pressed play.

"*Hello?*" I heard myself.

Silence.

"*Jay? Are you here?*" I heard myself again.

Silence.

WAIT! What was that? I thought. I hit stop, rewind, stop and play again.

"…here…yes."

The sound was faint, but I could hear it. It sounded like his voice, but I couldn't be sure, because it seemed far away. The tape continued to play.

"*I missed you. I miss you right now.*"

Silence.

His voice was low and sad, "I miss you, too, my dear."

This time a little louder, but still far away. My heart jumped back into place.

I hit record again.

"I'm sorry. Did I do something wrong?" I asked.

I waited while the tape ran in the silence.

"I wish I could see you."

I waited again as the tape still ran.

"What's wrong?"

Still running the recorder, I stayed still.

"When will I be able to see you again?"

I let the recorder run a little longer before hitting stop. I rewound the recorder to the spot where I had started asking the second group of questions.

"*I'm sorry. Did I do something wrong?*"

"No," he said.

"*I wish I could see you.*"

Silence.

"*What's wrong?*"

"Please don't be mad," he answered sadly.

My voice again. "*When will I be able to see you again?*"

"Soon."

I hit stop and hit record again.

"Why would I be mad?"

I waited.

"I'm not mad. You did warn me."

I waited.

"I really miss you. I wish that you could go to the dance with me tonight."

I waited.

"I....I....lo..." I couldn't believe what I was about to say. "Next time I'm in your arms, I want to tell you something."

I waited, still holding up the recorder in the air. After several more moments, I hit stop and rewound it to the third round of questions.

"*Why would I be mad?*"

"...____..._n't see me," was all I could make out.

"*I'm not mad. You did warn me.*"

I heard a long, breathy sigh.

"*I really miss you. I wish that you could go to the dance with me tonight.*"

He sounded even sadder. "I'm sorry. I would be honored to escort you to your dance."

"*I....I....lo...*" What was I saying? "*Next time I'm in your arms, I want to tell you something.*"

Silence. Had I scared him off? Even more silence. I was trying so hard to hear him that when the recorder clicked off, I jumped. I put the recorder in my back pocket and began speaking.

"I hope you can hear me," I started. "I don't know what you did to me, but I really like you." I sat on the stump of a fallen tree. "I wish you could give me a sign," I paused. "To let me know that you can hear me."

I waited....nothing...

"I have to start getting ready for the dance tonight," I know I must have looked incredibly stupid, but I really didn't care. "I'll miss you."

I started walking back to the edge of the clearing, my head down, wishing I could have seen him only for a moment. I felt a cool breeze on my face. I stopped in mid-stride. I stood up straight and closed my eyes, taking long, deep breaths through my nose in the hope of catching his scent.

I breathed out loud, "Yes!"

Barely, just barely, but I could smell him. I remained still while my breathing returned to normal. As soon I felt a cool sensation, followed by warmth on my cheek, I lifted my hand up to touch my face. As I did, I felt nothing. I opened my eyes, and my hand was moving in the emptiness of air. I raced home to start getting ready for the dance.

I didn't need as much time as other girls to get ready. I used only a powered foundation and lip gloss and did my hair. I got dressed and put on my shoes. My Mom knew I would get pictures at the dance, so she just sat at the table with a new book in hand.

I paced back and forth in the formal living room, waiting for Dave to show up. I saw lights pull up the drive and knew it had to be him.

"See you later, Mom!" I said, quickly opening the door.

"Are you going out afterwards?" she asked.

"Yup."

"The usual place?"

Our routine never changed. I don't know why she even bothered asking. "Yup!"

"OK, have fun," she waved from the table.

My parents only asked one thing from me – not to lie to them. I had never had a reason to before. Lying always created more hassle than it was worth. For every lie you told, you would have to create a new one to cover up the first lie. They had never inquired about Jay, so I never had to lie about him.

I stopped right outside Dave's car door, making sure I hadn't forgotten anything. "Got everything?" he asked.

"Yup," I replied, getting in.

"Excited?"

"Nope." We both giggled at my answer.

"You look beautiful," he said softly.

"Thanks," I said looking away. I added sarcastically, "Too bad we can't dress up more often."

"You're not like other girls," he grinned.

"Give me a pair of comfortable jeans and a t-shirt, and that's my prom dress."

"I would pay to see you go to prom like that," he chuckled.

"Yeah, me too. But you know prom is *formal* and they won't allow you in if you aren't *formally* dressed," I remarked.

The drive didn't take as long as it does on a school morning. The dance, just like any other school dance except for prom, was held in the gym. The theme, of course, was our school colors – red, white and yellow. There was a booth set up on one end for couples to get their pictures taken together.

"Come on," I said, pulling his arm.

He looked shocked. "*YOU* want pictures?"

"My *mom* wants pictures." I glared at him. "If I don't produce some type of formal picture, she'll be pissed at me."

Luckily we were early, and the line wasn't that long, so we got in and out pretty fast.

"Hey, there's everyone," he said, waving across the room.

"Let's go," I said. We walked over to where they were already gathered. "What's up, guys?"

"Val is mad," Lynn said.

"Mad why?" I looked over at her.

Val hissed angrily, "Because my dress didn't turn out like I thought it would."

Dave and I looked at her dress and couldn't see what she was talking about. What had been a long-sleeved black dress was now off the shoulder, accented by strategically-placed red squiggle stripes. Her shawl matched the design of her dress.

"What look were you going for?" I asked. "It looks great!"

"You're a bad liar," she growled.

"Yeah, on any other night, I would be," I smiled. "But tonight, I am telling you the truth."

"Yeah, your dress looks great!" Lynn agreed.

"Really?" Val asked, changing her tone.

"Seriously. What look were you going for?" I asked again.

"I was trying to do the overlay thing with the extra material, but it didn't come out right. I couldn't just sew it back on, so I created this shawl instead."

"Well, I don't care what anyone else says. It looks great," I said. "Just to prove you wrong, let's all get a picture together."

"Yeah, don't listen to yourself," Terry said, as he came up and joined the group. Everyone chimed in, agreeing with him. He looked really good all cleaned up.

"All *you* have to do is throw on a jersey," Val cackled.

He looked a little pissed. "Hey now, don't go there!"

"Sorry," she apologized.

"Since all the players are hanging out with, well, each other, do you mind if I join you all?"

Of course we didn't mind. The line for pictures was longer now, but still not too bad.

Aaron and Dave were trying to make Tim feel comfortable. Since he was the oddball, he didn't know what to say or how to act. It was like he was afraid of upsetting us. We really didn't understand why he was here, but we knew he wouldn't stay that long. I wished he would relax – we are a relaxed bunch. The worst we ever do is laugh about stuff.

After we had our pictures taken, we went back to the floor and started dancing. *Yeah,* me dancing. I look like an overgrown baby trying to walk for the first time. Not a pretty sight. A slow song came on.

"Do you mind if I dance once dance with Lynn?" Dave asked.

"Sure," I smiled.

But before Dave could get closer to her, Tim had already asked her to dance. Mike was not happy over that fact, even though Tim was her date.

"OK, forget that idea, then," he smiled.

He put his arm around my waist, and we started slow dancing together. Now even *I* can slow dance. Just sway back and forth.

Yup. I can do this.

We danced around in circles until the music turned back into a fast song. The DJ would play three or four fast songs before playing the next slow one.

I didn't know how long we had been dancing, but I was getting sweaty and needed a break.

I screamed into Dave's ear, "I'll be right back."

He screamed back, "Where are you going?"

"I have to use the little girls' room!" He gave the look like oh, oops.

I made my way through the crowd to the restroom. I was just coming out when something caught my eye.

I heard his voice, "Hello, beautiful."

My heart was in my throat. I looked around, and I saw him down at the end of the corridor. I quickly glanced around. Surprisingly, no one else was there, so I quickly and quietly went to where he was standing.

I whispered, looking around, *"What are you doing here?"*

He held up a finger and motioned for me to follow him. *"Come,"* he whispered.

We were behind the gym, but I could still hear the music. No one else could see or hear us. His hair was neatly in place, and he was wearing what could pass as a somewhat modern tux.

"Are you trying to get me admitted?" I played.

"Admitted, where?" he asked.

He didn't have to keep his voice low, since I was the only one who was able to hear him.

"The funny farm," I sighed. *"If anyone catches me talking to myself, there are going to be rumors."*

"Then don't speak," he smiled. "You look very beautiful tonight."

I mouthed, *"Thank you."*

"Do you mind if I have this dance?"

"I can't dance." I truthfully admitted.

He laughed. "Not this one, the next one."

"What if it's a fast one?"

"It won't be. Trust me, my dear," he smiled as he knew for sure.

Sure enough, the next song really was a slow one. He held his arm tight around my waist and held my hand in his free hand, twirling me around. I couldn't believe it! I was dancing! And not just in circles! He must have read my facial expression.

"I had to save my energy," his face next to mine. "So I would be able to have one dance with you tonight."

I lovingly whispered in his ear, "*Thank you.*"

The song was coming to an end, and we leaned into each other. His soft, warm lips pressed against mine, his arms tight around my waist. My heart felt like it was going to completely stop. We finished kissing as the song ended.

"I must go," he said.

"*I'll miss you,*" I said, giving him a kiss on the cheek.

"I'll miss you too my, lo…dear." He kissed me on the cheek and was gone.

I tried to hear whether people were in the corridor, but I couldn't make anything out. I peeked around the corner and no one was there. I was halfway back to the gym when Dave came up the stairs.

"There you are!" he said. "We thought you fell in!"

"I did, but I rescued myself," I teased, trying to divert his attention from wondering why I was here.

"Why are you down here?"

Crap. What do I say?

"I…ummm…thought I saw something," I sort of lied.

"They announced the last couple of songs," he said, putting his arm around me.

"Then off to watch Aaron eat a cow," I giggled.

"Then off to watch Aaron eat a cow," he repeated, amused.

Luckily, it was louder inside the gym, and more people were dancing. I did my pathetic excuse for a dance, while thinking about a few things that were different than the last time I had seen him. This time, I hadn't had that cool sensation. When he kissed me, I hadn't seen my breath. More importantly, he was going to tell me that he *loved* me. This time was different. He hadn't mentioned it at all since the last time, when I had chewed him out. One thing I really did wonder though. Since he didn't feel cool to me, would others have been able to see or hear him? The last song ended, and while everyone else stayed to chat and say goodbye, we were among the first ones out the door.

"It's too cold!" Val cried.

"We'll be in the car soon enough," Aaron said.

"Everyone have a ride?" Lynn asked.

"Can I ride with someone?" Tim asked. "I walked."

"Sure, you can ride with us," I answered. "That's OK, right, Dave?"

"If it's going to be a problem..." Tim started to say.

"I'll take him," Terry piped in. We just looked at him.

"Are you sure?" Dave was sincere enough.

"Yeah, I'm sure. If that's OK if I tag along with you all?" Again, no one disagreed.

We said our *see you laters* and headed off to our cars. The place wasn't more than five minutes driving. The car had just started to heat up when we arrived in the parking lot, all of us pulling up together at about the same time.

"Table for seven?" asked the hostess.

"Could we make it a table for eight?" I asked. We looked at one another and shrugged, saying it was no big deal.

"Table for eight," the hostess confirmed. We looked at the menus, deciding on what to order.

"I don't know why you even bother looking at the menu, Aaron." Val joked.

"What do you mean?" He sounded insulted.

"You order the same thing every time we come here!"

"Maybe they have something new? You never know," he laughed.

"We've been coming here for how long, and you order the same thing every time," she griped.

"Hey, maybe I wanna try something new. Is that OK with you?" Aaron snapped.

"Whoa, you two," I said. "We are here to have fun, remember?" They both said a pathetic excuse for a sorry and then shot each other a look that would have made a grown man cry.

"What can I get for you?" the waitress offered.

We stared at the menu as if we hadn't been there dozens of times, giving her our drink order. The restaurant staff knew we were a peaceful group, so they never gave us a hard time. I saw some kids from a more snobby group enter shortly after the waitress brought us our drinks.

"Great," mumbled the waitress. "Not this group again," she said, as she walked away.

"Was she talking about you guys?" Tim asked. Dave and Aaron just looked at each other.

"Remember, Tim is new in our group," corrected Lynn.

"I keep forgetting that," Aaron smacked his forehead.

Lynn whispered, "Anyway, she wasn't talking about us. It's the loud, obnoxious snobs that just walked through the door."

"Yeah, they complain about everything," Val rolled her eyes.

"They get pissy when mommy and daddy won't get them a limo so they can go downtown," I said holding my nose up in the air.

Dave stated in a snobby voice, "Yeah, they think it's all about the glamour and how much money they can spend in one night."

"It's not about the money or what you do, as long as you are with your friends," sided Tim.

"Hear! Hear!" We raised our glasses, clinked them and drank. The waitress back came and took our orders with a smile.

"I'm sorry you have to deal with people like that," Tim said.

"Oh," the waitress was taken off guard. "Well, let's just say, I would rather deal with a full house of you guys than an empty house with just them." She smiled and walked away.

"You made her night," Lynn said, flirting with Tim. Mike just sneered at him. Uh-oh. I smelled trouble.

"Don't we have history together?" Aaron asked Tim.

"I'm not sure, I'm the geek who sits in the back and pretends that he's invisible," he said, laughing.

"Oh yeah! Now I know you!" Dave chimed in.

"The teachers think you're hot shit," Lynn commented.

"I wouldn't say that," he blushed.

Val replied sarcastically, "You never get called on. Must be nice."

"Never mind her," I giggled. "The teachers like to pick on the ones who don't think they know anything." After an outburst of laughter, we went back to talking quietly.

"See," we heard the hostess speak. "It goes to show you that money can't buy manners."

We burst into a giggling frenzy. The waitress came with our orders, filled our drinks and went to go hide again. This was nice. Sitting around with a group of friends and enjoying ourselves.

"Oh! One thing I *have* to mention to the new person," Aaron said, through a mouth full of food. "No school talk."

"But they mentioned school," I said with a smile.

"That was before they knew the rules." Aaron was starting to piss me off.

"Yuck!" I gagged. "OK rule two, no talking with your mouth open and full of food."

"Hear! Hear!" We giggled as we clinked our glasses again.

Before we knew it the checks arrived, and it was time to call an end to the evening. We all hugged each other and said our goodbyes. Terry went to take Tim home, Aaron took Val home, Mike took Lynn home, and Dave and I started on our way. The sky was brightly lit, and the stars were shimmering. The moon shone bright in the dark sky, lighting up the night like a pale sun. Dave and I sat quietly in his car. There really wasn't much to talk about. We embraced the evening as it came.

"Where are you going?" I asked. He was pulling up to the curb next to the park near our neighborhood.

"It's too beautiful to call it a night yet," he said nervously. "Would you like to go for a walk?"

"I'm in a dress and heels," I motioned with my hands.

"We won't be out long."

"Ummmm. OK," I didn't like where this was headed.

"When you start to get cold, just let me know and we'll head back. OK?"

I stepped out of the car. "OK, I'm cold."

"Ha ha," he grinned. The park had soccer fields, baseball fields, a pond, and even football fields, although there was a rumor that these were going to be turned into more soccer fields.

"It is peaceful," I said, breaking the silence.

"Yes, it is," he sighed.

"What's wrong?"

"Nothing," he said, not looking at me.

"Liar! I know you enough to tell when you are lying."

"You look very beautiful tonight."

"Stop trying to change the subject," I demanded.

"Well, I'm trying to let you know," he hesitated. "Lexi, I really like you."

"I know you do. I really like you, too."

"That's not what I meant," he shook his head.

"Oh," *oh crap.*

"I know what you said about the friend thing…."

"Yeah. And you know I value our friendship too much to ruin that. You're my best friend, Dave."

"I know," he remarked.

"You'll be starting college next year, and who knows, you may realize that I'm not the one for you."

"You think that," he said looking at me. Not tonight. Please not tonight. I *did* think that. We sat again in silence. The cold wasn't bothering me as much as the uneasiness that surrounded us. He led me up to the middle of the bleachers.

"Are you jealous?" I asked.

"Jealous of what?"

"Jay?"

"How can I be jealous of someone I have never met?"

He had me there. "True."

"Look," he said leaning his body towards me. "You are very beautiful...on the inside and out."

"Pft!"

"Whether you believe it or not," he disregarded my dismissal. "Any guy would be lucky to have you. I just wish I was that guy."

"I know," I whispered. *Was he right, though?* Jay could never be around the way other guys could. I still hadn't figured out what Jay was, exactly. He wasn't human, nor did he fit any category of ghost. I really didn't know what was happening. Dave leaned in, and I followed suit. I wanted to pull away so bad. I tried to. But our faces grew closer. He put one hand out to keep balance and another one against my face. Our lips were just about to touch, when all of a sudden, a sharp breeze flew between us.

"NO!" cried the wind.

"What was that?" Dave asked.

"I have no clue," I lied.

I silently took a deep breath and smelled his sweet scent. I felt so bad about this – but how could I explain to Dave that I had fallen for another...well... just another.

"You're shivering," he said. "I'll take you home."

I hadn't felt cold, but I let him think I was. I repositioned my coat, and we started down the bleachers. Walking back to the car, I shot a quick glance over my shoulder. There Jay stood, by an old oak tree that I used to climb when I was younger. And he looked pissed. I had never seen him look like that before.

"I know you must be itching to get out of that dress and into sweats," he smiled as we walked up the drive.

"You know me oh so well," I grinned.

"Mother Nature," I heard him mumble under his breath.

"What?" I asked.

"Oh. Nothing. I'll give you a call tomorrow?"

"Sounds like a plan," I smiled.

He made sure I got inside before taking off. My parents were sleeping, and I crept slowly up the stairs to change into something more manageable. I gathered my clothes from my room and crept into the bathroom; after I was done, I slipped back into my room.

Why did Dave have to try to kiss me? Why couldn't he just leave things alone? If it ain't broke, don't fix it, and if it is broke, sometimes it's better to leave the broken alone.

But it did start to raise questions…

Chapter 13 – The Interference

"GASP!" My heart skipped a beat.

"Sorry," Jay, said frowning.

"Hold that thought," I whispered, as I threw on jeans over my sweats. I also struggled into two sweatshirts and my coat. Still whispering, "Meet me at the park."

He nodded and was gone. I got my running shoes and left a note saying that I had gone for a run. I snuck out the back door and over the fence. Fortunately, my parents' bedroom faced the front of the house. I ran to the park as fast as I could.

I called, just above a whisper, "Jay?"

"Yes, my dear," he replied, revealing himself from behind a big willow tree.

"You scared me earlier."

"I am terribly sorry. I did not mean to frighten you."

"It's OK," I smiled. "I'm glad you did!"

"You are?" He sounded bewildered.

"Yes. I can't even tell you how sorry I am," I said walking closer to him.

"You sorry? What do you have to be sorry about?"

"You didn't see what was about to happen?" I said, knowing he very well knew what had been about to happen.

"Yes, I know," he replied.

"I didn't mean for that, I mean I didn't want that, I mean...."

"I know. I could feel you," he said cutting me off.

I was lost. "Feel me?"

"I can feel feelings. Well, sort of."

"Oh," I was shocked. "So what am I feeling now?" I said with a sly grin.

"Something that I don't want you to be feeling," he said, with a sly grin back.

"Oh, how so?"

"I truly adore you, Alexandra," he paused.

"But?" There had to be a but, I've seen this a thousand times with other kids in my class.

"I never once in my life thought I would feel like this. Words cannot express or come even close to what I want to say."

"So, you thought you would see how I would react, scream and run away?"

"That is how I pictured it," his face was honest.

"I'm not your average ordinary girl," I flirted.

"I know. I can clearly see this," he said smiling.

I was growing annoyed. "I still hear a but coming."

"Please, my dear, don't be upset. I am trying," he said, coming closer.

"Trying?" I asked.

"I do not know what to ask of you," his tone said that he was unsure of what he wanted to say.

"I don't know what you mean," I was lost again. "What if I told you, that I wanted to be with you... no matter what?"

"I could never ask you to commit to that," he objected.

"OK, stop this," I held up my hands. "Stop this now." He lowered his eyes. "You can't do this to someone. Come into their life, tell them that you love them from day one, and then act like this is nothing but a huge mistake."

"Is that what you think?" His eyes grew wide. "And remember, I never told you that I love you."

"But I know you do."

"I will not lie. But you do not want me to speak such words."

"Well, correct me if I'm wrong," I demanded. I could feel my voice starting to rise.

"I can truthfully admit with an open heart, that I truly believe you are the one for me," he stared at me, scared at what I would do next.

"Then it's settled. We'll make this work," bringing my voice back down. "Unless you don't want to?" I added.

"I want to!" His voice now holding hope. "I just fear that I may not be enough for you."

"You let me decide that."

"Anything for you."

My voice was back down to just barely a whisper, "Thank you." I started moving towards him, my eyes on his. My heart seemed to stop. I reached my hand up and started to caress the side of his face. "You're so warm."

He looked at me in shock. "I am?"

"Yes," I said. "I can feel you as though you are really, well, here."

He touched my hand. Then the side of his face. His eyes grew with excitement and bewilderment, and then hopelessness. "It won't be that way for long." There was sadness in his voice.

"That's OK," I said, running both my hands through his soft, silky hair. "A little is better than nothing."

"You are more accepting than most," he said, staring into my eyes.

"If you want me to walk away and never look back…" I started.

His eyes grew wide. "I promise you, we *will* be together," he gently kissed my lips. "It will not be today, it may not be tomorrow. It may not be until years from now. But we will be together."

"Don't make a promise you can't keep," I teased. But although I was playing with him, I was also dead serious.

"I will keep my promise until such time as you order me otherwise." His smiled lit up the night.

"One thing that sucks about all of this," I said with sorrow. "One thing that I do wish for."

"What's that?"

"I wish we could take pictures together. I wish you could meet my friends. I wish I could take you to my school dances."

"Here," he said, handing me my camera.

"You thief!" I bantered.

"Let's try a picture now and see what happens." Well, if I could feel him like he was really here, maybe a photo would work this time. He held me close, grabbed the camera and snapped a picture. I had forgotten about the flash – I hoped no one noticed. "From my guess, the last set did not come out."

"They did." His eyes lit up. "But they didn't, at the same time," I continued. "I will show you later."

His eyes grew softer, and he kissed me again under the moon light. I pulled away, expecting to see my breath, but even with the cold in the air, I didn't see anything.

"This is great!" he cried.

"Shhhh," I said, giggling and putting my fingers to my lips. "If you are in this state, I know people can hear me, what if they can hear you?"

"So?"

"So, we'll get caught, and I'll have to explain it to my parents. That's what."

"Oh," he said in a lower tone. "Sorry."

"Say sorry by kissing me," I couldn't help but smile. "No one can hear us kissing. So I think we'll be safe."

"You....*kiss*....do....*kiss*...have...*kiss*...a....*kiss*...valid...*kiss*...point," and he continued kissing me. We were hidden by shadows of the mature trees that overlapped in the park.

"I have a question," I said pulling away slowly.

He kissed my neck before looking in my eyes. "Go ahead."

"How do you plan to keep your end of your promise?"

"Whatever do you mean?"

"You promised that we would be together," I said, dying to know the answer to my question.

"Yes, I remember."

"How can you promise that?"

"When the time is right, my dear."

"How will you know? How will I know?"

"Trust. It's all about trust and faith," he pulled me in closer to him. "Do I have to be worried about this Dave guy?"

"Dave?" I laughed. "No. We're just best friends."

"Do all your best friends try to kiss you?"

"No," I laughed playfully. "Dave, ummmm, Dave is an exception."

"So only Dave is allowed to try to kiss you?" I couldn't tell if he was serious or playing.

"Look, you are the only one I want," I said. "But I'm not going to lie – there will be times when it might be tough. Like, I had to lie to my friends and say you are away at college."

"Why?"

"They wanted to meet you. If I told them that I wasn't even sure if you were real, they would have me committed. So I had to say something, until *I* knew for sure what was going on."

"I see," was all he said.

"Do you want me to say that you are back from college and have you meet them?"

"You know I would love nothing more than that, dear. But I am unsure about how long I can stay like this without someone taking you away."

"See, now you know where I am coming from."

"I see now."

"Would you like to go for a walk?" I asked.

"Yes!" he exclaimed. "This feels new to me."

I hopped to my feet and held out my hand. He took it and stood. I could see that he didn't need my hand for support; I think he just wanted the contact. I kissed him, this time. I loved the way he held me when he kissed me. I pulled away, grabbed his hand, and we started walking side by side.

"So this is what it feels like," he looked a bit unsteady on his feet under the unaccustomed weight of his body.

"I have another question, if you don't mind."

"You are always full of questions when we meet," he laughed.

"As you probably are, as well," I smiled back at him.

"Most certainly."

"What are you?" I asked. He stopped, but still held my hand. I gave him a playful tug to continue.

He wasn't sure how to answer the question. "What do you mean, what am I?"

We started walking again.

"Well, I remember the times when we first spoke," I started. "Well, I mean you first spoke to me. The things you said. Followed by the things that happened. Like the coolness of your presence. I could see my breath when we first kissed. Your picture didn't develop. I couldn't hear you with my ears, I needed my recorder. You stopped a kiss that should never have happened. You appeared in my room without any sign. Now tell me where am I wrong to ask you what you are?"

"You ask with good reason, but I am afraid that I cannot answer what I am."

"Why not?"

"For, you see, it is not as simple as you might think," he looked straight ahead. "I know I was once a man. I mean, I am a man, I think. I thought at one time that I was ghost trapped between heaven and hell. I watched the decades pass, while no one even noticed I was here."

"You didn't let anyone know you were here, did you?"

"Sadly, that is true. But I never had a reason to," he turned to me and smiled. "A reason to before now. I know you may never love me in the same way that I love you."

"Whoa," I said.

"Just listen, please," he begged. I nodded. "I am willing to accept that. And I hope I have not made your life harder with my presence. That was not my intention, not by any means. For when I first saw you, many years ago, I knew there was something special about you."

"Why didn't you say anything sooner?"

"I was afraid to – I was terrified about how you would react. About what you would think of me."

"I'll give you that. I really don't know how I would have reacted." I was being truthful.

"So this is what you see when I see you out for your nightly runs," he looked around in amazement.

"Yup," I giggled. "Not too much to look at."

"It's everything to look at!"

"It is peaceful here, though, at night."

He sighed with enjoyment as we walked hand in hand, "So true."

This was great! It was so easy being with him. I didn't have to pretend to be something I wasn't. We walked along the small path that I take when I don't have much time at night. I didn't want this to end, but I didn't want to be out too late, either. We were almost back at the park.

"I wish this night didn't have to end," I said, frowning.

"I would give anything for this to never end," he said, giving my hand a squeeze. "But I do not know how much longer this will last."

"I don't care."

"What do you mean?"

"This is more than anyone could have given me." Standing on my tiptoes, I gave him a kiss on the cheek. "I do wish, though, that we could have had more time at the dance."

"Now," he said with a warm smile. "That wish I could grant. But only for tonight."

"How?"

He whispered something so low that I couldn't make out the words. After a few moments, I realized I could hear music.

I looked at him in bewilderment. "Only the two of us can hear," he said, as he put his arm around me and we began to dance.

"I don't even care if anyone can see us," I whispered. "I'm on cloud nine right now, and nothing can bring me down." He had the biggest, warmest smile I had yet seen on his face.

It was just the two of us in the shadows, dancing to music that only we could hear. I really don't know how long we danced – I was too busy staring into those big, beautiful eyes of his that twinkled every time the moon hit them just right. I had more questions to ask him, but I was afraid that it would spoil the moment. So I kept them to myself for now.

He twirled me as if I weighed nothing more than a feather. He was a great dancer; I couldn't believe that he had actually gotten me to dance. Dancing with him felt so natural and easy; I didn't even have to concentrate on my footing. When I came back in from the twirl, he held me close, never letting his eyes leave mine.

The music eventually stopped, and so did we. We gazed into each other's eyes, and he slowly leaned in to kiss me. His lips were soft as silk, his skin the same. His luxurious hair gently glided through my fingers. I could not only feel but also hear the beating of his heart. Our eyes were still closed when we slowly came to a stop. As I opened my eyes and exhaled, I could see my breath.

"Oh!" I gasped.

"What is wrong, my dear?" He looked into my eyes, but I couldn't speak. He looked down at our hands. "I am sorry," he said with sadness. "I felt that something had changed – I was just hoping that it was not what I thought it was."

"No," I knew it wasn't his fault. "Don't be sorry. It… just… took me by surprise."

"I am the one who is embarrassed," he whispered, looking away.

"Don't," I whispered, putting my hand on his cool cheek. "I was in complete bliss. I would never ask for anything more."

"As was I," he smiled shyly. "I cannot express the way you make me feel."

"I should get home," I said, dejected. "I don't want to, but the sun will be coming up soon, and I don't want my parents to worry."

"Of course," he said. "May I try something else with you? I have never done this before, and I would like to see what happens."

"Will it hurt?"

"I do not believe it will."

"I trust you," I said smiling.

"Hold on tight!" I did as he instructed, holding on to him tightly and closing my eyes. "You may open them," he said a moment later.

I opened my eyes, and we were right outside my house. "I didn't feel a thing," I whispered. I had no idea what time it was; I was really hoping my parents weren't up yet.

"Perfect," he smiled.

"I have to go. Until we meet again?" I was using his lingo now.

"Until we meet again," he hugged me and gave me a kiss on the forehead. "If you ever need me, I will be there. It may not..."

I put my finger to his lips to stop him from what he was about to say. I *knew* what he was going to say, and I didn't care. "I know you will. Will you be waiting for me in my room?" I kissed him gently on his lips.

"If you wish," he said with adroitness.

"I do, and a whole lot more," I flirted.

"Then yes," he beamed with delight.

With that, I dashed back through the fence and snuck into the house. Luckily, my parents weren't up yet. I threw away the note and silently crept back upstairs. When I reached my room, I felt a chill in the air and just smiled. I knew he was there.

"Hello," I whispered. I didn't want to turn my radio on now, because my parents were gonna be waking up soon. So I kept my voice as low as I could.

"Hello, my dear."

I whispered softly. "I'm so glad you are here."

"So am I," his voice said he was, as well.

"I can't wait until we are together."

"We are together," he snickered.

I yawned, "You know what I mean."

"You are exhausted. Sleep now, my dear," the sweet cool breeze made it hard to stay awake.

"I don't want to."

"You must," it was almost as if he were warning me.

"I'm afraid I won't see you again."

"I promise you that you will," he chuckled.

"Will I see you in my dreams?"

"Possibly. That depends on your dream state."

"What do you mean?"

"You must be in the right dream state for me to visit," he sounded concerned.

"How do I get into that state?"

"The brain is far too complicated. One cannot control that."

"I will find a way to be with you. I believe that we are meant to be together," I know I probably wasn't making much sense, but he understood what I was saying.

"Oh, you do?" he asked curiously.

"Yes. Don't you?"

"I do. Things will work out. I promise," he exhaled.

"You don't sound so sure."

"I have faith."

"Are faith and destiny male or female?"

"Neither and both."

"How is that possible?" I asked, trying to make sense of his answer.

"I cannot explain it. Nor am I able to show you as I did before."

"Well, you said have faith," I reminded, yawning again.

"I have faith in the power. Not in the form you think."

"That should be more powerful to override anything?" I was trying to be hopeful.

"I would like to think so."

"I forgot to tell you something," I said through a yawn.

"What's that?"

"You looked incredibly handsome tonight."

"Thank you. You looked incredible. I cannot fathom how lucky I am for this to have worked out."

"You're my right kind of wrong," I teased.

"What do you mean?"

I yawned again, "You are everything that I am looking for, but in the wrong form."

I really didn't know what I was saying. I was too tired and too blissed out to care about anything at that moment.

"I cannot disagree with you."

"One thing I am certain about," I said, barely keeping my eyes open.

"That you are about to fall asleep?" he chuckled.

"No," I laughed.

"Well, what are you certain about?"

"Nothing about our love makes sense."

"You've got that right," he burst into laughter.

I snuggled under the covers and closed my eyes. My mind ran over everything that had transpired that night. Right before I drifted off; I felt a pressure at my side, and the temperature dropped slightly. I didn't have to open my eyes to know that it was Jay. I knew he had placed his hand on my shoulder. I took my own hand and placed it where I could feel the slight pressure. My hand touched only my own shoulder, but the feeling of coolness let me know he was there.

I didn't know what I had said, for I was too far in my dreams.

All I know is that I heard, "I love you too," above my ear.

Chapter 14 – Irony

I can't remember what time it had been when I actually went to bed that night. For all I know, it could have been a dream. But if it was, it was the most realistic dream I have ever had. All I knew was that if it had been a dream, I never wanted to wake up.

As the hours turned to days, the days turned to weeks. He hadn't appeared again as he had since that night, but truthfully, it didn't bother me. We still had our long talks and our long goodbye kisses. Many questions lingered that I hadn't gotten around to asking. Every time we were together, I realized that the questions didn't matter, at least not until I was alone – alone with my own thoughts.

My friends only brought Jay up every so often. When the subject came up right before Christmas, I had asked Jay about it. I wondered if he could do what he had done the night of the homecoming dance, but he said "no," because he wasn't sure he could do it at will. Even he did not know how it happened. So when my friends asked about him over the Christmas break, I made the lame excuse that his parents wanted to spend as much time with him as possible, and he couldn't get away. Everyone understood, but they were still a bit skeptical. Even Dave had begun to grow more and more suspicious. On the days when we normally hung out, he seemed to be spending more time with Val, but that didn't bother me.

The emptiness that had once occupied my soul was gone. I knew I was still too young to think about getting married, even though I had always dreamed about what my wedding would be like. I didn't even think about having kids; I was way too young and still had college to think about. I wanted to have a career before starting a family. I lived the single life, but in a way I didn't. For reasons I couldn't fathom, I had always been oddly anxious about settling down. But when I was with Jay, all those worries seemed to disappear.

I said, holding down my camera, "Sorry, guys." I had used up my last shot.

They replied in unison, "Awwwww."

"I'm so glad football season is almost over," Terry sighed. "I miss these times."

"We've missed you, too," Val responded back.

"I'll buy more film tonight. Promise."

"When are you going to get those developed?" Lynn asked. "I want copies!"

"Of course," I said with a huge grin. "And I'll use the computer to enhance every detail."

She comically laughed, "No, you will not!"

"I haven't seen you use your camera that much lately," Val said, realizing that I had been camera-free for a while.

"Yeah," she was right. "But finals are coming up, and I needed to use up the last of this roll."

"I want a life size one of me," Aaron said, doing the superman pose.

"I'm sure Val would love that," Dave grinned.

"I can't believe the year is half over already," Tim remarked.

"Before we know it, you guys will be off to college. Well, Aaron will be off to college, and Dave, you'll always just be my Dave," I joked with a laugh.

"Hey now!" he snorted. "I'm saving money *and* getting the crappy classes out of the way."

Aaron snorted back. "I'm not spending a dime!"

Terry sighed, "College."

"Yeah yeah yeah," Lynn mumbled. "We can't all be lucky enough to get away with eating a cow...and getting paid to do it."

"He can keep the cow. I just want the steak," I said, laughing.

"Yeah, you can keep the fat, bro," Tim laughed back.

He was fitting in better than anyone of us would have thought. Lynn and Tim became an official couple over Christmas break. They were so cute together, but I knew it wouldn't last. But Mike never said anything to Lynn, and it had just happened between the two of them.

"I just chew the fat. Like this," he demonstrated with his gum. We all groaned.

"Hopefully, things will get better once you're away at college," Dave tried soothing Terry.

"I hope so. The last thing I need is for something to happen and they kick me off the team."

Aaron gently comforted, "Your dad is just making something out of nothing."

"I just hope he gets over this living vicariously through me phase."

"I think all our parents have done that," I said. "Mine are pushing me into college, period, because I'll be the first in my family to go."

"I wish I had that problem."

Then he noticed the look I shot him. "Sorry, I know, different situation, but the still same thing. I wonder how these pictures are going to turn out?" I changed the subject, rolling the film between my fingers.

"They are going to turn out great," Val stated.

"Have you ever thought about becoming a professional photographer?" asked Tim.

"Nah," I replied. "I like doing this just as a hobby."

"You know, if you do something you love as a career, they say you never truly work a day," quoted Dave.

"Yeah, but I don't want my hobby becoming burnt out either."

"Always the practical one," Val said, taking a drink of her water. "I am hoping to become a fashion coordinator."

"You would do great at that," Lynn said with enthusiasm. "Just think, we could wear what all the hot stars wear and wouldn't have to pay a dime for it!"

"Ha, ha," Val laughed. "OK, I won't charge you what I would charge the celebs."

Lynn stuck out her lower lip in a pout and then smiled. Things were back to normal. At least so I thought.

"When are you going to get the pictures developed?" Lynn asked.

"I'll drop them off soon. I'm not rich, so I can't do the one hour place."

"You *better* let us know as soon as they come in," Val pointed at me.

"Will do!"

"So how's Jay doing?" Val asked. Dave rolled his eyes.

"He's doing great. School has him overwhelmed with work, so I haven't been able to talk to him much lately." I was becoming a great liar. Not sure that was something to be proud of, though.

Dave was becoming more suspicious. "What is he going to school for?"

Huh. No one had brought up that subject before, so I had never come up with an answer.

"*RIIIIIIIIIIIIINNNNNNNNNNNNNNGGGGGG!*"

Aaron huffed grumpily, "Damn bell." We all picked up our trash and headed off to our classes.

"So what *is* he going to school for?" Dave asked. Our classes were close to one another.

"He's taking gen eds, just like you," I said.

"Isn't this his second year, though?"

"Third, so?"

"Shouldn't he be getting into his major?" He seemed determined to find a flaw with Jay.

"You will be going to community college for two years, right?"

"Right," he huffed. "I'm starting to doubt that this *Jay* even exists. And that you are just pretending."

"What do you mean, pretending?" I demanded. "You think I am making him up?"

"Well, yeah, sort of. I mean we've never even *seen* this guy you go on so much about."

"Wait a minute now! I don't go on about him. If I recall right, *YOU* guys are the ones who bring him up." I was getting mad, even though I knew that Dave was right in a way.

"Yeah, you're right. But that doesn't make it any better," he said. "I just want to know that he would take care of you like I would."

"Don't you trust me?" I huffed.

"Trust you? Of course I do."

"Then trust me when I say that he does take good care of me."

"Fine," he slumped against the doorway of his classroom. "But that doesn't change the fact that I still haven't met him."

"I promise you all will meet him soon," I didn't know how – I had the gut feeling that this was a promise I would have to break.

"Yeah, you said that at the beginning of the year, and look how long it's been," he folded his arms in front of him.

"I can't help that!"

"It had better be soon, or I'm going to hunt *him* down and have some words with him."

"Dave, stop being overprotective."

"I can't help it."

"Well, try," I said, storming off.

I knew he was right. I knew why he was being so protective. I would have been the same way if the roles were reversed. Since I still had some time before my photography finals, I would drop off the film to get professionally developed. I could always take the negatives in for my finals and produce more pictures.

After school I dropped off my bag at home, put the film in my front pocket and grabbed my wallet. I hopped on my bike and started off towards the shops in the middle of town. Ever since the neighboring towns had built more homes, there had been a lot more traffic, so I took the back roads as much as I could. I dropped off the film at the store; the sign said that it would be ready in three days. Three days, no big deal. My final wasn't for another week. I rode back home, my thoughts consuming me.

This weekend, my parents would be taking me to one of the colleges I planned to apply to when it was time. Normally, the college didn't allow a walk-through for those who weren't ready to apply, but my dad had explained the situation and they made an exception. Dave had asked my parents to go with us, because he wanted be there for moral support; my parents had agreed. They thought it was a great idea to have someone along who had already looked at colleges first hand.

I sat in the clearing, wondering what college life would be like. I had become sneaky since the first snowfall, using a broken branch to erase my footprints whenever I came and went. As far as I knew, no one else ever came here, and that's how I wanted to keep it. Jay had come to my dance that one time, so I knew he wasn't confined to the clearing, but I wondered how far he could actually travel. It was early enough in the day that the sun shone overhead. The snow lightly covered the branches of the naked trees. It was a beautiful picture.

"Hello, my beautiful."

"Jay!" I could hear him, but I couldn't see him. "Where are you?"

"I am sorry, my dear," just above a whisper. "I am terribly weak right now."

"I don't mind," I really didn't, just as long as I could hear his voice. "Can you come and sit beside me?" I felt the temperature drop, so I knew he was near. "I have missed you so."

"I have missed you too." He just didn't know how *much* I had missed him. "Are you strong enough to talk?"

"To speak, yes," he said. "Anything more, I am afraid not."

"That's fine. I have a few more questions burning in me, if you are OK with them."

"Go ahead, my dear."

"What's it like?" I looked at the place where I knew he was, but all I could see was the bare trees.

"What's what like?" He asked.

"To be in the state you are?"

"It's hard to explain. Some days I am stronger than others," he began. "Other days, no matter how hard I scream, I know you cannot hear me."

"Does it hurt?"

"There is no physical pain, just frustration."

"Do you remember who you were," I paused, adding quickly. "Who you are?"

"Very vaguely," he admitted. "All I remember is that I was about twenty one and lived in this area. Other than that, I don't remember where I used to live, who I was, or what I have become."

"Do you talk to any others?"

"No. You are the first person I have spoken to. I have told you this."

"That's not what I meant," I giggled. "Do you see others like you?"

"I used to."

"Used to?"

"Yes, before you came into my world." The air was a bit warmer than before. "I could see others, as you could see your friends. Then they became distant. Then not at all, after that night we danced."

"I wonder why?" I asked.

"Lately, though," he paused briefly. "I have been seeing them again."

"We *will* be together one day," I reassured him.

"I truly hope so," he sounded a bit distant.

"You're not giving up on us, are you?"

"Of course not, my dear," the chill returned. "Just with each passing day…"

"Our time is still young."

"You have much hope."

"Yes, I do. The hope that you once had…"

"I still do," he interrupted.

I looked at the ground and whispered, "It sounds like your hope is fading."

"I wish for nothing more than your happiness."

"I am happy! I wish you could see that," I was getting annoyed by his riddles. "Every time you say something like that, it makes me wonder if you meant what you said before."

"Please do not be upset, my beautiful. I am worried that one day, you will change your tone."

"I do not see that happening. But I can't see into the future, and from the sounds of it, neither can you. So stop talking like that."

"I apologize. I think that it just hurts too deeply that I cannot hold you."

"I wish I could hold you as well," I said, softening. "That day will come. I have faith."

"We shall see," he repeated.

"I must go," I said sadly. The sun was slowly starting to fall behind the horizon. "My parents are taking me to a college walk-through tomorrow."

"I need to say something to you before we part."

"Sure. Fire away."

"I know you will not want to hear what I am about to speak, but it must be said," his tone scared me. Uh-oh. This didn't sound good. But he always answered my questions, so it was only fair to hear him out.

"Go ahead," I nodded.

"I cannot remember having ever felt the way I feel about you. I love you more than you can know. I know that you are happy at this moment in time, although we do not exist in the same world. But there will always be a fear inside me that you will one day need something more. Until the day when our worlds become one, that fear will always be a part of me."

"I understand," I did, in a way. "I am sorry that I can't say the words that you want me to."

"You do not have to speak the words for me to know the truth."

"I do know that in a way it does bother you, if only a little."

"A little," I heard him sigh.

"Let me say this," trying to think of how to phrase it. "Would you rather have me say the words just so you could hear them? Or would you rather wait to hear the words because they would be from my heart?"

"I never looked at it like that. I believe you are right."

"I know I am," I chuckled. I could hear him chuckle back.

"Have a safe trip, my angel. I will always be by your side, please remember that."

"I will. I wish I could always be by your side."

"You are," he laughed. "When I am by yours."

"True. That's not what I meant, though. Until we meet again."

"Until we meet again," he agreed.

With that, I felt a cool breeze against my cheek. I slowly left the clearing and went home. His words really had me thinking. I knew I had developed tremendous feelings for him over the time we had been together, but he was dead right about one thing. As strong and deep as my feelings for him were, how long could I continue a relationship that was, but at the same time was not real? It mattered, and yet it didn't. Only time would tell the answer.

By the time I got home, the pizza that Dad had ordered was already there. *Sausage, YUCK!* I stuck my tongue out, grabbing a few slices on my plate. I picked the sausage off.

"That's the best part!" whined Dad.

"You know I hate sausage," I said disgustedly.

"You don't know what you're missing," as he took another bite. Dinner, as usual, was mostly uneventful. The normal questions with the normal responses.

Q. "How was school?"

A. "Fine."

Q. "How's Dave?"

A. "Fine."

Q. "Anything exciting happen today at school?"

A. "No."

The only question that varied slightly was the *"Any plans this weekend"?*

Q. "Any plans this weekend besides checking out the college?"

A. "I'm not sure."

After dinner was over, I headed off to my room. I wasn't in the mood to take my nightly run. Missing one night wasn't going to kill me. But before I could lie down and think about nothing, the phone rang.

"Lex, it's for you! It's Dave!" I heard Mom call from the bottom of the stairs.

"I'm coming!" I raced down the stairs and past her. She gave me this look like where I was going. "Tell him to hold on," I said, racing for the cordless.

"Hold on, Dave, she's grabbing the cordless," I heard Mom say into the phone.

"Hello," I said, as I hit the talk button.

"Talk to you later, Dave," Mom said, as she put the phone back in its cradle.

"What's up?" I asked.

"Not much. Just wanted to see how you were doing."

"Ummm, OK? I'm doing fine. Why, what's going on?" I was curious as to why he was asking such nonsense questions.

"Did your Mom tell you?" He sounded excited about something.

"Tell me what?" Of course I was confused again.

"Tell you that I'm coming with you guys tomorrow?"

"Cool," I said, without much tone.

"You don't sound too cool," he said, noting my unenthused tone.

"No, it's not that. I am nervous, that's all."

"Nothing to be scared about. It's just like high school, only you have the choice to live there or not."

"Lovely. I get to live *at* school."

"It's not as bad as you make it sound," he teased.

"Easy for you to say, you get to stay at home," I reminded him.

"Remember, you do, too, if you go to the same college as me."

"Yeah. I meant afterwards, though."

"Well, maybe we can carpool together?" he offered.

"What if we don't have the same class schedule?"

"I'll make it work," I could hear him grinning over the phone.

"I have a question for you."

"Shoot," his voice lit up.

"Why do you try so hard?"

"What do you mean?"

"I mean, it seems like you are trying even harder than you were before I met Jay."

"All honesty, Lexi, I don't believe that Jay is the right one for you."

"OK. Explain?"

"He's never around…"

"He's off at school," I snapped back.

"Calm down, Lexi. I'm just looking out for you, that's all."

I sighed, "I know." He was right again.

"I know I have never met this guy. But something is bothering me about him."

"Like?"

"Well, let me say this, first," he said thoughtfully. "And let's be honest. You've never had a relationship that lasted all that long."

"Go on," I was starting to get agitated.

"Remember that one guy you liked, and you found out that he was dating you and two other girls at the same time?"

"Yeah," I remembered it all too well. He had been taking bets on how many girlfriends he could have at once.

"And the one that told everyone he had broken up with you before he actually did?"

"Yes," I remembered that one as well. I caught him kissing another girl, and when I confronted him, he asked me about the message he had sent me.

"Or the one that you met online, once, and he said that you were too ugly?"

"Yup," I didn't know where this was going. I remembered that one too. I had been talking with him back and forth for a few months, and when we finally met, the next day he said that I was too ugly to be seen with him.

"Let me stress that you are *NOT* ugly. You are very beautiful, and those guys don't know what they are missing."

"And your point?"

"Do you remember when one guy told you that he loved you, and when you mentioned it the next day, he denied it and said that he had been drinking?"

"Yup, I remember all of them. What's your *point*?" I demanded, annoyed. The guy that had told me that he loved me was older; it had been his birthday, and he told me that he loved me. I hadn't said it back. When I asked him about it the next day, he acted like I was a fruit loop for even saying that he had said it, and he broke up with me right then.

"You were crushed," he reminded me, sounding depressed about my history of relationships.

"Hold on, I was crushed because of their actions, not because I was in love with them," I corrected.

"Same difference. This is the longest you have ever been with anyone, and we haven't met him yet."

"Now, let me ask you something," I snapped.

"OK."

"When have you *ever* liked anyone that I was dating?"

"That's not a fair question."

"Why? It's a simple yes or no."

He whispered, "Never."

"I know you haven't met Jay, but you do trust me, right?"

"I do, I just don't trust them. You know how I feel…"

"Yes and I think that's why…" I interrupted him.

"Let me finish, please," he said interrupting me. "You know how I feel, but at the same time, I don't want to see you get hurt."

"OK, let me ask you this. What if we did date and things didn't work out? Don't you think it would hurt me knowing I couldn't look at you the same way?"

"I told you that would never happen," he argued.

"How can you be so sure?"

"I have faith," he said with determination. *Faith.* How could it be true that one person was *meant* to be with two different people?

"Do you even know what faith is?" I asked.

"Yes. It means when two people are bound to be together, no matter what obstacles are thrown at them." Was he being stubborn, or determined? *Hmmmm.* What he had just said made me even more determined about Jay. *Thanks Dave!*

"Obstacles?"

"Yes," he chuckled. "The obstacle that you will not say yes to me."

"Very funny. Look, it's getting late, and we have an early and long day ahead of us tomorrow."

"Yeah. I'll see you tomorrow."

"Laters," I said, hanging up the phone. I ran downstairs to put the phone away and hurried back to my room. I put my favorite CD in the player and just lay in bed, staring at the ceiling.

Did I love him? Normally, when someone asks a question like that, the answer is no. Keyword being normally. This wasn't a normal situation. Yes, I did love him. Part of me was *in* love with him. The other part wasn't objecting to it; it was just the situation it was rejecting. I realized I had a smile that I couldn't wipe away. Every time I thought about him, it warmed my heart. Thinking about him warmed my soul.

At least I had my dreams to look forward to...

Chapter 15 – Off to College

I woke up to the sound of my alarm going off – I didn't even remember falling asleep. When I looked down at my CD player, the button was turned to the on position, but the display was blank. I crawled out of bed and started getting ready. I was scared, but excited at the same time. I had something to look forward to in life. Everyone thought that I would make a great attorney, because I loved to argue every chance I got. But somehow, I never saw what they were talking about.

"Hey Dave!" I could hear Mom letting him in.

"I'll be right there," I called down.

"We still have some time," Dad called back. *Oh great.* Dave's early. That shouldn't really surprise me. He's *always* early.

I had started down the stairs, but acted like I had forgotten something and went back to my room. I closed the door, and I could hear the three of them talking downstairs.

"Jay?" I whispered. "I'm leaving to check out the college. I'll be back soon. I'll miss you." I felt a cool breeze next to my cheek. I hope that was I'll miss you, too. I opened the door again and went down the stairs.

"What's the smile for?" Dave questioned. *Oh crap.* I had to think of something and fast.

I beamed, lying through my teeth, "Just excited about looking at my first college!" I was actually dreadfully nervous. I *was* becoming a better liar, although I wasn't proud of it.

"Maybe you two will go to the same college after the community one," Mom said with enthusiasm.

"Are we ready to go?" I said, ignoring her.

"Yes. All ready," Dad said, jingling his car keys.

"You have the directions?" Mom asked.

"Yes," he huffed. "They're in the car already."

In the car, Mom and Dad were playfully fighting over the radio station, as usual, so they didn't take much notice of the two of us talking in the back seat.

Dave softly whispered, "Have you told your parents about Jay?"

I whispered back, "No. Not yet."

"Why not?" he asked, still whispering.

"I'll tell them about him when he gets back into town. That way, I don't have to hear it from both sides of the fence."

"I better get to meet him first," he demanded.

"Fine, you get to meet him first," I mumbled. "Now let's drop it before my parents hear. Please?"

"Fine," he mumbled back. "I'll drop it now, but don't expect me to forget."

"I know you won't."

"What are you two kids mumbling about back there?" Mom asked, looking in her visor mirror.

"Nothing," we answered in unison.

"Doesn't sound like nothing."

Look at what you started! was the look I shot at him.

"We were just going over the college choices, mom."

"Oh. Okay." Mom didn't seem like she bought it, but she went along with his lame excuse. The ride was for the most part peaceful – Dad screaming his profanities at the traffic, Mom telling him to shut up. Yup, another ordinary ride in the car with my parents. Only this time, Dave was there to witness what I've always complained about. Fortunately, the drive itself didn't take too long.

"HELLO! Mr. and Mrs. Smith!" An older gentleman came out to greet us.

"Hello, Mr. Wick," my Dad said, as he shook his hand.

"It's a pleasure to hear that your daughter is thinking about attending our school!" He said this with such mirth that it made me wonder what my Dad had said to him over the phone.

We started walking up to the front offices.

I whispered, "What did you say to him?"

"I told him the truth about why you wanted to view the college so early," he smirked. "Plus, I told him that the money would not be an issue."

My parents never lied. Usually, they didn't exaggerate the truth, either. I knew my parents wouldn't be able to afford the schools I had picked out, but they had also told me not to worry about that. I heard Mr. Wick boasting about the school, my dad pretending to be excited. Every once in a while I threw in a *"Yes, that sounds great!" "This school has everything!"* and so forth. If I wanted a real opinion, I would turn to Dave to get his. Fortunately, he didn't even have to speak for me to understand what he was thinking. I really didn't know what I was looking for in a school, but I knew he would have a better idea to help guide me.

We walked through the classrooms. Nothing spectacular. Instead of desks, they were set out in a half circle in what looked like an auditorium, with one big desk sitting above each row of seats. Then Mr. Wick brought us to the library. *I was in my heaven.* It would take me a lifetime to run out of reading material here. I noticed the spark in his eyes.

"Your daughter loves to read."

Mom beamed with pride, "You can't get her out of the library."

Next, he had us check out the cafeteria, then came straight lecture halls. Then on to the dorms. *I wish I lived closer. Residence halls* was what they were called. *Icky.* Not dirty icky, just no bathrooms in the rooms. He proceeded to the upper level halls. *Phew,* these had bathrooms in them.

"I would *love* one of these," I said, as we looked around.

"Not this exact room, but one like this would be yours," Mr. Wick gave me a wide grin.

"I would get one with a bathroom *inside* the dorm? I'm just making sure I heard you right," I said, pointing at the bathroom.

"Of course!" *OK, his enthusiasm could be toned down a notch.* "The actual term is residence hall. The term dorms is more commonly used with the military."

He then proceeded to show us the apartment style or executive suites, as I called them. They were nice – like mini apartments. "Would you prefer one of these, instead, Miss Smith?"

"I really liked the other ones better," I echoed.

"It would be no extra money," he disclosed. I gave Dad a look, asking if he was insane.

Dad nodded, "It's your choice."

"I would still prefer the other ones. They are closer to the library."

Mr. Wick seemed shocked. "We've never had a student turn down an executive suite before."

"Our daughter won't be just an ordinary student," Dad gloated. "She sees things a whole lot differently than most."

Mr. Wick was even more delighted after hearing that. Dad had *never* paid a compliment to me or about me before. We went on with the tour.

"...and Mr. Smith, I did some extra research, and your daughter would not only get a top-notch education here, but the financing will not be a problem..." *Whatever that meant. I'll ask later.* I didn't hear the question that Mr. Wick asked next; all I heard was my Dad's response.

"Her grades aren't the greatest right now. That's why she's going to community college, to bring them up. She sort of knows that she won't get accepted at a major university." Dad shot me a look like that's what I should have been doing since day one.

"Come with me," Mr. Wick said, practically dragging my parents into his office. "Here is the *DIRECT* name of the person you need to speak with at our sister college. I'll call him first thing in the morning and let him know the situation."

They chatted away as Dave and I sat there bored out of our minds. *Finally,* it was time to leave.

He told my Dad as he shook his hand goodbye, "We can't wait to hear your daughter's decision."

"We'll be in touch," Dad pronounced.

My parents waited until we were back in the car before asking any questions.

"What did you think?"

"It's OK. I really loved the library, and my dorm would have its own bathroom, well sort of. That's a plus."

Mom added, "If you want not to do the community college and look at the sister college instead, we can arrange that."

"What about the money? What did he mean that the finances wouldn't be a problem? Would it really not cost extra to get the suite I want?"

"Money is all taken care of," Dad said with glee.

"What do you mean?"

"As long as you are a dependent of ours, you can go to any college you want, free of charge."

"I'm not following."

"Since I'm a retired veteran, the government will pay for your education."

It takes a lot to shock me, and this was the mother of all shocks. "What??"

"Really," Mom confirmed.

"I wondered why Mr. Wick was so upbeat," Dave chimed in.

"If the scholarship hadn't come through, we would have found a way to get you through college," Mom said.

"This just makes things easier," Dad stated. *I would say so!* I could tell Dave was and wasn't happy.

"Could we adopt Dave and have him go to the same first college as me?" I saw him smile wide at that idea. My parents laughed.

"We wish it were that easy," they said.

"What did you think about it?" Dave asked.

"It was OK. We still have the other one to check out. I just hope they will be cool with the finances like this one was."

"Watch, she'll like the one who won't work the scholarship," Mom cringed.

"I'll go where it won't cost you guys money," I said.

"We didn't mean that," Mom pointed out. "We want you to go where you'll be happy and do well."

"I know, Mom, but it does come down to the money, as well. If both schools offer a similar academic program, why not go for the one that won't cost anything?"

"True," agreed Dad. "What did you like about this college? You didn't look too thrilled during the walk-through."

"Oh, I was. It was just something missing. But I don't know what."

"Friends?" Dave asked.

"That could be," it did make sense. "I have to keep in the back of my mind that you all won't be there."

"We'll get a phone for your dorm so you can still talk to your friends." Dad sounded more excited than me.

"Really?" I asked, surprised.

"Since most likely we won't have to pay for your education, we can get you a phone."

I was thrilled. "Awesome!" My own phone!

Mom and Dad went back to discussing traffic and the radio. Dave was looking out the window in silence. And for a brief moment, I had completely forgotten about Jay. Not too much later, Dad was pulling into the driveway.

"Hey guys!" I tried to push my luck. "Since college will be free and you'll put a phone in my dorm, does that mean I get a car, too?"

Dad grunted, "Don't push your luck." Mom followed him up the stairs to the front door.

"I'll be in in a minute!" I called up to them.

"Take your time!" Mom called back.

"What did you really think about the college?" Dave knew I was holding something back. "It's not this Jay guy, is it?"

"NO! Considering I won't be attending that school; for at least another five years."

"What is it, then?" He looked at me, knowing I was holding something back.

"I don't know. I guess I'm just scared about leaving the nest," I shrugged, looking away.

"You, scared? I don't buy that."

I snapped, "Well, start buying it."

"What are you afraid of?"

"I don't know. Not doing well. Flunking out," I honestly said.

"You are very smart, Lexi."

"Yeah, look at my grades," I cringed, thinking that I couldn't get better than just a passing grade to save my life.

"There is nothing wrong with your grades. Remember, Einstein flunked out, and he was one of the smartest people in history."

"Yeah, that was back then, this is now."

"Quit being so hard on yourself; you'll do fine," he consoled me.

"I know. I still have one more year of high school left. It's not like I have to make a decision right away."

"Look, you've seen the first school. Check out the second and the sister college, and then make a decision."

"But..."

"No buts," he interrupted.

"Fine," I playfully stomped my foot on the ground.

"Yes, you are fine."

I gave him a playful shove, "Oh ha…ha."

"I gotta go and let my parents know I'm back. I know they'll have a lot of questions for me. I'll give you a call after dinner?"

"Sounds great."

"Later, sweetie," he hugged me goodbye and headed home. I went inside to change for my daily run.

"Everything okay?" Mom asked.

"Yeah. Everything's fine. I'm going to go for my run."

"Okay. Have fun."

Oh, yeah, lots, I thought to myself. I hurried to get changed and was out the door before they had a chance to ask any more questions. It was still early afternoon when I headed outside. I decided to see if Jay had enough strength to show himself to me today. I took the long way to the clearing; that way, *if* anyone saw me, they would think I had taken the outside trail. It took me a little longer than usual, but I finally made it to the clearing.

"Jay?" I breathlessly called out.

Nothing.

"Dangit!" I forgot to bring my recorder.

"Why?" He asked.

"JAY!" He wasn't as *there* as when I had seen him at the dance, but he was visible. To me anyways, and that's all that mattered.

"Yes, my dear?"

"I didn't think you were here!" I ran up, putting my arms around him.

"I apologize for being late." He barely returned my hug.

"What's wrong?"

"Nothing, my dear," he gave me a phony smile.

"Don't give me that, I can tell something is bothering you."

"I saw that Dave went with you."

213

"Dave is my best friend," I reconfirmed. "Please don't start this. He wants to meet you."

"He does?" His eyebrow arched.

"Yes. He wants to see that you are good enough for me."

"What did you tell him?"

"The same old story, that you are away at college, and when you come home next, he'll get to meet you," I said, trying to push away his worries. He sighed. I pulled away.

"It got him off my back, and what was I supposed to do, introduce him to air?"

"I understand your way of seeing it."

"Plus," I said, in a flirting manner. "You know I would love no better than to show you off to my friends." I put my arms around him again.

"I know," he said, holding me close.

"Even you knew this wouldn't be easy. So what's wrong?"

"I didn't think you would be this accepting."

"Well I am. Get used to it and get over it," I teased.

"You must bear with me while I do," he gently kissed my forehead.

I gave him a quick peck on his lips. "Valentine's Day is coming up."

"It's a holiday created by card makers."

"I don't care who created the holiday. It's the day every girl dreams about," I said, quickly kissing him again.

"How do you see it?" He was starting to get on my nerves.

"Well in the world *I* live in, girls get candy, flowers or a card." He sighed, and his arms gently glided down to his side. "What's wrong?" I asked.

"I cannot do any of those things for you."

"I didn't ask for any of those things, did I?"

"No, you did not, but..."

"But nothing. What I *do* want is you. That's it."

"You have me every other day. Why is this day so important?"

"Can you just play along?"

"I do not see…"

"You're not supposed to see," I whispered. "Not with your eyes," I trifled. I gently kissed him on the lips. He returned the kiss. I kissed again, a little longer this time. This went on till we had been lip-locked for quite some time.

"Hmm. I love what I have seen."

"See, that wasn't so bad now, was it?" I said, giggling. "I see you have a little more strength now."

"Some."

"Some is good enough for me," I flirted.

We sat in silence, just looking at one another. My hand traced his face over and over again.

"What are you doing?" he asked, watching my hand.

"Memorizing you," I whispered.

"Why?"

"So I never forget," I said, kissing him again.

"I already have you memorized," he said, with a warm smile, placing his hand on my face.

"How so?"

His warm smile faded. "You may become upset with me."

"Try me. You may be surprised at what I know."

His eyes drifted away, "I watch you sleep at night."

"I know you do," I giggled. That was no surprise there.

"How?"

"Well let's see here, you talk to me when I'm in my room, and that night of the dance you sat next to me on my bed."

"I did not know you knew! I do apologize."

"Apologize for what? You should know me by now, for you say you've been watching me from a distance for a long time. If something was bothering me, I would have said so. Right?"

"You are correct. So you are not upset with me?"

215

"Absolutely not. I couldn't be happier," I smiled so hard it was starting to hurt. "I do have one question about that, though."

"I will answer with the truth."

"You don't watch me while I take a shower or change, do you?"

"Absolutely not!" He blurted out. "That would be rude."

"Just making sure," I started kissing him again.

The night started to fall down upon us. The cool crisp air of the daytime was turning colder as the sun set.

"The time has come for us to part once more."

I playfully pouted, "I hate how time flies."

"So do I. So do I," he sighed, as he ran his fingers through my air and gazed into my eyes.

"Will I *see* you tonight?"

"Only if you wish."

"Now if I wish?" I laughed. "You have done it before without me knowing."

"I know," he looked down. "I know I have done wrong."

"No, you didn't do wrong. And yes, I do wish to *see* you tonight," I kissed him one last time and headed toward the edge of the clearing, looking back one last time before I sprinted for home.

After dinner was done it was the third degree on the college. *Lovely.* I hadn't even had time to decide what I thought.

"So what you think?" Dad asked.

"It's OK, I guess."

"What did you like the most?" asked Mom.

"My dorm room would have its own bathroom!"

"Besides that," she chuckled.

"It's a school to obtain a degree needed to function in the career path I want to take."

"That's true. You are the first person in our family ever to continue on to college," Mom beamed with pride.

No pressure there!

"It's just one school though. Nothing really to compare it to."

Dad seemed more excited about this than I was. "When are you going to set up the next college visit?"

"I'll set it up soon. I still have time."

"Yes, you do, but don't wait too long," Mom said, taking a sip of her coffee.

"I have at least five more years," I reminded her.

"Well, really just four," Dad corrected. "Just like high school, you'll have to decide by your junior year."

"OK," rolling my eyes. "Four years. I'll set up the appointment soon, that way I can dwell on which one."

Mom nervously questioned, "We thought this is what you wanted?"

"It is, but it's happening too fast."

"Well, get used to it, little one. Time doesn't stand still. Except when you're dead," Dad took a drink of his soda.

"Do you want me to call, or are you going to call that sister school?" I asked dad.

"I'll give them a call and let you know when. Sound good?"

"Sounds good. I'm gonna finish reading my book," I said, starting to get up.

"Night," they told me, as I hurried upstairs. I got washed up and headed to my room, closing the door behind me. I turned on the stereo to hide my voice.

"*Jay?*" I whispered.

It sounded like he was right next to me. *"Yes, my dear?"* he replied back.

"They can only hear when I talk, right?"

"No one can hear but you."

"Were you with me when I went to check out the college?"

"Yes."

"What do you think?"

"It's all about what you are looking for. For my opinion is just mine."

"OK. I am looking for your opinion. What didn't you like?"

"It wouldn't be my first choice."

"Why?"

"The school is not that old. It's only been around since the early 1900's."

"OK. That's pretty old to us," I softly laughed.

"You should wait to view the other university you want to look at."

"Why?"

"They have been around since the early 1800's, and I think you will like that one better."

"If I do, I just hope that they accept my dad's scholarship."

"Things will work out."

"I wish you could hold me right now."

"Soon," his voice held some excitement. "You're parents are going to head off to bed here shortly."

"How do you know?"

"Mortals are easy to predict. Especially your parents, they have a routine."

"Wow, you've noticed all that?"

"I notice everything. Remember, I don't sleep. I may rest at times. But I don't sleep. I have no need to sleep."

"True."

As he predicted, my parents headed off to bed. A short time later, Dad started to snore.

"See," Jay said, as soon as I heard the snoring. He started to materialize next to me on the bed. Again, not like he was at the dance, but enough so that I could see him.

"Better," I said, still whispering. I lowered the music so as not to draw attention and make my parents come knocking. I would keep up the whispering just in case, though. "I am worried about something, though."

"What worries you so? School?"

"No. The curse of this land. Is it true?"

"That depends," he lowered his eyes. I was embarrassed about the way my room looked.

"On what?"

"On whether you believe in curses or not."

"Well, the adults say that they don't, but then when a death happens, they blame the curse," I explained.

He hushed in a low whisper, "Then they believe."

"So if they don't believe, nothing bad will happen?"

"It is hard to give a precise answer. Anything could still happen, curse or no curse."

"So I'm safe? I mean since I made it past the age that people were talking about."

"Age has nothing to do with it. There are many factors that people do not realize, or they choose not to see."

"Like?" I asked, becoming a little standoffish.

"Like if your destiny had already held its course."

"I'm confused."

"I will do my best to explain," he said, smiling. "For you see destiny and fate are predetermined, but you do have the power and will to change them. The day you take your first breath, your fate is chosen by your destiny. But each breath that you take is not measured by what fate has decided – it is measured on what *you* have decided. I will give an example. Growing up, you are destined to become a teacher. When you reach maturity, you realize that you don't want to become a teacher, but, say, a doctor. Fate plants the idea of what you want. So you changed your course to become a doctor. If you followed the doctor course, you would not experience the same outcomes as you would have if you had become a teacher… a horrific accident on the traffic route you would normally have taken if you had become a teacher… an accidental fire in the house you would have bought if you had become a teacher. Mother Nature taking its course on the school that you would have taught in if you had become a teacher."

"Is there any way to know what course has been set for us?" I really hoped that there was.

"Not in your current state or in mine."

"Oh," I exhaled.

"Now, fate *could* override destiny. Given the example above, you chose your destiny by becoming a doctor. Fate could have mingled in somewhere to give the same outcome as if you had become a teacher."

"OK, that's confusing now."

"Yes, it is. That's why many mortals don't understand the concept, so they give up trying."

"I know my *fate* and my *destiny*," I said, turning to face him.

"Oh," he laughed. "How do you know when you were so confused a minute ago?"

"Destiny brought you into my life and fate has us to be together."

"So that's how it works?" He smiled, laughing. "So much easier than what I was trying to say."

"If I start asking too many questions, please tell me to stop."

"I love when you ask questions," kissing my forehead.

"OK, this is a really, really stupid question."

"No question is stupid."

"Yeah, that's what they all say. You've followed me in school. Can you honestly say that no question is stupid?"

He rephrased with a grin, "No life question is stupid."

"It's really stupid," I reminded him. "Besides being invisible, do you have any special gifts?"

"That is not a stupid question at all. It shows that you are observant. To answer your question, no, I do not have any special gifts. I cannot read another's mind, nor can I know the future, if that's what you are getting at."

"You lift me. I consider that a special gift," I giggled, and clapped a hand over my mouth. "When you talk, you say only I can hear you; is there like an option to have others hear you as well?"

"Well, yes I do have some strength, but only under extreme circumstances. I can't just lift something heavy to show off. Depending on the nature of what I am doing, others can hear me besides the person I want to communicate with."

"I know that Dave heard you, that night of the dance. Although he won't admit what he heard – he just talks about it being the cold breeze. Also, you moved me from the park to my house."

His eyes slowly gazed around the room. "I had not done that before. I don't know if I could again. I am sorry, I should not intervened between you and Dave."

I tried not to laugh. "I'm not mad. Dave probably is, though. But I'm really not."

"I have not yet met your friends, and I am already disliked by one."

"Dave dislikes anyone who likes me. If you follow him, you will see that."

"I will take your word for it. If I follow him, I cannot follow you."

"Good point," I smirked.

"You should sleep. It is late, and tomorrow is another day."

"You're just getting sick of me asking questions."

"No, I am no such thing. Look at the time, and I must go and rest myself."

"Wow," I yawned, glancing at the clock. "You are right."

"Now get some sleep, my angel," he kissed me on the cheek.

"Will you be OK?" I asked.

"Why do you ask such a question?"

"I just want to make sure that you'll be here tomorrow and not change your mind."

"I will be here as long as you allow me. You know where I stand. That has never and will never change." He wrapped his arms around me and gently started kissing me. I loved it when I was in his arms. I felt so safe – like I had truly found where I was supposed to be.

Was this the path that I was meant to be on? To have to work through a major obstacle to be with someone who made me feel this way?

Only time will tell...

Chapter 16 – The Picture

I hated finals. The tests were long and exhausting, and they could make or break your GPA. Really, the only final I was looking forward to was photography. In some ways, developing your own pictures was an art. You could customize the colors to exactly what wanted them to be. It wasn't easy, but it was something I enjoyed doing. Some of our teachers were cool; they allowed open books or open notes for exams. On the other hand, some kids were such horrible note takers that this did not help them all that much.

I had picked up the photos the night before. I wanted to create my own pictures in class before I looked at them, though, so I could compare mine to how the professionals had done. At least I knew I would be getting an *A* in that class. My other classes I wasn't too sure about. I still couldn't believe with my grades that two colleges wanted me.

"Did the pictures finally come in?" Val asked, as we sat down at our usual table.

"Yes, just picked them up last night," I said, holding up my bag.

"So? How did they come out?" Lynn demanded, bouncing up and down in her seat.

"Yeah, I wanna see!" exclaimed Val.

"Did you get my life-size one?" Aaron asked.

"If I didn't have the money for the one hour, I sure as heck didn't have money to get yours blown up to life size," I laughed.

"Well, let's see!" Dave said, reaching for my bag. I grabbed it before he could.

"OK, on one condition, though," I warned. They all looked at me like I was nuts.

Lynn motioned with her fingers for me to hand them over, "I don't care how they turned out. Because I know they came out great."

"It's not that," I started. "I don't want to see them until my photography final. I don't want any hint of how to adjust the colors."

They announced together, "DEAL!"

"Fine," I said, handing one set to Dave on my left and the second set to Tim on my right.

I could hear laughter, ooohs and ahhhs as the photographs were being passed around.

"Who's this guy?" Dave asked holding the last picture as he passed the rest to Val.

I really didn't remember what was on that roll of film. "Which guy?"

He hinted with a bit of envy. "Is this Jay?"

Since Tim was still new, he passed his set to Lynn. Lynn flipped through the pictures hastily to see which picture Dave was talking about.

"OMG, he's cute!" She wailed. "When was this taken?"

"Let me see that!" I snagged the picture from Dave. My face dropped. Lynn passed the extra copy around so everyone could see.

"He's beyond cute," Val exclaimed. "He's drop dead *gorgeous*!"

Aaron swung his hand over his shoulder, acting like he was sweeping back long hair. "I'm better looking."

"When was this taken? Why didn't you let us meet him?" Dave demanded.

"He... was... ummm..." I was trying to find an excuse. "Was only in town for one night. I figured that it would be too short notice to get you all together."

I was looking at the picture; I couldn't believe it. With the park around us, you could tell that the picture was taken at night. His dark sandy hair falling over his forehead, his eyes twinkling as the flash had gone off. His smile that looked too perfect. I had assumed that the picture would come out like all the others, so I hadn't given it a second thought.

"*See*," I gloated. "He's real."

"OK, OK," Lynn said, still analyzing the picture. "We believe you!"

"Are you sure she didn't doc the picture?" Aaron accused, swiping it from Lynn.

"How would I do that?" I questioned.

He mumbled, "Well you are in photography class, sooo, anything is possible."

I rolled my eyes, "OK, yes, he's fake."

"Pay no attention to him," Val said.

Everyone else started looking at the rest of the pictures I had taken. When both sets made it back to me, I took the one of both of us out and laid the extra set in the middle of the table. The other set I put away without looking, saving them for class.

"What's that for?" she asked.

"Well, I got two sets made, because you all wanted copies. So pick the ones you want."

Dave, Val and Lynn wailed, "Awesome!" They all grabbed for the pile at the same time.

"Calm down, guys," I said, laughing. "Or you'll ruin them! Here."

I broke up the pile into three sets.

"What about me?" Aaron asked. I re-divided them into four sets and gave one to each of them to pick out the pictures they wanted for themselves.

"This one looks like it was taken the night of the homecoming dance," Dave accused, taking out one of the pictures of Jay and me.

"Honestly, I don't remember when it was taken," I lied. I was hoping I could pull it off, since I had kept the film for so long before getting it developed.

Dave just looked at me like he knew I was lying. "You never wear makeup, and here you are wearing makeup," he knew me all too well. "And your hair is done."

"It might have been that night, now that you mention it," I said, pretending to think back.

"This had to be taken after I dropped you off, because I picked you up when it was still light out."

Oh crap! What could I possibly say to minimize the damage? "It was after." I couldn't lie about that. "He surprised me." That wasn't a lie. "It was a last minute thing for him, coming home that night, and he left early Sunday morning," again not a lie.

"He didn't call you beforehand? Ya know, to let you know that he would be there?"

"I don't know all the facts of why he was home. I think it had to do with a family illness or something. Remember, not everyone has a car phone. I don't know exactly what time he got in, and if he did try calling, remember I was with *you* at the dance and even afterwards?"

"OK, I'll give you that," he said admitting defeat. "Tell him next time he better call so we can meet him."

The rest agreed. "I'll tell him," I said finishing my water.

The girls were bartering over which pictures to trade for. It was quite comical to watch.

"I'll trade these two for that one," Lynn said, holding up two of the pictures she had first picked out.

"No way!" Val laughed. This went on for the rest of the lunch hour.

I was beyond stunned that the picture of him had turned out! I couldn't help staring at them as I walked to my photography class that afternoon. I hadn't even taken the first step into the classroom when Ms. Kohel started giving me the third degree.

"Why are you smiling like that?" she asked, smiling back.

"A picture that I didn't think would turn out came out great!" I still couldn't stop smiling.

"Let's take a look," she said, walking towards me. I held out the picture for her to see.

"My, my," was all she said at first. "This picture is wonderful. Look at the way the light catches the night around the trees. I'm impressed, no red eye."

"Yeah, I know, I can't believe how great it came out," even though I hadn't noticed the 'no red eye' thing before.

"Who is that?"

"That's... ummm... Jay." My smile got even bigger.

"Does he go to school here?"

"No, he goes to college."

"So I wouldn't know him," she returned to her desk, and I went to my seat. I held the picture carefully in both hands. There were still three minutes left before class started; I played that night over again in my head.

His voice whispered in my ear, *"Beautiful!"* Knowing exactly who it was, I mouthed *thank you* to the air.

The rest of the students started piling in the door; I put the picture behind the others so no one could start asking questions about it.

"Today your final will be on..." Ms. Kohel started as soon as the bell rang, "your imagination. Have fun!"

Some of the kids just looked at each other like, what was an *imagination?* Others couldn't wait to start playing with the film they had brought in. I wasted no time and dashed with my negatives into the dark room. I wanted to play with the negative of Jay and me. I laid the negative on the scope and started to enlarge it; carefully covering the areas where I wanted color. I then played with the black and white, getting the tones to precisely where I wanted them. I clicked off the special light and covered the areas that had only black and white. Then, I played around with the colors until they looked the way I wanted them to. I then continued the process to preserve the picture so I could bring it out into the light. Once I was done and the paper had dried just enough so I could bring it out without ruining it, I gathered all my materials and headed back to the classroom.

"Let me take a look," Ms. Kohel said, motioning me over. She spent a few moments looking at my work and then wrote something down in her grade book.

"You receive an A," she said, smiling. "You did great work!"

"Thanks," I couldn't help blushing.

I heard his voice again. *"Great job, beautiful!"* I looked around like an idiot, hoping that he would make an appearance.

"Something wrong?" Ms. Kohel asked.

"Nope, nothing," I said, shaking my head without looking at her. I just stared at the paper like it was a portable movie, and I was watching that night all over again. I was so lost in my thoughts that I hadn't even heard Russ and Will cracking jokes about the pictures that I was staring at. It was the bell that finally snapped me out of my daydreaming. I carefully placed the picture of us in my portfolio.

Once I left the classroom, it seemed to take forever for the school bus to depart. If anyone had spoken to me after class, I hadn't even noticed. I wasn't paying any attention to what I was doing; I just couldn't wait to get home. I sat on the school bus, with my bag clutched to my chest, looking out the window. I could swear that the bus was only going five miles per hour. Time just couldn't seem to move fast enough.

When I finally got home, I ran straight to my room to change. I needed to get to the clearing as fast as I could. I left my usual note for my parents and raced out the door, bee-lining it straight for the forest. I didn't realize how fast I was going; I was totally out of breath when I reached the edge of the clearing.

"Jay!" I managed to gasp out.

He was extremely faint, but I could hear him well enough, "Yes, my dear?"

Still gasping for air, "The... pictures..."

"I know, I saw," he said, coming towards me. "Calm down, sweetheart. You did not need to run."

"I…know…" I slowly started to catch my breath. "It's just that I couldn't wait to actually tell you." My breathing slowly returned to normal.

"You did a wonderful job, my dear."

"You showed up in the one!" I was so thrilled that I couldn't contain it.

"I am just as amazed as you are," he said, gazing into my eyes.

"At least now, I have proof and can tell everyone you are real!"

"I would not show it off quite yet."

"Why not?" I asked, disappointed. "The proof is in the picture."

"People will expect more than I can give at this moment," he said, with such sadness that I started to feel bad, too. "Look at how your friends wanted to meet me even more and sooner. But I cannot guarantee that is possible. Then they will blame you, which I do not like at all."

"Don't worry about them," I said, with a whiff of my hand. "I can take care of them. Remember they believe that you are off at college. In their minds, college is all year long."

He softly stated, "I do not like lying."

Now I was getting irritated. "Well, what would you like me to do? Lie and say I faked the picture?" What else was I supposed to do?

"No," he whispered. "I wish that I could grant your wish for you."

"You are granting me my wish." I placed my hand against his cool cheek; it felt as though my hand could go through his face – like I was resting it on silk water. "I have a picture, and that is more than I could ever wish for right now."

"Right now," he repeated.

"Let's not start on that road, please?" I begged. "You knew this was the only way things could be when you first came into my life."

"I know," he looked off to the side. "In some ways, I thought it would be easier, and in others a lot harder."

"I can only say one part is easy for me; the rest is a lot tougher than I would have imagined."

"Tomorrow is what you call Valentine's Day," he said, placing his cool silk water hand upon my cheek.

"Yes, I know," I frowned.

"What is wrong, my dear?"

"Nothing," I lied.

"You *are* a very bad liar," he grinned.

"It's just that, since you are very weak, do you think we'll be able to spend any time together?"

"Of course," he said, running his fingers through my hair.

"You sound so sure."

"I do not make a promise that I do not intend to follow through with," he said, as he lightly kissed me, once on the forehead and then on my lips. He was right, in a way. I wanted more. I wanted to hold him tight when we kissed. I wanted to hear the sound of his heart when our bodies touched. That was one thing that did confuse me more than anything else.

I lightly pulled away, but still held my arms around his neck. "I just thought of something."

"What would that be?"

"There are times that I can feel and hear your heart beat. Why is that?"

"I do not have the answer," he said. It seemed like it didn't concern him.

"You don't know, or you just ain't saying?"

"I speak the truth – I do not know the answer. The times you are referring to are probably the same ones I asked myself about afterwards. When I am in this state or weaker, I cannot feel or hear the beating of your heart. But when I am stronger, I can hear as well feel the blood that pulses through your heart."

Our fingers were now interlocked, hanging down in front of us.

"Do you think it's a sign?" I asked.

"I could not say," he said with sorrow. "You must go."

"Why?" I was stunned that he was telling me to go.

"Remember when I talked about mortal behavior and routines?"

"Yes, I remember. Why?"

His tone was saddened by the thought, "Dave, more likely than not, will be on his way to your home right now." The way he said that, with an expression of disgust, I couldn't help but laugh.

"Why are you laughing?" he asked, puzzled.

"The tone of your voice when you said that," I was still laughing. I could see the hurt in his eyes. "I'm sorry. I have told you before, you have nothing to worry about."

"I want to believe the words you speak."

"Trust. A relationship must have a foundation of trust. Right?"

He reluctantly agreed, "Right."

"Plus, how do you think it makes me feel when you talk about not being together."

His brown eyes looked deep in mine. "I guess you are right."

"I know I am. I will come back later on my usual nightly run, so we can spend more time together. Deal?"

"That sounds great!" he said, grabbing me with such intensity that it took me off guard. His kiss was more forceful than usually. "Until we meet again."

I kissed him back, but softly, like our kisses had always been. "I'll see you later," and I was gone, taking the back way to the house so I wouldn't run into Dave on the road. I snuck through the back door just in time to hear Dave knocking at the front door.

"Hey Dave!"

"Do you mind going for a walk with me?" He seemed nervous about something.

"Uh, sure. Let me just leave a note for my parents," I rushed over to the table and scribbled 'With Dave' on a piece of paper.

"Were you going out?" I looked at him, questioning. "You had your coat on and it looks like you are sweating," he pointed out.

"Oh." Oops. "Parents have the heat on full blast."

"Why didn't you take your coat off when you got home?" *What's with the third degree?*

"I knew you would be coming over?" I flirted.

"Yeah, right. What's up? Dish, now," he demanded. His look meant he was serious.

"Nothing is up, why?"

"You just have been acting strange lately. It's beginning to worry me."

I challenged him. "How have I been acting strange?"

"You have been more distant than usual. That's for one. For two, you have been answering questions very vaguely."

"Like?"

"Like, for starters, any time I ask you a question about *Jay,* you hesitate. Like you are thinking of an excuse or something. I know I haven't met him, and I trust you, I just don't trust *him*." He was trying to see through me. I couldn't blame him for getting upset. He was right. If I got angry now, he would know something was really going on.

"I'm sorry," was all I could manage to say.

"You're my best friend. I know I've said this before, but I know I don't have a chance in hell with you. But that doesn't mean that I want to see you get hurt, either."

"You know I want you to meet Jay. Things are, well, complicated right now."

"Complicated? How so?"

"Well, with his school, and I don't want to distract him from his school work."

He slowly formed an evil grin, "OK, let me start with the basic questions." *Oh-oh, this can't be good.* I couldn't think of any *basic* questions that he could ask that he hasn't already asked. "How did you meet?"

OK now, that would normally be an easy question to answer, but not in this case. I had to think of something fast. "We met when I was out on one of my runs." *Did that sound believable?*

"So you went up to a stranger in the dark?"

I know he was only looking out for me, but this was going far enough.

"No," I laughed, shaking my head. "You know I always go out for my runs when it's dark. It was dusk, and he was working on school work at the park when I ran by."

"And...?" he said, knowing there was more.

And what? I'm doing the best I can at trying to fabricate a story here.

"And... it was somewhat windy, and a piece of paper he was working on blew in my direction. What was I supposed to do, ignore it and not be helpful?"

"Which park?"

OMG, just stick a fork in me now, I'm done.

"The far south park."

His grilling was getting unbearable. "What was he doing at the far south park?"

Crap, that's right. I forgot. There are no homes over there.

"I really don't know. I didn't think to ask. I guess it was just peaceful, so he wouldn't be bothered while he did his work."

I sure hope he buys what I'm spewing.

"So you started talking to him, you have known him for how long, and you don't even know his last name?"

"I'm sorry, it never even crossed my mind. At first, I thought he would be like any other guy I gave my number to. You know, the excuse, 'I'm sorry I would have called but I lost your number/it went through the wash/my dog ate it, yadda yadda yadda'.'"

"Why didn't you tell me about this?"

"I didn't think I needed to inform you about every little thing that went on," which was the truth.

"You don't, but since you've 'been with him for this long'," he quoted his fingers around those words. "Let's be honest, most of your relationships last less than a month."

"Yes, and that's how I thought this one would be," I was truthful with that statement.

"You don't have a flavor of the month, you have a flavor of the hour," he said, cracking up.

"Gee, thanks," I said, rolling my eyes.

"Come on now, Lex, you know it's the truth."

He was right. My longest relationship was two weeks. We had met on the activity bus that took us home, and two weeks later he broke up with me. When I questioned his friend for the truth, they said it was because he didn't realize how ugly I was, since it was dark when we first met.

"I'm not denying what you're saying."

"Do you love him?"

His question threw me off guard.

Wow! That came out of nowhere! I knew Jay would be listening, so I had to be careful. "The relationship is still young. You know me, I don't fall in love fast."

"Yeah, that I know," he said.

"You're my best friend," I put my arm through his. "You would be the first one to know."

"On any other day, yes, but lately it's like I'm the last to know."

"Don't be like that," I batted my eyes. "Please?"

"I'll try," he said, pointing his finger at me. "Only because it's you."

"Thank you," I said sincerely.

"Do you really like him?"

Again, how do I answer this? I wanted to tell him the truth, but then he would never leave it alone.

"Yes, I do," I said truthfully. "I'm sorry."

"Lex, you have nothing to be sorry about if you really like him. I just don't want to see you get hurt like with that last douchebag."

I sighed, "I know."

"Will he be in town tomorrow?"

"Ummmm. I honestly don't know." *That was the truth.* "Why do you ask?"

"Well, I thought that maybe he would make the trip back so he could spend the most romantic day of the year with you," he cracked, then his voice trailed. "If he cared at all for you."

"He probably won't. He has finals, as well, and I don't know when they finish."

"Well, if he has to stay where he's at, do you think he would mind if I spent Valentine's Day with you? Strictly as friends?"

"I don't see why not."

For some reason, as I said that, I could feel that Jay would not like that at all.

"Good," Dave cried. "But remember, if he does come back into town, I *have* to meet him."

"Deal."

We walked back to my house, talking about other things besides Jay. Now this was the Dave that I missed. I could be myself around him. It didn't matter what I wore, how my hair looked, if something stupid came out of my mouth, or all three combined. We reached the end of the driveway, and as usual, he gave me a hug and told me that he would give me a call later to confirm tomorrow. My parents were already home. Mom was preparing dinner, and Dad, well, he was working on something or other in the basement again.

"How was school?" Mom asked as I walked in the door.

"It was good. Got an A on my photography final."

"That's great! Any plans with Dave tomorrow?"

I knew news travels fast, just not this fast.

"Maybe," I raised an eyebrow. "Why?"

She got quiet awfully fast. "Oh, just wondering."

"Why? What does he have planned?"

"Oh! Nothing! I just saw your note and figured that's why you two went for a walk."

"Need help with anything?" I offered. *I really didn't feel like going up to my room, in case Jay was waiting. I knew the inevitable talk would be coming tonight, anyway.*

"If you could set the table, please."

"Sure," I said, as I started setting the table. When I was finished, Mom told me to tell Dad that dinner was ready. Dinner was, well, dinner. Nothing out of the ordinary. Both of them told me that they had to work tomorrow. No big surprise there. Reminded me about no boys in the house. Again, no surprise there. After dinner was cleaned up, my mom asked me a question I had not been prepared for.

"So who's Jay?"

"He's... sort of a guy I'm seeing."

"Why haven't we heard about him?" Dad asked.

"It's nothing serious. Yet, anyways."

"Yet?" They both said, looking at each other.

"How did you know about Jay?"

Probably Dave.

"Dave," *Yup. Thought so.* "So how old is he?"

"He's 21."

"Don't you think he's a bit too old for you?"

"I'm 17 and a half. Plus, it's not like what you think."

"Really? How so?" Mom quizzed.

"Well first, I rarely see him," *truth.* "Two, he's away at some private college," *somewhat the truth.* "And three, I don't know how serious he is," *Oops. I probably shouldn't have said the last thing.*

"Don't throw your future away on some *boy.*" Mom put the emphasis on the word boy.

"I still plan on going to college," I remarked. "Nothing is going to change or stop that. Plus, he's very supportive of me going to college. That's why I don't think anything will happen until after I graduate from law school."

"Good. I'm starting to like him already," Dad said, raising an eyebrow.

"Do you have a picture of him?" Mom asked.

There was no way around it. She probably already knew the answer to that one.

"Sure, hold on," I ran up to my room to grab my portfolio. "Here," I said, handing the smaller professional one to her.

"He's cute," she said with a smile.

"Where did you meet him?" Dad asked. I told him the same thing I told Dave. "I don't want you going that far after dark, okay?"

"Agreed," I promised. *That wouldn't be hard to agree to since I never went that far.*

"When he's back in town, we'd like to meet him."

You and everyone else.

"Dave wants to meet him first," I said without thinking.

"Of course he does," Mom smiled.

"As soon as he comes home on break from school, I'll have you meet him."

"Good," Dad said, as Mom handed me back my picture.

"I'm going to go for my run. Is that OK?"

"That's fine. We'll probably be asleep when you get back," Dad said, heading back downstairs to work on whatever he was working on.

"I'll be quiet," I assured them.

"Have fun."

"Thanks, Mom. I will," I said, as I put my shoes back on and headed out the door.

I remembered to bring a flashlight with me this time.

I sort of knew what I was heading into.

I thought.

What did come next, I was not prepared for.

Chapter 17 – Jealousy Comes a-Knocking

I heard Jay speaking, as soon as I entered the clearing. "The truth has spoken."

"What do you mean?"

I figured I actually did know what he meant.

"You tell me one thing, and you tell others something else?"

"OK. Knock this crap off now," I said, with meanness in my voice.

"Please forgive me," he started.

"OK, first of all, stop the jealousy act. It's getting old. Secondly, we went through this before," I snapped. He was in his see-through silk water form. I was happy I could see him, but I hated it because it felt like my hands would go right through him.

"I don't know what more to do or say. You even heard Dave, I know you were with us, even though I couldn't see you, I knew you were listening. About what he said – you are my longest relationship."

"I heard everything."

"If you are going to act like this, then maybe we should rethink things," I snorted.

I really didn't want to. I knew what I wanted, but at the same time, I didn't want this. His eyes grew wide, like his heart had just been ripped out. I walked up to him so that we were standing face to face.

"I like you, I really do. How do I know you're not doing the same thing to other girls that you are doing with me?"

He strongly protested, "I'm not!"

"But how do *I* know? Think about it for a moment," I threw back at him. His face relaxed.

We sat staring at each other like we were enemies.

"You are right," he finally said.

"I don't accuse you, because I *trust* you. I know you would never do anything to hurt me."

"I feel like an ass." You could tell that his pride was hurt.

"Don't. I'm just saying," I started to chuckle a little. He looked at me funny. "I can't peek into the conversations you have with others. "

"You know I speak the truth."

"Just like you should know that I speak the truth."

"So where does that leave you and me?" he asked.

"You tell me," I said, as I crossed my arms.

"You already know how I feel," he said, as if that would be a good enough answer.

"I do. I need you to trust me on a few things if we're going to make this work."

"It's not that I do not trust you," he paused.

"Look, again, we knew this wouldn't be easy," I said relaxing my arms. "I am the one lying, putting up a front about who you are. Heck! I don't even know who you are!"

"Are you rethinking your decision?"

"NO! I'm just saying we knew this wouldn't be easy. I know that things eventually will be alright, but for now things are what they are."

"I am sorry…" he started to say.

"Please don't say sorry. Say sorry if you tried your best to save my life and failed. Say sorry for any other reason than how you think that I feel."

He just lowered his head.

"Look at me, and don't even think about disappearing!"

He looked at me with astonishment that I would even think he would do something like that. "I would never!"

"Don't," I said, raising my hand.

He softly admitted, "I am scared of Dave."

"It's that you don't trust Dave," I finished. He nodded. "How about I show you?"

"Show me? How?" He asked, not sure how I could possibly show him. I put my arms around his neck, stood on my tip toes and started gently kissing his lips. "Hhhhmmm," he said, after I slowly pulled away.

"Do you like my show and tells?" I giggled.

"More than you could possibly know," he said kissing me back.

"What time would you like to get together tomorrow?" I asked after our kiss.

"Would you like to hear something strange to your ears?"

"This isn't the 'do you think this is the most annoying sound' sound?" I asked, placing my hands on my hips.

"I do not know what you mean. But I am sure that is not it at all."

"Do tell, then," I whispered, as I played or attempted to play with his hair. His hair was no different than the rest of him – everything felt exactly the same.

"I had no recollection of time or day before I met you," our noses touching each other. "I lived in the dark, not caring about the light. I never watched the time, for I had no need to. I never knew what day it was, nor did I care. That all changed when you walked into my life. I want to know when it is light, to see your smile. I want to know what time it is, for then I know when we will be together next. I want to know what day it is, for every moment that I spend with you is a special moment I wish to treasure for eternity."

Our lips met. Something was happening to me that I had never felt before. I didn't know how to describe my emotions. Every part of me wanted him in every way imaginable. My heart would skip a beat and then stop. Skip a beat and then stop.

"So what time?" I exhaled, still holding onto him.

"Hmmm," he said giving a playful look. "How about when the sun is at its highest?"

"Noon. Sounds good."

"How did you know of what I spoke?"

"We studied it in history," I winked.

"I will wait for you here at *noon*," he winked.

I had completely forgotten. "Oh!"

"What's wrong, my dear?"

"I forgot I'm supposed to do something with Dave tomorrow. He's gonna call tonight to confirm plans."

"Hmmmm," he said stroking his chin.

"I can't cancel unless I have a really damn good excuse," I protested.

His eyes lit up when I said the word *damn*. I have never sworn in front of him before.

"I'm thinking."

"You very well know that I can't say that I've got plans with you," I said, reminding him.

"Leave it to me. I will make this work," he smiled.

Now he *had* me worried. "Make what work?"

"I will talk to you after you have spoken to Dave," he kissed me sweetly and disappeared.

What did I *get* myself into? I hate surprises. This was starting to really worry me. My parents were already asleep when I got home.

"*Dave called*," the note read on taped to my door. "*Don't call past 11.*"

It wasn't even ten yet. I still had time. I did my nightly routine and gave Dave a call.

Ring…ring…ring…

"Hello?"

"May I please speak to Dave?"

"Hey, Lexi!" I could never distinguish between his voice and his dad's.

"Hey, sorry it took me so long to call back."

"No problem. Your mom said you went for your run."

"Yes, it was nice and peaceful," I wasn't lying this time.

"What time did you want to get together tomorrow?"

I was really hoping he would cancel. "Ummmm, I don't know. What time were you thinking?" But I knew I wouldn't be so lucky.

"I was thinking around one-ish?"

I paused, waiting for a sign from Jay.

"Still there?" Dave asked.

"Yup. Sorry, just thinking," I said, still waiting for a sign.

"Take your time."

I heard Jay somewhere in my room. "That's fine."

"Yeah, that should work," I was groaning on the inside, because I had no clue what Jay had in store for tomorrow.

"I'll be there around one to pick you up then?"

"Yeah, where are we going, so I know how to dress?"

I could hear him grinning. "Wear something nice, I'm going to spoil you tomorrow."

I groaned, "Ugh. You know I hate to be spoiled."

"It's one day for a couple of hours. Get over it," he laughed.

"Fine. Where are we going?"

"It's a surprise," he said, still smirking.

"You know I hate surprises," I warned him.

"Yeah, well I already ran it by your Mom, and she said no problem," he was still chuckling.

I couldn't help but roll my eyes. "How did I figure?"

"I'll see you tomorrow."

"See you," I said, hanging up the phone. I turned the radio on low so my parents wouldn't hear me whispering. "What do we do?"

"What do you mean?"

I was freaking out a little. "Dave's taking me out. I don't know where he's taking me or what he has planned."

"Don't worry about it, my dear."

I grumbled, "Easy for you to say, you're not the one worrying."

"Trust me. It will all work out. After all, is not that what you said just a little while ago?"

"Yeah, but…"

"No buts. Now, get some sleep. I have to rest for this to work."

"For what to work?"

"Bring your camera, as well. Trust me," now I could hear him grinning.

"You know I hate surprises."

"I know. Again, you must put faith in me, you will love this one. I hope," I heard him chuckle.

"Alright."

"Sweet dreams, my sweetheart."

"Rest well," I said, closing my eyes.

I didn't go to sleep right away. *What* did he have in store? This really worried me. I wanted so desperately for Dave to meet Jay, because I wanted to be at peace with Dave and stop him from talking about my past. Stop talking about us being together and obstacles. The *obstacle* that Jay and I faced was being together as an *official* couple. That made sense. Dave was trying to get over the hurdle of us being together, and he's doing everything in his power for us to be. That all makes perfect sense now, I think.

I got up and searched for my flashlight, diary and pen in the dark. I haven't written in it since had I started running more often and had met Jay. I think it's time to catch up. This is the part where I'm lucky I don't have siblings that like to snoop.

Dear Diary~

I have to remind myself to update you more often. A lot has happened since the last time I wrote. I found the reason I am still alive after that near miss with death. I met a guy. Well, I think he's a guy. He doesn't fit into any category of a ghost, spirit or whatever you want to call it. He's like not me. Not human. Again, I think. I can't be sure. There are some days to where I can see him and feel him as I would anyone else. Then there are days where all I can do is hear his voice. Am I losing it? I know this isn't normal. But I'm not normal. I never felt normal before. I always knew there was something strange about me. Is this the strange thing, that I'm dating another life form? If you can call it that, life forms. There are a lot of things that don't make sense. The house that I can't help but be drawn to, it looks like there's someone there looking to buy the place. Not used to seeing anyone there before. Even though I've never seen anyone there before, the yard always looks like it's professionally kept. On a brighter note, the hole that was in my soul is completely gone. It has somehow disappeared. I can't explain it. I feel whole. I feel like I found where I am supposed to belong. I know that sounds crazy. What can I say? I'm crazy. I am crazy in l-o-v-e. I just can't bring myself to say the letters as one word.

I still couldn't sleep. I crept downstairs to grab something to drink. That didn't work. I was wide awake, and it was too late to give anyone a call. I had so much on my mind. I didn't know where to begin. I left a note and snuck out through the back.

The air was crisp against my lungs as I started to run faster and faster. I wasn't running anywhere in particular, I just felt like I wanted to jump through my skin. I wanted to be anywhere but where I was. I took the long route; I needed as much time as I could. I was in the back part of the subdivision when I saw lights flicker at the end of the street. I didn't think too much of it – most likely someone like me who couldn't sleep or whatever. I rounded the corner and saw where the light was coming from. The old Victorian house that I had never seen anyone in before. We kids used to joke about how it was so old that it didn't have modern electricity. Well, this put our theory to rest.

I just kept running along the side walk. I could see that someone had the curtain pulled back from a second-floor window and was looking out. I kept jogging by, still looking from the top of my eye until I couldn't see the window any more. With my back toward the house, I felt a sense of uneasiness – like something wasn't right.

I really don't know how long or far I had been running, but I knew it had to be late. I didn't want to look at my watch, for fear of how late it really was. Sneaking back inside, I removed the note from the table. I was happy that the run had worked, and I was actually getting tired. But everything that had been weighing on my mind was still there. I slowly and quietly crept up the stairs and sat on my bed, staring off into space.

I grabbed the photo album that Dave had gotten me for my birthday and opened it. I hadn't put any pictures into it yet. I was waiting to do that all at once and have everyone sign it at the end of the year. All of the pictures were loose in the front. I slowly flipped through each one until I came across the one of Jay and me. *He is real,* I thought to myself. We make such a cute couple. *I wonder what the future holds for us.* Like a star-crazed teenager, I kissed the photograph of us and put it back in its spot with the rest of the pictures. I replaced the photo album where it had been and crawled into bed.

I whispered to the air, "Sweet rest, and I miss you."

Sleep was always a hit or miss. Either I didn't dream anything, or I dreamt so much it was like living life on a rollercoaster. I started to dream about our first kiss, how we danced to music only we could hear. And then everything went dark.

I started to hear people whispering. I couldn't make out what they were saying; it was so annoying, trying to sleep and hearing people whisper, especially at this hour when no one should be out. I could just imagine the whispers waking Dad up and him being pissed off and yelling. I waited a few minutes for Dad to start going off, but I didn't hear anything. Could he even hear the voices that were whispering so loudly?

When I opened my eyes, the sun was shining. It didn't feel like I had slept at all. I walked past my parent's room, took a peek in, but didn't see them. They must be downstairs, I thought. Strange, I didn't have to use the bathroom. Very unlike me in the mornings. I continued downstairs, expecting to see my parents sitting at the kitchen table, as they do every morning. I reached the bottom of the stairs, and no one was there. The coffee wasn't even made. Maybe Mom's doing laundry and Dad's in the den. I walked down the next flight of steps and started to call out.

"Hello?" I asked.

I heard nothing.

I searched the whole house front to back and still didn't see them. I looked out the front to see if their cars were in the driveway. I didn't see their cars. That's strange. Mom's probably at the library, and Dad's probably at the computer store, then.

I started walking back to the kitchen when I heard the whispering again. Weird. I had just checked the whole house, and no one was inside. I grabbed my jacket, threw on my shoes and headed out the back door, standing there in the bright sun. I didn't hear the voices anymore. Was I going crazy?

I sat still and listened. I heard them again. They were louder, but still too faint to make out what they were saying. I started towards the front of the house, and the whispering grew quieter. I turned around and headed towards the back gate. The whispering grew louder. I started walking in the direction where they seemed the loudest, following them to the edge of the forest.

I heard a faint, unfamiliar voice taunting, "Why? Why risk it all? You have it all!"

I started into the forest. I was hidden in the shadows as I spotted a man I had never seen before. He was short and stubby with silver hair that wrapped around the shine of his balding head.

"Look at me! Look at you!" the man wailed. "Why would you want to give this all up?"

"Because I love her!" *That was Jay's voice! I would recognize that voice anywhere!*

But I could only see the short stubby man. "Oh, please, what do you know about love?"

He shot back in anger, "What would *you* know about it?!"

The short man acted like he wasn't entertained at all. "I know it's not worth risking all of this for."

"Says you!" He cried. Then he stepped out from behind a tree. Both of them were in what I guess you would call human form. It was like I was watching a soap opera on TV, but here it was, live.

"Destiny, will you listen!"

I gasped when I heard him call the man Destiny. Destiny was a guy! The two guys froze.

Destiny angrily demanded, "What was that?"

"I don't know," He replied.

They both looked around for an answer. I stood still where I was at – I could see them perfectly clearly.

"Look! You called me here for what? To tell me about your sorry excuse about love for a mortal?"

He lowered his shoulders and sighed, "No, to ask for a favor."

"I don't grant favors," he cursed, crossing his stubby arms over his chest. "Besides, you have been meddling in that *mortal's* destiny ever since last summer! And now you come to ask me for a favor?! I don't think so!"

"Why do *you* want her?"

"It's not *her* that I want. It's her soul! You know I don't care about the bodies of those *things*!"

"Why are you so grumpy?" Jay demanded.

"Grumpy? You think this is grumpy? You haven't seen anything yet!"

"NO! I will fight with every last breath that I have to save her! And you know that!" he wailed, jabbing a finger at him.

"Yeah, so?"

"What would Fate have to say about this?"

The short man grinned a scary grin, "Who cares."

"Fate, oh Fate, I need you now, don't be late, as here I bow," Jay was smiling even wider than the short man.

A colossal light emitted from nowhere. I had to close my eyes from the brightness. When I opened them, there were now two short, chubby men standing in front of Jay. They looked like twins; the only difference was that one had a full head of hair, and the other one did not.

"Fate, oh Fate, I am so regretful to have disturbed you. I need your help desperately," Jay said, with panic in his voice. "Your brother, Destiny, is trying to take the soul of the girl I love."

The one I guessed was Fate – the one with the hair –looked at his brother.

"Is this true?" Fate bellowed.

"It's not how it appears, brother," Destiny said, a little worried.

"Is Jay speaking the truth that you are trying to take the soul of the one he loves?"

"You see…"

"YES OR NO!" Fate screamed, so loudly that it hurt my ears.

Destiny, dropping his eyes, "Yes." Jay had a big grin on his face. "But she's a *mortal*," he added quickly.

Destiny looked at Jay with such evil that I wanted to go help him. "A WHAT?!"

Jay's grin had disappeared. "I cannot lie. She is a mortal, but I love her!"

"You know the laws. How could you have let this happen?" Fate demanded.

"You would never believe me, even if I spoke the truth. There is nothing you can do, I love her," he stated confidently. "You will have to kill me in order to take her soul. I will *NEVER* let that happen!"

"I have no desire for her soul right now," Fate said calmly. "Who said I wanted her soul?" Jay just glared at Destiny. "Why would you tell him that?" Fate screamed.

"*I* want her soul!" Destiny admitted.

"We cannot just go around stealing souls if their time is not up. *YOU* out of anyone know the laws!"

Jay just stood there, frozen. I was frozen, as well – not from the cold air, but from panic. I didn't want anything to happen to Jay. Fate turned back to Jay.

"Jay, how could you make this mortal fall for you?"

"She hasn't," he hesitated. "Not yet."

"You have fallen for her?"

"Yes," he stared him right in the eye.

"You know we cannot make you mortal."

"I know," he said, looking down. He looked up again, confused. "I have a question, if you do not mind me asking."

Fate motioned with his hand, "Go ahead."

"There have been times when I can appear just as the other mortals. Why is that?"

Fate appeared astounded. "You have?"

"Yes, I cannot explain it, either."

"This has only happened a few times before," he said, stroking his chin. "Brother, why did you not tell me any of this?"

"Does it matter? He's breaking the law. He's not allowed to be in love with a *mortal* and a *mortal* is not allowed to be in love with one of us."

"I know what the law is! But this doesn't follow the nature of *that* law."

Jay looked confused. I was confused. Destiny looked pissed. Fate looked thrilled.

"I think I know what you seek, and that is beyond our powers," Fate lowered his head. "I am truly sorry. But I will order my brother here to leave the soul of the one you love."

"Thank you," Jay said, almost in tears. "I don't know what to do."

"There is one person who can guide you, but he is very busy."

Why does everyone in power have to be a man? It's bad enough we have them here as humans, but whatever these are, all of them have to be men? At least the one called Fate seems a little more understanding.

"I'll do whatever it takes," Jay said, holding back tears.

Fate just looked down and frowned. "It could take years. I am being honest. I am sorry. It will not happen overnight. It could possibly take longer than years to get in to talk to the guide."

"I know I will wait as long as it takes. I love her far beyond any words."

"I know you do," Fate sighed. "But does she feel the same way? Even if she does, would she wait as long for you as you will for her? Remember, their forms are not like ours."

"I know," a tear rolled down Jay's cheek.

"Her soul is not ours to take," Fate looked at his brother again. "Do you hear me, brother of mine?"

"I hear you," he grumbled. "This is not over yet," he pointed at Jay and then left. Jay just stood there in panic.

"Don't worry about him. I will take care of it."

"Why is he so mad?" Jay asked.

"He just gets really upset when people stand in his way over the souls he wants to take."

"You said hers was not for the taking."

"I didn't say that the souls he takes are always ready to come."

"Oh..."

Fate stated very calmly but disturbed, "There are souls who are ready to come that get blocked, and he can't obtain them. So he gets angry and takes another one in its place."

"That's not right!"

"I know. His time will come for Justice. Please be patient."

"It's hard to stand by as someone tries to kill the one you love with a vengeance," Jay admitted.

"What you have done is wrong. I will side with on my brother on that."

He looked like he was ready to protest, but Fate held up his hand.

"But I know *why* you have done it. To be fair, I would have done the same thing," Fate said with a smile.

"I'm sorry for calling you. I just didn't know what else to do."

"No need to apologize. You don't call on me often. When you do, I know that it is no small thing you seek."

"Before you leave, how do I make an appointment to visit my guide?"

"Leave that to me. As I have said, you will need to be patient. Even I can't get in to see him on short notice."

"How will I know when? I would like to be ready to present my case."

"He sees all and watches everything that everyone does. Including us. It all depends on how urgent he believes the matter is."

Jay nodded, "Oh."

"I understand the intensity of your case. But I am afraid that he may not. He may find that other issues are more urgent."

"I understand," Jay said, another tear rolling down his cheek.

"This is the first time I have ever seen one of us cry," remarked Fate. "There is a transition taking place. I have only heard rumors about this, for those who have undergone this change have never returned to tell about it. No one knows exactly what is involved in the process, or even how long it can last. What I can say is that for those who had partial transitions, the effects did not last long."

"What do you mean by did not last long?"

"Their transitions came in spurts. It's hard to describe what a transition is, because no one who has gone through one can remember exactly what happened. Those who have had them remember extreme amounts of pain, and they were never wanted to go through them again. No one knows what a transition does, or what the outcome is, or why it happens. As much as we are a mystery to the mortals, the transition is a mystery to us."

"Thank you, Fate," Jay said, bowing.

"Any time. If you need me, just call for me. It was a pleasure conversing with you." As he spoke these last words, another flash of light erupted, and then all was black and silent.

Chapter 18 – The Break-Up

I woke up in a daze. I couldn't even describe what had just happened. I crawled out of bed to brush my teeth and stumbled downstairs for some breakfast. My parents were already gone for the day, so I didn't care what I looked like. Not that it ever mattered, though. Even though today felt like any other Saturday, I knew it wasn't. I had a date with Dave, where, I don't know. To make matters worse, Jay was up to something, and I didn't know what.

I knew Dave had always liked me as more than just a friend, but lately, it seemed like he was making more of an attempt than usual. *Maybe that's why Jay is jealous?* It made sense. If Jay had really been watching me all this time, then he would know that Dave had never tried this hard before. Well, maybe in the beginning, but then things cooled off, at least until now.

I had a few hours to kill before Dave was supposed to pick me up. I rummaged through the kitchen, thinking about what I was in the mood for. In the end, I decided just to grab a bowl of cereal. Easy enough. I was actually contemplating backing out of both dates and just spending the day alone. The last thing I needed was the boy that I liked to hate me and my best friend to stop talking to me.

I had just finished cleaning up when the phone rang.

"Hello?" I answered.

"Hey! Lexi!"

"Oh, hey, Lynn. What's up?"

"We were wondering what time to expect you guys today."

"Huh?"

You could tell she had spilled the beans. "Ooops…"

"So that's what he has in store for us today?"

"Ummmm, Ooops again. I'm sorry, I wasn't supposed to say anything."

"It's cool," I laughed. "I sort of figured something like this. So what else does he have in store?"

"Oh, no, I already ruined one surprise. I ain't giving the other one up."

"Oh, great," I moaned.

"What's wrong?"

"Nothing." I lied.

"You're so lucky," she remarked.

"How so?"

Really, how was I lucky?

"I have wanted to date Dave since we first met."

"Well, why didn't you say anything?"

"Because I knew how he felt about you, and I didn't want to seem like I was trying to compete or anything."

"He is a great guy," I couldn't keep myself from laughing.

"Why are you laughing?"

"It's not you. Seriously. It's just that Dave and I are like brother and sister."

"I can see that now, although I didn't in the beginning. Plus, as much as we have all hung out together by now, I only see him as a big brother, as well."

"Yeah. He just makes it look like we are together."

"That's what I thought. At first, I'll be honest, I thought you were leading him on. So I was sort of mad at you," she stated. "Then, as I got to know you more and figured out your creed against dating friends, it all fit together."

"Yeah. I have told him on more than one occasion that I just wanted to be friends and stop trying so hard. What do you think about Tim? You are officially a couple, right?"

"Yeah," she hesitated. "He's a great guy and all, but there is no chemistry."

"Yeah, trust me, I completely understand. It's the same way I feel about Dave."

"AAAHHHH! I gotcha! I thought it was just me," she sounded embarrassed.

"Nope, not just you. Tim's a great guy though. I would hate to lose him as part of our group."

"Yeah, I know."

I couldn't help but grin. "I really hate to tell you so." Because now someone else understood my rules. "This is why I *don't* date friends."

"But if you really think about it, we weren't friends like you and Dave."

"True. I'll give you that. But wait, you're not going to break up with him, are you?"

"I'm really thinking about it."

"I hate to say it, but not today. It's Valentine's Day, and that would break his heart."

"Yeah, I know. I don't know how to break up with him and still keep the friendship," she paused. "OK OK OK. I get it now."

I just smiled.

"I can hear you smiling," she teased.

"Sorry, but what can I say?"

"True."

"Do you think Tim feels the same as you? Or is he madly in love with you?"

"I don't know, that's the thing. I was wondering…" Her voice trailed off.

"If I would talk to him and find out?"

"Could you? Pleeeeeeeeeeeeeeaaaaaaaaaaaaasssssssssssssseeeee," she begged.

"I'll see what I can do. But you know this goes against everything that I stand for."

"Thank you, thank you, thank you!" she cried.

"Hey now, I just said I'll see what I can do, not that I *will be* able to."

"I know! You're still the best!"

"I'm going to get a run in before Dave picks me up."

"Alright, I'll see you later."

I just remembered something. "Hey, wait! I have a question!"

"What's that?"

I decided to press my luck. "What are we all doing?"

"Just act surprised when he *thinks* he's surprising you, OK?"

"OK. Promise."

She was hesitant. "We're all meeting up for a movie, and then he's taking you out to eat."

"Where are you all going to eat?"

"Since we couldn't agree on a single place, we're all going somewhere different."

"Ah. Gotcha. I won't say anything. I'll act surprised," I promised.

"Good, I'll see you later."

"Laters."

I hung up the phone and looked at the time. *Crap.* I didn't have time for a quick run. I knew with the way my mind was wandering my quick thirty minute run would turn into a two hour walk. So I plopped onto the couch and turned on the TV. Took me a good five minutes to learn how to actually get a picture on the screen. Dad had at least five remotes per electronic device in the house. One remote to turn on the TV, one remote for the volume, one remote to change the channels, one remote for the VCR, one remote for something else, and I couldn't tell you what the last remote did. To make matters worse, you never knew which remote operated which function. I was trying to figure out how I would be able to meet Jay at noon, then come home and change in time to be ready for Dave. I finally got everything to work in unison.

His voice came over the show that I was watching. "Good morning, beautiful."

"Hey! Good morning!" I could only hear him, I couldn't see him. That didn't bother me. I knew he said that he had to rest, which I was hoping would mean that I could see him better than I've been able to lately.

"There has been a little change in plans."

"Oh?"

"Not to worry, though. If all goes according to my plan, we'll see each other later." He sounded hopeful.

"OK," I paused. "I don't know what time I'm coming home, though."

He stated with joy, "That does not matter. I can work around whatever is thrown at us today."

"You sound hopeful."

"I am. Trust me. Don't worry about meeting me at noon."

I had been looking forward to that all night. "Why?"

"We are talking now, plus time will be tight for you," he sounded pleased.

"I can make it work," I argued.

"Please, my dear, everything will work out, and I promise that you will not be disappointed."

"OK," not liking it. But I *was* talking to him now. I had to trust him.

"Patience makes the soul stronger."

I snorted, "Well, then I don't have much of a soul."

"Yes, you do," he chuckled. "You have a very strong soul. You don't give yourself the credit you deserve."

"Whatever." I rolled my eyes.

"Relax, my angel. Have you heard the phrase, 'Single colors are bland until they are mixed to create a beautiful image'?"

"No."

"Each soul is a color. It's not until they are mixed with another that the colors will flow naturally as one, the way they were meant to be."

"I'm confused." *I really hated riddles.*

"You will see soon."

"I better," I teased.

"A piece of my heart belongs to you. When we meet again, it will become whole once more."

I whispered softly, "That was beautiful."

His voice trailed, "I will see you soon." I knew he was gone.

Crap! The time! I started hitting all the power buttons on the remotes, hoping that I was turning off the same electronics I had turned on. I ran to my room to get changed. I had no clue what to wear. I had completely forgotten to ask Lynn how I should dress today. All I knew is it was going to be cold; a late snowfall had made the air even colder than before. The only dresses I had in my closet were formal. I found a long, black velvet skirt and a nice sweater to go with it. I had one pair of high heels, three pairs of tennis shoes, and a pair of dressier shoes with low heels. I really didn't want to wear high heels, since I knew there would be patches of ice. If I could trip over air in regular tennis shoes, I would be a walking catastrophe if I wore heels when it was icy outside. I got ready in no time and was waiting by the time Dave pulled up.

Knock..knock...

I could hear Dave knocking at the door.

"I'll be right there!"

Purse...Check. Wallet...Check. Camera...Check. New roll of film...Check. Keys...Check. Left a note...Check.

"Ready!" I said, locking the door behind me.

"You look beautiful," Dave smiled.

"Thanks," I said, blushing. "Where are we going first?"

"First?" *Oops.* "Did Val call you?"

I made it down the stairs and across the drive without falling. This looked promising. He opened the car door for me, and I glided in. He closed the door as soon as I was seated and walked over to his side. I opened the door for him.

"Nope," not a lie.

"Aaron?" he asked again, as he carefully backed out of the driveway.

"Nope." Again, not a lie.

"Lynn?"

"Yes," I wiped the smile from my face. "She called because she had concerns about Tim."

"Riiiiigggghhht."

"Seriously, she did."

"What type of concerns?"

"You know, the usual girl problems." That was true. I just left out the '*I know where you are taking me first*' part.

"Period?"

"Nope."

"Wardrobe? Hair? Makeup?" He started asking the twenty question game. "Oh wait, I forgot, you don't do makeup, so that's a no brainer."

"Ha ha ha. And no and no."

"Well, I think I'm right about the next choice."

"Try it," I gloated.

"It *was* about Tim," he grinned.

"How did you know?"

"Tim called me this morning."

"He called *you*?" Even though Tim was becoming close with the group, it wasn't like he picked up the phone and chatted with us.

"Yeah. Poor Lynn."

I couldn't help but scream, "He's not going to break up with her today, is he?!"

"Well, not today."

"Phew," I said with relief.

"OK, spill, what do you know?"

"That the break up will be mutual," I said.

He added without much surprise, "She wanted to break up with him."

"Yeah. I told her not to do it today, though. But…"

"You know you are interfering," he judged.

"Yeah, I know. I hate it. But at least both parties are mutual about what they want."

"I'll give you that. So what should we do?" he asked, as if we were planning a war.

"Well part of me wants to just confront them both, since they both want the same thing. The other part says to stay out of it and let them handle it on their own."

"I know, it's a tough one. Usually, only one person wants to break up, and the other one gets hurt."

Normally, we don't intrude on each other's love lives. Only under extreme circumstances would we intervene.

"Let's play it by ear?" I asked.

"Sounds like a plan," he agreed.

"So where are you taking me?"

"You'll see," he mused. *He had no clue. I loved it!*

We were driving down the main strip in the neighboring town. You couldn't walk from place to place, like in some of the neighboring towns around here. Plus, this area was known to have more snobs than the others. When you traveled from one town to another, it sometimes seemed as though you had traveled a thousand miles. In this town, the people were upper class and more snooty. The town we usually went to was middle class – very down to earth, didn't care what type of car you drove, what kind of clothes you wore or what you did for a living. They treated you as human beings.

"So which movie are we going to see?" I grinned.

"How did you know? Lynn told you, didn't she?!"

"Uh, no. You're parking in the movie theater lot," I snickered.

He blushed with embarrassment, "Oh. Right."

"When are you going to believe me when I say girls don't gab as bad as boys?"

He firmly insisted, "Never!"

"You know it," I cracked. "You're just not man enough to admit it."

"Admitting it would be welcoming defeat. I will not be defeated!"

"Get over it," I teased. We walked up to the movie theater. I kept my hands in my coat pockets the whole time. I didn't want to give Dave a chance to try to hold them.

Aaron called, raising his hands, "DAVE!"

Dave called back in the same manner, "AARON!"

We started walking towards Aaron. If he was there, Val would be there, too.

"Here you go, guy," he said, handing Dave two of the tickets that were in his hand.

"Thanks. What do I owe you?"

"Buy me lunch for the week and we'll call it even."

"Deal," he agreed, as they shook on it.

"Is it just us four?" I asked. Aaron just grinned.

"We're waiting for the others to show up, that's part one of my surprise," he beamed.

"Even Terry?" I know that Terry didn't think about these holidays like couples did. I felt bad that he didn't have anyone.

Aaron snapped his gum. "Even Terry."

"Lexi!"

"Val!" We both shared a *how are you* hug.

"Lynn and Tim should be here soon," she stated tonelessly.

"You know?" I asked. She just shook her head. This was going to be awkward.

"Hey, guys!" Lynn said, gleaming as she walked up. "OK, what do you all of you know that I don't?"

Everyone just looked at each other like they were confused about what I was asking.

I whispered, "It's cool. Well, at least you both want the break-up."

Dave mumbled, "That should ease things up a bit."

I had just thought of something. "Wait!"

I could see this ending one of two ways. Lynn being pissed thinking that Val betrayed her trust, or happy that it would be a peaceful move on. Tim came walking up and did not look happy.

"OK, I can't take it anymore!" I cried. I could hear Aaron and Dave breath with relief. "You two, come here!" I motioned with my finger.

"What did we do?" Lynn asked, looking at me like she was in trouble.

"Nothing. Lynn, I'm sorry, but I can't deal with what I know."

She looked at me, confused. Val chimed in from the background, "We all know."

"You do?" Lynn blushed but seemed relieved at the same time. Tim looked confused.

"There is one thing I'm not sure that you do know, though, Lynn," I hesitated at what I was about to do next. "So don't be mad at me. It's better now than if it were to come out later."

"Just say it," she demanded.

"You both were going to break up, right?" They both just looked at each other with confusion, but utter relief. "The look says it all. There we go. Now..."

Lynn had an even more confused look on her face. I really hoped she wouldn't be mad at me for what I was about to say and do next.

"Since that's out of the way, Lynn," I paused. Her eyes grew wide, but she remained calm.

"That's fine," she said with a bit of sadness in her voice.

"We're not trying to start anything," Val said, coming to the rescue. "We just thought it would be better out in the open than to pretend that nothing was going on."

"I understand," she agreed.

Tim spoke up. "Listen, guys, I think it would be more comfortable if I took off. I'll see you later, OK?" We all felt bad, but we knew it would be easier on both of them this way. "OK, Tim, we'll see you on Monday, then, right?"

Tim had just walked off when Mike came jogging up the walkway.

"Hey, guys! Sorry I'm late."

"Just in time," Aaron handed a ticket over to him. Everyone greeted Mike, since it had been a while since we'd seen or heard from him. He comes in goes depending on his class load.

"How's college life, man?" Dave asked.

"It's going," he shrugged. "Homework is a lot tougher than I thought." He hadn't shown up in time to know about Tim and Lynn breaking up.

"Catch me up, what have I missed?"

Dave chuckled with relief, "It's a long story bro, we'll fill ya in later."

"Where's Terry?" Mike asked.

Dave started, "His Dad."

"Say no more," he said, holding up his hand.

We all knew when you brought up Terry's dad in a sentence, it wasn't good. It usually meant that his dad was making him train, even when the rest of the team wasn't. Mike took a quick look at everyone and noticed that Lynn was alone.

"Since it is Valentine's Day," Mike said, scratching his head. "Would you like to be my date for today?"

"Ummmm," she looked around to see if anyone objected. Of course we didn't. "Sure, OK."

He held his arm out, and she wrapped hers around his. We headed into the movie theater paired off. Of course they were playing some cheesy love story, since it was Valentine's Day. I had been so lucky that things worked out the way they had with Tim and Lynn. Lynn and Mike made a cute couple, but honestly, after seeing how things had gone with Tim, I could almost bet my life savings that she wouldn't date Mike. But I could be wrong.

The movie wasn't that bad. The guys groaned playfully after the movie was over. Us girls just rolled our eyes.

"What kind of love story is it when no one dies?" Aaron asked, snapping a new stick of gum.

Val retorted with hidden resentment, "It's called a happy ending."

"I'm starving," Aaron griped.

"You're always starving," I snapped.

"Whoa, looks like I'm not the only who's hungry," he shot back. We all laughed, said our goodbyes, and headed to our cars.

"What are you in the mood for?" Dave asked holding my door open.

"I don't know. Food?" I teased.

"Well, duh," he said, making a face.

"How about that little mom and pop place in town?"

He made an insulted face. "There?"

"Well I don't know then, you tell me where you are taking me."

"How about the Blue Circle?"

I groaned, "That place is going to be packed." I hated to wait to be seated.

"Nah. My parents know the owners. We have a reservation," he winked. That scared me. I hated any type of special attention.

The Blue Circle was a well-known chain. They had great food, so there was always a wait. It wasn't a fancy sit-down place, but it wasn't a mom and pop, either. Dave started driving towards the restaurant. The place would be even busier than it normally is, since it was Valentine's Day. The ride was peaceful; neither one of us said a word. Which scared me. When we pulled in, we had to drive around for what seemed like forever, waiting for a spot to open up. When one finally did, we snagged it. As soon as he was parked, he had my door open for me.

"Thank you," I gushed, as I stepped out.

"You're welcome. Today is your day to be treated like a queen."

"Oh stop that. I don't run a country," I joked.

"Humor me? Will you?"

I exhaled, not happy, "Fine.". He held his arm around me while we walked up to the large awning. There were people everywhere. I overheard one of them say that there was a two-hour wait. The smokers were off to the side, trying to kill time.

"Hello, Welcome to the Blue Circle," the host greeted us with a friendly smile. "Table for two?"

"Yes sir," Dave answered.

"The wait time is almost three hours," the host said, still with a smile but a different tone.

"Is Mr. Clard available?" Dave asked.

"Sure, let me get him for you," the host replied, with a confused look on his face.

A few moments later, a tall, beefy man came walking up. "Mr. Dave!" he grinned, holding out his hand.

"Mr. Clard!" Dave replied, returning the handshake. "My parents said that they talked to you last night?"

"Of course!" he waved. "Follow me. How's the family?" he asked, as we followed behind him.

"They are doing great. They said that you all need to get together soon."

"Most definitely! My wife asked about you guys just a couple days ago."

He said something else, but I couldn't hear what it was over the commotion in the room.

"Thank you very much," Dave said, pulling my seat out for me.

"Your server will be with you soon. Thank you, and enjoy!"

I didn't know what to say, "That was."

"Don't know what to say?" He smirked.

"Yeah, that about says it," I said giggling.

"My parents don't call in favors very often, but when they do, people will bend frontwards and backwards to help them."

"Wow."

His tone dropped, "Yeah, but they don't have the power your dad did with the colleges."

"That sucks."

"Everyone who owns, operates, or manages a business in this town was just about born and raised here."

"Oh, OK, that makes perfect sense now," I said, sitting back in the chair.

We sat in silence after the waitress took our orders. I just looked around the room in amazement. The place had changed a lot since the last time I was here. There were more pictures on the walls. They were older pictures taken in the surrounding area. One picture was fuzzy. A school, maybe a college, sat in the background, and kids were lined up in the front. Their faces were hard to make out, since the picture was a bit far away from our table.

"What are you looking at?" he asked, following my line of sight.

"Oh, just looking at all the old pictures," I said, motioning with my head.

"Every time he comes across one, he frames it and finds a space on the wall for it."

"Neat," I started to look at the others.

After dinner, he helped me put my coat on and walked me to his car with his arm around my shoulder. I tried to pull away, but it was too cold not to enjoy the warmth.

"Thank you," I said smiling. "That really hit the spot."

"You're welcome," he gushed. "They have great food."

"The atmosphere was so relaxed," I remarked.

"Their employees are taught to be courteous, the customers can be wrong and to have fun."

"Wow, you don't find too many places like that, where the customers know not to harass the staff."

"Yup. That's what makes this place so different from all the others."

As soon as he pulled out, a group of cars vied for his parking spot. He carefully maneuvered around the ice and cars, and we were finally on our way home.

"I can't believe how well you handled that situation," he complimented me.

"What, Tim and Lynn?" I asked, hoping that's what he was referring to.

"Yeah."

"Well, I would rather console her now than beg for her forgiveness for keeping the truth from her."

"True. I think she respects you more now because of that," he gushed.

"I wasn't looking for respect," I said, putting my hands over the vents.

"We know you weren't. It's just that you handle things cooler than any of the rest of us would."

"Yeah, OK," I said laughing.

"Do you honestly think that Aaron would talk things out?"

"Well," I started to say.

"No. He's a grunt. He would challenge you to a duel before he would actually agree to talk."

"You do have a point," I laughed.

We sat in awkward silence. I didn't know what else he had planned. If he had been planning to take me for a walk, I would definitely need to change. I was already ahead in the game today, since I hadn't tripped or broken anything. The roads were getting worse as the day was closing. Dave was crawling as he pulled onto the street between our subdivisions, the roads were so icy.

"Why don't you park at home, and I'll just walk to my house," I suggested.

"I am not letting you walk in this cold, in heels, in the snow," he retorted.

"The conditions are horrible. I don't want you driving any more than you have to."

"We're almost there – what's the worst that could happen at this point?"

I hated that phrase even more than I hated my nickname. I was more than terrified now. Whenever someone used that phrase, it never failed. He slowly turned onto my street. I would rather break a leg then have one of my friends get hurt because of me. We were not even six houses away, and I was starting to worry even more. He still had to cross back through one of the main intersections to get to his house after he dropped me off.

I looked up and I couldn't believe what I saw.

Chapter 19 – It was just an accident...or was it?

I turned and screamed in utter panic. "DAVE WATCH OUT!"

There was a car heading straight for us! The last thing I saw was Dave turning the wheel to avoid a collision, but his car kept moving straight – straight toward the other car, that was also out of control.

"SHIT!" I heard him scream as I closed my eyes. "DAMN ICE…"

I could hear horns honking. I felt Dave's car hit the curb, and then there was a loud crash. I still had my eyes closed, and I didn't realize it, but I was holding my breath. As soon as we came to a stop, I could hear the neighbors running out of their homes with the doors slamming shut behind them.

"ARE THEY DEAD?"

"ARE THEY OK?"

"ANYONE HURT?"

"HOW MANY PEOPLE IN THERE?"

"SOMEONE CALL 911!"

"DAVE, ARE YOU OK?"

"LEXI, ARE YOU OK?"

I kept my eyes closed. I didn't know what had just taken place. We should be dead. Dave had a small four-door sedan, and the other car was a large sport utility.

I could hear Dad's voice and a pounding on the window, "Lexi! Are you OK?"

I thought I was shaking my head yes, but I still had my eyes closed.

I heard Mom cry in the background, "Oh my God, is she OK?"

"Lexi, are you OK?" I heard Dave's voice. "LEXI!" He screamed, as he tried to shake me.

"DON'T SHAKE HER!" I heard someone yell. "She might be hurt!"

It had all happened so fast. I slowly started to open my eyes.

"Oh my God, she's alive," Mom started crying.

Dave turned off his car and unlocked the doors. I could hear the ambulance slowly making its way towards us. Dave opened his door and climbed out. Dad slowly opened my door. I could hear people screaming don't move them.

"I...I'm OK," I managed to whisper out.

"What happened?" Dave asked. "The SUV was headed straight for us, I turned the wheel but nothing happened."

"WAIT!" I cried.

"What's wrong?" Dad asked.

"Where is he?" I cried again.

"He...who?"

"Jay?!" I couldn't stop from screaming. "I saw him at the door. I swear I did!"

I hoped I had, or they would know that I was losing it. Well, if it had been my imagination, at least I could blame it on the accident.

"Jay?" Dad gave me a confused look.

So I had *imagined it.*

"He's fine," Mom said, slowly making her way over.

"He was waiting for you outside, and when he thought that the two cars were going to hit, he came and got us right away."

"He's here?" I asked. I looked around, but I didn't see him. "Where is he at?"

I saw her pointing, "He's right...."

"Weird," Dave said. He was looking to see how much damage had been caused by the accident.

"What? What's wrong?" I asked, still searching the crowd that had gathered.

271

"Nothing. That's what's weird," he said, shaking his head. "Are you OK? I'm so sorry!"

"Yeah," I said nodding. "Are you OK?"

"Yeah. I don't understand, though," he looked back at his car. Beside the fact that it was sitting in the middle of my parent's lawn, nothing was out of place on it. We could not say the same about the other vehicle. It had wrapped itself around a thick, concrete lamp post. Pieces of glass glittered in the snow around it.

I heard his voice! "Alexandra!"

"Jay!" I cried. So I hadn't imagined him!

"Jay? *Jay* is *here*?" I heard Dave. "Why didn't you tell me? You promised!"

I shouted back at him, "I didn't know! I really didn't. I am as shocked as you are!"

Jay finally managed to squeeze through the crowd and enwrapped me in a hug. "Are you okay?" He asked, concerned.

"Yeah, I'm fine. What happened?"

"I had enough time after finals to come by and surprise you," he said, playing out the idea that he was away at college.

"You...you're..." I didn't know what to say. I was surprised, because he was in human form.

He mouthed, "*Shhh*,"

"Hello. I'm Dave," Dave said, butting his way in between us.

Jay held out his hand for his. "Hello. I'm Jay. A pleasure to meet you."

"So what school do you go to?" Dave started to question.

"Sir, are you alright?" A paramedic was coming towards us. "We need to take a look at the both of you to make sure there is nothing wrong."

"I'm fine," Dave grumbled.

"I also need to get your statement," a nearby officer said.

A paramedic motioned for me, "You too, ma'am."

"I'll be right here," Jay smiled and kissed me on the forehead. "Promise."

The time dragged. I know the paramedics had to do their job, but I was fine. It probably wouldn't have bothered me if I had lost a limb or two – I was perfectly fine as long as Jay was there. He really was *here*; everyone could see him. The officer took my statement and said how lucky we were, and that fate was on our side.

Fate.

"Is there something wrong, ma'am?" the officer asked me.

"No, I'm fine, ma'am," I said, quickly shaking my head. "It wasn't Dave's fault, I swear!" Remembering why I was there.

"Relax," she said calmly. "I know. I followed the marks in the snow. Plus the other driver smelled of alcohol."

"Was there anyone hurt?" I asked, concerned.

"They are alive. The driver is the only one who's hurt really badly. His family is lucky they were wearing their seatbelts."

I choked out, "Family?"

"Yes," she looked down. "You are free to go. You should get back to your family now."

"Thank you," was all I had been able to say. Dave's parents were there, standing next to mine. Jay walked over to me.

"Are you okay?" Mr. Krivac asked. "Seriously?"

"Yes, I'm fine. Stunned a little. But I'm fine."

"You never did answer my question," Dave demanded.

"Dave! Not now! Please?" I begged, as I looked around.

"You're right. I'm sorry," he said, bowing his head.

We returned to our parents. Dave's parents wrapped him up in a hug. I told them that I had wanted him to drive home and let me walk the rest of the way; they reassured me that the accident was not my fault. They said that they had taught Dave to do the right thing, and that they never would have let me walk in this weather. They were just thankful that we were both OK. My parents and his were talking about what had happened; I could have sworn that they mentioned the curse, but I couldn't confirm it.

"Now," I said, as the three of us were somewhat alone. "Do you fully believe me now, Dave?"

"Yes, but you also promised that you would let us know when he was coming into town."

"That is my fault. Not hers," Jay defended me. "She did not know I would be in town. So she had no way of informing you that I would be present."

"What time are you from?" Dave questioned, remarking on Jay's pattern of speech.

"I attend a college up to the North of here," Jay stated. "They instill proper English in us."

"Which school would that be?" I rolled my eyes, when Dave asked the same question again.

"Barqueste."

Dave's eyes almost popped out when Jay mentioned the name of the school. "You go there?"

"Yes, I do."

"Wow," Dave seemed impressed. "I've heard of that school. I just never knew anyone who actually *went* there."

"Please do not be upset with Alexandra," he said, putting his arm around me. "I do not always know when my time off will be."

Dave seemed more relaxed with him now. "Nah, it's cool, man."

"Now will you lay off the twenty questions?" I sneered.

"Yeah. No more twenty questions," he held up his hands in defeat. "Look man, I just wanted to know that Lexi was being taken great care of."

"I completely understand," Jay nodded. "I would expect no less from a great friend. I most likely would have done the same as you."

Dave offered sincerely, "You should come out with us sometime."

"I will not make a promise I cannot keep. For school keeps us well occupied."

"Dave?" His mom called

"Yeah, Mom?"

"Time to go," his dad answered. Dave argued, but his parents wouldn't let him stay behind.

"Oh! Hold on!" I grabbed my purse out of Dave's car. "A quick picture?"

"Sure," Dave smiled.

"Anything," Jay grinned.

"Dad? Can you snap a quick picture of us?" Dave asked his father.

"Sure," he said slowly making his way over to us. I instructed him on which button to press. "Smile"

We all huddled together and smiled. "Thank you," I said, taking my camera back.

"I'll see you later, man," Dave said, holding his hand out.

"I will speak with you later," Jay returning his gesture.

"I'll give you a call later," Dave said, giving me a quick hug.

"I'll talk to you later," I said, waving.

By now most of the neighbors had gone back inside where it was warm. The ambulance had taken the other family to the emergency room, and the tow truck was hauling the mess of what was once an SUV away.

Mom hinted, "You guys come inside soon, okay?"

"Will do, Mom," I said. We stood outside while my parents returned to the house. We were now alone. "What happened?" I asked.

"Don't you remember?" he smirked. "You were in an accident."

"Yeah, I remember that. But the officer said something to make me think... and with what I saw..."

"You had your eyes closed."

"How could you have possibly known that? The only one I told that to was the officer, and you were standing over there when I said it."

He winked, "Good hearing?"

"No. Because you said that you don't have any extra powers. Now spill," I demanded, with my hands on my hips. "And I saw you on the stairs before I closed my eyes."

He lowered his eyes. "I saw Dave was frantically trying to get out of the way. His car was caught on a patch of ice," he said leaning to the other foot. "I hid behind the bush and asked to do what needed to be done to return to this state."

"Asked?"

"I would be so lost if anything had happened to you. My only concern was for your safety. I pushed Dave's car out of the way and went back to hide behind the bush. But not before I pounded on your parent's door. I stayed behind until I was sure that I could return to this form."

"What about the other family? You couldn't have helped them?"

"The reason I did not," he said with sadness, "was that I let their car take the course it was meant to go. Remember me telling you about the story of fate and destiny?"

I nodded. "Yes."

"They really discourage us from intervening. That's why I was surprised that I was able to return to this form. To return at all."

"What would happen to you?" I asked, throwing my arms around him.

He grinned, enjoying my body against his. "I do not know. This has never happened before."

"I heard the adults talk about the curse, and the officer mentioned fate."

"The curse and fate do not go hand in hand. As I mentioned before, if a person's fate is up, then there is nothing that person can do to change it."

"But you said a person can change their fate," I said, remembering our earlier conversation.

"Yes, they can."

"But if it was meant for them to die, then it doesn't matter what they change. It's quite confusing."

I deeply sighed, "You're telling me. You don't have to live it."

"I do not know why I was allowed to do what I did tonight," he said, holding me tighter. "All I know is that I'm glad that I did."

"Wait!"

"Yes?"

"If it's my destiny to die, not saying that I want to just yet, but if it's my turn, we would be together!"

"Yes, but," he looked away. "Destiny is not that easy. Destiny and the curse's way fight all the time."

"Fight?" Again, I was confused.

"Destiny may not want a certain soul. So they fight with the spirit of the curse to prevent the curse from taking it."

"How do you know who wins?"

"*You* don't. Sometimes the curse's spirit wins, sometimes Destiny wins."

"What about the Indians' spirits who protect the land?"

"They are here. The only thing though, is that they may not be near enough to help protect those whom the curse comes to call."

"Like tonight?" I asked.

"Like tonight," he confirmed. "Again, it is very tricky to explain. It is not something that can be easily understood."

"Would you like to go for a walk?" I asked.

"Very much so," he answered, with a smile.

"I'll be right back. Have to let my parents know and change quickly."

He nodded. I ran up to the house and started up the stairs.

"Everything okay?" Mom asked, worried.

"Yeah," I called back. "Just gonna go change, and then Jay and I are going to go for walk."

"Okay," she hollered back. I threw on a warm outfit with accessories and started back down the stairs. "Don't stay out too late," Mom cautioned. "It's supposed to be really cold."

"I won't," I promised. I grabbed an extra coat that Dave had lent me a couple weeks back. I hadn't realized how cold I was before. The shock from the accident had kept my body from knowing that I was freezing.

"Better?" Jay asked, with a smile. I handed him the extra coat to put on.

"Better," I smiled, grabbing his hand.

"I had forgotten what cold is like."

"The temperature is always the same where you're at?"

"Yes. I think. I never notice a change, even by one degree."

"Wow," I said, somewhat stunned. "Why didn't you tell me you would be like this today?"

"I had no idea. I did not want to get your hopes up in case things didn't work out."

"It looks like there will be a new moon," I said, looking up at the sky.

"Yes, it does. The stars are going to shine bright tonight as well."

"Yes, they are," I said, looking up but still walking forward. The stars were just starting to emerge.

"I hope that, aside from the accident, that this day has been good for you."

I gave his hand a tight squeeze with a loving smile I couldn't contain, "Better than I could have ever imagined."

"So what is on your mind on this now peaceful night?"

I couldn't stop smiling. "Nothing."

We walked in silence, but it wasn't awkward. I was happy that Dave and I were OK. I was happy that Dave had met Jay. I was ecstatic that Jay was here next to me. I knew that it wouldn't last long, but I didn't care right now. This one night, I was in bliss again.

We took the short route, as the air was becoming colder with the slight wind that blew. Again, I didn't care about the cold, as long as Jay was beside me. We were now at the same place where we had been on the night of the dance. I turned to Jay.

I asked softly, "Jay?"

Answering just as softly, "Yes, my angel?"

"There is something that I want to tell you."

"Do not be afraid, my dear," he said, stroking my hair.

I replied sheepishly, "I'm scared,"

"What are you scared about?"

"A lot of things," I giggled. I took his hands in each one of mind. "I have never said this to anyone before."

"What is it? Now you are making me nervous."

"Jay?" I paused, holding my breath for a moment. "I love you."

He was quiet, just staring at me. He had told me that he loved me before. Had something changed how he felt? I was afraid to breath.

"My dear," he paused.

I rolled my eyes. "I knew it," I harshly said. He looked at me with confusion. "I knew you would change the way you feel."

"Now, hush," he said, smiling. "You didn't let me finish."

I lowered my eyes, "Sorry."

He removed one of his hands and lifted up my face so our eyes met. "I knew since the first time I saw you. You gave me a heartbeat that I have never felt. I was afraid that you would reject who I was. My heart now and forever will belong to you. Only you have the key that unlocks the love that we share. Even if you fall out of love with me later on, I will have you to thank for these moments that I would have not had otherwise. But now that I know that you feel the way you do, I do not have to hide the words that I speak. I love you too."

We embraced with our most passionate kiss yet. His lips were warm against mine. His silky hair glided through my fingers. His hands on my back ever so gently pulled me in towards his body. I did not want this night to end. For a moment, I forgot all about the time as we were engulfed in our passionate kiss.

I forgot about the cold weather. I forgot about the snow. I forgot about everything that was around us. Our kiss was becoming more and more passionate. Jay was leaning against one of the old oaks, still holding onto me tightly. We softly glided down into the snow, never missing a beat. I could not only feel the beating of his heart, but I could hear it, as well. I removed my gloves and slowly slid my fingers under his shirt. His skin was so warm. I ran my fingers across his back, moving to his bare chest.

I could feel his breathing getting heavier. His bare hands were on my bare back. The heat that radiated from them made me feel as though we were sitting on a hot, sunny beach somewhere. To the snow that hard started falling, I paid no attention. The way we had slid down the stump, I had ended up sitting on top of him. He pulled me closer with each new kiss.

"I cannot," he breathed, in between a kiss. I kissed him hastily so he couldn't finish.

"I know," I breathed back.

My hands were combing through his hair. His body was magnetized to mine. His lips now kissed my neck with such sweetness, it felt like I was in a dream. A sweet dream that I hoped would never end. His lips moved slowly down my neck. I did not stop him. I was in such bliss that nothing could ruin this moment.

"LEXI!"

We stopped immediately. I grabbed my gloves as the cold came back worse than before.

"JAY!"

I recognized the voice, but in the gloom, I could not make out the figure.

"Dave?" I cried, squinting to decipher his shape.

"Who else would it be?" he snapped angrily.

280

"I knew it!" he cried.

We had stumbled to our feet by the time that Dave reached us. "What are you doing here?" I was pissed.

"I could say the thing about the two of you!"

"Keep your voice down," I threatened. "We don't want to wake the neighbors, or worse, my parents."

"I knew he was only after one thing," he said, lowering his voice a bit.

"Dave, you are most wrong in your accusations," Jay said, walking towards Dave.

"Really? It looked like you were taking advantage of her!"

Jay cried, resenting what Dave had thought we were doing. "I would not! I would never be so rude as to do what you are accusing me of!"

Dave folded his arms against his chest. "Really, that's not what it looked like to me."

"I love this woman with all my heart. And I know you do the same. I *would never* do such a thing as to hurt her in the way you are thinking."

"I have loved her since the first day I met her," Dave looked at me with heartbreak in his eyes. "How do you plan on caring for her? Supporting her?"

Dave was starting to sound more like my father than my friend. A friend would keep his mouth shut and open it only when it needed to be opened.

"With every fiber of my body will I care for, support and love this woman," Jay said, putting his arm around me.

Dave snarled with pure anger, "I don't believe that. You weren't there when she needed you." Jay looked at me, wondering what had happened that he didn't know about. Jay *always* knew what happened, because he was always there. Just that no one else could see him. "You, my *friend,* will have to make a choice tonight," Dave snarled, so fiercely that I thought he was going to explode right there.

"What do I have to do to fully convince you of the truth of the words that I speak?"

Dave calmed down for a moment while he thought about what to demand from Jay. "Transfer schools," he glared with hatred.

"That I cannot do," Jay softly argued. "You would have me risk my education?"

He was playing the role that I had given him.

"It shouldn't matter where you go to school," Dave said, tensing up. "If you are as high and mighty as you claim to be, then the school should not matter."

Dave moved as if he were moving a rock. Jay removed his arm from around me and kept pace with Dave until they were standing facing one another.

Dave continued with even more hatred for him, "I won't let her be hurt by you like so many others have."

"I have no intentions to hurt her. I love her. I will protect her until the end of my existence."

"When I'm done with you, that won't be too long," Dave hissed.

Before I could blink, they were in a brawl. They started pushing each other back and forth, swinging punch after punch. I'd heard and seen enough.

"Enough!" I said running in between them. "You two are acting like toddlers fighting over some toy. Dave, I love you, you're my best friend. Jay, I love you. You are my first love."

"You can't love two people at once," Dave said, coming to his feet.

"Yes I can. And I do. But I will *NOT* be the cause of two people I love fighting. *And* I will *not* choose if either one of you give me a choice. Because it will be neither of you. I don't want to lose either one, but I will not live knowing my best friend hates the one that I love. I will *not* live knowing that the one that I love hates my best friend that I love."

I don't think my words made any difference. They were still glaring at each other like two predators waiting for the other to show a weakness.

"I'm leaving," I declared. Their eyes grew wide as they stared at me. "You two can fight, but you know where I stand. If you chose to fight, I will have no part of it." I start to storm off. They followed. "No! Leave me alone. You both say that you will never hurt me," I was trying my best to hold back the tears that wanted to come out. "But you are hurting me right now!"

"But, Lexi," Dave started. I held up my hand to silence him.

"My dear Alexa," started Jay. I held my hand up again to him.

"Don't follow me. Don't call me. Don't bother me until tomorrow. I have some thinking to do."

I started off again. This time, the two guys were frozen in place. I don't know for how long, because as I turned the corner, I raced home as fast as I could. I was as quiet as I could be once I reached home. I really didn't want to explain to my parents what was going on. I knew Dad; he would go there to see what was taking place and address the situation very well knowing that it was what was causing me pain.

Back in my room, I took off the extra layers of clothes and turned the music on low. After I shut off the light, I peeked through my window to see if the two of them were still there. They were in the same position as I had left them. I threw myself on the bed and let the tears that had built up come streaming out. I just lay there. I didn't want to get up. I wanted to lie there and pretend that the fight had never happened. I wanted everything to go back to the way it was. I was mad at Dave for acting like that. I was mad at Jay, too. This was what I had been afraid of.

Then again, Dave had never acted like this before. I didn't want to sleep because I was afraid my dreams would be tampered with. I didn't want to remain awake, either, for fear of hearing sirens and knowing that the guys had not stopped fighting. I couldn't believe what was happening. Why couldn't Dave just see that Jay wasn't taking advantage of me?

Chapter 20 – Acceptance

It was all too quiet between Dave and me for the next month. We never mentioned that night, nor did anyone bring up the accident. I hadn't heard from Jay at all, either. That worried me, as well. It seemed as though I had lost both of my worlds in matter of seconds. Any time I tried to call Dave, I was lucky if the conversation lasted more than a minute. It killed me inside, thinking I was losing my best friend. It killed me inside knowing that I had lost my first love. How could I have been so stupid to think things would work out?

I had stopped returning calls. I stayed focused on school as much as I could. Even my parents were starting to worry. Anytime they asked me what was wrong, I would ignore their questions and change the subject. Everyone was starting to worry about what was going on. Lunchtime was even worse today than it normally was. The tension had grown so bad that I had stopped eating. I quickly glanced at Dave, who glanced at me and just as quickly looked away.

"OK!" Lynn bellowed. "This silence between you two has to stop!"

"It's Friday," Val spoke up. "You all are coming over to my place tonight." She pointed at everyone around the table. Dave and I started to protest. "I ain't gonna hear any excuses! Now is not the time or the place. I can see it's gonna take much longer than a lunch hour to resolve this."

"What time?" Lynn asked.

"How about six?"

Everyone agreed except Dave and me.

"I'll call Mike, and he'll be there as long as he doesn't have class," Lynn said.

"Good," Val nodded at her. "We'll order pizza once this crap gets hashed out."

"I have to see if my parents will drive me," I said, trying to get out of the blood bath that was coming.

"I'll pick you up," Aaron said. "This has gone on long enough."

I tried again, "But."

"No buts," Val reiterated. "I will call your parents if I have to and explain the situation myself."

I didn't want my parents knowing what was going on, so I reluctantly agreed.

"Good!" Lynn said without hesitation. "Now that is settled, anyone have any good news to share?"

Everyone started going back to their normal behavior. I knew it wasn't over. Dave and I glared at each other.

The rest of the day went quickly; each class seemed to last only a few minutes. Why is it that when you don't want to do something or go somewhere, time flies? Yet when you are itching to get somewhere or can't wait for an event to take place, time seems to stand still?

I knew I could not get out of tonight. Not with Aaron picking me up. I had a couple of hours to kill before he came. I knew that if I put up a fight, he would threaten to kidnap me. The snow had disappeared, and the weather was starting to warm up. The birds were chirping, and the sun was shining through the drawn blinds in my room.

I knew that I would be gone for most of the evening and would not return until late, so I decided to get my nightly run in while it was still light out. I quickly changed and left a note for my parents, as well as one on the door addressed to Aaron. My run shouldn't be that long but in case it was, I was prepared.

I didn't bother bringing my CD player, for I knew that whatever music I listened to wouldn't help. I ran a longer course than usual. I didn't care where I was going or how fast I was running; I just needed to release some tension before tonight took place. I stayed clear of the park that was behind my house. I didn't want any reminders of what had taken place that fateful night. I didn't even want to remember the good parts. I knew the good parts would remind me of the bad.

I didn't realize I had turned onto a path that would take me pass the park. When I became aware of my surroundings, I had had enough. I cut through the park, blocking out that night, and ran into the forest. Even though I hadn't been to the clearing in a month, I knew the forest like the back of my hand. I reached the edge shortly after making my way through the overgrown branches that had formed.

I stood there in silence, looking around. Something that hadn't been here before made the clearing feel distant. I felt like instead of the month, I had not visited it in years. I just stood there, wondering if I should call out for him. But I knew that he would know that I was there.

All I could hear was his voice. "Good day," he finally said.

"Hello." This wasn't starting off well. Something was going on.

"I am deeply sorry for not conversing with you sooner. You had stated that you wanted to be left alone. Alone I left you, for I knew that if you wanted to talk, you knew where to find me."

"Thank you," I replied, without much tone. "Can you make yourself viewable?"

"As you wish," he said, coming out of the other end of the clearing. He wasn't translucent, but he wasn't in the same form as I was, either. "Better?"

"Better," I agreed. "Now I can see when I am talking to you."

He lowered his face. "About that night," he started.

I held up my hand up to silence him. "I don't care what happened that night," I lied. "What is done is done."

"I know what you must think. I want to show my gratitude for your arrival before I depart."

"Where are you going?" I said, surprised.

"I do not want to cause you any more pain than I have already inflicted. I think it would be best if I leave."

"I didn't say that I wanted you go," my voice lightened up a bit. "I just said I needed some time."

"Dave is right. I cannot offer you what you need."

"Wait?" I couldn't believe what I was hearing. "So what you said to him that night was a lie?"

"No, it was the truth," he protested.

"Then why are you saying what you say now?"

"I have had time to think, just like you."

"Wait," I sighed lowering my shoulders. "So that's it?"

"I was only fooling myself into thinking that you would ever want me without wanting something more."

"OK, that's the one thing I can't stand," I straightened up. He looked at me with confusion. "People thinking they know what I am thinking."

"My beautiful," he said, taking another step closer. "I have not meant to offend you."

"This has killed me for the past month. Not hearing from you, and my best friend won't speak to me."

"I am sorry," he remorsefully said.

"I have made up my mind on what I want and who I want. But the issue comes down to how to make it all work out."

He looked at me, puzzled. "What do you mean?"

"Before I tell you what I want, I need to know what you want."

"My feelings have never changed," he said, taking my hands in his. "I love you and would do everything in my power to make you happy. If leaving you would make you happy, then I will honor your wishes."

"Jay," I said squeezing his hands. "I love you. What do I *have* to do for us to be together?"

"I wish it were that easy, my dear."

"Things are only as hard as you make them," I said, getting closer.

"It's not as easy as you might think. I couldn't even describe what would need to be done, for the truth is I don't know."

"You mentioned fate and destiny. The way you described them, they were actual, well, I don't know what you would call them. But I could talk to them!"

"They are worse than Death. Believe me, I've seen it."

"Well, what do we do then?" I asked, losing hope.

"If you could trust me one more time, I promise you, things will work out."

"You know I hate surprises."

"I know. Before I can explain the details, I have to work them out." His hopefulness was coming back.

"Don't make a promise," I started. He held his finger to my lips. The air was cooler than around us.

"A promise I cannot keep. I vow to keep this promise," he kissed me lightly on the lips. "You must go. Time is running low."

"Wait! I thought you said you had given me my space?"

"I did. I only just came back today. You have had no sensory of my presence."

"What do you mean sensory?"

"Others 'feel' when I am around, but since they do not see me, they brush it off. You do not even 'feel' when there is someone watching you."

"Could it be that I don't care if there is?"

He shrugged, "That could be very well true."

"I've missed you so much," I threw my arms around his neck. A shot of cool air breezed behind me.

He exhaled very softly, "I have missed you, too."

He gently kissed me on my lips. His lips were velvety soft, but cooler than usual. He pulled away and vanished at the edge of the clearing. As soon as he vanished I looked at my watch and realized I had to get home as fast as I could. As I flew through the door, Mom and Dad just looked at me.

"Sorry guys," I was out of breath. "My run ran longer than expected. Do you mind if Aaron picks me up? I know you don't like driving to Val's, and the gang is getting together for pizza tonight and watch a movie or something."

It's not that my parent's didn't like Val; they liked all my friends. They just hated driving all the way into the other town.

"That's fine," Dad replied, still in a daze. I looked at Mom.

"Have fun," she smiled. "You need a night out with your friends."

"Thanks!" I rushed upstairs, took a quick shower and changed. When I was headed back to my bedroom, I heard Mom call for me.

"Aaron's here!"

I hollered back, "Tell him I'll be there in two minutes!" I gathered the usual for going out and headed down the stairs.

"Is Dave going to be there?" Mom questioned.

"Uh, yeah."

"Why isn't he driving you?" Mom looked kinda suspicious.

"He's got something to do and will be there later."

"Only call if you're in trouble," Dad said. "Most likely we'll be sleeping by the time you get back home."

"Will do," I raced out the house and towards Aaron.

"If I didn't see your note, I would have thought your parents were lying for you," he said, holding the note up.

"Sorry, I didn't think that I would be gone that long for my run."

"No problem. At least you're coming," he grunted.

"I was thinking about crawling out my window and making a run for it, though," I teased.

"Second floor? Yeah then you would have all of us pissed off because we would have to go to the emergency room to make sure you were OK. Once we knew you were OK, we would have killed you."

"Ha ha," I mocked.

"You think I'm joking?" he said, laughing. "At least you seem like you are in a better mood."

"Yeah," I agreed. "Come to think of it, I am in a better mood."

"Good. Cuz if you weren't, Val was thinking of ways to hurt you."

"Hurt me? For being in a bad mood?"

"Yeah for ruining *her* mood!" he playfully snapped.

"Oh. Sorry," I said, with my head down.

"Hey, it's OK. Tell me when everyone gets there. That way you don't have to repeat your story twice."

"Deal."

The car ride was long and boring without either of us talking after that. Aaron cranked the radio to some rock station. I kept thinking about what Jay had said about trusting him. I knew there wouldn't be books on the subject, so it's not like I could go check out a book and read about it. What was Dave going to say tonight? Now I was starting to question what had happened that night. I was going in blindfolded. I didn't know whether Jay had done something to tip Dave off to what he was.

Well, even if Jay had done his disappearing act, Dave would think that he had some type of special powers or something. I didn't want that, either. Something *was* said though. I just didn't know what. No matter how mad Dave was at me, he always talked to me. He never gave me the silent treatment. Well, one time, but it was for only an hour, and then he came back laughing and saying how he couldn't stay mad at me. We were now pulling onto Val's street.

"We're here," Aaron announced, parking. After he climbed out, I opened my door and started towards the house.

I heard Aaron scream in surprise, "LEXI!"

I don't know what I tripped over, but I lost my balance and started falling to the cement. Then I was watching the concrete as it started coming closer. I just closed my eyes, waiting for something to break or my head to hit the ground. I saw my life start flashing before my eyes.

"Oh my God, Lexi, are you OK?" Aaron asked, running over to me.

"Lexi!" screamed Lynn. "Is she OK?"

I heard everyone calling my name and asking if I was OK. "What happened?" I asked, dazed. I was lying on the ground. Nothing was broken. Not even my head hurt.

Aaron breathed in astonishment, "That was the strangest thing."

"What happened? Do I need to call 911?" Lynn asked, ready with the phone in her hand.

"No, I'm fine. Please don't," I begged.

"What happened?" Val impatiently demanded.

"I don't know. She got out of the car and started walking towards the house, and she tripped."

"Did you hit your head?" Lynn asked.

"No, really, I'm fine."

"Then, as if she hit water, she slowed down, and slowly ended up where she is," Aaron finally finished.

"LEXI! I'm so sorry. Are you OK?" Dave asked, with tears in his eyes.

"Why are you sorry?" I asked. "You didn't trip me."

"You must have a guardian angel," Mike taunted, from behind Aaron.

"Huh?"

"You know, a guardian angel. Someone who watches over you to make sure that nothing bad happens to you."

Dave and I just looked at each other.

"Well, her guardian angel is working overtime lately," Lynn snorted. "First with Dave's car, and now this."

Was Jay there? I couldn't ask out loud if he was. They would think I had hit my head and definitely call 911. Dave helped me to my feet, and we all headed inside.

"So since Lexi is OK," Val started. "You *are* OK, *right*?"

I nodded my head. I just wanted this night to be over with.

"We can either order pizza first," she said, giving options. "Aaron your vote doesn't count." Everyone laughed. "Or we can get this *thing* out of the way."

"Can we order pizza while we talk, eat, and continue talking?" Aaron offered.

"Guys?" Val said, looking around.

"Order first," everyone said, in agreement.

I was an easy one to please. Cheese. I didn't like all the extra toppings. I couldn't help but think about what Lynn had said. I knew Dave was thinking the same thing, as well. He wasn't glaring at me like he had been for the past month. His look was now more peaceful. We ordered the pizza and had about an hour to kill before it would be delivered.

"OK, guys, spill," Lynn said.

I lowered my eyes. "I don't know where to begin."

Dave gave up and started, "I met Jay about a month ago."

Everyone started to get upset with me, because I had promised that I would have them meet him when he got into town. Dave saved my butt when he told them that even I didn't know that he would be in town. Then they started asking him questions about Jay.

"We're getting off track, here," Lynn said.

"You don't like Jay?" Aaron asked.

"He seems like a great guy," his eyes turned toward me. I knew he had been going to tell everyone the truth about what happened that night when he caught us. After what had just happened, his face wasn't so sure any more. "I just didn't want Lexi getting hurt."

"If he seems like a great guy," Mike said, "Then why would he hurt Lexi?"

"I don't know," he lowered his head. "I guess I was just jealous."

I knew he was sort of making it up to avoid saying what he had actually seen that night. "Can Dave and I have a few moments?" I asked, looking at everyone.

"Sure," Val said calmly. "Pizza should be here soon anyways. Let's go wait outside for the guy. For some strange reason, he keeps going to the wrong address."

Everyone slowly got up and headed out the door.

As soon as I heard the door close, I whispered, "Thank you for not telling everyone exactly why you were upset."

"I am, was, worried that he was taking advantage of you."

"What happened that night after I stormed off?" I inquired.

"He told me everything," he looked at me, asking me why I hadn't said anything before.

"*Everything?*" I choked.

"Yes, everything," he nodded. "At first I didn't believe him."

"What made you? Believe I mean?"

"He disappeared in front of me. I became even more upset at you than him after that."

"How so?"

"Well, you had chosen *him* over someone like me."

I just lowered my face.

"And then," he continued. "After what Lynn said, about the guardian angel. Do you love him?"

"Yes."

"Why didn't you tell me before?"

"Because I didn't know before," I was being honest. "I mean the last time you asked me."

"Oh. I just want you to be happy. I still don't like the guy all that well. I'll be honest. You deserve better."

"Shouldn't that be up to me, not you?"

"True," he said, looking down. "Look, I'm sorry. I mean, look at it from my point of view. I didn't want you doing something stupid just to be with him. You *are* my best friend and I don't want to lose you."

"I don't want to lose you, either. Do you think it was Jay who saved me from crashing my head on the concrete?"

"I hate to admit it, but yes, I think it was. After that night with the drunk driver and tonight, he has me thinking that he isn't *all* that bad."

"How so?"

"If he wanted you with him, we would both be dead from that night. Instead, here you are, still with us. And I have him to thank for that," he was admitting more to himself that Jay wasn't all that bad of a guy.

"So what did you two talk about that night?"

"We mostly talked about you and what we thought would be best for you."

I rolled my eyes. "Let me make that choice from now on? Please?"

"OK. I'm sorry. I love you, Lexi. More than you will ever know."

"I know. But look at what almost happened because of it. I don't want that happening again."

"I'll try to back off a little more. I promise," he said, holding his arms out.

"Friends?" I asked, halfway putting my arms out.

"No. Best friends," and we embraced in a hug.

"Pizza's here!" exclaimed Aaron.

"Couldn't wait, huh?" I laughed.

"Nope," he said, with a mouth full of pizza.

"Everything better?" Val glared.

"Yes, everything is better," I said, smiling. It was nice to have my best friend back. And now I didn't have to lie to him anymore.

"Good. Now that's out of the way," Lynn said aloud from the kitchen. "What are we going to do for prom?"

"Prom? Already?" I groaned.

"Come on now, we're going to be seniors next year," Lynn gloated.

"Seniors," I said. "OK, here's a better one, anyone applied to any colleges yet?"

Dave, Aaron and I laughed while the rest of them groaned.

"Let's stick with prom for now," Val said, returning with soda and cups.

"So we all know who's going with whom," I looked around the room.

"So are you two an item?" Aaron asked, grabbing for another piece of pizza.

"No," we said, in unison.

"We're just best friends again," I finished. "Now hand over a slice or someone is going to get hurt."

"Sheeeeeeeeeeeeee's baaaaaaaaaaaaaaaaaaaaaaaaack," Mike roared.

The night that I had dreaded actually turned out to be really fun. After we were done eating, we played a round of monopoly, and then we watched some lame movie. May not have sounded like a relaxing night to some, but to us, combining relaxing, laughing and just having fun was as good as it could get.

The night was coming to an end, and we all said goodbye.

"Stop trying to kill yourself," Lynn said. "You don't want to burn out your guardian angel."

"I'll take her home," Dave said to Aaron. "She lives practically across the street from me, and you still have to drive home yourself."

"Thanks bro. Oh wait," he said, looking around. "Oh OK, no snow, you should be fine."

"Thanks, man," Dave said sarcastically, doing the handshake hug thing.

Dave opened the door for me as usual and got in on his side. We were the last ones to drive off.

"Look, I'm really sorry again," Dave started in.

"Forget it, OK? I know that you were only looking out for me."

"Yes, I am."

"Can you please just try to be a little nicer to Jay? For me please?"

295

"I'll try. I'll say this though. If he does one thing to hurt you, I will *kill* him," he said seriously.

I nodded with a smile, "Deal."

Chapter 21 – The Story

The rest of the school year flew by in a flash. I still hadn't set up an appointment to check out the second law school, but I figured that I had plenty of time, since I still had five more years. Dad had called and set up the main college visit for the coming summer. At first, they had given him the cold shoulder. Then, when they found out who he had talked to and that the financing was all taken care of, they couldn't wait for us to come. I had so much to cram in next year, since I had put off a lot this year.

I was so happy that everything was back to normal. I had my best friend that I could now tell *everything* to. Dave has been a little more understanding. I still know he wishes that he was the one and not Jay, but he's been very supportive. As if dealing with colleges, my last year of high school, and not having the usual gang around every day wasn't hard enough. I was determined to make things work, though. I knew the day would come when I would *have* to make a decision about colleges, but that part I was still keeping locked up for a later date.

The worst part about the end of the year was PROM. We had decided to all chip in and rent a limo. Well, the guys wanted it more than the girls. Not saying that we weren't thrilled about taking a limo, but we didn't care that much either way. The guys wanted a limo since it would be their last prom. Thankfully, Aaron's parents had contacts, and they were able to get a limo to sit all of us. We were all meeting at my house, since I was the only one who lived on a street that could accommodate extra parking.

Lynn and Mike were going together. I had been surprised that Lynn said yes when Mike asked her to be his girlfriend; I just sort of shook my head, thinking about what she had said when things were going sour with her and Tim. But it was her choice. Aaron and Val of course were going together.

One day, Dave said that he needed to talk to Jay alone. It worried me, because I didn't know what it was about, but Dave pestered me until I got him and Jay together. After they were done talking, they told me that I could rejoin them. Dave had asked Jay's permission to ask me to prom. I was surprised that Jay agreed. It wasn't a male bonding thing that had happened, but some kind of mutual respect.

On the last day of school, you could see kids crying, hugging, laughing and acting like any other normal day. It was a half day, and you could tell the teachers didn't want to be there any more than the students. In fact, they were just as anxious as the kids to get out of there. Today was what we liked to call a free-for-all. No tests, no homework, no lectures, and more important, no teaching.

Prom was tomorrow, and tonight, we were all meeting at Dave's house. His house had a small bonfire pit in the backyard, and we had decided to cook hot dogs and s'mores on sticks. Tomorrow, after prom, we were going out to eat at our usual place and then head over to Lynn's to gather and continue the prom celebration.

The half day finally ended, and you could hear cheers throughout the hallways. The cheers were mostly coming from the graduating seniors. The juniors were excited because they had one year left. The sophomores were excited because they were halfway done. The freshmen were thrilled that they had survived their first year, but groaned because they had three more to go.

I told Dave that I would walk over to his house, since it wasn't that far and that would make up for the run that I would miss tonight. I took my time, since we weren't meeting until six. I called Mom at work to let her know the plans for this weekend. She was excited, since she would be able to get pictures before we left for prom. I got changed and packed an extra set of warmer clothes just in case, then got everything ready for prom the next day. I also got my overnight bag ready, since the girls were going to be spending the night over at Lynn's. I was going over my mental check list when a voice broke my concentration.

"Hello, my love."

"Jay! Hello to you, too, my love," I greeted back with a huge smile.

"Are you excited about this weekend?"

"Sort of," I said, with a bit of disappointment.

"Why do you not sound happy?" he asked, concerned.

I depressingly breathed, "I wish you could be there this weekend." I knew he couldn't.

"I know," he said with sadness in his voice. "But I will always be near you."

"I know. That's not what I meant, though."

"I know. The time will come. You will see," he promised.

"It's just killing me inside."

"Well, stop," he teased. I made a face at the air. "Your face is going to freeze like that," he chuckled.

"Yeah yeah yeah," I hissed.

"Just promise me one thing?"

"What's that?" I asked.

"Promise me that you'll have fun this weekend."

"I know I'll have fun, but it would be even better if you were there." He deeply sighed. "I know."

"Would it be too much to ask if I can see you before I leave tonight?"

"Well," he said. "Just for a moment," he sounded far away.

I smiled even bigger than before. My parents weren't due back for another hour or so. He materialized in front of me. I wrapped my arms around his neck, and I could feel the slight chill as he placed his arms around me.

"I love you," I said, looking into his eyes.

"I love you, too," and he quickly kissed my lips. "I must go now."

As much as I wanted to argue, I knew he had to. I did and didn't know why he had to, but I never questioned his motives.

"I'll see you later," I said. I felt the coolness of his body becoming colder and more water-like.

"I'll see you soon," he said, and then he was completely gone.

I grabbed my things, left a note in case Dad came home first, and headed over to Dave's. The air smelled of freshly cut grass. I loved that smell. I walked just a little slower so I could inhale the scents for a bit longer. The trees were in full bloom, and the streets looked like something off a painting. By the time I reached Dave's house, I could see everyone else was already there.

"We thought you got lost!" Lynn teased.

"We were about to send the feds to come get you," Mike chuckled.

"Oh, yeah. I got lost walking the couple blocks over," I cracked back.

The three of us walked around to the back, where the rest of the gang was preparing the fire and hot dogs. The fire pit was larger than I remembered. There was a cooler off to the side that held the drinks and ice. A table was set up with metal skewers and the things we needed to finish the off hot dogs once they were cooked.

We heard Terry behind us. "Hey guys?"

"Hey Terry!" I said. "What brings you here?"

"I was wondering if you guys minded if I join you." He looked uncomfortable.

"Terry, man, we've told you before, you're always welcome here," Dave said, giving him one of those half high fives, hug type of deals.

"Thanks! And I have some great news, too!" He sounded like he had just won the lottery.

"What's what?" Lynn asked.

"I don't know what happened, but Dad laid off the football thing." You could tell that was such a relief off his back.

We were all so happy for him. "That's great!"

You could tell the difference in Terry's attitude; he was more relaxed and didn't look like he was crawling out of his skin. *This* was the Terry we all knew and loved.

"Hey, Lexi!" Dave cried.

"Don't tell me that *you* were worried?"

"Nah," he said, then whispered. "Did you say hi to Jay for me?

I softly whispered back, "No, I'm sorry. He didn't stay long." He just looked at me to see if I was telling the truth. "We only talked for a few minutes, and then he was gone." It was the truth. "He did tell me to have a great time with you all."

"Well, he should know better than that," he teased. "You *always* have a great time with us."

"That is the truth," I smiled, grabbing a stick and a hot dog.

Everyone filed behind, and we sat around the fire trying to maneuver the hot dogs.

Terry breathed with much relief, "I want to say thank you so much, guys."

"Quit thanking us," Aaron moaned, as he was trying to manage a hotdog on the stick.

"You don't know what it meant to know I could count on you guys during the thing with my dad."

"That's what friends are for," Mike said, giving him a pat on the back.

"It meant so much to know I wasn't alone," he smiled.

I knew where he was coming from. Not with the college thing so much, but with Jay.

Aaron groaned, "Oh, crap."

"How can you handle a baseball if you can't handle a hotdog," Dave teased.

Aaron had dropped his third hot dog in the fire before anyone else had their first dog over the fire.

"You know what they say," he grinned. "The bigger the better."

"I don't think that's the case with you," Terry teased. We all groaned and laughed at the same time.

Dave's Mom got in, "When you said Aaron and hot dogs in the same sentence, I figured I needed to pick up extras." She came walking up with four more packages of hot dogs. We all burst out laughing. Aaron, who had turned beet red, didn't see the humor.

"Hey, long time no see, Terry. How have you been?"

"I've been good, mom."

"That's great. You kids dig in and have fun," she smiled warmly, walking to the back to the house.

We all called in giggling unison, "Thanks, Mom!"

We were such a close-knit group that everyone's parents were mom and dad to us. "You're welcome, guys. Have fun."

"We will," we replied, giggling.

After Aaron managed to fully cook five hot dogs out of a package of twelve, he announced his night a success. We put away the leftovers and cleaned up the table, and then proceeded to discuss prom and graduation. We were meeting at my place at six so we would have time to get pictures in. Aaron and Dave had the brilliant idea to combine their graduation parties. Dave's Mom was cool. She didn't mind having twice the giggling teenagers. I offered to come early and help set up; I just had to remind myself to tell my parents when and where. Later, after the hot dogs had settled, we started roasting marshmallows for the s'mores. Aaron had brought his own bag of marshmallows.

"Do you think we'll still have nights like this?" I asked. "I mean, once the guys are off at college?"

We just looked at one another, the depression kicking in.

"Let's make a pact," Aaron proclaimed, holding up his burning marshmallow, "that we'll keep in touch with one another and get together whenever Mike and I are back in town."

"And I don't care where I am, what I'm doing or what Dad says. I will be here," Terry added.

We all cheered in agreement. Dave was going to community college close by and staying at home. Mike just attended the university a couple of towns away. Aaron was moving towards the border of the state. Terry was going to college in the south, I think mainly to get away from his dad. Dave motioned me with his eyes towards the house.

"We'll be right back, we're gonna grab more sodas," Dave announced.

"Can you grab me a bottle of water?" Lynn asked.

Val chimed in, "Me too."

"Sure, be right back," I said. I was waiting until we were closer to the house to ask him what was going on so the others wouldn't hear. "What's up?" I asked with curiosity.

"Nothing," an evil grinned was forming on his face. "Is Jay around?"

"I don't know," I honestly answered. "Most likely. But he never lets me know when he's actually present."

"How would you like to have some fun with the guys?" he said, grabbing a case of soda while I grabbed the water.

"How so?"

"We tell scary stories…"

"Jay isn't going to materialize in front of us," I warned him.

"I'm not saying he *has* to," he chuckled. "When I had talked to him that one day to ask about taking you to prom, I could feel a cool breeze around me."

"Let's take these back to the guys and walk around front and see if it's OK with him," I said, looking around. He nodded, and we headed back out to where the gang was still roasting marshmallows. He threw the soda in the cooler, and I handed the girls each a bottle of water. "We'll be right back, guys," I said. "We have to do a favor for Dave's Mom real fast."

"Do you need help?" Aaron asked, stuffing a whole s'more into his mouth.

"No, we're good. We won't be too long," Dave quickly said. Dave and I raced off to the front of the house. We did a quick sweep to make sure that no one was around to hear us.

I asked, whispering, "Jay?"

Nothing.

"Jay?" Dave whispered, as well. "We have a favor to ask of you."

"Sweetheart? If you can hear us right now, can you play along with our ghost story?"

"You don't have to materialize," Dave added quickly. "Just something to freak everyone out. Something small. It won't take much to freak them out."

We listened carefully for a sign. We heard a faint chuckle, and a cool breeze passed by us. I smiled. "Let's go," I said, starting back.

I knew Dave had heard it, too, and I heard him whisper thank you. It didn't take him long till he was racing right alongside me. We were trying our best not to burst with laughter.

"Why are you two so happy?" Mike asked.

"Oh nothing," I replied. "I couldn't wait for another s'more!"

"You two are up to something," Val warned. "And I don't like it."

"What?" Dave asked. "We're not up to anything."

"Yeah, sure," Terry said. "What do you guys want to do now?"

"They probably have something cheesy cooked up," Aaron smirked.

Dave and I just looked at one another and grinned.

"OK, now I know you two are up to something," Val remarked. "That's the only time you two grin like that."

I quickly asked, "How about ghost stories?"

Aaron snickered, "Yup, told you."

"That's why you two are grinning?" Lynn asked. "Because you want to tell ghost stories?"

"Why not?" Dave grinned wider.

"Don't you think we're a little too old for ghost stories?" Mike grunted.

"Unless you are *afraid*," Dave teased.

"Try your best!" Aaron tested.

"Go for it!" Mike retaliated.

I loved s'mores. We made a few more before starting in on the stories. Aaron had offered to go first. His was a cheesy ghost story. Val went next, trying to outdo him. Lynn and Mike ganged up together and told one. You could tell each one was trying to outdo the last. Next was Dave's turn. He just winked at me. I didn't really know any ghost stories so I helped him along.

Things were going great. Dave was a natural at telling ghost stories. I chimed in here and there to try to enhance the level. I saw Val straighten up, and hoping it was what I thought it was, I started grinning. Dave took over, and he could see that Mike had straightened up with surprised look on his face. Once the two relaxed again, the story was close to being over.

The climax was coming, and I could see the clear water silk form of Jay sitting in the background with a huge grin on his face. I pretended to stretch by putting my arm behind Dave's back. I was giving him the sign that it was good to go. Everyone was too enchanted by the story to notice even what I was doing. I saw Jay mouth *I love you,* and then he disappeared.

Everyone screamed and jumped up right after Dave finished the last word. That's when you knew that Jay had passed by everyone. Dave and I just burst into complete and utter laughter.

"How did you do that?" Mike demanded, looking around.

"Do what?" Dave asked, through his tears.

I was on the ground with tears in my eyes from crying so much. I felt a cold sensation on my forehead. Dave and I were laughing so hard that we couldn't stop crying. Everyone went to search around to see what they had felt. When they couldn't find anything, they came back to the circle and started accusing Dave of using some type of fan. I grabbed another s'more and put it in the fire. Some followed, and some groaned about how full they were. The night was coming to an end. We cleaned up, put the fire out and said our goodbyes. Mike offered to drive me home, but I refused. I waited until everyone had left to say goodbye to Dave.

Dave exclaimed, through laughter, "That was fun!"

I couldn't stop laughing. "Did you see the looks on their faces?" I bent over, putting my hands on my knees.

Dave whispered in the air, "Thank you."

His voice floated by, "*You're welcome.*"

"I'll see you tomorrow," I told Dave, giving him a quick hug. "Thank you for a great night."

"Are you sure you don't want me to drive you home?" Dave offered.

"I'm sure. I have my guardian angel with me," I said, looking at the air.

"True. Take good care of her," Dave said.

We gave each other another hug, and I headed home. This was so nice. Dave wasn't afraid of Jay any more. I had my best friend back. He had been a lot more understanding than I had thought he would be. Dave knew that I was happy, and he was taking it better than he had with any other guy I had *dated*. Something wasn't sitting right, but I ignored it, because for once I felt complete.

Well, almost complete. But complete as complete could be at the moment. I could say that I was in love. I was in love with everything. And the best part of it all was that everything seemed to be working out. It seemed like nothing could go wrong. I knew that it still bothered Dave a little about Jay, but each day it seemed like he came around a little more and that he had accepted my decision. I could tell, though, that in the back of his mind he thought that something was going to go wrong. But I kept faith that it wouldn't.

I was home, but I didn't go inside. It was such a beautiful night, I decided to continue my walk. There was a full moon, and the stars shone bright. I couldn't believe what had transpired in just one year. It felt as though a lifetime had passed. I remembered my dream as I passed by the old Victorian. I don't know what had brought that on. Was it fate and destiny working against one another? What did it all mean? I had a lot of unanswered questions that would have to be answered in the next the couple years. I felt a tear halfway down my cheek when I heard Jay.

His voice was strong in my ear. "I love you, my dear."

I just smiled and wiped the tear way. I hoped he didn't think that it was a tear of sadness. I looked at my watch; it was getting late.

I knew I had to get some sleep before tomorrow came.

Chapter 22 – One Dream Comes True

The next day, my parents let me sleep in. It felt great not to have to get up at a certain time. I moseyed around the house, debating on how to kill the time. I asked my dad if I could go online for a bit and went into a few chat rooms to see if anything new was going on in the world. Nope. Nothing. I checked out the website of the college that we were going to visit over the summer.

Finally, I decided to take a quick run before I had to get ready for prom. I set my watch's timer to make sure that I didn't lose track of time. The air was a bit stickier than it had been. I loved summer, except for the fact that by the time I got home from my runs, my clothes were always drenched. Passing by the old Victorian house, it seemed drearier than usual.

Mostly, everyone knew everyone, since the neighborhood wasn't that big, but no one knew anything about the people that lived in this house. As I was running by, I noticed again that someone was watching, peering from behind a curtain on the second floor. When I looked up, they had disappeared, and you could see the curtains swaying back and forth.

Strange.

I shrugged it off and continued on. I was five minutes ahead of my run when I got home. Chugging a glass of water, I headed off to shower and change.

It took me a few minutes to get used to my heels; I looked like a kid who was trying to walk in her mother's shoes. Mom just laughed.

I mumbled under my breath, "I'll get used to them."

"What time is everyone expected to show up?" She asked.

"Any minute," I answered.

"I'll get the camera and some more film," She replied, setting her book down and getting up. I was walking back and forth in the formal living room, trying to get used to the heels; I saw movement coming from behind the curtains and took a peek out.

I called to Mom, "They're here!" I grabbed my purse and headed out the door.

Please don't let me trip. Please don't let me trip.

Everyone was parking along the street and getting out. Instead of the four cars, there were eight – some of the parents had come to take pictures and send us off. The limo arrived and parked right in front of the house, and the driver got out and came over to introduce himself to us. He was very nice and polite. He apologized for not asking us sooner, but he wanted to know if it was OK if his wife rode in the front with him. We didn't have a problem with that and said it was fine. He said to let him know whenever we were ready to go.

For about twenty minutes, it felt like we were movie stars. Flashes going off, everyone telling us how beautiful we looked and wishing us a great time at prom. Once all the pictures were done and our parents had hugged us goodbye, we gathered in the limo. We asked the driver if we could put the divider up, and he was pretty cool about it. He said that normally, since there were people under the age of 18, he wasn't allowed to close the divider, so he kept it open a crack just to get around the policy. Again, we didn't mind. He joked with us and said that we couldn't drink the champagne, but we could help ourselves to the water and sodas.

The ride was very smooth, and before we knew it, we had arrived at the banquet hall where prom was being held. He asked us what time they should be back to pick us up and whether it was OK if they went somewhere; we said that was fine. He held the door open for us and closed it when we were all out. We just stood there, hesitating. We knew that the sooner we went in, the sooner it would end. Well, I did anyways.

The prom committee had done a wonderful job – the place was beautiful. There was a huge banner that read 'From This Moment.' Red, yellow, clear, white and silver balloons filled the room. Streamers glistened in the dim light. The tables were beautiful. Each one had a centerpiece that held more balloons, and confetti was spread strategically between the prom programs.

We found an empty table and claimed it as ours, then headed off to the dance floor. I had gotten better at walking in my heels, so at least I didn't look like a toddler any more. The dancing part, well, that was another story. The night was going by wonderful. I was so glad that Dave was being more accepting of Jay. A slow song came on, and I went to sit down.

"Where are you going?" Dave asked, taking my hand.

"It's a slow song," I groaned. "My cue to take a break."

"I don't think so," he said, grabbing my hand and leading me back to the dance floor. It was nice to actually be taller in my heels, since I didn't need to break my neck to look at him.

He whispered apologetic in my ear, "I know you wish I was Jay."

"You're my second choice," I teased. "You know I probably wouldn't have come if anyone else had asked."

He pulled me in closer. But not too close. Well, you know what I mean. We started to hear whispers. We didn't know what everyone was whispering about; we gathered close together and started questioning what was going on. No one had a clue. When the whispers seemed to stop; we went back to dancing. Dave had a strange look on his face and backed away.

"What's wrong?" I asked, more confused than I usually was.

"May I cut in?"

I turned around and gasped. "JAY!" I screamed, throwing my arms around him. He looked incredibly HOT! He was wearing a black tux with his hair in place and those brown eyes that sparkled.

"Yes, you may," Dave said, with a smile.

I whispered, "What are you doing here?"

"Just think of it as a fairy tale in reverse," he sweetly smiled. We danced the rest of the slow song together. After the song ended, everyone came up and started throwing questions one after another.

"Slow down, everyone," I said, holding a hand up. "Jay, these are my friends." I pointed, as a stated everyone's name. "Everyone, this is Jay."

"Why didn't you tell us that he was coming tonight?" Val playfully accused.

"I..ummm...." I said, scratching my head.

"I wasn't sure if I would be able to come," Jay said, when he saw I didn't know what to say. "I didn't want to say yes and let her down if I wasn't able to make it."

"Well, now we know he ain't a ghost," laughed Lynn.

A ghost. Nice, Lynn. Dave and I just looked at each other and silently snickered. Jay was trying his best to answer the questions that were snowballed at him. He glanced at me – my cue to rescue him.

"OK, OK, guys. Enough with the questions. We're here to dance, not to interrogate."

"You guys thirsty?" Aaron asked. "Mike and I are gonna grab some drinks. Anyone want anything?"

Everyone gave them their orders, and they took off through the crowd to gather the drinks. We took a seat at the table. I felt bad for Dave, since he was the one without a date now. I just prayed that this wouldn't turn into what happened last time.

"Thank you," Jay leaned over toward Dave. "I am sorry if I have ruined your evening."

"Nah," Dave whispered back. "I can tell she's happy with you, and that's all that matters."

You could tell there was still a look of hurt on Dave's face. Aaron and Mike returned with the drinks. After we were finished, we all headed back to dance floor. Things were going great until another slow song started to play. I looked at Dave with sorrow and confusion. He just nodded with a look that said it was OK.

I whispered to him, "Thank you," looking into his eyes.

This was so cool. My heels gave me just enough height.

"You are welcome," he whispered, in my ear. "But you are the one that I must thank."

"How so?" I asked, as he twirled me around the crowded dance floor.

"For giving me a second chance. You look so beautiful tonight," his brown eyes were so gorgeous, I was becoming lost in them.

"I don't know how you managed this pull this off. But I am so grateful that you did."

We danced close together. I could smell his sweet scent as my head lay against his shoulder. Every hair on his head was perfectly placed. I was afraid to run my fingers through it, in case I messed it up. As he spun me around again, I noticed that a girl with features similar to mine was talking with Dave. I didn't remember ever seeing her in school before. Not that I actually paid attention to all how many thousand students. Dave was smiling and flirting with this mystery girl. You know how they say you don't want someone until they are with someone else? Not me. I wasn't jealous. I was actually happy. The song we had been dancing to came to an end.

He breathed into my ear, "I love you, my sweetheart."

"I love you, too," kissing him on his lips.

The prom was coming to an end. The DJ announced the last dance; and everyone was dancing with their dates; Dave was dancing with the mystery girl.

I whispered, "Do you know when?"

"Yes," he answered.

"Would you be able to come out to eat and then over to Lynn's afterwards?"

"Yes," he sweetly smiled.

He held me close while we danced the remainder of the song in silence. I could feel his heartbeat against my chest. I never wanted this night to end. You could hear groans as the DJ thanked everyone for coming out. There was one little problem that I knew that was coming up. I couldn't tell everyone that Jay could pop in from place to place.

"Did you drive here, man?" Aaron asked.

"I was dropped off," Jay answered.

"Is your ride here?" Lynn asked, concerned.

"Not yet. You guys go. I don't want to hold up your evening."

Aaron sounded threatened, "Do you think the limo dude would have a problem with an extra person?"

"It doesn't hurt to ask," I replied.

"Before you ask, do you guys mind if the girl I just met tonight tags along?" Dave wondered.

"I don't have a problem with it, if no one else does," I answered. Everyone looked at one another and shrugged.

"Thanks! I'll be right back," he said, starting to take off.

"Wait! Will she be riding with us?" I asked. I needed to know how many extra people were coming so I could be honest with the limo driver.

"Let me find out," he answered back.

I decided to talk to the limo driver, who was holding the door open for us. He greeted us with a friendly smile. I explained the situation to him and asked him if that was OK. I told him that he didn't have to drive us to the restaurant, and he could still get paid for the extra two hours. He said that we didn't need to do that, but I wouldn't take no for an answer.

"It's all set up," I said.

"She said that she would meet us at the place," Dave told us.

We all climbed in the limo.

"There's one little compromise," I explained to everyone. "The driver is going to drop us back at my place, and we're gonna have to drive to the restaurant. I didn't think that would be a big deal."

Everyone agreed and thanked the driver.

"Can we scrape any change together for a tip?" I asked, whispering. Well, more mouthed it. Us girls dug through our purses and the guys through their wallets.

"I'll take care of it," Jay said.

I just looked at him in utter confusion. *Where would he get money for a tip?* Scare the guy? OK, that was harsh. I was mad at myself for even thinking that. He did earn brownie points with everyone though. The limo ride was just as fast on the way back as it had been on the way to the prom.

Once we were at my house, as much as we weren't ready to get out of the limo, we *were* ready to get something to eat. The driver opened the door, and we all got out. We thanked the limo driver for a great ride, and Jay, being the last one out, personally thanked the driver and shook his hand. The driver looked down and stared in disbelief. I thought something was wrong, but when I went to go ask if everything was alright, the driver had a huge smile. Thanking us again, he handed us his personal business card. He stated if there was anything we needed, not to hesitate to call. We thanked him back and just looked at each other like what the heck just happened.

"Dave?" I asked sweetly.

"What's up?" He asked, turning to me.

"Do you mind if we catch a ride with you?"

"Sure," he smiled back. "I kinda figured."

"Thank you so much," I said. My parents didn't see the need for me to have a car yet. I had the bus for school, and pretty much everything was within a bike ride's distance. I ran inside to grab my overnight bag for Lynn's. When I returned, the guys were in the car, laughing away. Dave seemed to be in a better mood. "I'm ready," I said. "What are you laughing about?"

"Nothing," Dave replied.

"So who is this girl that you met at the prom?" I asked.

"Her name is Angela," he started. "No, she doesn't go to our school. Her date hooked up with someone else at prom and left her alone. She's also going to be attending the same college as me next year."

It was awesome having a best friend that knew every question you were going to ask. "I hope you're not a rebound for her," I said sadly. "I just don't want you to get hurt."

"I know," he agreed. "I am being cautious, though."

I knew he didn't want to be the lone man, that's why he'd invited her. This was actually the first time that everyone had a date in our group. It had never bothered us before if one of us didn't have anyone; we never put pressure on anyone, and we didn't flaunt it when we had someone. I was a little sad because Jay was sitting shotgun while Dave drove, and I was alone in the back. I wanted as much time with Jay as possible, because I didn't know how long I would have with him in his current state. But I was ecstatic that my best friend was becoming chummy with the guy that I loved. So I just sat back and basked in the thought that everything would work out.

In a short time, we had arrived at our restaurant. We knew it would be dead, since the rich snobs would be off in the city at some fancy restaurant. We walked in knowing we were well over-dressed for the place; we didn't care, though.

"Usual table for six?" asked the hostess.

"Yes," Aaron said, without thinking.

"Hold on, guys. How many do we have?" I knew there were more than before. "Eight please."

"No problem," the hostess said with a smile. "Right this way."

"Is Angela coming?" I asked.

"Angela's right here," Mike said, giving Lynn a hug.

"Not *Lynn*, Angela," I chuckled. "The girl Dave met at prom." Lynn's name was really Angela, but she preferred to be called by her middle name.

Aaron crowed, "You met a girl at prom?"

"Yup. Her name is Angela."

"She's coming here tonight?" Lynn asked, delighted.

"Yup. She goes to the school west of here."

"OK, we'll wait to order to give her time to get here," Lynn said.

We ordered our drinks and an appetizer. Everyone talked about what they would be doing over the summer. You could see that Dave was getting frustrated, because Angela hadn't arrived by the time we finished the appetizer.

"Do you want me to go with you to see if she's outside waiting?" I asked Dave. He nodded solemnly. I looked at Jay, and he nodded. Dave and I excused ourselves and began walking towards the door. We told the hostess that we would be right back, that we were waiting for the last member of our party to arrive. "Are you OK?" I asked him as soon as we were outside.

"Yeah," he answered glumly. "I should've known."

I offered support, "She could be running late."

"How should I have known?"

"Don't give up. Maybe she left a little later than us?" I tried, sounding hopeful. I didn't know what more to say. I felt so bad for him. If she really had stood him up, she and I were going to have some words.

"Do you know what kind of car she drives?"

"No, I didn't even think to ask," he angrily admitted.

The place was dead, as I had known it would be. I looked around to see if I noticed anyone that looked lost and confused.

"Is that her?" I asked, pointing at a car that was pulling in.

As the car got closer, I could see there was an older couple driving. "Nope," he said with despair.

A girl's voice from behind our cars, "David?"

"Angela?" he asked, confused.

"So sorry I'm late," she breathed.

"It's OK. Are you OK?"

"Yeah, I'm fine. My ride was being an ass and didn't want to leave."

I mouthed, "See, I told you she would make it," and walked back in to be with Jay. I smiled and nodded at the waitress. "The last member of our party has finally arrived," I joked with her. She just laughed back. I walked through the restaurant and took my seat next to Jay.

"Is she finally here?" Aaron asked.

"Yes," I replied.

"Good, now we can order!" he cried, motioning for the waitress.

She came over and started taking our orders. By the time she was through the group, Angela and Dave had joined us. The interrogation started all over with Angela, as they had with Jay. Jay laid his hand on mine under the table. Aaron was babbling about graduation. Lynn was listing the teachers she hoped she wouldn't have senior year. Val was thinking about starting a portfolio for her outfits. Lynn was asking Val to redesign her dresses from last year. Terry was talking with Mike about the colleges he had applied to and heard back from. The food came, and the noise level in the back room that we occupied was a few decibels lower than before.

After we were done, we paid our tabs and headed outside to our cars.

"Hey, Lynn?" Dave asked.

"What's up?" She answered.

"Do you mind if Angela tags along?"

She gave him a look, "What do you think?"

He chuckled, "I just wanted to double check."

"Hey, Dave?" I asked in my sweet voice again.

"Here," he said, laughing. "Don't crash it, OK?"

"Ummmm," I started.

He threw me the keys to his car. Any other teen would be excited, but I didn't have my license yet, so I wasn't insured.

"Do you mind if I drive?" Jay asked, taking the keys from me.

"Even better," he laughed. "Take care of both of them?"

"You know I will," Jay said, looking at me with that smile of his I couldn't resist.

I whispered unsure, "Are you sure?"

"Yes. Trust me," he answered. He opened the door for me as I carefully got in. He closed my door and went around to the driver's side. I opened the door from the inside for him, and he gave me the oddest expression. I just shrugged it off. I was very nervous about driving with Jay. Something told me he hadn't driven in a very long time. But he said to trust him. So I had to do just that. Dave trusted me. It worried me just the same. He giggled as he started the care. "A little nervous, aren't we?"

"A little," OK, I lied.

I was a lot nervous. He pulled away from the parking spot slowly and started to follow the others over to Lynn's. I just sat in silence, monitoring the road like a good passenger.

"I told you to trust me," he said, with a smile.

"I do trust you," I sort of lied. "Well, I do, but…"

"Oh stop that. Remember, I have special powers."

"No you don't, except for that transport thing you did once. You said you don't have any special powers."

"That's true. I guess I lied," he said, with a chuckle. "My special powers are I can do anything you guys can do."

"Oh. I think."

"Have faith," he said, as he took my hand in his. "I love you, and you know I won't let anything bad happen to you. Remember what – who was it? Lynn said? I'm your guardian angel."

"Yeah, she did say that," I said, with a half-smile. "But that doesn't make me any less nervous."

"Just relax," he said, giving my hand a squeeze.

"I don't know how you pulled it off, but thank you. It was the best night."

"You're welcome. But I shall warn you now I cannot do this very often. So it may be a great while until you are able to see me with your eyes again."

"I sort of figured that," I stated sadly.

"Hey now, do not be sad. I did this for you. I wanted to see you smile. That means more to me than all the stars that light up the dark night."

"I love you so much. I can't wait until we are together."

He breathed a heavy sigh, "Me too."

We arrived at Lynn's without a scratch. We all went inside, and us girls pardoned ourselves to go and change. We giggled and chatted as we got out of our dresses and into something more comfortable. When we came out, we could tell that the guys were itching to get out of what they call monkey suits.

We popped the movie in, had the sodas ready and were waiting when the guys returned. I had to laugh when Jay came out with the guys. He was wearing an extra outfit Mike had brought. It just didn't look right on him. Maybe I was too used to the old-fashioned outfits he wore.

The guys had something planned. They just stood at the top of the stairs with huge grins on their faces. As soon as all the guys were ready, they came sat down next to someone other than the girl who they came with. They sat back and put their arms around us. The girls just looked at each other like what the heck is going on. The guys stood up.

"Oops, wrong girl," they laughed, standing up and going to their dates. We all cracked up. Tonight had been the best night ever. Everything was right where it was supposed to be.

If there was a Heaven, this was it.

Book 2 Preamble

If you have made it this far, I want to say a big thank you. I know this book was no easy to read. I can promise you, that with each book you'll see the characters grow. There will be obstacles, harder choices, more laughs and greater rewards.

Now, will Lexi find a way to bring Justin into the mortal world? Will Lexi join Justin in his world? Will Justin be able to handle the mortal world? Will Lexi be able to handle Justin's world? More secrets are revealed as the pages turn to the next chapter. Will either one be able to handle the secrets about their past? To where it will ruin their future…

Or will they overcome all odds?

ABOUT THE AUTHOR

Lilibeth grew up in a smaller town, acknowledging her life was different than most. She grew to know she felt things most of us weren't aware of. Even at a young age, she was aware of the spiritual existence and struggled to comprehend and make meaning of it. At the same time she used it to overcome many of her life struggles and turmoils. With the help of her friends, Lilibeth strives to understand more about her past while living in the present. Lilibeth's memories have been documented in her diaries and are being shared with everyone, so that we may all benefit from her gained knowledge.

A SPECIAL THANK YOU TO YOU!

On behalf of everyone at Freedom Of Speech Publishing, thank you for choosing The Mystic Diaries: The Whispered Secret for your reading enjoyment.

As an added bonus and special thank you, for purchasing The Mystic Diaries: The Whispered Secret, you can enjoy discounts and special promotions on other Freedom of Speech Publishing products. Visit www.freedomeofspeech.com/vip to learn more.

We are committed to providing you with the highest level of customer satisfaction possible. If for any reason you have questions or comments, we are delighted to hear from you. Email us at cs@freedomofspeechpublishing.com or visit our website at http://freedomofspeechpublishing.com/contact-us-2/.
If you enjoyed The Mystic Diaries: The Whispered Secret, visit www.freedomofspeechpublishing.com for a list of similar books or upcoming books.

Again, thank you for your patronage. We look forward to providing you more entertainment in the future.

The Mystic Diaries

The Whispered Secret

By Lilibeth Muscato

For more books like this one, visit the Mystic Diaries page on my website at:

http://lilibethmuscato.com/

or visit the series pages at:

http://themysticdiaries.com/

Printed in the United States of America

The publisher offers discounts on this book when ordered in bulk quantities. For more information, contact Sales Department, Phone 815-290-9605, Email:

sales@FreedomOfSpeechPublishing.com

Freedom of Speech Publishing, Leawood KS, 66224

www.FreedomOfSpeechPublishing.com

ISBN-13: 978-1470046163

ISBN-10: 1470046164

14112562R00177

Made in the USA
Charleston, SC
21 August 2012